THE PRICE OF JUSTICE

Printed in Australia
Cover Design: Jess Chaplin, Layout: Luke Harris

First printing: November 2023

Paperback: 978-1-7637549-3-5
Hardback: 978-1-7637549-4-2
ebook: 978-1-7637549-5-9

A catalogue record for this work is available from the National Library of Australia

Angry Cat Publishing

THE PRICE OF JUSTICE

ROBERT M. SMITH

Also by Robert M. Smith

Purgatory

For the people of the Mallee

NOTE

While some of the peripheral characters and incidental events are based on real people and occurrences, the main storyline and central characters are entirely fictional. The location and warmth of the community where the novel is set are authentic.

PROLOGUE

Adrian Weston could see an orange glare reflecting off the shotgun's barrel, but not the face of the person silhouetted against the blazing afternoon sun. However, he knew the voice – a voice from decades past, a voice cemented in his memory.

'There's no need for this,' Weston said nervously. 'I've paid my dues. Thirty-one years in prison is more than enough, don't you think?'

The gun barrel wavered slightly.

'No,' was the reply.

'Would forty years have been enough for you? Or fifty, perhaps?'

'No.'

'This won't fix things.'

This time, there was no reply.

'I'm sorry, alright?' Weston's voice was feeble. 'Would it help if I got down on my knees and begged forgiveness?'

Again, the gun barrel wavered a little. 'No.'

'I don't deserve this. You understand what happened wasn't really my fault, don't you?'

The silhouette's head shook, but there was no answer.

'I'm about to come into some money,' Weston said, more confidently. 'Well over a million dollars is the estimate. Perhaps we can come to an agreement. Surely what happened is chickenfeed compared with a million dollars.'

The muzzle flash reached Weston's retinas just milliseconds before the tight formation of lead pellets, way too quickly for him to appreciate that he was paying the true fee for his atrocities.

CHAPTER 1

Detective Inspector Greg Bowker put down the phone and stared out the window of the police headquarters on Spencer Street. *What goes around, comes around,* he thought. *An eye for an eye, and all that. But who squared the ledger?*

He pondered this for a moment or two before turning in his chair and calling across the room. 'Sherlock. You got a minute?'

Detective Sergeant Darren Holmes wandered over and dragged a chair up to Bowker's desk. 'What's the go?'

'Fancy a trip to the Mallee tomorrow?'

'No can do,' Holmes replied. 'In court for the next two days. The Trigoni trial. Thursday would be a goer, though.'

'That'll have to do. I'd like you in on this one with me. You were born up there in the sand, so you won't start sooking about the heat and isolation. Murrayville, wasn't it?'

Holmes chuckled. 'Yeah. Capital city of nowhere.'

'I think I'll drive up in the morning. If you come up on Thursday, that'll still work.'

'What have we got?' Holmes asked, crossing his legs and linking his hands behind his head.

'Body of a male. An Adrian Weston. Found between the grain silos at the Cocamba siding, just south of Manangatang.'

Holmes grinned. 'They're racing at Manangatang. Isn't that how the saying goes?'

Bowker leaned back in his chair. 'Yeah. But this bloke won't be doing much racing. Face blown off with a shotgun, according to the Swan Hill boys.'

Holmes raised his eyebrows. 'Subtle.'

'Yeah. Whoever killed him really meant it.'

'Aren't you still working the Madigan investigation?'

'Louise can handle that. Peter will give her a hand if she asks for it.'

'What's the attraction of this Mallee case?'

Bowker folded his arms across his chest. 'The victim was released from prison a month ago. Just finished a thirty-one-year sentence for the murder of a schoolgirl and incest with his stepdaughter.'

Holmes shook his head. 'What a depraved prick!'

'I put him away back in the mid-eighties.' Bowker paused for a moment. 'Well, me and Jack Moloney.'

Holmes raised his eyebrows. 'The legendary Jack Moloney?'

'Yeah. Top operator.'

'Thirty-one years ago? Shit, you were young to be working Homicide.'

'I was a senior constable in the one-copper station at Manangatang. Was up there for twelve years.'

'Twelve years?' Holmes laughed. 'Don't get that for murder, these days.'

'Ha, ha. Believe it or not, Rachael and I could've happily stayed there forever. But the kids were growing up, and my ambitious itch needed scratching. Applied for a move to Homicide and, unbelievably, I got in first try. I think Jack might've put in a good word.'

'You must've impressed him.'

'The schoolgirl went missing a month before her body was

found, so I'd done most of the legwork before Homicide became involved. Everything pointed to the girl's boyfriend. Jack charged him, and he was remanded in Melbourne. I wasn't fully convinced he was guilty, but no other suspect fitted the facts of the case, so I put my feelings down to inexperience. A month or so later, new information came to light that proved we had the wrong bloke, and that Adrian Weston had murdered the girl. He spent thirty-one years inside, and now he's met his fate.'

'And you reckon the two cases are connected?'

'Yeah.' Bowker looked to the window again, as decades-old memories resurfaced. 'The schoolgirl's body was left at the Cocamba silos as well.'

* * *

Bowker stepped off the Number Three tram on Balaklava Road and jogged across the street to his home in Caulfield North. He found his wife, Rachael, in the kitchen preparing dinner. She turned and smiled when she saw him, and they kissed gently. Rachael was in her mid-fifties but looked twenty years younger. Her brown hair displayed no hint of grey, and she was still in great physical shape. She played sport several nights a week and conducted a jazz ballet class on Thursday evenings.

Bowker dragged off his tie and unbuttoned the neck of his shirt. 'Want to go up to Manang for a few days?'

Rachael looked puzzled. 'Manang?'

'You're not due back at the kinder until next week. Got a few days of leave left. Thought we could go for a drive back to God's country.'

Rachael sat down at the kitchen table. 'What's suddenly brought on all this nostalgia?'

Bowker joined her. 'Remember Yvonne Bryant?'

'Of course I remember Yvonne,' Rachael replied sadly. 'I often think of her, and what she'd be up to if she was still alive.' She smiled. 'Whether she'd still be a hellraiser, or dancing with the Australian Ballet.'

'She'd be a bit old for the ballet. If Weston hadn't killed her, she'd be forty-seven years old now.'

Rachael sighed. 'How time flies. So, what's a trip to Manang got to do with Yvonne?'

'Adrian Weston was released from prison about a month ago.'

'Yeah, I know. You told me he was out. I was hoping the bastard would die in jail, then rot in hell.'

'He's been found dead. Shot in the face.'

Eyes widening, Rachael put her hand to her mouth. 'You're joking, right?' she asked. Bowker shook his head. 'Killed at Manang?'

'It's more bizarre than that. They found his body at the Cocamba silos.'

Rachael leaned back in her chair. 'It has to be a square-up for Yvonne, surely?'

'That's my guess. Why leave his body there if it wasn't to avenge her murder?'

'No doubt you'll be looking at those who were hardest hit by her death.'

'That'll be our starting point, yeah,' Bowker said. 'But in my eighteen years at Homicide, I've learnt not to rule anything out until you can rule it out.' He thought for a moment. 'Occasionally, when I remember that Bryant case, I wish I'd dug a bit deeper around Adrian Weston. Once we had him dead to rights on the murder, and on the molestation of his stepdaughter, we drew a line under his name.'

Rachael frowned. 'I've got a feeling this might be another jigsaw puzzle.'

'The first question we'll need to answer is why Weston was back in the Mallee after his release,' Bowker said. 'Unless, of course, he was shot somewhere else, and his body was dumped at Cocamba as a symbolic gesture.'

'There was a Back-To-Manangatang celebration about a week or so ago,' Rachael said. 'Remember? We were keen to go, except that Jacinta had her graduation that weekend.'

Bowker screwed up his face. 'A Back-To isn't the kind of event the most despised man in the town's history would attend. Unless he was looking for someone.' He shrugged. 'Like Jimmy Cobb, maybe, or Skeeta Allender, if they're still around.'

'Or you,' Rachael added quietly.

'Easier ways to find me than hoping I'd be at a reunion in a place I hadn't lived in for the best part of twenty years.'

'Who else is going up?'

'Sherlock Holmes. But he's in court until Thursday. I thought you and I could take a little trip down memory lane, drive there in our own car, and Sherlock can bring a police vehicle up later in the week. If the investigation drags on, then you can head back in time to start work.'

'It'll take you half a day alone to brief Darren on the intricacies of the Bryants' family tree.'

'Thought I'd leave that until he's up in Manang and I can go through Yvonne's murder file with him. If I try to explain the various connections in the abstract, he'll be totally confused before we even start the inquiry.'

'Where will we stay? Can't really impose three visitors on the local policeman.'

'I've already booked a couple of rooms at the pub.' He smiled. 'A twin for you and me. A single for Sherlock.'

'I'm surprised the pub's still there.'

'There'll always be a pub in Manang.' Bowker walked around to Rachael's side of the table, took her hands, and hoisted her to her feet. He put his arms around her. 'This could be our second honeymoon, Rach. Romance under the Mallee sky.'

Rachael laughed and kissed him on the nose. 'A twin room at the Manang pub in the middle of a murder investigation. Gee, you know the way to a girl's heart!'

* * *

The next morning, the couple set off early and were in Swan Hill by lunchtime. A more direct route would've taken them through Sea Lake via the Calder Highway, but Bowker was keen to retrace their journey of thirty years earlier, when they'd been banished from Ballarat and sent to the purgatory of the one-copper station at Manangatang. The route may have been the same, but the weather couldn't have been more different. The spring day was fine and cool, a light southerly breeze barely disturbing the leaves in the eucalypts beside the road. Thirty years earlier, their journey had been brutal. Temperatures in the high forties had generated a blistering inferno, and a roaring northerly had lifted dust, leaves and bark into a swirling maelstrom. Their old Peugeot had struggled with the heat, its air conditioner finally giving up just a few miles short of their destination.

'Remember when we first came up here, Rach?' Bowker said, with a smile.

'I'll never forget that day. I honestly believed we were driving through the gates of hell. If you'd suggested giving it a miss and finding another job, I would've turned the car around.'

Bowker put his hand on her knee. 'Think what we would've missed, eh?'

'Yeah.' She put her hand on top of his.

As they passed through Nyah, Bowker indicated a boarded-up milk bar with faded ice cream and newspaper advertising hoardings. 'That was the shop where I bought drinks that first day. Remember? My shoes got stuck in the melting bitumen.'

Rachael rolled her eyes. 'I thought the wind would tip the car.'

'I wonder what happened to the grumpy old bastard who ran the shop. Called me a dickhead for being out in the heat.'

Rachael laughed. 'He was right.'

Although the weather was pleasant, the drive took a depressing turn where the highway paralleled the river. Most of the verdant grape blocks that had once lined the road had now returned to nature, as small-scale sultana growing became unprofitable in the face of cheap imports and the rising price of diminishing irrigation water. Former orange orchards had also been abandoned, or the trees removed, as they followed the grapes into unprofitability. Even the scenic Nyah golf course that formerly followed the river like a green snake lay abandoned, indistinguishable from the landscape that had reclaimed it. Had it been a lack of membership from the departing population that led to its demise, or the advent of the monolithic Murray Downs Country Club across the river from Swan Hill? Particularly sad for Bowker was the demise of the Nyah Harness Racing Track, with meetings now being conducted on a new circuit inside the thoroughbred track in Swan Hill. Gone were the colour and close-up excitement of the picturesque riverside track, ditched in favour of a circuit so distant from spectators that the few patrons who attended watched the races on monitors in the dining room.

Bowker made the familiar turn onto the Mallee Highway at Piangil, one he'd made hundreds of times in the twelve years he and Rachael had lived in Manangatang. Piangil had always been a one-horse town, but it was looking shabbier and more neglected than the last time he'd seen it.

Stunted mallee scrub soon replaced the river red gums and irrigation, but unlike on their initial journey, the paddocks were an undulating carpet of green, the light wind carving waving patterns in the crop. Early spring rains had promised a bumper season, and a bumper season was required to cancel a series of wipe-outs from the preceding few years.

Bowker smiled to himself as he remembered the good times he and Rachael had spent in this area. He was well over six foot and measured a good axe handle across the shoulders, still fit despite closing in on sixty. His hair was greying at the sides, but he maintained the good looks of his earlier years. Fellow officers in Homicide were surprised when he spoke of retirement, assuming he was well short of the minimum age.

The kilometres slipped by without the angst of their first journey, and the couple marvelled at how they still knew by instinct how far they were from Manangatang. Rachael laughed as she recalled the Saturday they'd run out of petrol ten kilometres short of the town after a morning's shopping in Swan Hill. Bowker had been due on the football field at two o'clock, so had to jog into town and send out one of the locals to rescue her pregnant self, left abandoned on the side of the road with a toddler.

Over the final rise, the town came into view. From a distance, nothing appeared to have changed in a decade and a half. But as they crossed the railway line and came to a stop at Manangatang's main intersection, any illusion of a town trapped in time was shattered.

On the corner diagonally opposite, a new construction housed the Arenz agricultural business, but the rest of the main street was a shell of its former self. Most of the shops were vacant or boarded up. Gone was the old post office, and gone were the pharmacy, the supermarket, the banks, the newsagency, Pengilly's, Herbert Solicitors, and basically everything else in between.

Rachael stared sadly at the town's carcass. 'Oh, Greg. What's happened to the place?' she whispered.

'What's happened is exactly what Tom McColl predicted thirty years ago when I rode in his Cessna searching for lost sheep. He forecast Manang would eventually go the way of Chinkapook and Chillingollah. Unfortunately, that's happening.' He pointed up and down the street with his left hand. 'A couple of ag businesses, the café and the pub. That's it, by the looks of things. Shit, it's depressing.'

Neither of them spoke again until they pulled up in front of the motel-style accommodation attached to the Manangatang hotel. Bowker dragged their suitcase from the rear of the Subaru and placed it under the grapevine-lined walkway outside the rooms. 'I'll go grab the key,' he said, as he left Rachael to retrieve the last few items from the car.

The lounge was empty when he entered the hotel via the side door, so he made his way through to the public bar. A group of middle-aged men sat around a veneer-topped table, each fondling a pot of beer. An elderly man, his forearms on the bar, balanced on a stool as he chatted quietly with a woman washing glasses behind the counter.

The woman, who Bowker estimated to be in her sixties, walked to his end of the bar. 'What's your poison, mate?'

Bowker raised both palms. 'Nothing to drink right now, thanks. I've booked a couple of rooms for the rest of the week. I'm just chasing the keys.'

'I'll go and grab them. Won't be a minute.' She lifted a hinged section of the bar and started towards the lounge door.

'Booking will be under Greg Bowker,' he called after her. One of the men at the table looked up.

'I figured that,' she said. 'You're the only booking we've got this week.'

The man stood and strode over, hand outstretched. 'Greg Bowker, our ex-copper. Haven't seen you up here for twenty years. Shit, you've aged well. Hardly changed at all.' They shook hands. 'You remember me?'

Bowker thought for a moment, scanning his cerebral filing system for a name to fit the man with the bald, bowling-ball head. Finally, he had it. 'Yeah. Ball-Bearing Brodie. Got a farm out Daytrap way.'

Bowling-Ball-Head burst out laughing. 'Ball-Bearing was my old man. Died a couple of years ago. Hit the piss a bit too hard. Still, he made it to seventy-six, so his liver did a pretty good job.'

Bowker frowned. 'Sorry to hear it.'

'I'm Jim. Jim Brodie. Most people call me Pellets – you know, little ball-bearing.' Brodie chuckled. 'You would've known me as James when you were here.'

'Can't place you off the top of my head,' Bowker said. 'Must've kept your nose clean.'

'Went away to school in Ballarat, then to Longerenong Ag College, and played footy over at Nandaly. I wasn't around Manang much when you were here. You scared the shit out of me when I was a kid, so I wasn't keen to poke my head up again. You probably don't remember that night, but I bloody well do, I can tell you. Especially after what happened later.'

Bowker shrugged. 'You better remind me, mate.'

'Me and Donno Donovan were drinkin' piss under the pepper tree out there with Yvonne Bryant. You sprung us. You remember that?'

Bowker remembered the blond-headed fifteen-year-old version of Brodie but remained noncommittal. 'Vaguely.'

'You remember Yvonne, though? You solved her murder.'

Bowker nodded. 'Yeah, I remember Yvonne,' he said wistfully.

'She the reason you're back here? Heard you were a bigwig in the homicide squad nowadays.'

As the barmaid returned with two sets of keys, Bowker played a straight bat to Brodie. 'Yvonne Bryant's case was closed over thirty years ago.'

'Yeah, but you're here to investigate who killed that Weston prick.'

Bowker gave nothing away. 'You think that's got something to do with the Bryant girl's death?'

'You're takin' the piss, right? Body of her killer found at Cocamba where he dumped her all those years ago? Somebody's taken revenge, and good on 'em, I say.'

The barmaid was happy enough to throw in her two bob's worth. 'I wasn't around when the girl was killed, but from what the locals say, getting his head blown off with a shotty was too good for the pervert. Rooting bloody kids. It doesn't get any lower than that.'

'People around here will be barracking for you to solve this one so we know whose neck to hang a medal around,' Brodie added. 'Shouldn't be an offence to kill fuckers like him.'

'Well, it is.' Bowker accepted the keys from the barmaid. 'Thanks for these. Do I need to sign anything?'

'Fix it up when you leave. Rooms Four and Five.'

CHAPTER 2

Room Four was basic, but clean and tidy. Bowker threw the case on one of the single beds as Rachael hung their coats in the wardrobe.

'This will be a tricky investigation, Rach. Got a feeling the community won't be jumping out of the trees to help us find Weston's killer.'

'They reckon justice has taken its course?' Rachael asked.

'It seems that way, if the attitude in the pub is anything to go by.' Bowker snapped open the suitcase and began transferring clothing to a small chest of drawers. 'Remember that blond kid we sprung drinking stubbies under the peppercorn tree on our first night in town?'

Rachael screwed up her face, trying to recall. 'Was that when we first ran across Yvonne?'

Bowker nodded. 'Yeah. Well, that baby-faced kid is now a bald, fat, middle-aged pisshead. The spitting image of his old man. He's sitting in the bar knockin' down pots in the middle of a weekday.'

'Apple hasn't fallen far from the tree. Is that what you're saying?'

'Right beside the trunk.' Bowker tested the bedsprings with his hand. 'Might have to move these beds together if this is our second honeymoon.'

Smiling, Rachael put her arms around his neck. 'I'm sure a single bed won't slow you down, Detective.'

Bowker kissed her lightly on the lips. 'Was thinking of heading down to the police station and introducing myself. You be okay here on your own?'

'I might have a wander myself, or take a nana nap. Even though I'm not a nana. Yet!'

* * *

Bowker walked north up Wattle Street, pausing briefly in front of the town's public hall. There, his mind was instantly whisked back thirty-one years to when he'd stood at this very spot, contemplating the disappearance of a wayward teenage girl from the school's end-of-year social. He looked up, catching his reflection in the glass double doors at the top of the steps, and pondered how this simple instance of an absent student had led to a brutal murder committed to mask unspeakable acts of depravity by one of the local school's most senior staff.

Continuing northward, Bowker surveyed the giant grain silos across the road to his right. He was certain they'd multiplied since he last served in the town. At the corner of Coghill Street, he was stopped in his tracks by his first glimpse of the police station in nearly fifteen years. The front garden was choked with long, straggly weeds, most of them thistles going to seed. An overgrown melaleuca made the path up to the station door difficult to negotiate. He could've avoided the trouble. A sign on the glass door notified visitors that the officer was presently off duty and emergencies should be directed to the Robinvale station. A phone number for Robinvale was scrawled underneath in thick black Texta.

Bowker stood for a moment, hands on hips. This hadn't been

the way things operated when he ran the show up here. He'd always been on duty, arranging his free time around when he was needed, and had kept the yard neat and tidy, viewing the station's surrounds as a reflection of his attitude to the job and commitment to the community. *Still, each to their own*, he thought.

He walked around to the door of the attached residence. The backyard was in worse shape than the front, any remnant of the vegetable garden long gone. He thought of the snakes he'd bailed up out here on a green kikuyu lawn and wondered how many lurked in the long grass that now grew from the concrete verandah all the way to the back fence. A silver late-model Commodore wagon with three wide mag wheels fitted with high-end Bridgestones was parked in the carport. A standard wheel and tyre were fitted to the driver's side front. With the Commodore under cover, the police vehicle had been relegated to the street.

Bowker knocked on the back door. There was no answer. He knocked again, more urgently. A voice came from inside. 'I'm off duty. Ring Robinvale if it's an emergency.'

Bowker rolled his eyes. 'It's Greg Bowker from Homicide.'

He heard footsteps from inside and the sound of the door being unlocked. A shortish man in a tee-shirt, shorts and thongs opened the door. 'Sorry, mate. I didn't expect you till later in the day.' He thrust out a hand. 'Shane Parker.'

As they shook, Parker removed his hand quickly with a grimace. 'Sorry. Cut my thumb on a broken glass. Had to break up an altercation between two yokels at the pub a week or so ago. Went to the hospital, had a stitch put in, tetanus injection, the lot. Only just starting to heal up.'

So, you're not off duty all of the time, Bowker wanted to say, but kept his own counsel. Parker showed Bowker his taped finger, then invited him inside. The senior constable had a round, puffy face with short-cropped dark hair receding on each side. In the 1980s, there was no way he would've qualified as a policeman, being well below the minimum height requirement at that time. His stretched tee-shirt betrayed the start of a premature middle-age spread.

'Can I get you a coffee?' he asked, as he rifled through a bench covered with dirty plates and cooking utensils.

'No thanks, mate.' Bowker dragged out a chair at the kitchen table. 'Just came over to introduce myself and grab the Weston file to read over tonight.'

Giving up on the bench, Parker sat down opposite him. 'Bet you got a shock when you drove into this shithole.'

Bowker raised his eyebrows. 'Got a shock when I saw how much the town had died since I worked up here.'

Parker sat bolt upright. 'You worked here? What, as a copper?'

'Yep,' Bowker said, smiling. 'Senior constable, just like yourself.'

'I didn't know that. Shit. How long did it take you to escape the place?'

'Came up in the mid-eighties, stayed here twelve years. That was my own decision. Absolutely loved it. In a way, I regret having to leave.'

Parker shook his head. 'Fuck me! I'll be gone as soon as I can get a transfer. Boiling hot, shitty weather. In the middle of bloody nowhere. Nothin' to do.'

Bowker shrugged. 'You get to like the isolation after a while. The heat, not so much. And there was plenty to do when the wife and I were up here.'

Parker scratched his chin. 'The mid-eighties? So, you must've been here when the girl was killed.'

'Yep. First year in Manang.'

'I should've put two and two together when you introduced yourself.' Exhaling loudly, Parker shook his head. 'Thanks, mate. Made it tough for the other poor bastards following you. Fuck me. Not a day goes past where I don't hear about bloody Greg Bowker, the local hero who cracked the Yvonne Bryant case. That's between taking on a gang of bikies, or nailing a drug dealer, or doin' this, or doin' that. Gun footballer and tennis player into the bargain.'

Bowker leaned back in his chair and smiled to himself. 'Big fish in a small pool. How long you been up here?'

Parker closed his eyes. 'Came in January. Worst decision of my life.'

'Why'd you apply? Surely you did a bit of research.'

Parker folded his arms on the table. 'Wanted to be my own boss – I was sick of big-headed senior officers, and there wasn't much competition for the position. 'Sides, my mother was born up this way, and she said it'd be a pretty easy gig. Lots of reasons.' He shrugged. 'You're right. Should've come up and had a look first, I suppose.'

'Where you from?'

'Melbourne, but born and brought up in the Western District near Hamilton. Used to go camping at Lake Bolac. That's got a one-copper station. Thought one small country town would be pretty similar to the next.' Despondently, Parker looked at the ceiling. 'Fuck me, did Laura and I get an education when we drove into this hole!'

'Is Laura your other half?'

Parker spat out a half-laugh. 'Was. Lasted less than a month.

Heat and wind cracked her in the end.' He shrugged. 'Then again, we'd been having problems before we came up here. This probably brought everything to a head.'

Bowker frowned. 'Sorry to hear that.'

'What makes it worse is that there's not a single female within fifty k's of this dump.' He laughed. 'And in a town this size, you'd never get away with rooting a married one.'

'Nice wagon in the carport,' Bowker said, keen to change the subject.

Parker beamed. 'My pride and joy. Dropped a V8 into it, now it goes like a cut cat. Hit the accelerator too hard and it'll put you in the back seat. Absolute chick magnet.'

Not working too well at the moment, Bowker thought, but didn't say. He suppressed a smile as he recalled Rachael's theory about hotted-up cars and their attraction to women. *Usually driven by little weeds*, she'd said, and *most females don't give two hoots about muscle cars.* 'Did you have a blow-out on the right front?'

Parker huffed out a breath. 'Ran over a bloody echidna. I rang up the Ouyen tyre place about getting it fixed, but apparently, it's totally fucked. You can't even put a tube in because of all the little spikes coming through. They've ordered a replacement, but it'll have to come up from Melbourne, so it might take a while.'

'Set you back a quid or two, I'll bet. Probably need a new spare as well. The one on there now is nearly bald.' Leaning forward, Bowker placed his forearms on the table, fingers knitted together. 'Tell me what we know about the Weston murder. Let's start with who found the body.'

'A Netcor maintenance team replacing the feeder cable into the Cocamba silo's control room. The body stunk to high hell.

They called it in to me, and I went out, had a look, then rang the boys from Swan Hill. I took a statement from the power workers and told them to move on to their next job, expecting Cocamba would be tied up as a crime scene for days. When the Swan Hill detectives arrived, they ID'd Weston from the licence in his wallet, then called you blokes from Homicide.'

'Any gut feelings on who might've done it?'

Parker shrugged. 'That's well above my pay grade, mate. But from what the locals have said about Weston, my advice would be not to waste too much time on him. Bastard got exactly what he deserved, apparently.'

This had Bowker seething, but he said nothing.

Parker continued. 'Someone obviously waited patiently and took revenge when he was released from prison.'

'So, you've been through the Bryant murder file looking for people with a possible motive?'

Parker shook his head. 'Nope. You don't call in the dogs and bark yourself. But I fished it out in case one of you big dicks wanted it.'

Bowker was desperately trying to keep his annoyance in check. 'I'm afraid it doesn't work that way, Shane. Detective Sergeant Holmes will be here on Thursday, and the three of us will operate as a team. We'll divvy up the work between us. You know the locals and the social networks. Your input will be crucial to the investigation.'

Parker shrugged. 'You're the boss.'

'We'll meet in the station at eight each morning and map out our strategy for the day.'

Parker frowned. 'Fuck, eight o'clock? Can I bring in my brekky?'

Ignoring this comment, Bowker stood up. 'Now, I'll just grab the Yvonne Bryant file and your notes on Weston's death.'

Parker led Bowker through the house and into the station. The files Bowker had requested were on a disorganised desk covered in its fair share of takeaway food wrappings and lolly papers. Bowker put the files under his arm, bade his farewells, and resisted the temptation to tear down the *Station Closed* sign as he left through the station door.

CHAPTER 3

Rather than retracing his route back to the hotel, Bowker headed west down Coghill Street, past Prong Lyon's house and into the lane running to the rear of the homes on Pioneer Street. After a hundred metres, he was behind Red Cameron's house. He was delighted to see a couple of standardbreds in the horse yards and two jogging carts close by, their shafts pointing to the heavens. *Red's still got his horses*, Bowker thought, smiling. He wandered across and gave a chestnut filly a pat on the nose before she shied sideways and turned her rump towards him. A gelding in the yard next door gave a jealous whinny, and Bowker obliged him with a scratch between the ears.

Bowker returned to the pub via Pioneer Street, passing the hospital where his three kids had been born. Unlike the main street, Pioneer hadn't changed much in the twenty years he'd been away. The houses had obviously aged, and the odd new residence had been built, but all in all, the population of the town itself appeared to have remained fairly stable. Bowker theorised that the decimation of the business sector had been due to the consolidation and mechanisation of cropping properties, and to the relative accessibility of larger towns on the back of modern transport.

Rachael wasn't in the room when Bowker arrived, so he decided to quickly peruse the file Parker had started on the Weston murder. He pulled up a chair to the small table, where he had room to spread out the contents of the file. Much to his disgust, the manilla folder contained just four pages with scant handwritten notes. The first sheet simply bore a record of the date and time Parker had been called by the Netcor team, and a one-sentence summary of where the body had been found. The second and third each contained a one-paragraph statement describing the discovery of the body, signed by the power company workers.

Bowker flipped to the other page, expecting a diagram of the body's location in relation to the road, the railway line, the grain shed, and the various silos. To his disappointment, all he found was Adrian Weston's name, address, date of birth and driver's licence number. The fact that the listed abode read Lockett Street, Altona told Bowker that someone had updated Weston's address and kept his licence current while he was in prison. Obviously, no attempt had been made by Parker to follow up on his details. When Bowker finally deciphered the three letters scrawled in capitals at the bottom of the page, he knew why the file was so minimal and why more current details hadn't been sought. *NMP.* Not My Problem.

Bowker shook his head and closed the folder. Picking up the two-inch-thick Yvonne Bryant file that he'd compiled three decades ago, he opened it to the first page. He took a writing pad from his briefcase and scribbled a heading. *Those with Motive to Kill Weston.*

*   *   *

The main street was virtually deserted, but Rachael finally encountered a familiar face in the Five Star Café. Prong Lyon's wife Lenore was collecting *The Herald Sun* and *The Swan Hill*

Guardian from the small shop, and procuring a few household items from the tiny range available. The two women exchanged hugs and pleasantries, each commenting on how the other hadn't changed in the last twenty years.

'What are you doing up here, Rachael?' Lenore asked, as she paid for her purchases.

'Just came back for a look. Greg's working a case up here.'

'Oh, the Adrian Weston murder,' Lenore said matter-of-factly. 'That's certainly created a buzz around the town. The bugger isn't getting much sympathy, that's for sure.'

Rachael shrugged. 'Still, all crimes have to be investigated, regardless of circumstances.'

'Police must think it's pretty important if they've sent up one of their most senior detectives.'

'Greg was keen to run the investigation,' Rachael replied. 'It would take a fortnight to bring another detective up to speed on the goings-on of thirty years ago.' Keen to move the conversation away from what was really her husband's prerogative, she said, 'Gee, Lenore, the town's changed a lot.'

'Yes, it's sad for those of us who remember what the place used to be like. The population of the district has collapsed, but the town's stayed pretty similar, since there's cheap housing available to people living on Struggle Street. The number of farming families has dropped through the floor, though. The football and netball club merged with Tooleybuc over the river a few years ago, and the town has one tennis team that travels every second week to play.'

Rachael frowned. 'What happened to Terry Rivers and the chemist shop?'

'Terry retired back to Elmore, where his family came from. Passed away three years ago, unfortunately.'

'That's awful,' Rachael said. 'If Greg had known, he would've attended his funeral, I'm sure.' She paused for a moment. 'Tim and Pam?'

'Bought a post office in Melbourne somewhere. They've sold that, and live in a retirement village now, I think. Supermarket closed decades ago, then gradually, most of the other businesses followed. We held a big Back-To-Manangatang a few weeks ago, and thousands came. Most got a hell of a shock when they saw the main street.' Lenore smiled. 'Anyway, enough of the doom and gloom. How long are you up for?'

Rachael shrugged. 'For Greg, it depends on how long the investigation takes. For me, I resume work at a kindergarten on Monday, so I'll probably head back over the weekend.'

'How about you and Greg come around for tea tomorrow night?' Lenore asked brightly. 'We can discuss old times.'

Rachael screwed up her face a little. 'That might be a bit tricky, unfortunately. Another detective will join Greg tomorrow, and–'

Lenore cut her off mid-sentence. 'Then bring him along as well. He'll be sick of pub meals by the time he leaves Manang.'

Following another couple of minutes of social chit-chat, much of it centred on the fate of Rachael's old netball teammates, the two women again exchanged hugs and went their separate ways. When Rachael arrived back at the hotel room, Bowker was only partway through rereading the Yvonne Bryant file. She walked behind his chair and kissed him lightly on the top of the head. 'Been asked out to tea tomorrow night, over at Prong and Lenore's. Darren's been invited too.'

Bowker smiled as he leaned back in his chair. 'Why don't you call him Sherlock? Everyone else does. Don't think he answers to Darren unless his mum calls.'

'I feel stupid calling a grown man by a nickname. I'd have trouble calling Prong that. I notice Lenore calls him Ian.' Rachael sat down opposite him. 'How'd you go with the local bloke? Got it half-solved for you?'

Bowker shook his head, a disgusted look contorting his face. 'He's absolutely useless. As far as he's concerned, Weston's murder isn't his problem. *Above his pay grade*,' he said, using air quotes. 'If I'd taken that attitude, Skeeta Allender would've spent twenty years in jail. Shit, it's not as though he's overloaded with other work.' Exhaling loudly, he dropped the four-page file in front of Rachael. 'There's his case notes.'

Rachael opened the folder and looked up at him, open-mouthed. 'You're joking.'

'If he thinks he's getting a free ride while Sherlock and I do all the legwork, he's got another thing coming. I'll take an old photo of Weston down to the station in a couple of minutes and see if it rings any bells with him. Tomorrow morning, I'll get him to drive me out to Percy Bryant's place at Winnambool, and fill him in on the background to the Yvonne Bryant murder on the way.'

Folding the file, Rachael returned it across the table. 'I walked up the main street while you were away, Greg. Two out of every three shops are closed. Gee, it looks sad.'

'Yeah, well, the police station looks pretty sad too. The gardens you spent so much time developing are gone, and the building looks as though it's been closed down for good.'

'His other half mustn't be a gardener. Then again, keeping a garden is a tough gig in a climate like this.'

'His missus only lasted a month, Rach.' Bowker shrugged. 'I suppose I should cut him a bit of slack, the poor bastard. I'm not sure how I would've coped without you.'

Rachael smiled. 'We coped well enough to have three kids.'

* * *

When Bowker arrived back at the police station, he made his presence known with a long whistle as he walked towards the back. Parker ushered him inside, and they adjourned to the station, where Parker had at least made some attempt to clean up. He motioned for Bowker to sit in the office chair behind the desk, but Bowker declined the invitation.

'That's your chair, mate. I'm here to use your office, not take it over.' Bowker pulled up a second, cloth-covered chair.

Parker opened the top drawer of his desk and removed a key from a tray of paper clips and other stationery accessories. 'This is a spare key to the station. If you're going to operate out of here, you'll need access when I'm out and about somewhere.'

'Better exchange mobile numbers too,' Bowker replied.

Parker nodded. 'What's our next move?'

Bowker smiled to himself. The use of the word *our* was an improvement on their earlier conversation. 'I'd like to go through everything you know, or might've observed, regarding Weston. And I don't just mean after the body was found.'

'Seeing his body was the first time I'd laid eyes on the prick,' Parker replied quickly.

'Well, we can't be totally sure of that, because he'd had his face blown off before you were called to Cocamba,' Bowker said. 'You might've seen him earlier in passing, but not connected him with the body. He may have been wearing different clothes, or whatever.'

Parker shrugged. 'I wouldn't have a clue what he looked like.'

Bowker opened Parker's Weston file and removed a picture. 'This old photo of him was in the Yvonne Bryant file.'

'I didn't open the Bryant file,' Parker muttered. 'Didn't think it was my investigation.'

Bowker handed the photo across the desk. 'It was taken when he was a teacher at the school thirty-one years ago, so he probably looked a lot different after three decades in prison. But it might ring a bell.'

Parker stared at it blankly. 'Haven't seen that face around, although as you say, he might've looked a lot different.' Squinting, he examined the picture more closely. 'That gold chain's the same one he had on when we found his body, though.'

Bowker smiled. They were getting closer to verifying Weston's ID. They had his driver's licence, and now the jewellery, but no face. They'd need his DNA and prison dental records to fully confirm he was the victim. 'Did you go to the Back-To reunion at the racetrack a week or so ago?'

'I was there for a while, until it was my knock-off time.'

Bowker felt his annoyance rise again, but bit his lip. 'And you can't remember an older version of that face in the crowd?'

'There were hundreds of people. Most of them strangers to me. I'm not saying he wasn't there, but it's a big ask to remember someone who might look like a thirty-year-old photo.'

Although Bowker had known it was a long shot, he'd hoped that an incident at the reunion might've brought Weston to Parker's attention. 'Seen any strange cars parked around Manang since the Back-To?'

'What sort of cars?'

'Any that you haven't noticed around the town before,' Bowker replied. 'Parked in the same spot for a week or more.'

'Weston's car – is that what you're getting at?'

'Well, there was no car reported out at the silos where his body was found, so *something* was used to transport him there, either dead or alive. If that trip originated from Manang or surrounds, then he must've come up here under his own steam prior to his murder. If that was the case, then he either drove a car or came on the bus. If he did drive a car, then he was obviously in no condition to drive it away. Logically, it must be still sitting around somewhere. Or someone's hidden it.'

'Have we got any idea what sort of car he owned?'

'When he went to jail, he had a bright red Valiant Charger. We'll need to see if he still owned it and whether it's still registered after all these years. But I can tell you one thing: if he drove it up here, it would've stood out like dog's balls.'

Parker shook his head. 'I don't even know what a Valiant Charger looks like.'

Bowker smiled. 'That's because it was built before you were born. Big, heavy, two-door coupe, made to compete with the Holden Monaro and Ford's Falcon GTHO. They were the muscle cars of the time.'

'Can't recall seeing anything like that around town.'

Bowker nodded. 'If he did drive it, it should be easy enough to track his journey, because it runs on leaded petrol, and it'd struggle to get from Melbourne to Manang on one tank of juice. Even if it had, I suspect he would've fuelled up before he got here, in case he couldn't find the additives he needed to get him home.' He beckoned to Parker. 'Hand us your phone, and find me the number of VicRoads, please.'

Parker slid the phone across, then googled the number on his desktop computer. Bowker punched it in, identified himself with VicRoads, and quoted the Charger's rego number, which he'd scribbled on the back of Weston's photo. After receiving the information, he replaced the receiver and looked at Parker. 'The plates have never been handed in, so the car's still in Weston's name. But it hasn't been registered for thirty years. So, what does that tell us?'

Parker looked unsure. 'Fuck nothing?'

'Not quite,' Bowker said. 'It helps crystallise things just a little, and if you keep making these baby steps, eventually you reach your destination. There's an old Chinese proverb: every long journey starts with one small step.'

'Yeah? So, Confucius, what little step did that phone call help us make?' Parker asked with a smirk.

'We now know that if Parker drove the Charger up here, it was as an unregistered vehicle. So, there's a possibility it's come up on numberplate recognition software somewhere – on the Citylink toll scanners, for instance. If it did, then an infringement notice will be somewhere in the system. We just need to make some enquiries and see if we can find anything. Can I leave that with you?'

Parker frowned. 'Yeah, okay.'

'It'd be particularly interesting if anything showed up on the major city arterials leading to Ballarat or Bendigo.' Bowker smiled.

'We've made a bit of progress in the last ten minutes, Shane. We now know Weston was either brought up here, dead or alive, by an unknown party who dumped him at Cocamba, or he drove up of his own free will, in the unregistered Charger or another vehicle. Unless, of course, he came by bus or got a lift with someone.' He laughed. 'Close to nailing it, eh, mate?'

'Yeah,' Parker replied blankly.

'I'll slip around in the morning, and you can take me out to Winnambool to have a chat with Yvonne Bryant's family,' Bowker said. 'Not sure if old Percy is still alive, but his son should be there.'

'Where the fuck is Winnambool?'

'Look it up,' Bowker said, as he stood. 'See you at eight in the morning.'

* * *

When Bowker arrived back at his room, Rachael was lying on her bed reading *The Age*. He sat beside her and kissed her gently. 'Want to come with me to visit Yvonne?'

'What, out at the cemetery?'

'Yeah. She wouldn't get a lot of visitors, given her history. Besides, I'd like to see what other graves have appeared since we left. Might be able to cross a few names off the list of people I need to speak to.'

The Manangatang cemetery was located on Robinvale Road, to the north of the town. In today's spring weather, it was the picture of serenity, with new growth on the trees, green grass flourishing between the plots, and birdsong providing a soundtrack for the departed. It was a far cry from the day Yvonne Bryant had been buried, when the blistering heat and a dusty northerly gale had made conditions close to unbearable.

Rachael and Bowker walked up the closest row of headstones, stopping at the graves of people whose names they recognised. Most had been elderly when they'd passed away, and their presences in the cemetery came as no surprise. But two nameplates jumped out at Bowker. The first was the double grave of Pete and Dawn Allender, the long-suffering parents of Yvonne Bryant's boyfriend Skeeta, who'd originally been charged with her murder before additional evidence led to Adrian Weston's arrest.

Bowker stared at the grave. 'At last Pete and Dawn are at rest. They spent every waking hour trying to squeeze a quid out of that crap piece of dirt they owned. And for what? To pass it on to bloody Skeeta, who probably sold up and pissed the money against the wall straight away.'

The other grave of interest belonged to Cath Bryant, Percy's second wife. Cath's grave was beside that of her eldest son Bernard, who'd committed suicide in his twenties, leaving behind a wife and kids. Bernard was born of Cath's first marriage to Keith 'Crayfish' Harris, who'd died under a falling slasher. Keith's grave was on the other side of their son's.

Shaking his head, Bowker put his hands in his pockets. 'Bloody old Cath's gone to meet her maker. Wonder if she'll be able to plead her innocence up there? Or maybe she'll go straight down below to join old Crayfish.'

Rachael put her arm through his. 'Come on, Greg. Don't speak ill of the dead. Let's go find Yvonne.'

They found the teenager's modest grave in the second row back, next to her mother Lynette's, who'd died of a drug overdose in

Melbourne in her early thirties. Red dirt covered most of the granite slab, but Bowker noticed that up near the headstone, the granite had been brushed cleaner. An old glass bottle sat below Yvonne's name. A bunch of badly withered red flowering gum blossoms buckled over its neck and gradually decayed against its sides.

'Somebody remembers Yvonne,' Rachael said sadly.

'Yeah, but judging by the dirt on her grave, she doesn't get too many visitors.' Bowker took one of the flowerheads and rubbed it between his fingers. The dead petals crumbled to powder. 'How long do you reckon these flowers have been here?'

Rachael thought for a moment. 'If it was the middle of summer, I'd say about five minutes. But in this weather, it could be weeks. Hard to tell. You reckon someone might've left them during the Back-To?'

'That's what I'm wondering.'

'Do you think it might've been Adrian Weston, feeling a pang of conscience after all these years?'

'Maybe,' Bowker said. 'It was his first chance to visit since he killed her.' He walked to a nearby sugar gum and found a stick, which he poked in the bottleneck, lifting it away from the grave. 'I think I'll take this with me. Might have prints that'll give us a clue in solving this case.'

'Here's Shirley Bryant's grave,' Rachael said, as she stood afoot a double grave next to Lynette's. 'Looks like there's room for Perce when he passes away.'

Bowker raised his eyebrows. 'Interesting that he'll be buried beside his first wife rather than Cath.'

'Not necessarily. This grave would've been created on Shirl's death, years before he hooked up with Cath. His plans ccould've changed.'

'I don't think so,' Bowker said. 'Cath's grave was a single. We just saw it, remember? Percy would've buried her, so by the looks, he wasn't planning to join her.'

Rachael nodded. As they returned to their car, she howled in pain, then looked at the sole of one of her runners. 'Three-cornered jacks. I'd forgotten about those bloody things!'

Embedded in the heel of her shoe was the bane of every Mallee resident's life, after snakes – a seedpod of the noxious weed emex. The pod was as hard as steel and had three spikes projecting from it. It grew on vines that spread along the ground, sometimes covering an area of ten or more square metres.

Bowker placed the bottle on the ground and extracted the brown three-cornered pod from Rachael's shoe. He knew her foot would be bleeding inside her sock. Tracking the vine back to the short stem, he reefed the whole plant out, taproot and all. When he held the plant above his head, the tendrils cascaded to the ground on all sides. He threw it in a heap away from the walkway and returned to retrieve the flower bottle.

'You right, Rachael?'

'Yeah, I'm okay,' she replied, as she limped towards the car.

* * *

That evening, it was chicken parma for two, as Bowker and Rachael patronised the pub for tea. The lounge was quiet, with just a young couple at a table near the window and a group of four in the centre of the room. As Bowker led Rachael past them, an elderly man grabbed him by the wrist.

'Has to be Greg Bowker, surely?'

Bowker looked down at the man, who had red hair and blistered skin, and recognised him in a flash. 'Red Cameron. You haven't changed a bit.'

'Still a bullshit artist, I see, Greg. And Rachael. *You* haven't changed.'

'You're too kind,' Rachael replied, before turning to Red's wife. 'Still teaching, Pam?'

'Been retired a few years now. Only one left from your time there would be Anne Stapleton, or Anne Ronke, as you would've known her.' Pam motioned to the couple sharing their table. 'This is our son Sean and his wife Danielle.'

'Knew they'd send some big boys up to sort out the Cocamba murder, but I didn't expect the local hero to come up himself,' Red said, with a chuckle.

'I know which way the land lies up here, so it made sense for me to handle the case,' Bowker replied, then quickly changed the subject. 'I notice there's a couple of horses behind your place.'

Red laughed. 'Didn't take you long. When are you due back in Melbourne?'

'Depends on how the case goes. But it'll be a few days at least, I'd imagine.'

'Wander down one morning and we'll work them up the roads for a few miles. Just like old times.'

Bowker smiled. Working pacers again would be an unexpected bonus.

CHAPTER 4

Bowker arrived at the police station a little before eight and found Parker half-dressed. He assured Bowker that he'd be ready by the agreed time, so Bowker left him to don his uniform, wandering to the carport and leaning against the police vehicle. The morning was cool by Mallee standards, with a few drops of rain painting splotches on the concrete footpath. Bowker looked up Coghill Street to the west, where the sky was darkening with the arrival of the promised cold front. Half an inch of rain had been forecast – a godsend at this time of year, with the heads of grain starting to fill.

Parker arrived at the vehicle, still tucking his shirt tails into his trousers. He threw the car keys to Bowker. 'All yours, mate.'

Bowker caught the keys and immediately tossed them back, suspecting that Parker had little idea how to find Winnambool. 'It's your vehicle, Shane. You drive. I'll just sit back and take in the delights of the countryside.'

'I planned to have a quick glance at the CFA map before you came, but my alarm didn't go off,' Parker said sheepishly.

Bowker remained po-faced, keen not to alienate an officer he needed as part of the investigation, although his hope that Parker would be a source of local intel was weakening by the minute. 'You must approach the job differently than I did when I was up here, mate. In my first two days, I travelled all the backroads and found every locality in my patch. Three thousand square kilometres of turf, and I knew every acre of it.'

Parker screwed up his face. 'To each their own, I guess. I tend to work on a need-to-know basis. If I'm contacted by somebody out of town, I drive out and find the place. Can't see much point travelling around dirt roads that all look the same just for the hell of it.' He laughed. 'Suppose that's why you're a detective at Homicide and I'll always be a flatfoot in some godforsaken backwater.'

Although Bowker agreed, he said nothing as he climbed into the passenger seat.

Parker fastened his seatbelt and started the vehicle. 'In your vast experience of the area, what's the quickest way to get out there?' he asked, without any attempt at hiding his sarcasm.

Bowker turned in his seat and faced him. 'Listen, Shane. I've come up here to investigate a murder, not to engage in a pissing competition, okay? You might feel I'm a bit obsessive for your liking, but that's the way it is. So, let's cut the schoolboy sniping, okay? To be honest, I'm way too old to be interested in that shit. We both are.'

While Bowker was thirty years older than Parker, there was no doubt who would prevail in a physical altercation. After a pause, Parker shook his head, and finally spoke. 'You're the boss. Which way's the quickest to Bryant's?'

'You could follow the Robinvale Road as far as Annuello, then turn left. Better road that way, but I always preferred to go there directly via Winnambool Road. Turn-off is just before the cemetery. Lot more to see that way as well.'

Parker smirked. 'We must be lookin' for different things.'

'Probably,' Bowker replied. 'What do you know about Percy Bryant?'

'Nothing. Never met him. But I'm assuming he's related to the girl murdered at Cocamba thirty years ago.'

'He's Yvonne's grandfather. She came up to live with him and his second wife after her mother died. Although Percy treated her like the daughter he'd lost, his wife Cath and her son hated Yvonne's guts. For a while, we suspected that Cath or Yabby, or both, may have had something to do with Yvonne's death, but it didn't turn out that way. Adrian Weston was the bastard who killed her, no doubt.'

Parker chuckled. 'Yabby?'

'Kevin Harris. His old man's nickname was Crayfish, so the two sons got Lobster and Yabby.' Bowker smiled. 'Surely you've noticed that everyone in this district has a nickname.'

Parker nodded. 'Yep. Bloody hard to keep track of who's who.'

'You'll probably get one if you're here long enough.'

'The only name I've been called is Dickhead.'

Locals usually get it pretty spot-on, Bowker thought, but didn't say. 'You wouldn't have seen Yabby in Manang,' he said instead. 'Does most of his socialising over the river at Tooleybuc, where his wife hails from.'

Flicking on his left indicator, Parker headed up the gravel-covered Winnambool Road. 'You thinking the old bloke murdered Weston? A revenge killing?'

'I'm not even sure he's still alive, but I couldn't find his grave in the cemetery, so I'm assuming he's still with us. Cath is gone, though.'

'Bryant will be pretty long in the tooth by now, surely?' Parker said.

'Yeah, he'll have to be in his mid-nineties, I reckon. He was sixty-odd at the time of Yvonne's murder.'

'Shit. Sounds a bit old to be shooting a bloke and carting him out to Cocamba.'

Bowker shrugged. 'Yeah, probably. At this stage, we can't count him out simply because of his age, though. We'll have to wait for the forensic report, but Weston may have been shot where his body was found. Perhaps Percy had help in the killing, or in transporting the body. Too early to dismiss anything.'

After a few minutes, they were at the sandy intersection of Winnambool and Webster Roads, where corner-cutting tracks created a diamond shape. In a patch of scrub in the centre was a homemade sign that read *Piccadilly Corner*. Finger boards pointed in various directions, displaying the names of local families.

Parker guffawed. 'Somebody's got a sense of humour. Couldn't be more different to Piccadilly Circus.'

Bowker smiled. 'Believe it or not, this district is officially called Piccadilly Corner. You'll find it on some of the older maps.'

'Fuck me,' Parker said, shaking his head. 'Delusions of grandeur!'

A couple of kilometres went by, and the rain became heavier, requiring Parker to click the wipers up a notch.

'First time I've ever been out here in the rain,' Bowker said. 'Normally hot as buggery with a wind picking up dust. Nice change.'

Parker looked across at him. 'Out this way a lot, by the sounds of it?'

'Yeah,' Bowker replied wistfully. 'More times than I wanted.'

'Were the Bryants hard work?' Parker asked.

'When Yvonne was creating havoc around town, I knew this trek pretty well. Even more so when she was found murdered.'

A trio of kangaroos bounded across the road, and Parker slowed a little, waiting for the last one to clear the fence into a paddock of barley.

'But it wasn't just the Bryants I came out here to see,' Bowker continued. 'Her fuckwit twenty-three-year-old drug-dealing boyfriend, Skeeta Allender, lived next door. And just up the road was this young bloke who was close to Yvonne as well. Travis Urdevic. He lived with his mum in a derelict farmhouse on the Bryant property. She was a junkie, and I needed to visit her, as well as Travis. End result was that I spent a lot of time at Winnambool.' Bowker looked across at Parker. 'If you'd read the murder file, I wouldn't have to explain all this shit.'

Parker's eyes remained on the road, and he was silent for a few moments. 'There's a bloke called Urdevic who works on a farm down at Chinkapook.'

'That's him. He was labouring for Steve Brain when I transferred to Melbourne, doing a bit of contract shearing when cropping was quiet.'

'Steve Brain? Is that Shitfa?'

Bowker chuckled. 'Yeah, Shitfa Brain. Nickname's not only clever, but appropriate, from what I can remember.'

'The Robinvale blokes picked up an Urdevic in Manang one night when we did a swap,' Parker said. 'Over the limit.'

'Travis Urdevic would have to be in his late forties by now. Should know better,' Bowker replied.

'Nah, the kid they booked was only eighteen, from memory,' Parker said, as he turned on the demisters. 'Still on his red Ps. Double zero limit.'

'Most probably Travis's son, if he's got one.' Bowker shook his head. 'Shit, time flies.'

'I'm guessing Urdevic Senior and this Skeeta bloke are high on your list of suspects for this murder? They wouldn't have had a lot of time for the bastard if they were both keen on the Bryant girl.'

'They're part of the group we'll need to talk to first,' Bowker replied.

* * *

While Bowker and Parker were absorbing the wondrous sights of Piccadilly Corner and beyond, Rachael visited the school, hoping to catch up with any former colleagues that remained before classes started. Her twelve years of working there as an integration aide gave her a sense of belonging when she entered the school, bypassing the general office and heading directly to the staffroom.

This feeling evaporated when she walked through the door. Fifteen unfamiliar and mostly young faces stared at her, and Rachael realised she was a stranger in a not-so-strange world. The sudden silence was only broken when an older woman she recognised strode across the room and threw both arms around her neck.

'Rachael Bowker!' the woman exclaimed. 'How come you never change?'

'Anne Ronke,' Rachael replied, as she hugged her former premiership wing defence.

'It's Anne Stapleton nowadays. Married Bryan Stapleton from Chinky.'

'Good get,' Rachael replied, with a chuckle. She looked around the room. 'I know it's stupid, but I had visions of walking in here and seeing the staff from twenty years ago. Thank God you were here, otherwise I would've looked sillier than I already do.'

'Lucky you caught me, actually. I only work part time these days, teaching VCE English four mornings a week.'

'Are you the sole survivor from the old days?'

'Donna Scott's here. Just came back from long service leave. You would've known her as Donna Cavanagh – she married Spider Scott from Daytrap, and they've got four boys now. Rebecca Johns is married to Sammy Moore. Had a kid of their own to go with the two she brought up here with her in your day. Drives up from Chillingollah every morning.'

The two women exchanged updates about their children and life in general and agreed to meet after lunch for coffee at Anne's house on Church Street. The school bell rang, and the room quickly disgorged its human contents, leaving Rachael sitting at the main table on her own. She skimmed a couple of industry publications, then left the room via the corridor that led through the library and primary section of the school. She passed several classrooms where small children were sitting on the floor in groups around their teacher. As she passed the Grade Six room, a voice echoed down the passage behind her.

'Miss Stow!'

Miss Stow? I haven't been called that since I worked here, she thought, as she turned towards the voice. In the corridor was a slim woman of around forty years of age, with short, mousy hair and a friendly smile. Her face was vaguely familiar, but a name or a context refused to materialise in Rachael's mind.

The woman walked closer. 'You don't remember me, do you? Then again, I did leave here when I was eleven. Bernadette Weston.'

Rachael's jaw dropped. What was Bernadette doing back here? Back in the place where her father had molested her stepsister? Back where her father had killed Yvonne Bryant to cover his tracks? And now, back where her father himself had just been murdered?

Rachael did her best to remain matter-of-fact. 'Bernadette, I haven't seen you for thirty years. What brings you up here?'

'I'm a teacher. Not my first preference for a school, obviously, but positions were hard to get when I graduated. Still are, apparently. This one was available, so I took it.'

Rachael frowned. 'Pretty courageous decision, after all that happened here.'

Bernadette shrugged. 'I was a bit too young then to remember most of it. Thought I'd put in a year or two up here, then transfer somewhere else. But I started going out with Travis, we got married, and here I am.' She gave a weak laugh. 'Pretty ironic, eh?'

Surely she didn't marry Travis Urdevic, Rachael thought. 'So, who's the lucky Travis?' she asked instead.

'Travis Urdevic. You must remember him from when you were here. Really good friends with Sophie, and with Yvonne.' She looked down at the floor. 'Before she was killed, of course. Before my father…'

Rachael tried to lift the mood. 'Of course I know Travis. Good basketballer. Nice kid.'

'Not a kid anymore,' Bernadette said, with a laugh. 'He was forty-seven his last birthday. We've got two children – an eighteen-year-old son, and a daughter just about to turn fifteen.'

Rachael shook her head. 'Seems like just yesterday that you and Sophie were kids sitting under a tree out there eating your lunch.' She paused, unsure if she should ask the question. 'How *is* Sophie?'

Sadness seized Bernadette's face. 'Ah, she has her days. She works part-time at a women's shelter. Had a couple of relationships, but they both went belly-up.'

'Does she still dance? She had real talent.'

'To my knowledge, she hasn't danced since your classes here at school.'

'That's a pity,' Rachael said, genuinely. 'How's your mum?'

'She just plods along. She was really anxious when Dad was released from jail. Worried he might go looking for Sophie and make things worse, I think.'

'Well, say hello to both of them for me when you see them, okay?' Rachael said, to break the funk. 'And let Travis know I said g'day too.'

'Will do. I know they all liked you, and Travis absolutely loved Constable Bowker. Reckons he wouldn't still be here if it wasn't for him.'

'I'll tell Greg that. He had a lot of time for Travis.' Rachael sobered a little, recalling those old days. 'Travis had a tough row to plough as a kid. Is his mum still alive?'

Bernadette shook her head sadly. 'No, Wendy died thirteen years ago. Finally at peace, the poor woman. You know her story. Drugs, alcohol, domestic violence. Had Travis when she was fourteen. Kicked out of home. Miracle she survived as long as she did.'

She began to tear up, and Rachael put a hand on her shoulder. 'What about you, Bernadette? Still having those heart issues you had as a kid?'

Wiping her eyes, Bernadette took a steadying breath. 'Gee, you've got a good memory. No, my heart's all good now, thanks to the big advances in coronary surgery over the last few years. Got a valve from a pig's heart inside my chest.' She laughed. 'Oink oink.'

Rachael laughed with her. 'Glad to hear you're fit and well.'

Suddenly, Bernadette became more serious. 'Are you up here with Senior Constable Bowker? To investigate my father's murder?'

Rachael smiled. Everything appeared caught in a time warp. 'It's Detective Inspector Bowker nowadays. And yes, he's here to investigate that case. I just came up for the ride. I'm returning to Melbourne on Sunday, and back teaching kindergarten kids Monday.'

'Suppose it makes sense for him to do it,' Bernadette said. 'He knew all about Yvonne's murder. There's a good chance they might be connected, I guess.' She looked back towards her classroom. 'I better return to my class before they start climbing the walls. Good to see you again, Miss Stow.'

'It's Rachael, Bernadette. Rachael Bowker. Great to see you again too.'

Bernadette hesitated a moment longer. 'Tell your husband I won't be too disappointed if he doesn't catch the killer. What happened to my father was better than he deserved.'

CHAPTER 5

Following Bowker's directions, Parker turned into the Bryant property, crossed a cattle grid, and travelled down the kilometre-and-a-half-long track to the farmhouse. The old home with its high gables and wide verandahs had been allowed to run down since Bowker had last visited. A metal panel was missing from the large air conditioning unit on the corrugated iron roof, and the roof itself was badly in need of repainting, with patches of green flaking off to expose the old silver frost coating underneath. The formerly verdant garden was now non-existent, with no evidence of the extensive kikuyu lawn that had helped cool the residence. Even the normally indestructible agapanthuses had surrendered to the Mallee's four horsemen of the apocalypse: high temperatures, hot wind, lack of water and sandy, infertile soils.

In contrast to the house, the sheds to the north of the residence still looked in excellent condition. An array of modern farm machinery hibernated in their shelters, awaiting the call for sowing or harvest. The closest bay contained an extensive workshop where Percy's stepson Yabby Harris was servicing an enormous four-wheel-drive tractor. Parker followed the dirt track to the sheds and parked the vehicle in an empty bay out of the rain. When they alighted from the car, a tan kelpie sheepdog exited its forty-four-gallon-drum kennel and strained at its chain, waving its tail incessantly. It suddenly thought better of the exercise as the rain became heavier, shaking its body vigorously and retreating to a drier environment.

Bowker approached Harris, hand outstretched. 'Long time no see, Yab.'

The farmer looked him up and down, then smiled. 'Well, well, well. Greg Bowker. I didn't expect to see you up here again once you became a big knob.'

'God's country, Yabby. Couldn't resist the chance to renew old acquaintances.'

Bowker introduced Parker and the two men shook hands. Harris had aged well. Now in his seventies, he didn't look too different to when Bowker had last seen him twenty years prior. Constant labour had maintained his wide shoulders and strong physique, and his weathered face closely mirrored that of two decades past. His piercing blue eyes had lost none of their intensity.

'How's Marlene?' Bowker asked.

Harris shrugged dejectedly. 'Not good. She's had two bouts of breast cancer. Thought she'd beaten it the first time, but it came back after eight years. Right through her now, so it's just a matter of bloody time, unfortunately. Still having chemo to try and string it out a bit longer.'

Bowker closed his eyes and dropped his head before looking up again. 'Shit. I'm sorry, mate.'

Harris stared out into the rain, tears welling in his eyes. 'Makes you wonder if it's all bloody worth it. When Marlene goes, it'll be just me and Percy left. And he's ninety-three, for fuck's sake. Not too far down the track, it'll be just me on my own, bustin' a gut on this piece of useless dirt with nobody to pass it on to.' He chuckled. 'Might see which distant relative I detest the most and leave this bloody albatross to them.'

Bowker laughed. 'How *is* Percy?' he asked, nodding towards the old house. 'Still living here?'

Harris shook his head. 'Nah. Moved over with Marlene and me a couple of years after Mum died. He's going alright for a bloke his age. Drove one of the chaser bins last harvest, and still drives the ute around the farm.' Harris looked at Parker. 'Robinvale cop took away his licence, so you won't see him out on the roads.'

'Wise move,' Parker said, clearly happy to have an opportunity to break his silence.

Bowker pointed to the farmhouse. 'Pity to see the old place go to rack and ruin.'

Harris pulled a face. 'No point in maintaining two houses. Hell, when I'm gone, one will be too many. The place will be swallowed up by one of the neighbours.'

Bowker remembered the hovel on the other side of the property that Travis Urdevic and his mother had lived in. 'I presume Percy's original old house has fallen down.'

'That's been gone for twenty-five years. Wind blew it over, so we heaped it up with the dozer and burnt the bloody lot.' Harris leaned back against the work bench. 'So, what are you doing out this way? I'm presuming it relates to Adrian Weston's murder.'

'Yeah,' Bowker said. 'But our visit's just routine. Preliminary stuff. I've been up here less than a full day, and my Homicide partner doesn't arrive until this afternoon. We haven't even got the forensic report. Asked Shane to take me for a drive so I could show him one of the best grain properties in the Mallee.'

Harris's face didn't acknowledge the compliment. 'So, Yvonne returns from the grave to torture the family again. Fuck, she's got a talent.'

'We haven't come out here to make accusations, mate.' Bowker paused for a moment, searching for the most diplomatic phrasing. 'Look, Yabby, I know you wouldn't have wanted anyone to go the way Yvonne did, but her death did solve a lot of issues plaguing your family. So, unless anything has changed over the last thirty years, I can't see you having any interest in killing Weston.'

Harris folded his arms across his chest. 'But you think Percy does? Loved Yvonne like his daughter and all that.'

'As Detective Bowker explained, these are just preliminary investigations,' Parker replied quickly.

Ignoring Parker, Harris stared straight at Bowker, his blue eyes burning. 'So, you think a tottery old man in his nineties is capable of taking down a bloke thirty years his junior?' He shook his head. 'Bloody preposterous.'

'A man that age is certainly capable of pulling the trigger of a shotgun,' Parker said before Bowker could reply.

Harris chortled sarcastically. 'What, all the way down there at Cocamba? Twenty-five miles from home? When he doesn't drive anymore? Come on!'

'Weston may not have been killed at Cocamba,' Parker replied. 'For all we know, he was shot in Winnambool and dropped off down there.'

'That's even more absurd,' Harris countered. 'Percy can hardly lift his feet, let alone a dead body.'

Parker put his hands in his pockets. 'May have had help, Mr Harris. Somebody keen to clean up the mess he'd made. Somebody keen to protect the family.'

'Nice theory, Constable,' Harris retorted.

'It's *Senior* Constable,' Parker fired back.

Bowker decided enough was enough and put a hand on Parker's forearm. 'Nobody's accusing Percy of anything, Yabby. Shane was just describing a theoretical scenario.'

'Sounded like a bloody accusation to me,' Harris replied.

'Sorry if it came across like that.' Bowker looked at Parker. 'That wasn't your intention, was it, Shane?'

Parker stared out into the rain. 'Just floating possibilities. Just doing my job.'

Bowker was keen to move on. 'Before we go, can I ask a couple of quick questions?'

'Should I have a lawyer present?' Harris asked sarcastically.

Bowker smiled and ignored the comment. 'Is there any chance Weston visited Percy in the days leading up to his death?'

'Why the fuck would he do that?' Harris said.

Bowker shrugged. 'I dunno. To apologise for killing Yvonne, maybe. He had thirty-one years to think about what he'd done. Perhaps his conscience got the better of him.'

'A bloke who roots his daughter *has* no conscience,' Harris said, staring at Bowker.

Bowker persisted. 'So he didn't visit Perce?'

'Not to my knowledge,' Harris said. 'I have no idea what Weston looked like, anyway. I had nothing to do with Manang when he was teaching there. Wouldn't know him if I fell over him.'

'Has Percy received any visitors?' Bowker asked.

'Look, a strange car would stand out like a turd in a wineglass around here, and I haven't seen any for a month. So I'm pretty sure Percy's had no visitors.' Harris shook his head. 'Satisfied?

Can I get back to work? This tractor's not going to service itself.'

'Will Percy be home at your place?' Bowker asked.

'If he's not there, he won't be far away. Marlene should be there as well.'

Once back in the car, Bowker had some words of advice for Parker. 'Came on a bit strong there, didn't you, mate? Only succeeded in getting Yabby's back up.'

Parker sniffed. 'Just thought I'd hit him with a few possibilities. You know, good cop, bad cop. Throw in an accusation or two and see where the shit falls.'

Bowker smiled. 'You've been watching too much television, Shane. In my experience, you trap a lot more flies with honey than you do with vinegar.'

Parker started the car without responding. The Harris residence was located less than a mile across the paddock, set among a copse of sugar gums. Unlike the old Harris farmhouse, this was a young, modern dwelling, one designed to rely entirely on air conditioning systems when the summer inferno arrived. The structure lacked the high gabled roof and wide verandahs of the older houses, and its brick veneer skin made things worse in the warmer months. But today, water cascaded down the red Colorbond roof as the rain became heavier and the horizon quickly disappeared into a white haze. A double garage sat at one end of the house, with a carport at the other. The garage was occupied by a Nissan one-tonner, most probably Percy's vehicle. In the carport was an aging silver Toyota Camry, the car likely used by Yabby and Marlene when they left the farm.

As Parker brought the police car to a stop on the gravel driveway beside the house, Bowker caught sight of a woman pulling aside a curtain to monitor their arrival. As Bowker was about to knock on the front door, it opened to reveal a morbidly thin woman who he guessed to be Marlene Harris. He hadn't known her well when he was stationed in Manang, and twenty years and the ravages of cancer had rendered her unrecognisable. She wore a Manangatang-Tooleybuc Football Club beanie, and a cheap red and blue tracksuit hung off her bony frame.

Bowker thrust out a hand. 'Hello, Marlene. Greg Bowker. This is Senior Constable Parker from Manang.' Marlene lifted a skeletal hand and invited them inside.

In the neat but basic kitchen, Marlene offered them coffee in a feeble voice. Bowker politely refused, mainly to save her unnecessary effort. 'Is Percy home, Marlene?' he asked.

'In the lounge room.' She pointed shakily towards a brick arch. 'Through there.'

Percy Bryant was sitting at a picture window, staring at the rain forming shallow puddles in the paddocks. He looked across, his face breaking into a smile as he saw Bowker. 'Greg Bowker. Long time no see.'

He tried desperately to stand, but Bowker put a hand on his shoulder. 'Don't get up. We'll grab a couple of chairs.'

Bowker and Parker each dragged an ornate dining chair from under a carved French table, which sat anachronistically among cheap veneered particle board furniture, the centrepiece of this basic, low-ceilinged room.

'How are you, mate?' Bowker asked, as he sat down and shook the old man's bony hand, its skin like opaque tissue paper.

'As well as can be expected, I suppose. Old age is an absolute bastard,' Bryant said weakly.

'There's only one alternative to getting older, Perce,' Bowker replied.

'Sooner the better, as far as I'm concerned. I've had enough, mate.'

'Percy, this is Senior Constable Shane Parker,' Bowker said. 'He's part of the team working on the Weston murder.'

Bryant shook Parker's hand gently. 'Stay close to Greg here, young fella, and you'll learn all there is to know about the police caper.'

Parker smiled. It looked forced. 'That's what I've heard, over and over.'

'I assume you know Adrian Weston was found dead at Cocamba,' Bowker said.

'Yeah. Only pity is it wasn't thirty bloody years ago,' Bryant replied. 'That bastard didn't deserve to live a minute longer after he murdered young Yvonne. And what he did to his daughter makes me want to vomit every time I think about it.'

'His killing looks like a square-up, don't you think?' Bowker asked.

Bryant looked him in the eye. 'I'll make it easy for you, Greg. I killed the bastard. Blew his face off with a twelve gauge. My granddaughter can rest in peace, now.' He thrust out his arms, wrists together. 'You can cuff me if you want.'

Parker stood up. Bowker pulled him back into his seat by the sleeve. 'Better start at the beginning, Percy. How'd you know Weston was out of prison and back here in the district?'

'Weston phoned me and asked to meet so he could explain how sorry he was for killing Yvonne,' Bryant said, looking out the window.

'Was anybody else here when he called?' Bowker asked.

'No.' Bryant met his gaze. 'I was here on my own. Yabby and Marlene had gone somewhere. Might've been down to Bendigo for more chemo.'

'Did you tell anyone Weston called?' Parker asked.

'Nope. Didn't want anybody else involved. Didn't want anyone to stop me from what I planned to do.'

Bowker leaned back in his chair. 'How did Weston know how to find you?'

Bryant rubbed at his ear. 'Since I moved in here, there's only one Bryant in the phone book for Winnambool. Would've been pretty easy to track me down.'

'Okay,' Bowker said. 'Weston wanted to meet. What happened next?'

'I told him he couldn't come out here because I wanted to keep Yabby and Marlene out of it. He asked me to suggest somewhere, so I told him the Cocamba silos would be an appropriate place to make peace with his conscience. Thought Yvonne's spirit might even hear what he had to say. You never know about these things.'

Bowker scratched his cheek. 'You drove down to Cocamba, even though you don't have a licence?'

Bryant chortled. 'I had a loaded shotgun across my lap, ready to blow the bastard away. Do you think I'd be worried about being done for driving without a licence? Besides, from what the locals tell me, the new copper in Manang wouldn't know if his arse was on fire until the local brigade turned up. I reckoned I was pretty safe.'

Bowker struggled to keep a straight face. 'Actually, Shane here is the copper you're talking about.'

Bryant smiled. 'Sorry, officer. I thought you'd come up from the city with Greg. No offence intended. I was just going by what I'd heard.'

Parker rolled his eyes in response.

'So, you drove down to Cocamba and met Weston,' Bowker said. 'Was he there when you arrived?'

'Yeah. Just leaning against one of the silos. I got a shock, with how old he looked.'

'I bet he thought the same when he saw you,' Parker said, evidently still seething at Bryant's quip.

Bowker thought for a moment. 'What sort of car was he driving?'

Bryant shrugged. 'Dunno. Suspect it must've been around the back of the grain shed, out of sight from the road.'

'What did you talk about?' Bowker asked.

'Didn't talk much. I drove the ute up close to him. It took me a while to climb out of the cab while he was blabbering on, saying how sorry he was about Yvonne. I held the shotty down below the window level, then I brought it up and pulled the trigger. He fell backwards against the silo, and I gave him the second barrel for good measure.'

'Then you drove off?' Parker asked.

'Threw the gun on the front seat, climbed into the ute, and drove back out here with a big smile on my face all the way.'

Bowker raised his eyebrows. 'Nice clean hit, by the sounds of it, Perce. Any cars come past on the highway while you were out there?'

'Not that I noticed.'

'What size shot did you use?'

Bryant thought for a moment. 'Number fours, probably.' He smiled. 'Didn't want him to walk through the pattern.'

Parker chortled. 'No need to be particular from that range.'

'Where are the spent cartridges?' Bowker asked.

'In the garage, in an old kerosene tin with hundreds of others. I dropped the cartridges in there when I got home.'

'And the gun?'

'In the gun safe at the back of the garage. Key's on a nail above it, so it doesn't get lost.'

'Fuck me,' Parker said, shaking his head.

'I'll go and open it up for you. I guess you'll have to take me in, right?'

'Stay where you are, Perce. I know where to find you if we need to ask any more questions.'

Parker frowned at Bowker, shook his head, and wandered towards the front door. Bowker stood and looked down at Bryant. 'I'll be in touch.'

*   *   *

As rain pattered down on the garage roof, Bowker took a handkerchief from his pocket and retrieved a double-barrelled shotgun from the gun safe. He broke the weapon to ensure it was unloaded and smelt the muzzle.

'Been fired in the last couple of weeks, I'd say,' he said, and replaced it in the safe. 'We know where to find it if we need Ballistics to take a look.' He checked through the boxes of cartridges stacked alongside the gun. 'Just number fours and fives. Nothing heavier in here. Yabby must go duck shooting, or blasting cockatoos digging up his crop.' Shutting the safe, he looked at Parker. 'These cartridges should be stored separately to the gun. When this is all over, you might need to come out and have a word to Yabby about firearms security. But for now, just grab a couple of spent shells from the tin. If we find any others related to this case, we can compare brands and pin indentations.'

Once in the car, Parker frowned at Bowker. 'Why didn't you arrest the old bastard and take his gun for evidence?'

Bowker snapped on his seatbelt. 'Because he no more killed Adrian Weston than you or I did.'

'He just confessed to blowing Weston's face off with a shotgun,' Parker said sharply. 'It doesn't get any more clear-cut than that.'

'Percy's too frail to have done what he said. You saw him in there, Shane. He struggled to even stand up from his chair. He'd battle to lift a shotgun, let alone whip it out from behind a ute door and take Weston by surprise.'

'People can find amazing strength when they have to,' Parker replied, as he started the car. 'You hear stories of folk who lift tractors off loved ones or hold up a falling wall to let others escape.'

'Not ninety-three-year-olds with nothing left in the tank. And I don't buy that story about Weston wanting to say sorry. He was an amoral bastard without a conscience.' Bowker shook his head, watching rain spatter on the windshield. 'Even if he did ring Percy, why not apologise over the phone? Agreeing to meet at Cocamba is another bridge too far for me. Besides, where's Weston's car if he drove it to the silos before his murder?'

'Someone might've knocked it off,' Parker said. 'The keys were probably in the ignition.'

'If it was out of sight behind the grain shed like Percy said, then no one's going to see it from the Sea Lake Road. Only locals use Miralie Road, and they're not going to steal a car. More likely to report it to you in Manang.'

'Bryant seemed to know where the body was located. Relative to the silos, I mean.'

Bowker shrugged. 'Lucky guess, I reckon. Plus, things spread like wildfire on the bush telegraph.'

It was quiet in the vehicle for thirty seconds before Parker spoke aggressively. 'Why the fuck would Bryant confess if he didn't do it?'

'Because he's happy that Weston's been killed,' Bowker said. 'Probably would've loved to do it himself, if truth be known. He's ninety-three, and he knows he'll be dead before any trial is finished. No judge will imprison him at that age, anyway. He's happy to take the blame as a gift to whoever avenged his granddaughter's murder.'

Parker steered the vehicle back onto Winnambool Road, splashing through a large pool of water. 'Do you think he might be covering for his stepson? Perhaps he helped the old bastard take out Weston.'

'Yabby? Not a hope in hell,' Bowker replied. 'He hated Yvonne with a passion. Can't see him putting his head on the block to avenge her. I don't reckon Percy has a clue who killed Weston, but he's thankful to whoever did.'

They fell quiet again for a few moments as the rain continued to hammer the car and the road ahead became a shiny ribbon. But for once, the shimmer in front of them was water, not a blistering mirage.

Parker glanced across at Bowker. 'Are *you* sorry that Weston's no longer in the land of the living?'

Bowker stared straight ahead. 'Nope. He was a pathetic excuse for a human being. Disappointed there was a murder involved, but I don't mourn his passing.' He looked at Parker. 'Why?'

'Just asking. Everyone I've spoken to agrees Weston was a piece of shit. The common view is that his murderer deserves a medal rather than a jail sentence. And as you say, it appears the murder was a revenge killing, so whoever did the deed is probably no danger to anyone else.'

Bowker frowned. 'Where are you heading with this?'

'I was just thinking that maybe it's in everybody's interest to go with Percy's confession. Percy gets what he wants, the perpetrator doesn't go down for doing society a favour, and the police can move on to more worthy cases.'

Bowker was briefly dumbfounded. 'Are you suggesting what I think you're suggesting?'

'It makes sense, doesn't it? We've got a conviction in the bag. We can draw a line under the case and move on.' Parker saw the expression on Bowker's face. 'What's with the dirty look? You'd keep your local hero status by solving the case in less than a day. Everybody wins.'

Bowker struggled to contain his fury. 'I'm going to pretend I didn't hear what you just proposed, Shane. And if I get the slightest sniff of that attitude again, you're fronting Internal Affairs. Do I make myself clear?'

'Fuck. Settle down, mate,' Parker said, reddening in the cheeks. 'I was just trying to find a solution to a tricky case.'

'We don't look for *solutions*. We look for the facts.' Bowker was seething.

'Okay, okay. My mistake. I won't mention it again.'

'Bloody hope not, because we don't work like that.'

The conversation for the remainder of the return journey was subdued. It was still raining steadily, so Parker dropped Bowker back at the hotel. 'I'll catch you in the morning. Eight bells,' Bowker said, as he climbed out of the car. 'I'll have Detective Sergeant Holmes with me, so the full team will be on deck.'

Parker screwed up his face. 'Usually don't work Fridays if the footy's at home the next day.'

'No rest for the wicked in a murder investigation, mate,' Bowker replied. 'See you at eight.' He closed the car door before Parker could protest, or his own anger could bubble over.

CHAPTER 6

Rachael was stretched out on a bed when her husband entered their motel room. 'Triumphant return for the dancing queen, was it?' Bowker asked, as he kissed her on the forehead and tried to keep his annoyance with Parker under control.

Rachael rolled her eyes. 'Pfft! Only one person recognised me when I walked into the staffroom. Anne Ronke, or Anne Stapleton, as she's known now. The staff are mostly babies. They stared at me as though I was an alien from another planet come to invade their hallowed space. I'll tell you who I *did* run into, though – and the story will knock your socks off.'

Rachael proceeded to relate her conversation with Bernadette Weston, giving particular emphasis to her marriage to Travis Urdevic.

Bowker sat on the bed beside her, his irritation slowly dissipating. 'So, Adrian Weston's daughter is married to Travis Urdevic. Or to put it another way, the sister of the incestuously molested Sophie Weston is married to Yvonne Bryant's closest childhood friend. There'd be a ton of malice towards Adrian Weston in that family, don't you reckon?'

Rachael screwed up her face. 'Yeah. But enough to fuel a murder?' she asked. 'I know Travis was quick-tempered and had the serious hots for Yvonne, but that was thirty years ago.'

Bowker shrugged. 'Plenty of time for the anger to ferment and erupt if the opportunity presented itself.'

'Can't see Bernadette being party to the killing of her father. She's a bit of a mouse.' Rachael thought for a moment. 'But she did say she wouldn't be too disappointed if you didn't find the murderer.'

Bowker scratched his chin. 'This case is the reverse to most murders I've investigated, Rach. There's raw hatred for the victim, and virtual hero-worship for the killer. It's like a Robin Hood scenario, where the outlaw is the good guy. Solving this case will be tricky when I've got most of the community working against me. Even the local policeman wants to call it quits.'

Bowker recounted their visit to Winnambool and Shane Parker's suggestion of letting the ninety-three-year-old Percy Bryant take the rap.

Rachael was gobsmacked. She was about to speak when there was a loud knock on the door. 'I'm not interrupting anything, am I?' a voice yelled from outside.

Smiling, Bowker looked at Rachael and whispered, 'Another five minutes and he would've been.' Rachael hit him playfully on the shoulder with the newspaper.

Bowker unlocked the door and welcomed Holmes in, who brushed droplets of rain from his suit coat as he entered. The men shook hands, and Holmes gave Rachael a peck on the cheek. Holmes was a tall man in his early forties, only slightly shorter than Bowker and not quite as wide across the shoulders. He had sandy hair that was receding quickly, a brown moustache and sparkling green eyes.

'Good drop of rain,' he said, as he took off his coat. 'Started the other side of Bendigo and hasn't stopped since.'

'Yeah. Set in, I reckon,' Bowker replied. 'Have much trouble finding the pub?'

Holmes laughed. 'Bloody town's gone downhill, hasn't it? Played a practice match over here in the mid-nineties. A lot more hustle and bustle then.' He shrugged. 'Same everywhere, I suppose. Went into Culgoa and Berriwillock on the way up. They're both buggered. Shouldn't be surprised – Murrayville is sadder every time I go home.'

Bowker helped Holmes unload his luggage into the room next door, and the trio ambled down Wattle Street for a casual lunch at the Five Star Café. On their return, Bowker suggested a quick drive out to Cocamba to survey the scene of Weston's murder. He knew the silo complex like the back of his hand, after his work on the Yvonne Bryant case, but wanted to see if changes had been made since his last visit decades ago. He was also keen for Holmes to get a feel for the site. Due to the rain, Rachael asked to be dropped off at Anne Stapleton's Church Street house on their way.

During the short drive south along Sea Lake Road, Bowker brought Holmes up to date on his visit to Winnambool and his discussion with Percy Bryant. His description of Senior Constable Shane Parker's attitude induced the biggest reaction from Holmes.

'*What?*' Holmes enquired, wide-eyed. 'He was happy to let the old bloke take the fall so we could all move on?'

'Win-win, he reckoned. Percy was happy to protect the person who avenged Yvonne, the real killer gets to go free because everyone agrees he deserves a medal, and the police can close the case quickly and get back to more important things.'

Holmes chuckled. 'What's more important than solving murders?'

'Lying on the couch with a *Station Closed* sign permanently pasted on the window,' Bowker said.

'What are you going to do?' Holmes asked. 'Cut him loose from the investigation?'

Bowker shook his head vigorously. 'No way. That's what the lazy prick wants. He can pull his weight, as far as I'm concerned. But I'll tell you one thing, Sherlock. If his attitude doesn't improve, I'll report him. This community deserves better than a bloke sitting on his arse waiting for his chance to transfer out. Problem is, he's so fucking slack he probably won't get a position anywhere else. Manang will be stuck with him for good.'

Holmes shrugged. 'If he hates the place so much, he might resign and chase another career.'

Bowker looked straight at Holmes. 'I'm going to ride the prick. It'll either make him or break him.'

Holmes laughed. 'This should be fun to watch.'

The Cocamba grain receival centre hadn't changed much since Bowker had last seen it. Located ten kilometres south of Manangatang, the silos sat adjacent to the railway line at the intersection of Sea Lake and Miralie Roads. The two towering steel cylinders today resembled brutalist metal fountains, as rainwater cascaded from their roofs in a skirt of miniature waterfalls. The long grain shed that had hidden the body of Yvonne Bryant thirty-one years prior remained as an ugly memorial to the wayward meteor that, for a celestial instant, had flamed across the local sky.

'This is Cocamba, mate,' Bowker said. 'The whole box and dice. Two silos and a grain shed.'

Holmes shook his head. 'Nearly as many murders here as there are buildings.'

Bowker drove to the rear of the grain shed. He stopped the car and pointed to a section of its wall. 'That's where we found Yvonne's remains. One of the wall panels had blown in, and her body had been dumped inside. One of the worst sights I've seen. Half the body had been eaten by animals and insects. It was a hundred and twenty in the water bag that day, so you can imagine what the smell was like.' He took a laboured breath. 'And the bloody flies! Fuck.' He shook his head. 'She was wild as Ned Kelly, but a good kid at heart. Didn't deserve to die like that. Nobody does.'

'Except Weston, p'haps,' Holmes said.

'Somebody must've thought that way,' Bowker replied.

On their return to Manangatang, they adjourned to Holmes's room to discuss Yvonne Bryant's murder, the case they agreed held the key to Adrian Weston's demise. Holmes had read the file back at headquarters on Spencer Street, but Bowker spread out the Manangatang copy on the table in case they needed to check any details.

Holmes leaned back in his chair. 'So, Weston was a teacher here in town, who had a long history of inappropriate interactions with underage schoolgirls. Yvonne Bryant got wind he was sexually molesting his own stepdaughter, and she was murdered by Weston to prevent her going to the police. Tell me if I've missed anything, Greg.'

Bowker nodded. 'It was a long and complicated investigation, but that's it pretty much in a nutshell.' He paused for a moment. 'Just on your own reading of the file, who jumps out as a suspect?'

Holmes removed a folder from his briefcase and withdrew a sheet of paper. 'There are half a dozen people with a good reason to wish Weston dead. I'm talking just motive here, ignoring means and opportunity. Okay?'

Bowker nodded. 'Okay.'

'Yvonne's grandfather was originally top of my list, despite his age. After what you've told me about your visit to Winnambool this morning, though, I can probably cross him off.'

Bowker shook his head. 'If we're only talking motive, leave him on. My gut says he's not involved, but there's always a chance he organised the killing, I suppose. For now, let's leave every possibility open. Next?'

'The stepdaughter, Sophie,' Holmes said. 'Physical and mental trauma, abuse of trust, life ruined, depression. Plenty of reasons to want to kill the bastard.'

'Agreed.'

'Weston's wife, Belinda. Biological mother of Sophie. Betrayal, mental pain, destruction of the daughter's childhood and probably her life in general.' Holmes shook his head. 'I'll tell you what, Greg. If some bastard did that to one of my kids, I'd be happy to blow him away.'

Bowker rested his forearms on the table. 'Where have you ranked Travis Urdevic?'

'Next. From his statement, he had the hots for Yvonne and was devastated by her death. Fiery temper, spent time in juvenile detention.'

'And Rachael discovered this morning that he's since married Bernadette Weston,' Bowker added. 'Wheels within wheels, eh, Sherlock?'

Holmes sighed. 'Bloody hell. She was the next one on my list. There'd be hatred of Weston baked into that household, then.'

'Just to put a cherry on top, Travis had an abusive father who broke parole and came here to belt up Travis's mother. If I hadn't got wind that he was in the area and turned up at their place in Winnambool, Travis would've killed the bastard. I've never seen a kid so angry. Was punching the shit out of his old man.'

'You think he'd kill Weston?'

'Possibly, from what I remember of him. Not a bad kid when he was younger. Survived an absolute shit upbringing.' Bowker leaned back and folded his hands behind his head. 'But he's forty-odd now, with a wife and two kids. Would he risk that to settle old scores? I honestly don't know.'

Holmes looked down at his notes. 'The last one on my list is Daryl Allender, or Skeeta, as he's called by a few others in their interviews. Boyfriend of the Bryant girl. From his testimony, he seemed genuinely distressed by her death, so I guess revenge is a potential motive there.'

'You can add the fact that Weston put him in the frame for Yvonne's murder. He served time on remand before we nailed Weston. If a snippet of information hadn't luckily come our way, Skeeta would've spent twenty years inside himself.'

Holmes tapped his fingers on the table. 'Do you think Allender's the type to blow a bloke's face off with a shotgun?'

'Skeeta was a prize piece of shit when I knew him. He was twenty-three and rooting a sixteen-year-old. He gave his parents bugger-all help on a marginal wheat block while he was driving around supplying weed to the area. The moment the prick was released from remand, I nailed him for drug trafficking, and for belting up Yvonne on the night she was killed.' Bowker frowned. 'I've got my doubts he'd have the guts to take on a grown man. I reckon thumping teenage schoolgirls is more his go.' He snorted. 'I might be wrong. I guess it doesn't take a lot of guts to shoot a bloke in the face.'

Holmes closed his folder. 'Well, that's my list. You got anyone I should add?'

'In terms of Yvonne Bryant's murder, the only other name I'd mention is Jimmy Cobb.'

'The intellectually disabled kid who pointed you towards Weston?'

'Yeah. It was at Yvonne's funeral. He was devastated by her death, because she always stuck up for him and treated him well, and he thought it was his fault she'd been killed. He was scared of Weston and hadn't reported seeing him with Yvonne on the night she died. Everyone assumed Weston was at a teacher's conference in Melbourne at the time, but Jimmy's story led to us nailing the bastard.'

'Is that a motive for killing Weston after three decades?'

'I doubt it. I'm just throwing out the names of anyone who may have been impacted by those events.' Bowker rubbed a hand down his face. 'We're in the early stages of this investigation, and everything is speculative at this point. Hell, I don't even know who still lives in the district. I know Percy Bryant does, and Rachael said Travis Urdevic and Bernadette Weston are still here. I think we can assume that Belinda and Sophie Weston aren't. But Skeeta Allender?' He shrugged. 'His parents are dead. I assume he sold the farm, but I don't know that for sure. Shit, I can't even be certain he's still alive. And Jimmy Cobb? He'll now be nearly fifty. Is he still with us? Is he still around Manang? Are his parents still alive to keep an eye on him? There are so many unknowns.' He sighed. 'Hopefully we'll find out a bit more over dinner tonight.'

Holmes raised an eyebrow. 'What, at the pub? Are we going to grill the publican?'

Bowker laughed. 'We've been invited out to Prong Lyon's place. Played tennis with the fat little bastard for twelve years. One of the best players I've taken to the court with. When you see him, you won't believe me, but you'll just have to take my word for it.'

'And you reckon he'll have all the goss on where our suspects have ended up?' Holmes asked, folding his arms across his chest.

Bowker nodded. 'Absolutely. Of course, we may be barking up the wrong tree. Weston's death may have nothing to do with the Bryant murder. Might've been set up to look like it does.'

Holmes frowned. 'By who, for example?'

'Dunno. If it was a hit ordered from inside prison, they wouldn't be too worried about covering their tracks by setting up the Cocamba thing.'

Holmes screwed up his face. 'Why would anyone order a hit on a bloke like Weston? It's not as though he was part of the underworld, or anything.'

'He was a paedophile who abused his own daughter. Even crims don't like rock spiders.'

'I don't buy it. They'd have got him in jail.'

'Neither do I – I'm just saying we need to keep an open mind on this. Tunnel vision leads to mistakes. As I said, there are just so many unknowns at this stage. Right now, we don't even know if he was actually killed at Cocamba.'

'When do we get a look at the forensics?' Holmes asked.

'I've been assured they'll be emailed to the Manang police station first thing tomorrow,' Bowker replied.

Holmes smiled. 'The senior constable might have the case solved by the time we get there.'

Bowker laughed. 'Count your lucky stars if he's even out of bed.'

* * *

Rain tumbled down outside the large lounge room windows at Anne Stapleton's house as Rachael and her host sipped coffee, nibbled on homemade Anzac biscuits, and caught up on twenty years of news. Anne and Bryan's daughter played centre for the combined Manangatang-Tooleybuc A-Grade netball team, while their two sons played in the club's senior football side. Life had generally been good to them, despite several severe droughts where Anne's teacher's wage had been crucial in maintaining a cash flow for the family. On the flip side, the good years had been very good, and their lifestyle was comfortable.

Rachael took a long sip of her coffee, then retrieved a biscuit from the floral plate in the centre of the teak veneered coffee table. 'I ran into Bernadette Weston as I left the school this morning,' she said.

'Yeah, she's a primary teacher here,' Anne replied. 'She's Bernadette Urdevic now. Married to Travis Urdevic, who you might remember from your time up here. They're a nice couple.' She settled back further into the couch. 'Travis is a hard worker. As a matter of fact, he'll be shearing ewes at our place at the moment, if Bryan got them shedded before this rain. Bernadette's a good teacher and has been a terrific mother to her kids. I guess she thought she'd purged all the bad vibes from Manang until what happened to her father a week or so ago.'

'What's the town think about the murder?' Rachael asked.

'Good riddance to the bugger, is the best way to sum it up. As you'll remember, anybody who had a kid when Adrian taught here was shocked and gutted by what he was up to. Right under everyone's noses, too. And I'll tell you what's sad, Rach – things still haven't returned to what they were before Weston came. Parents have permanently lost their trust in teachers. Remember when we used to take groups of kids to sporting events in our own cars, or drive them home if they missed the bus, or offer them one-on-one tutoring in our own time? That's all out the window now, unfortunately. Thank you very much, Mr Adrian Weston!'

Rachael drank the last of her coffee. 'Any rumours around town as to who might've killed him?'

'Not that I've heard. But you lived here long enough to know how Chinese whispers take off in this place. Even if I heard about someone doing him in, I'd take it with a shovelful of salt. Remember when young Yvonne was murdered? Everyone in the town was guilty at some stage.' She chuckled. 'Except for Adrian Weston.'

'Many of our old crew come up for the Back-To?' Rachael asked, taking the last biscuit from the plate. 'Greg and I had one of the kids' uni graduations, unfortunately.'

Anne shook her head. 'Not a lot. Bob and Judi Wikman were here, Peter and Paula Hindmarsh, Dwayne and Michelle Jones. Not too many of the youngies.' She laughed again. 'Well, they were youngies when we knew them, but they'd all be in their fifties now!'

Rachael nodded. 'I've heard there was a big roll-up.'

'More than a thousand over at the racetrack for the main do, and about a hundred and fifty hung around for the reunion ball at the hall. Saw a lot of the kids I've taught over the years who went away to uni or work and never came back to live.'

'Was Adrian Weston there?'

'Not that I noticed.' Anne shrugged. 'And I haven't heard anyone mention he was there. If he *was* seen, I think somebody would've said something, given the events that followed.'

'I guess the local policeman would've been informed,' Rachael said.

Anne chortled. 'I wouldn't count on it. People are sick and tired of reporting things to the lazy bugger. There's never any follow-up, and the station's always closed if you've got any police business. After Greg left, we've had half a dozen really good coppers.' She sighed. 'I suppose we were due for a dud.'

There was the sound of a vehicle pulling into the carport, and after a minute or two, Bryan Stapleton entered, sans boots. The Bryan Rachael remembered had curly fair hair and a broad, smiling face. The smile was still there, but most of the hair had disappeared. Rachael couldn't believe his resemblance to his father. Stapleton instantly recognised her, and he kissed her on the cheek as they exchanged pleasantries. Anne fetched more biscuits and returned the kettle to the stove.

Stapleton pulled up a chair and sat down. 'If the rain had held off for another half hour, I would've got 'em all into the shed. The forecast said it wasn't due till this evening. Trav will be back tomorrow arvo to finish them, provided they dry out.'

Anne placed the biscuit plate in the centre of the table, but remained standing, awaiting the kettle to boil. 'Greg's up here to investigate Adrian Weston's murder. Rachael's come up for the ride, and to check out her old stomping ground.'

Stapleton grinned. 'Not much to see. The old place is going backwards, I'm afraid. But I see we're in the news again. Murder capital of the central Mallee, apparently.' He laughed. 'Two murders in thirty-one years, and we cop that reputation? Bit harsh, I reckon. Although this one is pretty gruesome, by the photos.'

Rachael was puzzled. 'What photos?'

'Photos of Adrian Weston after he was shot. I think one of the Netcor blokes took them when they found the body at Cocamba. Messaged them out to a few mates, and now I reckon everyone in Manang's got copies on their phone.'

CHAPTER 7

Roast lamb, potatoes, pumpkin, carrots, peas and old-fashioned gravy, followed by bread-and-butter pudding topped with thickened cream, had immobilised the three guests as they relaxed in the warm comfort of Prong and Lenore Lyon's lounge room.

'Still playing tennis, Prong?' Bowker asked.

'Nah. Hips are shot. Plus, you have to travel every second week. I'm too old for all that now.'

Holmes sat on the couch, still coming to terms with how this short, rotund man could've been the player Bowker had described, who'd once been in a development squad coached by the legendary Harry Hopman in Melbourne. But the trophies around the room bore witness to his tennis prowess and that of his wife and their five children.

'Pity you're not still playing,' Bowker said. 'I threw a racquet in the car in case you wanted a hit while I was up here. Thought we could put the old pair back together and take on any local upstarts.'

Prong laughed. 'No local upstarts, mate. Bugger-all people play sport nowadays. Kids are too busy on their computers and iBoxes, or whatever they're called, to go out in forty-five-degree heat and chase a ball. Rather sit under the cooler and do jack shit.'

'Speaking of doing jack shit, is Skeeta Allender still around the district?' Bowker asked.

'Pissed off when his father died,' Prong replied.

'Which was only six months after poor old Dawn's heart called it a day,' Lenore added. 'Skeeta probably had a lot to do with that, truth be known. She tried everything a mother could do to keep him on the straight and narrow, but in the end, I think her body just chucked it in.'

Bowker shook his head. 'And bloody Skeeta walks away with the fruits of their efforts. Sometimes, there's not a lot of justice in this world. And I bet he's blown the lot already.'

A giant grin pervaded Prong's round face as he shook his head. 'Never got a cent. It was all left to the elder daughter, Cynthia. She's married to Skid Marx's son. Name's Jeff, if I remember rightly. They've got a property further west, over closer to Kulwin. Hard workers. Good farmers.'

Bowker's mouth fell open, his expression a mixture of surprise and glee. 'Years ago, Red Cameron told me that Skeeta was the only son. Somehow, I got it into my thick head that he was an only child.'

'It's a story typical of around here, actually,' Lenore said. 'Pete and Dawn tried for years to have kids but had no luck. Adopted Cynthia, the pressure came off, and what do you know? Dawn's pregnant with Skeeta.'

Prong snickered. 'You can't help bad luck, eh?'

Lenore dismissed her husband's comment with the wave of a hand. 'There's a lot of adopted kids in the district. Sounds a bit sexist these days, but I can name more than one family who produced a tribe of girls then adopted a boy so they'd have someone to leave the farm to.'

Rachael's eyes widened. 'You're joking?'

'No joke, Rachael,' Lenore responded, shaking her head. 'The assumption was always that their daughters would marry a farmer anyway and get their own place.'

Rachael clicked her tongue. 'What if they went to the city or followed a career outside of farming? It seems so unfair.'

'Adoption's always been a puzzle to me,' Prong said. 'Lenore and I only have to pass each other for her to get pregnant. One-Hit Lyon, they call me.'

Lenore rolled her eyes as the others laughed.

'Was Skeeta here for the Back-To?' Bowker asked.

'Didn't see him,' Lenore replied.

'He wouldn't have come back,' Prong added, shaking his head. 'He hated the place when he lived here, and apparently, he was apoplectic when the solicitor showed him the will. I don't think there'd be too many positive memories up here for old Skeeta.'

'Can I ask you about another name from the past?' Bowker said. 'Jimmy Cobb.'

'Still in the area,' Prong replied. 'Lives in a farmhouse on one of the Cobbs' blocks at Bolton. On the Kooloonong Road, not far past the Myall reserve.'

'Lester Green's old place? Massive dam near the front gate?' Bowker asked.

'Yeah, that's it. Jimmy's mum and dad are only five miles away on another block they bought. They're close enough to keep an eye on him, but far enough away to give him some independence. Wise move, I reckon. They're both in their seventies now, so they won't be around forever. Jim's brother farms his own block at Annuello, so he's only fifteen minutes away in an emergency.'

'Jimmy copes alright, then?' Rachael asked. 'When we left here, he was still living with his mum and dad.'

'Seems to,' Prong replied. 'Must be what you taught him at school.'

Rachael smiled. 'Thanks for your confidence, Ian, but I was only his integration aide. I think most of the credit goes to his parents. Hopefully, his brother will keep an eye on him when they pass on. You hear some horrific stories about what happens to disabled adults when their parents die.'

Prong leaned forward in his lounge chair and put his hands on his knees. 'Couldn't tell you what arrangements the Cobbs have put in place for when that happens. Jimmy's fairly handy with cropping and sheep work, apparently, but I don't think he'd handle all the planning and finances that go into running a big property like theirs.' He shrugged. 'But knowing Corn and Marilyn, they'll have something in place. Whether that involves selling the property, or having his brother run the lot, or appointing a manager, I'm not sure. They were Red's clients before he retired, so he might have an idea what they've worked out. Landmark in Swan Hill looks after them now, I think.'

'Has Jimmy got any close friends?' Rachael asked. 'It'd be sad if he was out there on his own all the time.'

Prong scratched his head. 'He's pretty friendly with the Barber brothers on the property next door. And he goes spotlighting with Leigh Davidson every now and then. According to the cockies out that way, they've got a lot of foxes this year. They've lost a shitload of lambs.'

Bowker frowned. 'My memory says the Davidson property is the other side of Chinky, though.'

'Yeah, that's where Leigh lives,' Prong replied. 'He married a lovely young teacher, and they had a couple of kids before the isolation and weather finally cracked her and she moved back to the city. He lives out there on his own now, poor bugger. His parents retired to Swan Hill a decade or so ago. Old Tom Davidson and Corn Cobb have been close mates since school. Used to go fishing and shooting together. The boys often went along, so I guess they've kept up that connection.'

Bowker nodded. 'Ever see Jimmy in town?'

'Not much. I don't think he drinks, and if you're not chasin' the pub, there's bugger-all reason to come into Manang these days. Sad, really.'

'Was he at the Back-To?' Holmes asked.

'Didn't see him.' Prong looked at his wife. 'You see him, Lenore?'

Lenore shook her head. 'Is this in relation to Weston's murder?' she asked.

Bowker feigned surprise. 'Hell, no. Just interested in a few people I dealt with closely when I was up here.'

Bowker went on to question the whereabouts of another half dozen locals to disguise his interest in Skeeta and Jimmy. Whether Prong and his wife's suspicions were allayed was debatable.

By the time the visiting trio said their thankyous and goodbyes, it was after midnight. The rain had cleared, the wind blew cold from the south, and the shadows danced on the footpath under the streetlights. Clouds scudded across the full moon, and the still-wet silos on the other side of the railway line glistened in the moonlight.

*   *   *

The sun shone brightly in a cobalt-blue sky as Bowker and Holmes made their way to the police station the next morning. The front door was propped open, letting fresh air into the office, where Parker had placed two cloth-covered chairs aside the large desk.

'This looks promising,' Bowker said, raising his eyebrows at Holmes. He dropped a cardboard box on the desk and knocked on the connecting door to the residence before leading Holmes through it. Parker was in the kitchen, scoffing down a slice of Vegemite toast and gulping a cup of black coffee. Bowker introduced Holmes to Parker, and the two men shook hands. Bowker saw Parker wince a little as Holmes squeezed his sore thumb.

Parker rinsed his cup under the tap and placed it upside down on the draining board beside the sink. 'You blokes like a tea or coffee?' he asked. 'Got a few stubbies in the fridge if that suits better.'

Holmes smiled. 'Bit early for me, mate,' he said.

'Just had breakfast at the pub,' Bowker added. 'But I might trouble you for a glass of water.'

Parker grabbed three glasses from an overhead cupboard, rotated the rims against his shirt, then removed a jug of water from the fridge. He took them through to the station, where Bowker and Holmes took the seats opposite him at the desk.

Bowker opened up the box and used his hanky to remove the glass bottle he'd collected from the cemetery. 'This was sitting on Yvonne Bryant's grave with some withered flowers. I'd like to dust it for fingerprints. The publican told me that yesterday was the first rain for a fortnight, so if there are any recent prints, they should've survived. If they've been degraded by dew, then we'll send the bottle to Melbourne. See if the lab can lift any prints with molybdenum disulphide.'

'Do you think Weston's killer might've put the flowers there as a way of saying the Bryant girl could now rest in peace?' Parker asked.

'Possibly,' Bowker replied. 'Or maybe it's just a simple case of someone visiting the cemetery, seeing Yvonne's grave, and feeling the need to leave something honouring her memory. People put flowers on graves for any number of reasons. Love, respect, grief, guilt. What's interesting is that I reckon it was a spur-of-the-moment thing. If you planned in advance to leave flowers, you'd surely come up with something better than an old bottle and a few gum blossoms.'

'Maybe it was Weston himself who left them,' Holmes suggested. 'He may have come up here to pay his respects or seek some sort of redemption, perhaps.'

Bowker shrugged. 'I suspect we won't get a match with the prints unless it was Weston. But you never know. Might give us a lead.' He looked at Parker. 'Now, Shane. Do you know anything about photos of the murder scene being circulated around the community?'

Parker looked puzzled. 'No. The forensic team took a shitload of photos, but there's no way the public would get access to those. Have you seen some?'

'Got them on my phone,' Bowker said, leaning back in his chair. 'Looks as though you're the only bloke in the district who hasn't seen, then.'

Parker sat up straight. 'You implying I took photos and distributed them?' he asked indignantly.

Bowker raised both palms. 'No, I'm not, so settle down. The story is that one of the Netcor blokes took them when they found the body. But if photos are being shared around, it would explain how Percy Bryant was able to give us a pretty accurate description of where the body was located at Cocamba.'

Before Parker could respond, his computer beeped as a new email arrived. He looked at the screen, then back at Bowker. 'Forensic report.'

'Good,' Bowker replied. 'Print it off, please, and we'll see if it leads us anywhere.'

Within thirty seconds, the report was in Bowker's hands. He scanned it briefly before delivering a summary. 'Okay, gentlemen, this is what we've got. Autopsy was conducted last Tuesday. The victim has been confirmed via DNA comparison with his mother as Adrian John Weston of Altona. On the basis of tissue decomposition and the maturity of maggots found in the body, it is estimated that his death occurred approximately ten days prior to his body being autopsied.'

Holmes closed his eyes and did the mental arithmetic. 'That puts time of death at two weekends prior. The Back-To-Manangatang weekend.'

'That's the way I see it,' Bowker said, nodding, before continuing to read. 'Cause of death, a shotgun blast to the head. Pellet pattern and powder residue suggest he was shot from a range of between two and two point five metres. Cartridge pellets were of the lead variety, and BB in size.'

'Percy said he used number fours,' Parker said. 'Got that one wrong, didn't he?'

'Yeah,' Bowker replied. 'Examination of the site where the body was found revealed an absence of blood spatter, powder residue, and pooling of blood, all indications that the shooting took place elsewhere. Small droplets of dried blood were detected where the head came into contact with the grass around it, suggesting that the victim was still seeping small quantities of blood when deposited at the silos. Based on the aperture of the wound and the prevailing temperatures in the region at the time, it is estimated that the victim was shot less than one hour prior to his body being deposited at Cocamba.'

Bowker turned to the next sheet. 'Fingerprints were lifted from the steel silo surface against which the body was located. Five different sets of prints were found. Only two of these remain unidentified. One belongs to a female—'

Parker interrupted. 'How the fuck would they know if it was a female? Could just as easily be a small bloke.' He shook his head and exhaled loudly. 'Shit, these guys are up themselves. Fair dinkum.'

'They lifted DNA with the print,' Bowker said. 'As I was saying, only two sets remain unidentified. One belongs to a female, a finding supported by analysis of DNA embedded in the print residue. The second unknown set was also found on the wallet recovered from the victim's front trouser pocket. Analysis of residues established the prints belong to a male, but insufficient material was recovered to allow a more detailed mapping.'

Holmes smiled. 'Sounds like we're looking for Bonnie and Clyde.'

Bowker chuckled and returned to the report. 'The other three sets relate to the discovery of the body. Two of those belong to Netcor employees, Campbell Kilmartin and Damien Cowton. The third set belongs to the police officer attending after the body's discovery had been reported to the Manangatang police. Senior Constable Shane Parker.' Bowker looked at Parker in bewilderment. 'Fuck me, mate. Ever heard of using gloves when you're at a crime scene?'

'I didn't intend to touch anything, did I?' Parker shot back angrily. 'When I saw the bloke with just raw meat for a face I nearly keeled over. Just steadied myself on the bloody silo. I told the forensic techs that.'

'I bet they were happy,' Holmes said.

Parker huffed. 'Fuckin' pissed off they were. But they see that sort of stuff every day. I've seen one gunshot death in my life, and that was a rifle bullet through the chest. Couldn't even see the entry wound for the bloke's jacket.' He looked at Bowker. 'I'm sorry, alright?'

Bowker took a deep breath. 'I suppose there's no harm done. But do things by the book next time, okay?'

Parker rolled his eyes. 'Right, boss.'

'The Netcor blokes were obviously fingerprinted at some stage,' Holmes said.

'Yeah,' Parker said. 'Up in Mildura the next day. Just for the purpose of elimination, presumably.'

'You get printed again, or did they use the ones on record?' Holmes asked.

'Ones on record. The set they take when you apply to join the force.'

Bowker continued to read. 'Two long strands of hair were found adhered to the cranial blood. DNA analysis of the follicles matched the hair samples to the same female whose prints are mentioned above.'

Bowker quickly scanned the rest of the page, then flipped to the next part of the report. 'A small quantity of short polyester fibres were found in the cranial blood, indicating that the body had been transported to the site by motor vehicle. Small quantities of soil and vegetable matter were recovered from the clothes and the wound of the victim. These couldn't be matched to samples taken in the area where the body was found. There was no evidence of alcohol or other drugs in the victim's system. Analysis of the stomach contents revealed undigested diet cola, saveloy components, bread, and tomato sauce, suggesting a recent meal of hot dogs and soft drink.'

Bowker scanned the remainder of the report. 'The rest is just the supporting technical data.' He dropped it on the desk in front of him. 'Okay, team. What does all that tell us?'

Holmes spoke first. 'Weston wasn't killed at Cocamba. He was shot elsewhere and transported to the discovery site, most likely by a male and a female. Given that he was still oozing a little blood when he was dumped, it's likely he was killed relatively close by. Within a hundred k's, if the lab's timings are right.'

'Which means he must've already been in the district,' Bowker added, before taking a mouthful of water. He put down the glass and looked at Parker. 'What else?'

'Well, obviously he had a hotdog and a drink not long before he was shot,' Parker replied.

'Which means?' Bowker asked.

Parker smiled. 'He didn't die hungry?'

Holmes spoke before Bowker could react. 'I'd say there was a very good chance he purchased them at the Back-To celebrations. Hot dogs aren't the type of food you buy from a milk bar or most servos. Especially when the forensic report specified that the stomach contained saveloy rather than frankfurt. When I've seen hot dogs in a servo, they're those long pale frankfurts.'

'Didn't know there was a difference,' Parker replied, as he played with his pen.

'Savs are a seasoned pork sausage,' Holmes said. 'Frankfurts are usually made of reclaimed scraps of anything. That's why they're always cheaper.'

Parker screwed up his face. 'Shit. That's the last time I'll buy those fuckers.'

Bowker was keen to move on. 'I agree with you about the Back-To, Sherlock. He was there, I reckon. We just need a witness to confirm it.'

'Obviously, the key is finding the owners of those unidentified prints,' Holmes said. 'There's your killer or killers. Or at least someone who can tell us who they are.'

Bowker nodded. 'Agreed,' he replied. 'This is how we'll work it from here. Sherlock, you and I will catch up with Travis and Bernadette Urdevic. Travis is at the Stapletons' property shearing their ewes. We'll take a run out to Chinky and talk to him first. Hopefully, we'll be back in Manang in time to catch Bernadette at school during her lunch break.' He placed his forearms on the desk, folding his fingers together. 'Shane, I've got some research I'd like you to do. Got a piece of paper?'

Parker opened a drawer and withdrew a notebook, ripping the cellophane wrapper from it. 'Okay, shoot,' he said, with pen poised.

'Number one. I want you to ring Barwon Prison and see if you can get them to send up a record of Weston's visitors. I'd like to know if he had any friends left in the world when he got out. If he did, they may be able to help us sort out his movements from the time he was released until he was shot. And ask them to send us the most recent photo they have on file.'

Parker took an eternity to write down Bowker's request, before looking up. 'Okay.'

'Number two. See if you can get into contact with Weston's mother. Forensic took DNA samples, so that might be the best place to start. I'd like to tee up an interview with her.'

Again, Parker laboured over the transcription. He put down the pen and leaned back. 'I'll get onto those when we finish up here.'

Bowker smirked at Holmes. 'Number three. See if you can track down Skeeta Allender. Daryl Allender. Try his sister first, then see if he's come up on the crime computer in recent times. Number four–'

'Hold on a minute,' Parker said, as he struggled to keep up. 'They didn't teach shorthand at the academy.'

Bowker waited until Parker had finished writing. 'Number four. This is the easy one. Find out who organised the food stalls at the Back-To, and check if they served hot dogs on the day. If they did, see if you can get a roster of who worked on the stall.'

'What'd your last slave die of?' Parker said.

'Number five. Check with firearms registration and see if there are shotguns registered to Skeeta Allender, Travis Urdevic, or Jimmy Cobb. May as well check Mark Cobb as well. If Jimmy uses a shotgun, I doubt it would be registered in his name.' Bowker took another drink as he waited for Parker to catch up. 'There are a few other things I'll need you to chase up, like the contents of Weston's wallet and whether it contained a credit card. If there's not one listed, we'll need to find out whether he owned one.'

When Bowker saw the look on Parker's face, he smiled and tapped Parker's notepad with an index finger. 'But what's on your list here will probably keep you busy for today.'

Parker tossed his pen on the desk in front of him and threw himself back in his chair. 'Thank God. There's only so many hours in the fuckin' day.'

'Can you grab the fingerprint kit?' Bowker asked. 'We'll do this bottle before we go.'

Parker unlocked a steel cabinet at the side of the room and removed a plastic box. He handed it over to Holmes, who opened the lid, retrieving a fine, feathery brush and a bottle of light grey carbon-based powder. Holmes held the brush over the small office wastepaper bin and sprinkled powder on it, giving it a quick twirl to remove excess material. He daubed the bottle with the powder, then smiled.

'Here we go. Looks like we've got some good ones,' he said, as a series of prints began to appear. He covered one of the most distinct prints with a length of clear tape, removed the tape from the bottle with the print attached to its sticky side, and stuck it to a clear acetate card, securing the print between the tape and the acetate backing. This process was repeated until all the usable latent prints had been lifted. Bowker took each of the prints, enclosed them in an official police envelope, stuck down the flap and signed his name across the seal.

'We'll drop these off in the city next week. Sherlock and I need to go back to Melbourne to conduct interviews with Adrian Weston's mother, Belinda and Sophie Weston, and Skeeta Allender, if Shane establishes he lives down there.' *God knows that won't be pleasant*, Bowker thought grimly.

CHAPTER 8

The drive south to Chinkapook was a pleasant one. The blue sky seemed to stretch on forever, and the crops undulated in the light southerly. A flock of pink galahs, enthusiastically feasting on spilt grain, lifted from the road when the police car approached. As it passed, they flew in formation in a wide circle, then resettled on the road behind it.

'On a day like this, it's hard to imagine how brutal the climate can be up here in summer,' Bowker remarked.

'Or how cold it gets when that Antarctic sou'wester rips across the flats and through whatever clothes you're wearing,' Holmes replied. 'I've never been so cold as one night when I was sowing canola for the old man in May. The heater in the big Versatile gave up the ghost and fair dinkum, Greg, I couldn't feel my toes for the whole bloody night. Got one of the dogs to lie across my feet to try and keep them warm. Fuck, it was awful. Stood under a hot shower for half an hour after my stint. Took that long to get feeling back in my hands.'

'Spare a thought for the poor bastards before Gason started making tractor cabs. Froze in the winter and melted in the summer.'

'According to the old man, the worst thing in summer wasn't the heat. It was the bloody dust. Particularly crop dust off the header. Got down the neck of your shirt and into your undies. Itched like something shockin', he reckons.' Holmes grinned at

Bowker. 'Good excuse for a bloke to scratch his balls, I s'pose.'

Bowker laughed. As they passed the Cocamba silos, he pointed at the road ahead. 'Thirty years ago, the surface of this road was an inch deep in mouse guts. Swan Hill Shire had to put *Slow Down* signs because cars and trucks were sliding sideways.'

'So, you were up here in a mouse plague?' Holmes asked.

'Yeah. And if I hadn't seen it with my own eyes, I wouldn't have believed what people were saying. You get that one over at Murrayville?'

'Absolutely. It was Mallee-wide, I think. But I was stationed down at Morwell, so I didn't see much of it. Mum and Dad were raving on about it over the phone, but I thought they were just adding a bit of mayo.'

'Whatever they told you would've been a fraction of what it was like,' Bowker replied. 'Something I'll never forget, that's for sure.'

When they reached Chinkapook ten minutes later, Bowker took Holmes on a tour of the town, an excursion that lasted no more than thirty seconds. William Street, the main drag, had even fewer buildings than when Bowker had last been there. Little now remained of the once-thriving town except for the odd house dotted along the two remaining streets. The main structures, of course, were the five giant silos and the massive grain shed that adjoined the railway line.

Bowker pulled up in front of a dilapidated house, which, amazingly, still showed signs of habitation. An old-model Datsun was parked in the falling-down carport.

'This was where the Westons lived before Adrian's arrest,' Bowker said. 'Totally vacated the day after we locked him up. Belinda and the girls departed for Melbourne at sunrise. After they left,

I arranged for Travis Urdevic and his mother to move down here from Winnambool – it's a sight better than their old house.'

Holmes frowned and shook his head. 'Fuck! If this was an improvement, the place they came from must've been a palace.'

Bowker smiled. 'It blew down in the wind, so that should tell you something.'

On their way out of the township, Bowker parked briefly beside the well-kept Chinkapook public hall, which adjoined the local tennis courts. 'See those three courts, Sherlock? They were the scene of many a great battle, especially before Manang installed lights. For the first couple of years I was up here, this was home base for our night team.'

'Fuck me,' Holmes said. 'Hard to believe anyone's played here in the last fifty years.'

Most of the fencing was still intact, but beginning to rust loose of the corroding posts. Old-fashioned lights with green and white metal shades swung gently in the breeze, still attached to wires strung between corner poles. The gypsum surface was quickly returning to nature, bushes growing among the bark and leaf litter, and the three-cornered afternoon tea shed was now a steel skeleton. Its corrugated iron walls and roof had either been removed or blown away by the fierce winds that could howl through the area.

Holmes caught Bowker's faraway stare and suspected his partner's mind had wandered back a few decades. Back to the laughing and shouting, the whack of racquet on ball and the general bonhomie of sport in the bush.

'They call it progress, mate,' Holmes said. 'I'm not so sure.'

'Yeah, it's sad, really,' Bowker replied, as he started the car and headed west towards Templeton Road. 'Listen, when we talk to Travis and Bernadette, let's keep the female prints to ourselves, okay? That probably goes for any potential suspect. We might be able to use it to our advantage later on.'

'Sounds like a plan,' Holmes replied, staring ahead.

*　*　*

The Stapletons' shearing shed was a modest affair comprising just two stands, a far cry from the corrugated iron monoliths of the enormous sheep stations to the north in New South Wales and Queensland. In terms of a Mallee farmer's annual income, their sheep enterprise was a sideline to grain production, but a profitable way to utilise stubble left behind after crops were stripped.

As the detectives climbed from their car, they were immediately struck by the stereotypical bucolic soundscape of bleating sheep, barking dogs and the high-pitched modulating buzz of shearing machines. Parked beside the sheep yards were three vehicles: a battered Holden ute, an old-model Ford one-tonner, and a late-model grey Nissan Navara twin-cab.

Inside the shed were a smell and vista redolent of quintessential rural Australia. Except for the mechanical shearing equipment, the scene mirrored Tom Roberts's iconic masterpiece *The Shearing of the Rams*. Travis Urdevic had his head down, crouched over a young ewe, removing her belly wool. A younger man was sweeping the board of locks and dags, and as Bowker approached the wool table where Bryan Stapleton was skirting a fleece, Urdevic's shearing partner crashed backwards through the swinging doors of the catching pen, dragging the next upended animal to have its fleece removed.

Stapleton looked up from his skirting duties and backhanded a fistful of dirty wool into a jute woolpack suspended from the rafters by lengths of rusty wire. 'Come out to shear a few?' he shouted, smiling, over the din of the shearing plant.

'I'll leave that to the experts, mate,' Bowker replied. 'Just wanted a word with Travis when it's convenient.'

Stapleton looked at his watch. 'Nearly morning smoko, but I'll tap Trav on the shoulder when he's finished this one and you can have a yarn outside if you like.'

Bowker gave a thumbs up.

After a minute or two, Urdevic finished shearing the ewe and guided her headfirst into a chute in the side of the shed, where she nervously descended a ramp to join her naked friends in the pen below. Urdevic stood up straight, hands behind his hips, and stretched backwards. Stapleton spoke to him briefly, pointing to the detectives at the other end of the wool table. Urdevic wandered across, and the three men adjourned outside to where the noise level was bearable.

Bowker shook Urdevic's hand and was struck by the softness of his skin, conditioned by the incidental application of lanolin. 'Long time no see, mate.'

Urdevic smiled. 'Twenty years, it'd have to be. You're one of the big boys now, I hear.'

'Yeah, but believe it or not, Travis, there's plenty of times I miss being up here as just a little cog in a big machine.'

Bowker introduced Holmes, and the two men shook hands. Urdevic was no longer a skinny kid with a long rat's tail and pierced ears. He'd grown quite tall, into a Collingwood six-footer, as Bowker would later describe him to Rachael. Broad across the shoulders and not carrying an ounce of fat, Urdevic was the picture of fitness. He still retained his boyish looks, although like all men in the district, his skin was brown and weathered. He wore the unofficial shearer's uniform: a blue singlet, heavy-duty denim trousers, and desert boots with a leather buckle-up lace overlay.

'Married to Bernadette Weston, I hear,' Bowker said.

Urdevic's face lit up. 'Got lucky. We have two teenage kids, believe it or not. Trying to teach them what you taught me.'

Lost for words, Bowker just nodded appreciatively.

'I assume you're here to ask me what I know about Adrian Weston's murder?' Urdevic said.

'We're asking a lot of people, so don't take it personally,' Holmes replied.

'I expected a visit. Most people believe his murder was tied up with Yvonne's death all those years ago. There are half a dozen people I thought would be your first ports of call.'

'Yeah?' Bowker said, raising his eyebrows. 'I'd be interested in who you have on the list, just in case we've missed somebody.'

Urdevic leaned against the wall of the shed. 'Me, Bernadette, Belinda, Soph, Old Percy.' He thought for a moment. 'And Skeeta, probably.'

Bowker winked at Holmes. 'Better sign him up, I reckon, Sherlock.'

Holmes nodded. 'Got better instincts than a lot of blokes we work with.'

'I'll make it easy for you in my case,' Urdevic said. 'I'm bloody thrilled beyond words that the bastard is dead, but I had nothing to do with shooting him, and I don't know who did.'

'You know why we're talking to you, though, don't you?' Holmes replied. 'You were really close to the Bryant girl, and from what Detective Bowker here tells me, you had a pretty fiery temper back when he knew you.'

'I'll level with you, okay? If I'd found out that Weston killed Yvonne before you blokes put him away, I probably *would* have killed him. I really liked Yvonne, and I was an angry young man with a drug-addicted mother and an abusive jailbird for a father. I had very little to lose. But not now. I have a wife I adore, two beautiful kids, and a regular job. People respect me because I work hard and I'm honest. I'm not about to throw all that away to get even with a piece of shit like Adrian Weston. It wouldn't bring Yvonne back, and it wouldn't undo what he did to Sophie.'

Bowker nodded. 'What was Bernadette's reaction when she heard about the murder?'

'Mixed feelings, I think. She understood how he'd systematically broken her mother, and effectively destroyed her sister's life. And then committed murder to cover his fucked-up perversions. But he was still her father, so I suppose it saddened her a bit that he'd been shot. She only knew him until she was twelve, so all her memories of him were pretty positive.'

Holmes put his hands in his pockets. 'I have to ask you this, mate. Do you think your wife could've had anything to do with the murder?'

Urdevic laughed. 'Bernie? Shit, she wouldn't know how to fire a gun, let alone kill anyone. When you see her, you'll realise the recoil would knock her over backwards.'

'You and Bernadette live in the old house in Chinky?' Bowker asked.

Urdevic shook his head. 'Too many bad memories there for both of us. We bought the Wikmans' old place in Manang when we got married. On Pioneer Street, just up past the hospital.'

'Who lives in the Chinkapook house now?' Holmes asked.

'An old bloke called Peter Cowan. Moved up from the city a few years ago.' Urdevic rolled his eyes and smiled. 'Loves the serenity, apparently. Grows his own vegies. Got a couple of yapping little dogs.'

Holmes was keen to avoid being sidetracked. 'Did you or your wife attend the Back-To-Manangatang celebrations?'

'We both went to the racecourse for the big get-together in the afternoon,' Urdevic replied.

Holmes nodded. 'What about the reunion ball in the evening?'

'Nah. It was booked out pretty early. Besides, Bernadette and I are pretty much homebodies. It was a Saturday night, so I probably watched the footy.'

Bowker folded his arms. 'Did you notice Adrian Weston hanging around at the racecourse during the big shebang?'

Urdevic shook his head. 'Didn't lay eyes on him after I pissed him off from our place in the morning.'

Bowker and Holmes exchanged glances. 'Why didn't you tell us you'd been talking to him?' Bowker asked, a little annoyed.

'You didn't ask me,' Urdevic replied, in a totally matter-of-fact manner.

'How long was he there?' Holmes asked.

'About ten minutes. Arrived around midday, wanting to bury the hatchet with Bernadette. She was caught off-guard by him just turning up out of the blue and didn't really want to talk to him. He was raving on about being misunderstood, saying how

Jimmy Cobb had got everything arse-about. Reckons he came back to Manang to set things right. In the end, I just pushed him out and slammed the door behind him. Good riddance, as far as I was concerned.'

'Was he driving a car?' Holmes asked.

'Buggered if I know. I didn't look. I just went back and gave Bernadette a hug. She was pretty upset, as you can imagine. Mainly about how he was trying to justify what had happened.' He looked at Bowker. 'Fair dinkum, Greg, it was fuckin' sickening.'

Bowker scratched the side of his head. 'And you didn't see him at the racecourse?'

'Nope. I've told you that.'

'Have you heard of anyone who did?'

'Nope. But then again, Bernadette and I keep to ourselves. Maybe some people saw him there who we just haven't spoken to.'

'How'd he find out where you live?' Holmes asked. 'If he asked around town, someone might've recognised him.'

'He said he went to his old house at Chinky. Peter Cowan must've told him. Cowan wouldn't know Weston from Adam, so there'd be no alarm bells ringing there.'

'And Cowan knows where you live?' Bowker asked.

Urdevic shrugged. 'Obviously he must. Fucked if I know how.'

The two detectives questioned Urdevic for another few minutes before they shook hands with him and turned to leave. The mechanical buzzing from inside the shed had ceased, and the air now rang with the sounds of sheep and dogs. Urdevic pointed to the door of the shed. 'It's morning smoko. Come inside and have a cuppa. There's always more than we can get through.'

As they walked towards the steps up to the shed door, Bowker said, 'Sorry about your mum, Travis. I heard she died a few years ago.'

'For the best, I reckon. She had a shit life from start to finish.' Urdevic blinked away tears. 'At least she outlived the old man. The bastard died in prison, which was poetic justice, if that's what it's called.'

Bowker pointed to the Navara. 'That beast yours?'

Urdevic smiled. 'Not made of money. Belongs to my shearing mate, who owns a farm and does a bit of shearing on the side.' He laughed. 'The boss drives the old Holden shit heap.'

Inside, the other shearer and the rousie were sitting on the floor, backs against the shed wall, both with a rollie in one hand and a steaming cup of black tea in the other. Stapleton stood chalking up the numbers for each shearer on a small blackboard hanging on a nail beside the wool press. Bowker and Holmes walked in through the blinding light of the doorway, and Urdevic ushered them to the wool table, where he poured them tea from a large thermos. He then filled his own mug, which had an Essendon Bombers logo, and slumped against the wall with his workmates.

Bowker felt totally out of place in his woollen suit and knew Holmes would be feeling the same way. Both detectives sat on bales of pressed wool while they sipped their tea, knowing how ridiculous the scene must've looked. But the shearing team made no comment as they tore into cream-and-jam-covered scones and rainbow sponge cake. Stapleton introduced the policemen, then pointed to the other shearer and the roustabout. 'Our rousie is Matty McIver. One-Ball's oldest son.'

Bowker smiled as he blew on his hot tea. 'You the same bloke who spewed up at the school social when you were in Form One? Gutful of grog, if I remember rightly.'

Urdevic laughed. 'Couldn't hold your grog back then either, Matty.'

McIver looked down at the floor as if he were a schoolboy being admonished.

'Naughty, naughty boy,' the unnamed shearer said, shaking a finger in McIver's direction.

Bowker raised his eyebrows but kept a straight face. 'Perhaps not as naughty as smoking weed at school, eh, Leigh? It is Leigh, isn't it? Leigh Davidson?'

Davidson looked at Bowker, wide-eyed. 'Shit, you've got a good memory, mate,' he said. 'That was over thirty years ago.'

'You're the spitting image of your old man,' Bowker replied.

'I've never touched the stuff since, I promise. I was so shit-scared you'd put me in jail if I smoked it again.'

'You blokes up here looking for whoever killed Adrian Weston?' McIver asked.

'Yeah, mate,' Holmes replied, as he licked jam off his fingers.

'Why waste your time? Prick deserved what he got. Whoever pulled the trigger did it on behalf of the whole community, as far as most people are concerned. Haven't you blokes got a big red stamp that says *Unsolved* you can put on Weston's file?'

Bowker shook his head. 'Afraid it doesn't work like that, Matt.'

'Pity it doesn't,' Davidson said, and scoffed down his fourth scone.

Bowker didn't react. He turned to Stapleton, thanking him for the unexpected morning tea. The two detectives waved to the shearing team and disappeared into the brightness outside.

Once in the car, Holmes buckled his seatbelt as Bowker started the engine. 'What do you reckon about Urdevic?' Holmes asked him. 'Telling the truth, you think?'

'I'm inclined to believe him. Fair bit to risk to settle an old score.'

'Happened plenty of times before. He might've thought about getting even for years. Then, out of the blue, Weston appears at his place, he gets his chance, and *bang*. All over, red rover.'

Bowker frowned. 'Someone would've heard it, surely. How about we go back through Chinky? I'd like a word with this Cowan bloke, just to confirm that Weston was there looking for Bernadette.'

'You worried Urdevic could be lying about his visit?'

'No. I'd just like to hear exactly what Weston and Cowan spoke about.'

*　*　*

After ten minutes, the detectives were back in Chinkapook. Bowker turned into Cowan's drive and pulled up behind an old Datsun. They made their way along the half-rotted verandah and knocked on the front door. There was no answer after a second attempt, so they walked through the carport and into the backyard. There, they found an elderly man stretched out in the sun on a battered old cane chair. His mouth was wide open as he snored loudly, despite two Jack Russell terriers trying their best to wake the dead. A large book lay open across his chest. Bowker read the title before rousing the sleeper with a poke to his shoulder. '*The Complete Sonnets of Shakespeare* is a bit out of place in Chinky, don't you think, Peter?'

Cowan woke up with a start, gaping at the two suited men in front of him. Bowker put a hand on his shoulder. 'Don't get a shock, mate. My colleague and I are police officers from the homicide squad. We'd just like to ask you a few questions, if we can.'

Cowan closed the book and sat up in his chair, rubbing his eyes with the backs of his hands. 'Of course, officers. Is this about the gentleman they found deceased at Cocamba a week or so ago?'

'That's right,' Holmes replied. 'His name was Adrian Weston.'

'That's what I heard from the locals here. But I'm quite new, so I didn't know the man at all.'

'He lived in this house at one stage,' Bowker said.

'Yes, I've heard that too,' Cowan replied. 'But it must've been a very long time ago. When I bought the residence from the McKay estate, I was told that Travis Urdevic, a local shearer, had last lived here. I was given his address in Manangatang if I needed advice on how the pumps and water tanks work.'

Bowker nodded. 'We know Travis and his wife quite well.'

'Thank goodness I've not needed to call on his services thus far. But I keep his details on my fridge, just in case.'

'Did you have any visitors on the weekend of the Back-To-Manangatang celebrations?' Holmes asked.

'Yes, a man I hadn't seen before, on the Saturday morning of that weekend. He thought that Travis and his wife might still reside here and was looking to visit them. I fetched my note from the fridge and conveyed to him the address and phone number I'd been given.'

Holmes folded his arms. 'Can you describe this man for us?'

'He would be in his mid to late sixties, I would estimate. Quite short, with a pinched face, grey hair, and a moustache. He wore wire-rimmed glasses and a gold chain around his neck, under a very brightly coloured open-necked shirt. He had a... what do they call it – a *retro* look to the way he was dressed. Nice manners.

After I gave him the information he was seeking, he thanked me and drove off in a small white car.'

Bowker removed a photo from his inside coat pocket. 'This was taken thirty years ago. Does it resemble the man who visited?'

Cowan took the picture and perused it closely, before returning it. 'Yes, that's him. Looking a lot older now, obviously. But that's him, I'm sure.'

'Do you remember what make of car he was driving?' Holmes asked.

'No. I'm hopeless with cars. I have no interest, as you no doubt have deduced from the vehicle I drive. All I remember was that it was small and white.'

Bowker shook Cowan's hand. 'Thank you, Mr Cowan. What you've told us has been very helpful.' He took out a business card and handed it to Cowan. 'If you think of anything else, don't hesitate to call me.'

'We'll leave you to your sonnets,' Holmes said. 'Great day for it.'

Cowan looked at the business card. 'Detective Bowker, can I ask who this man is, and why his visit is of interest to you?'

Bowker looked at Holmes before answering. 'It was Adrian Weston, Mr Cowan.'

Cowan's palm flew up to cover his mouth. 'My God!'

'You weren't to know what awaited him. Again, thanks for your time, sir,' Bowker said, as he turned towards the carport.

'There was another thing he asked just as he was leaving,' Cowan said belatedly. 'He was after another address, but it was for someone I'd never heard of.'

Bowker walked back. 'And who was that?'

The old man's brow furrowed. 'A Jimmy Cobb,' he replied.

CHAPTER 9

On the short return journey to Manangatang, the detectives reflected on what they'd learnt during the morning's investigations.

'Well, Sherlock, the mystery's solved on how Weston travelled to Manang. One tiny step forward,' Bowker said. 'He didn't come by bus, he didn't hitch, and he didn't drive the old red Charger. He drove a little white car, just like half the people who attended the Back-To would've driven.'

'But where *is* the bloody thing? Our local constabulary said he hasn't spotted any stray cars.' Seeing Bowker's expression, Holmes chuckled. 'Yeah, I know. That's hardly conclusive evidence.'

'My gut feeling is that Weston's car will still be where he was murdered. And I doubt that'll be in the town itself.'

'Do you reckon it could be out at Jimmy Cobb's?'

Bowker screwed up his face. 'I can't see the Jimmy Cobb I knew killing anybody, or having the intellectual wherewithal to dump the body at Cocamba. But his name does keep coming up in relation to Weston's visit.'

Holmes nodded. 'Urdevic said Weston was blaming Cobb for his woes, and asking Cowan about Cobb's address would imply Weston was keen to catch up with him.'

'Agreed. What we need to find out is whether he actually got that address, and whether he visited Jimmy before he was taken down. We'll see if Bernadette corroborates what Travis said about her father's visit and his apparent obsession with Jimmy Cobb.'

'Urdevic may have already rung and tipped her off about our discussion,' Holmes said.

Bowker shook his head. 'Bloody mobile phones. Geez, they make things hard. When Jack Moloney and I investigated Yvonne Bryant's murder, there was no such thing. You could make assumptions about who could've known what and when, and you could play one person off against another. Now there's instant communication.'

Holmes shrugged. 'We can get phone records if we need them.'

'Yeah, but they don't tell us what was said.'

There was quiet in the car as the detectives drove north along Sea Lake Road. Off to their right were the Cocamba silos, glistening in the late morning sun, set against a backdrop of bright yellow canola flowers. It was difficult to envisage this postcard panorama as the epicentre of two heinous crimes.

'It'd make things a bit easier if we could just fingerprint anybody we saw as having a motive for the shooting,' Holmes said, gazing out his window to the far western horizon.

'Yeah, but you know the rules, Sherlock. Reasonable grounds. I hardly think a possible motive, and bugger-all else, would constitute reasonable grounds for printing half a dozen people. Even if we got no match, it wouldn't prove they were in the clear anyway.'

'On the other hand, if one or two did match, it'd be game on.'

Bowker nodded. 'Can't disagree with that, mate.'

'The unidentified prints belonging to a male and a female points to a couple working together,' Holmes said, after a pause.

Bowker didn't respond for a minute or two. 'I might request

the national database run a specific comparison of the prints with Skeeta Allender's, just in case the computer missed a match. Haven't heard of that happening, but in terms of our major suspects, Skeeta is the only one with prints on file. As far as we know, anyway.'

'His prints would've been destroyed when his murder charge was dropped,' Holmes responded. 'Well, within the prescribed six months, anyway.'

'But I did him for drug trafficking and assault as soon as he was released. His prints should still be there.'

Holmes stroked his moustache. 'If you request another comparison for Allender, you may as well do the same for Urdevic. As a juvenile offender, he would've been printed.'

Bowker shook his head. 'According to the LEAP database, he's been as straight as an arrow since his days in Turana, and–'

Holmes beat him to the punch. 'And a juvenile's prints are destroyed if they reach age twenty-six without reoffending.'

'Correctamundo, my friend,' Bowker replied, as they approached the same flock of galahs they'd temporarily dispersed earlier in the morning. Again, the birds lifted together, but this time, they turned back towards the car, before all but one climbed to avoid the vehicle. The low flier hit the bonnet of the car then bounced lifelessly off the windscreen, leaving a circular opaque mark on the glass.

Bowker watched the receding image of the dead bird in his rear-vision mirror, its pink breast feathers fluffing up in the light breeze. 'Poor bastard,' he said quietly.

Holmes sighed. 'Interesting how much time and effort we put into explaining the deaths of human creatures, isn't it? When it happens to other animals, we just shake our heads and move on. That bloody galah deserves a lot more regard than fuckers like Weston.'

Bowker nodded but said nothing.

By the time they were back in Manangatang, it was lunchtime at the school. Rather than entering the grounds via the main gate, Bowker drove a few hundred metres east along the highway before turning right onto the bitumen drive that led to the bus assembly area. 'Bloody hell, this has changed,' he said. 'This used to be the site of the old disused consolidated school. There was a cluster of relocated rural schoolrooms brought in from surrounding districts in 1946.' Bowker gestured to the modern buildings further west. 'The new school was built over there much later. I was going to show you the Winnambool school that educated Percy and his generation in the thirties when it was still out in the sticks. It's also the room where Rachael conducted her dance lessons.' He shrugged. 'But it's gone now, obviously.'

Holmes pointed through the front windscreen. 'Not a bad replacement.'

Ahead, beyond where the buses lined up, was a massive gymnasium-cum-assembly hall, strategically placed to cater for drive-in traffic. 'Can't believe a structure like that was built for a pissant school in the middle of nowhere, and in a town this size,' Holmes said.

'Go easy on the pissant school business, mate,' Bowker replied, with a smile. 'My wife worked there for twelve years, and our kids all went there, as did a shitload of doctors and other high-fliers.'

Holmes grinned. 'Sorry, mate. A bloke who grew up in Murrayville shouldn't comment on pissant schools. Although ours was pretty modern for its time.'

Bowker followed the dirt track around the rear of the school and pulled into the carpark west of the main buildings. The biggest change he noticed from his last visit nearly twenty years ago was the growth of the vegetation. Trees that had been mere saplings when he left now shaded the roofs of most of the buildings. The grounds had been beautified, which helped disguise the harsh Mallee environment. He noted new outdoor seating areas and a rotunda in the midst of shady gums. The concreted quadrangle, where he'd delivered inspiring addresses on road safety to the children, was now surrounded by verdant shrubs in large red gum boxes. In all, the school grounds represented the yang that balanced the yin of the landscape enclosing them. Overlaying this picturesque background was the soundscape of screeching parrots in the trees above and unseen children at play on the other side of the buildings.

Bowker introduced himself and Holmes to the young receptionist and asked if Bernadette Urdevic was available for a quick chat. The receptionist phoned the staffroom, and after a minute or two, a petite woman appeared, cradling a half-eaten sandwich on greaseproof paper.

'Good afternoon, officers,' Bernadette said. 'The principal is away at a conference, so perhaps it would be best if we used her office.'

The policemen followed her to a room beside the front counter. Before he sat down, Bowker examined an original oil painting on the wall next to his easy chair and noted the small commemorative plate honouring one of the young teachers who'd been killed in a horrific car crash during his first year in the town. The artwork, which had been painted by the young woman's mother, immediately evoked vivid memories of the devastating conversations he'd had with a trio of unprepared families three decades before.

'Saw Rachael the other day,' Bernadette said, as she sat across the coffee table from the two detectives. 'Wondered how long it would be before you spoke to me.'

'I'm not sure what your relationship was like with your father before he died, but Detective Holmes and I would like to pass on our sympathies,' Bowker said sombrely. 'Everything else aside, losing your father can't be easy.'

'Thank you. We had no relationship, really. How he treated Mum and Sophie was unforgivable, let alone what he did to Yvonne. I didn't wish him dead, but at the same time, I'm not going to mourn too deeply either.' Bernadette brightened a little. 'So, what can I help you with?'

'I know this is what all coppers seem to say, but I can assure you that this chat is strictly routine,' Bowker said.

'Okay.' She took a bite of her sandwich.

'We're particularly interested in your father's movements leading up to when he was shot. We're almost certain it was on the weekend of the Back-To celebrations.'

'He came to our place on Pioneer Street the morning of the big get-together over at the racecourse,' Bernadette replied. 'Just turned up out of nowhere.'

'What sort of mood was he in?' Holmes asked.

'Anxious, nervous, snappy. Annoyed that I didn't go to see him when he was in prison. He thought it was a daughter's duty to look out for her father. In spite of all that, he wanted us to re-establish a relationship.'

'What was your answer?' Bowker asked.

'Told him I wasn't interested. Asked him why, if he thought

family duty was that important, did he treat Mum and Sophie the way he did?'

'Did he see the irony?' Bowker asked.

'I don't think so. He blamed all his troubles on Jimmy Cobb – seemed to believe if Jimmy had kept mum about his relationship with Yvonne, none of the other things would've happened.'

Bowker threw his head back and sighed loudly. 'Did he say how that would've worked?'

'Skeeta Allender was already in jail for her murder. My father said Skeeta was a worthless drug-dealing pothead who deserved to be in prison anyway. He admitted he'd done the wrong thing with Sophie, but swore he wouldn't have touched her again. According to him, life would've gone back to normal if Jimmy hadn't shot his mouth off.'

'Trying to rewrite history, by the sounds of it,' Holmes replied. 'Happens a lot with the people we deal with.'

'How did Travis take this visit?' Bowker asked.

'He was angry,' Bernadette replied. 'Worried that I was becoming upset. In the end, he showed my father the door and told him to never come back. I rang the local policeman to let him know my father was in town and there could be trouble.'

The detectives exchanged a glance. 'And you didn't see your father again?' Holmes asked.

Bernadette shook her head.

'Did you attend the reunion over at the racecourse?' Holmes asked.

'Yes, but I didn't see my father there, if that's your next question.'

Bowker paused before asking, 'Were you with Travis for the rest of the day?'

Bernadette dropped the remains of her sandwich onto the coffee table and stared at him with steely blue eyes. 'Yes, Detective, I *was*,' she said irately. 'And we didn't go to the ball on Saturday night, and we worked around the house all day Sunday.' She paused for effect. 'He didn't kill my father.'

'Does Travis own a shotgun?' Holmes asked.

'No, he doesn't. He has a .22 that he keeps in a locked gun safe in our shed down the back.'

After obtaining the current addresses of Bernadette's mother Belinda and sister Sophie, Bowker thanked her for her time and returned with Holmes to the carpark. It was after one o'clock when they reached the police station, following a counter lunch with Rachael. The station was locked, with the *Station Closed* sign on the door. Bowker called the station's number and received an answering machine message to ring the Robinvale police if the matter was urgent. He rolled his eyes, then walked with Holmes around to the residence and banged on the back door. Parker opened it in casual clothes, holding a half-eaten meat pie in one hand.

'You closed up for the day?' Bowker asked, with a tinge of irritation.

Parker frowned. 'Can't stay open to the public and run your case at the same time,' he said. 'I've been following up on what you asked me to at sparrow fart this morning.' He invited them inside with a sweep of an arm. 'Just finishing my lunch. Do you want a coffee?'

'Just had a countery at the pub,' Holmes replied, as he and Bowker followed Parker through to the police office. The blinds were all down, and a reverse-cycle air conditioner was blowing warm air into an already uncomfortably hot room. Papers and

Fantale wrappers adorned the desk. Parker pushed the remnants of his pie into his mouth and switched on the lights. Two overhead fluorescents buzzed and flickered to life.

'It's a bloody oven in here,' Bowker said. 'If you like it this hot, then the summers shouldn't worry you too much.'

Parker flicked off the air con and stared at Bowker. 'Satisfied?' he asked loudly, expelling fragments of pastry into the air.

'Will be, if you open the blinds and let a bit of light and fresh air in,' Bowker replied.

Parker swallowed deeply, then burped. He opened the blinds with annoyance. 'Now every bastard who comes to the door will be able to see there's someone in here,' he said. 'Not much good having a *Closed* sign up, if people can see there's a cop inside.'

'Hard to disagree with that,' Bowker replied sarcastically, as the three men sat down. 'You didn't tell us Bernadette Urdevic warned you that her father was back in town.'

Parker shrugged. 'Nothing came of it.'

'Except that he was murdered that same day,' Bowker said.

'I kept an eye out for him, alright?' Parker replied irately. 'But I wouldn't have known him even if I'd seen him.'

Bowker exhaled loudly. 'Have any luck with Barwon Prison?'

Parker grinned, clearly happy to be on more positive ground. 'Hit pay dirt. A prison officer pulled Weston's file, and he was able to answer two of the questions you had.' After shuffling through the mess on his desk, Parker handed Bowker a torn-out notebook page. 'These are Adrian Weston's mother's details. She owns a house in Altona at that address. Apparently, that's where Weston went to live when he was released.'

'Good,' Bowker said. 'What about visitors? Must've had a few over thirty years. Any regulars, especially over the last few months?'

'Barwon are emailing a copy of his file, plus a photo, as you requested. But the officer said that except for his mother, very few others came in to see him. One bloke was a constant for decades though, apparently.' Parker again rifled through papers until he found what he was after. 'A Hayden Tomlinson, of Swift Crescent in Niddrie. Visited on a fortnightly basis. I checked on the Law Enforcement Assistance Package to see if he has any criminal history or has come to police attention, but there's nothing recorded.'

Bowker was pleasantly surprised by Parker's initiative and impressed that he remembered the formal name of the police database. Every officer used LEAP on a regular basis, but most would have long forgotten what the acronym stood for. 'Well done on that, Shane. Whether he had a record would've been my next question. Did you make any progress on the other things I wanted chased up?'

'I checked the firearms register. Daryl Allender has a Browning five-shot automatic registered in his name. Nothing for Jimmy Cobb, although his father has a registered Beretta under-and-over shotty and a couple of rifles. According to Firearms, Travis Urdevic's only registered gun is a Rimfire .22 rifle.' Parker passed another scribbled note to Bowker.

Bowker nodded. 'Okay. What about the hot dog stall? Make any progress there?'

'Haven't had a chance yet. Same with Allender – planned to do those this arvo. But I did chase up the red Charger like you asked. Nothing on Citylink or any traffic cameras.'

Although Peter Cowan's observation of Weston driving a small white sedan had already eliminated the red Charger from their inquiries, Bowker decided against downplaying the importance of Parker's information. He was just happy that Parker had followed it up. 'Thanks, Shane. Sherlock and I are taking a drive out to Jimmy Cobb's to have a quick chat.'

'Do you want me on that one?' Parker asked. 'Could help you find the place.'

Bowker looked at Holmes, then shook his head. 'Nah, we can handle it. I'd prefer you chase up the hotdogs and get in touch with Skeeta's sister. See if you can get a contact from her.'

'We also need a list of what was in Weston's wallet, so if you're at a loose end, you can follow that one up too,' Holmes said, winking at Bowker while Parker wrote on his pad, swearing under his breath.

* * *

The journey out to Cobb's Bolton property took less than twenty minutes. On this occasion, Holmes drove while Bowker navigated to the farm formerly owned by Lester Green. In an earlier life, while investigating the theft of a scarifier, Bowker had attended the property on three or four occasions. Holmes followed Robinvale Road north as far as the Bolton silo complex, turned right over the railway line, and travelled east for a few kilometres along the Kooloonong Road.

After they bore left at the Myall bush reserve, Bowker knew they were close. A couple of crows lifted from the road near a concrete culvert. Holmes veered slightly to avoid the roadkill. Two or three minutes later, Bowker recognised the big dam near the front gate, with its towering Southern Cross windmill beside an enormous poly water tank. A mob of sheep in full wool were lying in the sun on the northern bank. 'Turn in here, mate.'

Holmes turned into a gateway beside a ten-gallon-drum letterbox supported by a short length of heavy drag chain, its links welded together to create the illusion that it stood vertically. The car crossed a cattle grid between two ancient header wheels with rusty spokes and progressed up the pot-holed drive towards the house. Off to his right, Bowker spotted a tractor towing a boom sprayer. He indicated to Holmes to follow a fork in the track towards the paddock being sprayed. Holmes pulled up at the opened double gateway to the paddock, and the two detectives alighted from the car. Beside it was a quadbike with the keys in the ignition.

'Most dangerous thing on the bloody farm,' Holmes said, pointing to the four-wheeled machine. 'You can throw in tractors, power take-offs, slashers, you name it. Combined, they don't kill as many people as these death traps. I read somewhere that around a hundred and fifty people using these fuckers were killed over the last seven years. And about a quarter of them were kids.'

Bowker straddled the quadbike's seat and grasped its handlebar grips. 'Why haven't they got roll-over protection?'

'They will from next year,' Holmes said, leaning his backside against the car. 'Manufacturers have been dragged into it, kicking and screaming. They reckon fitting roll bars is equivalent to admitting they're dangerous.'

'There's no way you could control one of these if you were a young kid,' Bowker said. 'The bloody thing is as heavy as buggery.'

'And they go like the powers of piss,' Holmes said. 'On uneven ground, or turning sharp corners, they flip like nobody's business. If you're trapped underneath, you're fucked. Crushed or asphyxiated, take your pick. It's goodnight nurse either way.' He pointed into the paddock. 'And unless your mate has taken his helmet with him, I'd say he doesn't wear one of those either.'

'Ever seen a farmer wear a helmet, even on a normal farm bike? They all reckon they're too smart to have a prang.' Bowker dismounted the quadbike, went over to Holmes, and nodded towards the crop in front of him. 'You're the cocky, Sherlock. What's he spraying?'

'It'll be a post-emergent herbicide of some sort. Kills the weeds coming up in the crop.' Holmes placed his forearms atop a strainer post.

'I wonder if he's using 2,4-D or 2,4,5-T, like they sprayed when I was up here.'

'Shit, no,' Holmes replied quickly. 'That's all been banned – contained dioxin, especially the stuff coming out of China and India. Caused cancer all over the place. Mix the two together and you have Agent Orange.'

'Fuck me,' Bowker said, and grinned. 'Apparently, the Lands Department bloke in Manang drank some to prove how safe it was. Before my time. Not sure if he's still in the land of the living.'

Holmes didn't smile. 'Bloody idiot either way. The big danger with the stuff is that sometimes, the dioxin boils off before the spray is dry and blows away on the wind. That's why it even affected people who were nowhere near the paddock being sprayed. Course, in the old days, cockies were slack with protective equipment. Just handled the stuff like it was water.'

Bowker shook his head. 'Looking back, it was a bloody time bomb. Bit like DDT. One day a miracle pesticide, the next an environmental disaster.'

'Cobb's intellectual disability mustn't be too bad if that's him spraying out there on his own,' Holmes said. 'He's handling the tractor and spray rig pretty expertly, by the looks of it.'

'You'll find he's a bit slow on the uptake at times, and he tends to mangle the English language, but he's not exactly Robinson Crusoe there.' Bowker chuckled. 'I didn't have much to do with him once he left school. As a kid, though, I always found him open and honest. Whether that's still the case, I don't know. People with these sorts of impairments sometimes cop a lot of shit as they grow up, and they can withdraw into themselves to cope.'

Across the paddock, the tractor stopped. The driver closed down the spray pump and wandered through the ankle-high crop towards the police car. As he approached, Bowker confirmed quietly to Holmes that it was Jimmy Cobb, now a strong and fit man in his late forties. Cobb's face had grown rounder since Bowker had last seen him, and his hair showed a little grey where it protruded from his green John Deere cap. He wore the obligatory elastic-sided boots, dirty jeans and checked flannelette shirt with the sleeves cut out. Bowker thrust out a hand. 'G'day, Jimmy. Long time no see.'

Cobb looked at Bowker quizzically, then his face lit up. 'Consable Bowker. Youse not wearing uniform. Must be your days off.'

Bowker laughed. 'I have a different job in Melbourne now, Jim. This is Detective Holmes, who works with me.'

Holmes shook hands. 'Heard a lot about you, mate. What are you spraying?'

'Weeders,' Cobb said.

Holmes smiled. 'I mean, what chemical?'

'Atlantis. Got to be careful with chemicals. Have to wear gloves and mask,' Cobb said. 'Dad comes over and mixed 'em for me. Then I spray.'

'You're doing a good job,' Holmes said. He pointed to the rows of foam dots deposited by the boom sprayer to indicate which areas had already been treated. 'All your spray marker lines are nice and straight.'

'I'm a real good driver,' Cobb replied proudly. He looked at Bowker. 'Is Rachwell up with you? She is the nicest lady I ever knowed.' He smiled. "Cept for mum, but that don't count.'

'She came up for a few days. She's staying in town at the pub.'

'I'd like to see her, but I don't drived into town. Only around the back roads and on the farm.'

Bowker pulled his phone from his pocket. 'How about I take your photo so I can show her what you look like now? I'll tell her how well you've done since you left school.'

Cobb smiled and leaned up against the gatepost, striking a pose straight out of a men's fashion magazine. 'Wait!' he yelled, just as Bowker was about to snap the picture. Cobb licked his fingers and smoothed down a few stray hairs on the top of his head. 'Good now.'

After Bowker had taken the photo, he showed it to his model. Cobb nodded his approval, then frowned. 'Have you come to Manang to catch Mr Weston's murderer, like you catched him when he killed Yvonne?' he asked.

'That's right,' Bowker replied, slipping his hands into his trouser pockets. 'How did you find out he'd been murdered?'

'Dad told me. He told me Mr Weston was found at Cocamba, just like Yvonne was. 'Cept he was shooted.'

'That's right, mate. When was the last time you saw Mr Weston?' Bowker asked.

Cobb thought carefully for a moment. 'When he was at school. When he was a teacher. Before he went to jail.'

'You haven't seen him in the last couple of weeks?' Holmes asked.

Cobb shook his head. 'No. Not since school. A long, long, long time ago.'

'Did you go to the Back-To-Manangatang celebrations in town a couple of weeks ago?' Holmes asked.

'No. No. I stayeded at home. On Sadays I go with the ferrets, down the back paddock to the big sandhill. Lots of burras.'

Bowker folded his arms across his chest. 'Do you take a gun with you when you go ferreting?'

'No, no. Rabbits go into nets, and you kill them with your hands.' Cobb mimed breaking their necks, making a cracking noise with his mouth.

'Do you have a shotgun, Jimmy?' Bowker asked.

'Dad has a Bretta,' Cobb replied. 'I get a lend when I go spotlightin'.'

Holmes scratched his cheek. 'Where's the gun now?'

'At Dad's, I think,' Cobb replied. 'Lockeded up in a steel box.'

Holmes and Bowker looked at each other, wondering what other questions they needed to put to Cobb. 'Have you seen a little white car out this way in the last couple of weeks?' Bowker asked. 'A car you haven't seen before?'

'No, no. Just utes on the road. And Dad has a big grey car.'

'Are you here on your own all the time, Jim?' Holmes asked.

Cobb nodded. 'Yep. 'Cept when Dad comes over to help with the farm. Mum comes over on some days with food for me to cooked.'

Bowker pointed to the quadbike. 'You wear a helmet when you ride that thing?'

'Don't needed to. I'm not on the road,' Cobb explained, with great authority.

'It's not about the law, mate,' Bowker said. 'It's about keeping you safe when you ride. What happens if you flip this machine over down the paddock?'

'I'm really careful, Consable Bowker. Don't goed faster than twenty-five unless I'm chasing a foxes or something.'

Bowker closed his eyes at the futility of trying to give safety advice to Cobb, or to any farmer, really. 'Just be careful, okay, mate? I'd hate to hear of you being killed on one of these things.'

After another five minutes of establishing Cobb's normal daily routines, Bowker handed Cobb his business card and bade his farewells. Cobb tucked the card into his shirt pocket and trudged his way back to the tractor. Rather than retracing their path to the front gate, Bowker suggested they return to the fork in the track and turn back towards the homestead.

'Might just do a lap of the house and sheds before we go, I think, Sherlock.'

'Looking for a stray small white car?'

'Yeah. I don't think Jimmy is telling lies, but let's just take the long way home. Okay?'

Holmes drove past the neat weatherboard residence with a rudimentary garden at the front and a garage-cum-workshop to the side. In the garage was a Toyota one-tonner, which had rolls of wire and steel pickets on its tray, inside a steel frame used for spotlighting. Behind the house, among half a dozen pepper trees, was a long shed sheltering a large grain-carrying semitrailer, a self-propelled combine harvester, a large air-seeder with its booms folded, and an enormous chisel plough. Two bays were empty, obviously homes for the tractor and the spray equipment. Further along the tree line were a large chaser bin parked under a sugar gum, several field bins, and a cluster of permanent silos. Two kelpies ran up and down a mesh dog run, barking at the police vehicle as it passed.

'Everything that opens and shuts here,' Holmes commented.

'Everything except a small white sedan. May as well head back to the station and see what our favourite senior connie has found out for us.'

As the car passed the dam, a pair of black ducks lifted from the water, their wings whistling as they climbed into the clear blue sky. Bowker found himself incrementally reconnecting with this familiar Mallee milieu, and for the first time on a homicide case, didn't resent the time it was taking to make meaningful progress in his investigation.

CHAPTER 10

Back at the station, the *Closed* sign was still up, but the glass door was unlocked and the lights were on. Senior Constable Parker was at his desk making notes when Holmes and Bowker returned. Bowker précised their discussion with Jimmy Cobb and their cursory search for Weston's car.

'I'm surprised you didn't go over the place with a fine-toothed comb after what the Chinky bloke said about Weston looking for Cobb,' Parker said.

'At this stage, there's nothing to suggest that Weston went out there, or even that he found out where Jimmy lived. And Jimmy seemed pretty sincere when we asked him about whether he'd seen Weston.'

Parker spread his hands. 'He's a halfwit. Do you think he'd even remember?'

Bowker arced up. 'He has an intellectual disability, Shane, and doesn't deserve to be labelled a halfwit!'

Parker rolled his eyes. 'Sorry, didn't mean to upset the PC brigade.'

'This has nothing to do with political correctness. It has to do with respect,' Bowker said irately, resisting the urge to tell Parker that the biggest halfwit he'd met on this trip was sitting across the desk from him.

'Okay, okay. I get the message,' Parker replied.

'I thought Cobb was pretty straight down the line with us,' Holmes said. 'He never hesitated on any question we asked him. If Weston did visit his farm, I'm willing to bet that Cobb didn't see him. There's plenty of other places to be on five thousand acres if he's not at the house.'

'Fair enough,' Parker replied. 'We give him the benefit of the doubt.'

'No, that implies he's our number one suspect, which is certainly not the case,' Bowker said. 'Not at this stage, anyway. If something comes up that points to him, we'll take a closer look.' He leaned back in his chair. 'Now, what have you been able to find out?'

Parker exhaled loudly, seeming happy to venture into safer territory. 'I checked the list of items found at Cocamba as you requested – more specifically, the contents of his wallet. There was a Medicare card, his licence, obviously, and a Woolworths loyalty card. No cash. No bank cards.'

'Bit strange for a bloke we presume travelled five hours from Melbourne,' Bowker said. 'I assume you rang around the banks?'

Parker smiled. 'Contacted the big four. Took ages to get through all their security protocols. Bottom line is, Weston has a debit account with NAB and a Visa credit card with ANZ.' He leaned back smugly in his chair. 'So now we know whoever killed him robbed him as well. Just another small step along that long road, eh, Greg?'

Bowker smiled. 'Well done. Did they estimate how long it'd be before we receive the transaction statements for those cards?'

Parker looked at him blankly. 'What do you mean?'

Bowker shot a glance at Holmes. 'We need a printout for each of those cards to see if they've been used since the murder. If they have, that'll give us a heads up about who we're looking for and where they might be.'

Parker was crestfallen. 'Never thought of that. I just assumed you were wanting to know if anything had been taken from the scene.'

Bowker resisted the temptation to scream out loud and spoke quietly instead. 'As soon as we finish here, ring back and request that a copy of those statements be emailed to you.'

Parker checked his watch. 'Banks will probably be closed by now.'

'They'll have a twenty-four-hour helpline,' Homes replied. 'Go through that.'

Bowker was keen to move things along before he said something he might regret. 'What about the other things I asked you to suss out?'

'I tracked down Skeeta Allender's sister out at Kulwin. She doesn't know where he lives, but he did visit her on the weekend of the Back-To trying to scrounge some money. Apparently, he arrived on a loud motorcycle with a tough-looking woman riding pillion. They were both in full leathers with an insignia on their backs.' Parker rifled around on his desk until he found the piece of paper he was after. 'Barbarians, they're called.'

'Never heard of them,' Holmes said.

'Did she say anything else?' Bowker asked.

'Only that the bikie gang was on a ride up to Mildura. When they got to Ouyen, Allender decided to make the quick detour to Kulwin. Said he was going to meet up with the others at Merbein, where they planned to camp on the river. Sister told him to piss off. He got shitty and accused her of stealing his inheritance.

Told her she was only adopted and not a real daughter. Told her she had no right to his old man's farm.'

Bowker shook his head in annoyance. 'As if he had a right to it after treating his parents like shit, and sponging off them until they dropped dead of hard work. Did she say whether he kept going into Manang or rode back to Ouyen?'

'I asked her that. She didn't know. Their house is half a mile from the road and behind a couple of sandhills, apparently, so she couldn't see which way he headed. Said she wouldn't have taken notice anyway. She's got no time for the bastard. Her husband had to tell him to piss off and not come back.'

Holmes took a notebook from his inside coat pocket and scribbled on it. 'Barbarians. That gives us a starting point.'

Bowker smiled. 'The sister didn't say whether Skeeta had a shotgun slung over his saddlebags, did she?'

Parker didn't get the joke. 'Not that she mentioned,' he said seriously.

'Could've had a sawn-off shotty hidden among his stuff, though,' Holmes said. 'Often par for the course in these gangs.'

'Hadn't thought of a sawn-off,' Bowker replied.

'And then there's the prints found at Cocamba. A male and a female.' Holmes frowned. 'Allender's didn't match, though, did they?'

'I want confirmation of that before I write Skeeta off,' Bowker said. 'Besides, a lack of prints doesn't prove he's in the clear.' He sat forward and looked at Parker. 'Anything else?'

'I chased up the food stalls at the Back-To. According to Kaye O'Riordan from the organising committee, there was a hotdog stall run by the school. It was mostly manned by kids with a staff member supervising. The school closed at 3.30, so I haven't got any further with that.'

Bowker nodded. 'Sherlock and I are returning to Melbourne to conduct more interviews, so we'll leave that to you to follow up on Monday. Hopefully, by then, an up-to-date photo will have arrived from Barwon to go with a description of how Weston was dressed.'

Parker wrote on his pad. 'No worries. And I'll chase the banks for those statements as well.'

Bowker stood up. 'We're having a counter tea with my wife Rachael tonight, so how about you come down and join us around 6.30? Unless, of course, you've got a better offer.'

Parker leaned back in his chair, hands folded behind his head. 'There's never a better offer in this place, mate,' he said, with a smile. 'Pub sounds great.'

* * *

Two chicken parmas, a mixed grill, and a plate of fish and chips arrived at the table in the sparsely populated hotel lounge. The occasional older patron warmly greeted Bowker and Rachael upon recognising the detective and his wife. None of the locals acknowledged their senior constable.

When Bowker went to replenish their glasses, he spotted a familiar face in the public bar next door. Rick Brennan, his old footy coach whose family formerly owned the pub, was seated at a round table with a trio of younger men Bowker didn't recognise. Taking the two beers, a lemon, lime and bitters, and his Coke Zero back to the table, Bowker patted Holmes on the shoulder. 'Grab your beer, Sherlock, and I'll introduce you to an old mate of mine.' He looked across the table at Parker. 'Can you take care of Rachael for me, mate? Make sure she stays out of trouble while we're away.'

Parker raised his glass. 'I'll make sure that lemon, lime and bitters doesn't send her off her head.'

'Won't be long, Rach,' Bowker said. 'Just want to catch up with Rick Brennan. He's in the bar next door.'

Rachael smiled and nodded. 'Say hello from me.'

As the two detectives made their way to the bar, Parker shot Rachael a puzzled look. 'Who's Rick Brennan?'

'He coached the footy team for most of the years we were up here. Ex-AFL, or VFL as it was when he played for Melbourne. His knees were shot when he came up here, but he still dominated the comp, and Manang was pretty successful under his guidance. His in-laws owned this hotel. Last I'd heard, he'd settled further south. In the Wimmera at Horsham, I think.' Rachael took a sip of her drink. 'Do you play footy, Shane?'

Parker shook his head. 'Nah. Sport's not really my thing, unless you count playing on the Xbox.'

'It's a good way to meet people up here. Helps make you feel at home.'

'I never want to feel at home in a dump like this. To be honest, if I was offered any other placement in the state right now, I'd take it, no questions asked. Except Werrimull. That's even more one-horse than here, apparently.'

'Greg said your mum was from around here, and she's the one who encouraged you to apply for a one-copper station.'

'Yeah. She and Dad had a farm between Chinkapook and Nyah. The family played sport in Nyah West and had a fair bit to do with the policeman there. Mum said it seemed like a pretty easy, laid-back gig. There was no vacancy at Nyah, or at Piangil further along the river, so I applied for here, thinking they'd all be pretty similar. Worst decision of my life. The other towns had the river for fishing and skiing. This hole has got nothing. Zilch. Zero. One big duck egg.'

Rachael frowned, trying to marry her own happy experiences with Parker's dystopian assessment. She was also keen not to make his depression worse by mentioning the departure of his ex, so she elected to follow an easier path. 'What's your mum's name?'

'Lorraine. My dad's Andy. Also got a sister a fair bit older than me, Katherine, who's married with a couple of teenage kids. She lived up here too, before the family sold up and moved south.'

'Can't place her, but she must've gone to school in the years I was here.'

'Went to primary at Nyah, then followed her friends to Swan Hill before the old man bought the place down near Dunkeld. He became more interested in growing fine wool than scratching sand in the middle of a desert. That's where I was born and raised. A Western District blue blood, I am.' Parker spread his arms wide. 'Can't you tell?'

Rachael smiled. 'You weren't interested in staying on the farm?'

'Nah. Mug's game, farming. Mum's brother was a copper, so I followed his lead, much to my father's annoyance. He finished up sending my sister to Glenormiston Ag College, but she had no interest in that area either. Happy running a takeaway food shop with her husband.'

'Your uncle still in the force?'

Parker shook his head. 'Supered out after he was stabbed trying to break up a gang fight in Footscray, ten years ago. When I joined the force, he told me to apply for the country and stay right away from city problems.' Parker laughed. 'I guess I took his advice too far. I bypassed the country and ended up on another planet!'

'No gang fights, though,' Rachael said, with a grin.

Parker held up his Band-Aided thumb. 'Still enough aggro to get myself cut on a broken beer glass. Barely compares with a stabbing, I suppose.'

Rachael chuckled. 'Hardly gets you supered out, either,' she added. 'Did the Chinky farm originally belong to your grandfather?'

'Yeah, but it's quite ironic. He originally owned a sheep farm in the Western District. During the war, he was up here, servicing the Catalina flying boats at their base in Lake Boga, when he met Grandma in Swan Hill and decided to stay on. So he bought the block on the Chinky-Nyah West Road.' He shook his head. 'Things have come full circle.' He gulped a mouthful of beer.

'Greg and I went to the museum at Lake Boga years ago. Apparently, the Air Force wanted a secure place to do maintenance on the sea planes. Somewhere remote. Somewhere they couldn't be attacked by the Japanese.'

Parker smiled. 'And you don't get a place more remote than Lake Boga. Unless you're talking about…' He pointed his finger at the floor.

Bowker and Holmes returned to the lounge, and Bowker recounted their conversation with Rick Brennan. It was the second time in a fortnight that Brennan had visited Manang, having been to the Back-To earlier. This time, he'd come up for an award presentation after the football the following day.

* * *

The next morning, Holmes packed his gear and headed back to the city. Bowker and Rachael had lunch at the local football, where a clear azure sky and the smell of cut grass brought a smile to both their faces. A pie and a pastie hit the spot for Bowker, while Rachael selected a healthier plate of mixed sandwiches. Bowker was delighted to see that the club had retained its red, white, and black colours in its amalgamation with Tooleybuc. As a trade-off, the majority of home games would be played across the river at the Tooleybuc ground.

Rachael strolled across to the netball, and Bowker mingled with the local footy supporters. It was as if he'd never left. He was greeted warmly, and conversations seemed to be picked up where they'd left off twenty years earlier. The faces were decades older, but the personalities and banter hadn't changed. The locals reminisced about the football glories of the past, when Bowker controlled centre half forward and Rick Brennan dominated the league.

Word had spread quickly that Bowker was in town, and everyone seemed aware of his mission. The reaction to Weston's murder was universal. His killer had done the district a huge favour. The slate had been wiped clean and the ledger squared. They all encouraged Bowker to let sleeping dogs lie, even though they knew it wasn't in his nature to do so. No one had seen Weston at the Back-To, several saying that he wouldn't have made it as far as Cocamba if they'd caught sight of him earlier. In spite of the unanimous support for Weston's killer, there appeared genuine ignorance about the perpetrator's identity. Everyone had their theories, all of which mirrored the lines of investigation the detectives were already following.

Over at the netball, the situation was exactly the same. Rachael was embraced by the locals, and past glories and premierships were relived. The common impression was that she hadn't changed in appearance since she left the district, but Rachael found that hard to believe when she saw daughters of her former teammates among the senior players, and even a few grandkids playing in the underage teams. The attitude towards Weston's murder was identical to that encountered by Bowker. There was no sympathy for Weston, and the hope was that the police would fail in their pursuit of his killer. No one at the netball had seen Weston on the weekend he was killed.

Manangatang-Tooleybuc ground out a narrow victory over Tyntynder in the main football game, while the club had an easier win in the A-Grade netball. As the sun slid behind the town's buildings, most of the spectators remained for a barbecue, followed by entertainment from local musician Jeff Gibson. Bowker and Rachel danced and nattered the night away as if time had been swept back twenty-five years. A presentation was made to Rick Brennan, recognising his years of service to the football club, before festivities resumed under a blanket of stars.

Bowker and Rachael returned to their motel room well after midnight, exhausted but still exhilarated by their day from the past. When Bowker returned from the shower, Rachael stood beside the bed in a pale blue satin nightgown with cream lace around the décolletage.

Her husband was stopped in his tracks. 'Where'd you find that?'

'Well, you did say this was our second honeymoon,' she whispered, as she draped her arms around his neck.

CHAPTER 11

The Bowkers slept in on Sunday morning before a late breakfast in the hotel dining room. The day was overcast, with the odd fluffy white cotton pillow slowly traversing a blanket of high stratus cloud. Out towards the northeast, the weather looked more threatening. A front of black clouds was banking up, threads of lightning illuminating its interior, the thunder too distant to hear. Bowker and Rachael decided to return to Melbourne via the most direct route through Sea Lake and down the Calder Highway and were on the road by 9.30.

In the Yvonne Bryant murder case three decades earlier, Bowker had found it profitable to lay the facts out in front of Rachael. Not only had this helped get his own thoughts in order, but Rachael's insights had helped solve the case.

As they passed Cocamba, Bowker explained what they knew. 'We've established that Weston came to Manang on the weekend of the Back-To in a small white sedan. He stopped at his old house in Chinky, looking for Bernadette and chasing an address for Jimmy Cobb. The old bloke who now lives there pointed him towards Bernadette and Travis, but couldn't help with finding Jimmy. Weston arrived on Bernadette's doorstep in Manang, criticising her lack of contact during his stint in prison, and espousing that Jimmy Cobb was responsible for him losing thirty years of his life.'

Rachael shook her head. 'So, he sexually abuses his stepdaughter then kills a sixteen-year-old schoolgirl, and it's a disabled kid's fault for dobbing him in?'

'That's about the strength of it. Thirty years behind bars, and he still sees himself as the victim.'

'What was the Urdevics' reaction?'

'Travis arseholed him and told him not to come back. Forensics found evidence of a hotdog in his stomach, so we're assuming he purchased that at the racecourse during the Back-To. We haven't yet been able to confirm he was definitely there.' Bowker shrugged. 'After that, his movements are a complete mystery.'

'He ended up at Cocamba, obviously. Was his car out there as well?'

'Nope. Disappeared off the face of the earth. We don't even know what make it is, let alone its rego number.'

Rachael wound up her window a couple of inches. 'Did the crime scene tell you anything?'

'Only that Weston wasn't killed at the silos. He was transported from somewhere unknown, in an unknown vehicle, by a person or persons unknown.' Bowker laughed. 'Got it nailed, really, eh?'

Rachael chuckled. 'Pretty close, I'd say.'

'They lifted five sets of prints, one left by a female. Of the four remaining sets, three are explained. Two are from the Netcor workers who found the body, and the other belongs to our local senior constable, who must've missed the academy lecture on the use of gloves at a crime scene.' Bowker shook his head. 'Actually, from what I've seen, he must've missed a lot of lectures, to tell you the truth.'

'So, I presume you're looking for a male and a female.'

Bowker slowed down a little as he bypassed the remnants of

the Chinkapook township to his left. 'Yeah, probably. Forensics also found two strands of female hair adhered to the blood on Weston's skull. DNA belongs to the same female as the prints but doesn't match anything on record.'

'I'd guess your first thought was Travis and Bernadette until the prints didn't match the ones on file for Travis.'

Bowker snapped on his right-hand blinker and cruised around an empty B-Double cattle truck. 'The prints were destroyed when he turned twenty-six, so he and Bernadette are still suspects. Theoretically, anyway.'

Rachael looked at him, puzzled. 'Why theoretically?'

'Can't see them killing Weston, particularly Bernadette. Too much to lose. Plus, they would know they'd top the list of suspects.'

'Percy? Perhaps with some help?'

'He's already confessed, but it's all bullshit. He's only got a few years left, and no judge would send him to jail at his age. He just wants to say thank you to the real killer by taking the blame.'

'You reckon he knows who did it?'

'Nah,' Bowker said. 'Less idea than we do, in my opinion.'

'What about Skeeta?'

'We know he visited his sister at Kulwin on that weekend. He had a woman with him, but there's no evidence he came any closer to Manang. Besides, the prints at the scene don't match his.'

'So progress is slow?' Rachael asked, frowning.

'Yeah. The only other person needing a closer look is Jimmy Cobb.'

Rachael was aghast. 'Jimmy couldn't kill anybody, Greg. It's just not in his nature.'

Bowker raised his fingers on the steering wheel. 'Settle down

– I don't think he did it either. But we need to be certain before we put a line through anyone's name. Jimmy really liked Yvonne and hated Weston, so he had a motive.'

Rachael shook her head. 'Not possible.'

It was quiet for a few minutes as the kilometres slipped by, until Rachael finally broke the silence. 'What's in Melbourne that you need to chase up?'

'Interviews. Routine ones, mostly. We'll talk to Belinda and Sophie Weston, and have a chat with Adrian Weston's mother, as well as with a friend of his who visited him regularly in prison. We'll also talk to Skeeta if we can track him down. He runs with some bikie pack, so hopefully they have a clubhouse somewhere that might head us in the right direction.'

Rachael chuckled. 'Good luck with that.'

'Looking forward to it,' Bowker said, with a faux smile.

'I bet!' she replied.

'Sherlock lifted prints off the flower bottle we found on Yvonne's grave. I'd like Forensics to run them against the national database. And there were credit cards missing from Weston's wallet. The bank statements might take us somewhere.' Bowker grinned. 'So there's plenty to keep us busy.'

The Sea Lake Road paralleled Lake Tyrell as they approached its junction with the Calder Highway. Rather than turning south towards Sea Lake, Bowker went right and followed the highway north before heading onto the side road that led to the Lake Tyrell viewing platform. Lake Tyrell was a shallow salt lake with a flat, highly reflective surface. It was popular for photography and stargazing, and in recent times had become a magnet for overseas tourists, particularly those from China. As a result, the nearby town of Sea Lake had experienced a renaissance, with new accommodation and eateries developed for the ever-increasing tourist trade.

Once out of the car, Bowker and Rachael were struck speechless by a panorama stretching to infinity. The billowing tempest in the north was perfectly reflected on the lake's mirrored surface, with threads of lightning seemingly fusing mid-sky. Bowker put his arm around Rachael's shoulder and the couple stood transfixed for several minutes as the lightshow continued unremitting. Finally, Bowker spoke. 'I could stay here all day, Rach, but we better keep going. Need to stay ahead of that weather.'

Swirling anvil-shaped clouds illuminated by lightning filled the Subaru's mirrors all the way to Inglewood, where the couple pulled in for lunch. Two toasted sandwiches and milkshakes later, the sky grew darker and the streetlights in the small country town flickered to life. A massive thunderclap announced the arrival of the storm front. Hail hammered the bakery's tin roof, making conversation impossible. The gutters on the verandah filled quickly, and when the hail gave way to heavy rain, a curtain of water segregated the footpath from the street.

The Bowkers watched in awe as Mother Nature unloaded outside. It wasn't until thirty minutes later, when the violence of the storm had abated somewhat, that they ventured back to the car. The street gutters were flooded, with water covering the nature strip. Bowker splashed through the torrent and moved the Subaru to where Rachael could clamber in without soaking her jeans to the knees.

Constant rain was their companion for the remainder of the journey. Bowker drove conservatively, not only to suit the road conditions, but because he was in no hurry to revisit the tempest that now lay ahead of him.

* * *

Holmes was already at his desk on Monday morning when Bowker arrived at the police headquarters on Spencer Street. Bowker shook his hand and sat down, placing the envelope containing the cemetery bottle fingerprints down in front of him. 'I'll send these out to the McLeod centre and see if Forensics find a match.'

Holmes nodded, and Bowker continued. 'Can you ring the organised crime squad and see what they've got on the Barbarians? Hopefully, they can tell us where to find Skeeta Allender. I'll give Erin O'Meara a ring at Forensics and recheck that Allender's prints are still on file. That's if she hasn't died of lung cancer or emphysema since we spoke last.'

'Don't worry, mate – she's been on death's door for as long as I've known her, so my money is on her still being alive and kicking. Hope so, anyway. In terms of forensics, she's irreplaceable.'

'Yeah, I agree entirely.' Bowker tapped his fingers on the table. 'Then I reckon we should take a run out to Altona for a chat with Weston's mother. According to the prison, Weston lived with her after he was released from Barwon. With a bit of luck, she'll give us a clue about his movements and state of mind.'

'Sure thing,' Holmes said.

Plan confirmed, Bowker went to his nearby desk. He dropped into his chair, consulted a list of contacts pinned to a shelf, and punched in a series of numbers. After a few moments, he had a connection. 'G'day, Erin.'

'Greg. Long time, no hear.' O'Meara's voice caught, provoking a few seconds of coughing. When it settled, she asked, 'What can we do for you this time?'

'Was wondering if you could check something on the National Fingerprint Database for me.'

'What's the case?'

'The murder of an Adrian John Weston in the Mallee a couple of weeks ago. You've already run a comparison of the prints from the scene.'

Bowker heard her clear her throat noisily, spitting out the product before she spoke. 'So, what are you after?'

'An answer to a simple question. Are the prints of a Daryl Peter Allender on file? Thirty-one years ago, he spent time in prison for drug trafficking and assault.'

'How old was he when he was put away?'

'Twenty-three.'

O'Meara sounded puzzled. 'Why wouldn't his prints be here? If he's an adult with a criminal conviction, we keep them.'

'Just double checking in case there was a balls-up. He was charged with murder and spent weeks on remand before the charges were withdrawn. Dropping them would've triggered a mandatory order to have his prints destroyed within the following six months. As soon as he was released, I did him for drugs and assault. At that stage, his prints were already on file, so he was never reprinted.'

'You're worried about the time lag, then – that the order to destroy might've been executed after he was convicted on the new charges.'

'Don't think it's likely, but I'd like to be certain. He's a suspect in this new murder case and I'd hate him to slip through the net because of an administrative error.'

'I'll have a look.' For a minute or two, Bowker could hear hacking and retching in the background, before O'Meara came back on the line with a lilt in her gravelly voice. 'Well, what do you know? No prints on file for Daryl Peter Allender.' She chuckled. 'Fine work, Detective Inspector Bowker. Hope there aren't too many other cases like this.'

'Wouldn't think so,' Bowker said. 'Pretty unique for a bloke to be exonerated, then charged again on different counts within a week or two.'

'Agreed.'

'There's another set of prints on their way I'd like you to run for me. Found them on a bottle at the local cemetery. I suspect they're related to this case.'

'I'll keep an eye out,' O'Meara replied, as she was caught in another fit of coughing.

Bowker had just hung up when his mobile rang. It was Jimmy Cobb.

'Someone stoled my gun, Consable Bowker,' Jimmy blurted out as soon as Bowker answered.

'Slow down, Jim. Stolen which gun?'

'The Bretta, under'n'overs. The shotgun.'

'You said it was locked in a safe at your dad's place, remember?'

'No, no, no,' Jimmy replied in a panic. 'I thinked it was. But Dad said I had it last. Then I 'membered that I used it fox shooting with Leigh Davidson. Left it on the bench in the workshop. Now it's gone.'

'Look, I'm in Melbourne at the moment, mate. I'll be back in Manang later in the week, so we can talk about it then, okay?

You have another good look around your sheds in case you put it down somewhere else.'

'Okay, Consable Bowker. I'll have a really, really good look.'

Bowker pocketed his phone and wandered back to Holmes, who was just finishing a call himself. 'Just got off the phone with Jimmy Cobb. He reckons someone's stolen the family shotgun. I suspect he's put it down somewhere in one of the sheds and forgotten where he left it. We'll sort it out when we go back to Manang.'

Holmes nodded.

'The other interesting news is that Skeeta Allender's prints aren't on file. Mistakenly destroyed after the murder charge was quashed.'

'So Allender's back on our list?' Holmes asked.

'He was never off it, really. Absence of prints doesn't automatically clear anyone.'

Holmes raised his eyebrows. 'S'pose he could've pulled the trigger and touched nothing else.'

'Exactly,' Bowker replied. 'Any luck with Organised Crime?'

Holmes smiled. 'Yeah. Barbarians are a small-scale bikie gang into cooking and supplying methamphetamines. There's nothing specific on your mate Allender, but a few of his colleagues have spent a bit of time inside. Got an address for the gang's clubhouse in Northcote.'

'That's a good place to start.'

'Organised Crime said to be careful. They're tough bastards, apparently.'

Bowker patted Holmes on the shoulder. 'So are we, mate.'

They both laughed.

CHAPTER 12

t wasn't a lengthy drive from Spencer Street to Altona. Just a short hop over the Westgate bridge and a few kilometres down Millers Road, past the Mobil refinery and into a suburban labyrinth close to the bay. Altona was a classic example of gentrification. Once a shunned working-class region close to factories and industry, its residential land was now highly sought after for its close proximity to the city. Many of the older fibro cement and weatherboard houses so typical in days of yore had been replaced by twin-storey rendered townhouses, often in a duplex configuration. A home on a quarter-acre block with a sprawling backyard, once so typical of Australian suburbia, was a dying dream in the face of developers' determination to cover every square metre of available land with oversized and pretentious residential dwellings.

Adrian Weston's mother had resisted the temptation to sell her modest double-fronted weatherboard, or to renovate to keep up with the numerous Joneses who shared her street. The house made no attempt to hide its age. The exterior was in urgent need of a major paint job, starting with timber primer. The garden must've once been a feature, but the roses had since gone wild, their tendrils now climbing two silver birch trees near the partly fallen front fence. The lawn had long needed mowing. Tufts of grass grew from the roofing gutters. The concrete drive leading into a rickety carport had cracked, and several segments were lifting under pressure from the roots of a badly located Norfolk pine that grew against the side fence. In the carport was an old-model Austin sedan heavily clad in dust and cobwebs.

Bowker led the way to the front entrance and pushed the button on an ageing doorbell he suspected was out of order. After thirty seconds with no answer or noise from inside, he knocked loudly on the door's rippled glass pane.

'I'm coming,' a shaky voice said from inside. What seemed like minutes later, the door opened slowly to reveal a frail elderly woman clutching a walking frame. She breathed with a loud rasp and was bent at the waist, needing to tilt up her head to look at her visitors. Her hair was pure white, her face wrinkled, her tissue-paper skin translucent. Worn-out pink slippers covered her bony feet and a coloured floral dress, five sizes too large and covered in food stains, hung from her scarecrow frame.

Bowker confirmed the woman was Ester Weston before introducing himself and Holmes. Mrs Weston invited them inside, apologising profusely for the state of the house. The interior was as depressing as the outside. The smell of stale food, or mice, or both, permeated the whole house, but was less overpowering in the formal lounge where Mrs Weston asked them to sit. Bowker thought it likely that this room wasn't often used. In his experience, elderly people living on their own spent most of their lives in their kitchen, their bedroom and somewhere warm with a television. This room had no TV.

'Can I get you a cup of tea, officers?' Mrs Weston asked. 'I'm sorry, but I haven't got any cake or biscuits to offer.'

'We're fine, thanks, Mrs Weston,' Bowker replied quickly, knowing Holmes was as keen as him to get this over with.

Mrs Weston lowered herself carefully into a lounge chair opposite the worn-out couch where the detectives were seated. 'I assume you're here in relation to the death of my son?'

'Yes, Mrs Weston,' Bowker replied. 'And I pass on our condolences. Regardless of the circumstances, no mother deserves to go through this.'

'Adrian doesn't merit any sympathy, Detective. What he did was unforgivable. Out of a mother's duty, I visited him in prison and gave him a place to stay when he was released. But any affection was long gone.'

'I take it he lived here up until his death?' Holmes asked.

'No, he only stayed here for a couple of weeks after he was released. He constantly complained about the state of the house.' Mrs Weston smiled. 'He didn't make any attempt to clean it up or do any maintenance, mind you. Always been a taker. Just like his father.' She looked out the window wistfully. 'Like his father in many ways, really. Always had an eye for the young ladies. The younger the better. Got more than one bloodied nose from an irate father, my husband did. Then he'd come home and take it out on me.'

'Is your husband still alive?' Holmes asked.

Mrs Weston shook her head. 'Died forty years ago, thank God. Hit by a train at the Altona station. One minute he's standing beside me on the platform, the next minute, *bang*, I'm a widow.'

'You said Adrian stayed with you for a couple of weeks,' Bowker said. 'Where'd he go after that?'

'Rented a flat in Geelong North. Said it would tide him over until my will was executed. Wonder who's had the last laugh now?' She chuckled. 'He tried to get me to sell the place, you know. The house is worth nothing, but the block would fetch well over a million. He reckoned I'd be happier in a nursing home.' Sighing, she clasped her wizened hands in her lap. 'The stupid thing is, he was getting nothing from me anyway. It's all going to young Bernadette and the boy Adrian fathered with a schoolgirl when he first started teaching at Kilmore. Sophie will get a share too, even though we're not related by blood. The Weston family owes her at least that much after what Adrian did to her, poor little thing.'

Bowker raised his eyebrows at Holmes. Holmes smiled. Mrs Weston was clearly relishing the opportunity to get a few things off her chest.

'Fancy thinking he had a God-given right to be an instant millionaire after he lived the life he did,' she scoffed.

Bowker was keen to get back on topic. 'Do you have an address for his flat in Geelong?'

Mrs Weston nodded. 'Yes. He even left a spare key, if you'd like to go down and have a look around. He took most of his stuff with him. His old car is still here in the backyard garage, though. I think it has a few old suitcases on the back seat.'

Holmes leaned forward. 'Was here his forwarding address while he was in prison?'

'Yes. Not that much came for him except his rego, car insurance and driver's licence renewals. I let the rego and insurance lapse, but I paid to keep his licence up to date in case he needed it when he came out. Save him having to do another test, you know? Any personal stuff would've been addressed to the prison, I assume.'

Bowker folded his arms. 'Did your son say anything about visiting the Mallee when he was released?'

'Bernadette teaches up there, and he talked about making peace with her. He also carried on about squaring things up with some disabled kid he reckoned was responsible for him going to prison. Seems like somebody else might've had squaring things up in mind too.'

'Did you know he'd actually gone up there?' Holmes asked.

She shook her head. 'Not until the police officers visited to inform me of his murder.'

'Have you heard of a man named Hayden Tomlinson?' Bowker asked.

Mrs Weston pursed her lips. 'One of Adrian's sick mates. Visited him in jail on a regular basis. I don't know if Tomlinson's ever been caught, but I reckon he's got a thing for young girls as well. They met up when Adrian taught at Kilmore High, and Tomlinson was at Heathcote. The schools used to take combined camps.'

'Have you ever met him?' Bowker asked.

'Crossed paths with him a couple of times when I visited the prison. He brought Adrian's car and belongings down after he was put in jail and delivered him here when he was released.' Mrs Weston gritted her teeth. 'Slimy piece of work, if ever I've seen one. He said Adrian had been hard done by. Said most of these underage girls ask for what they get. I was livid and told him I've never met a girl yet who asked to be murdered. That shut him up, quick smart.'

'Good on you, Mrs Weston,' Bowker said. 'Do you think Tomlinson could've driven Adrian to Manangatang?'

'No idea. As I said, I didn't know Adrian was up there until the police came around last week.'

Bowker looked across at Holmes. 'The old bloke at Chinky

didn't mention there being anyone else in the car when Adrian visited, did he?'

'Nope.'

'Pop outside and ring VicRoads,' Bowker said. 'Check if any cars are registered to Tomlinson, or anyone else who might live at the address in Niddrie that Shane gave us.'

Standing, Holmes removed his notebook and mobile phone from his coat pocket. 'I'm on it.' He walked out into the front yard.

Bowker shifted forward on the couch. 'Do you catch up with Bernadette very often?'

Tears welled in Mrs Weston's eyes. 'Haven't seen her since Adrian went to prison. Belinda wouldn't let the kids have anything to do with our side of the family. Don't blame her.' She took a dirty tissue from her dress pocket and dabbed at her eyes. 'The girls used to spend some of the school holidays here with me, and I'd take them down the street to the beach. Even though Sophie was my step-granddaughter, she still called me Nana.' She blew her nose on the tiny portion of the tissue that wasn't already sodden.

'Did Adrian ever mention if he was afraid someone might be out to hurt him?'

Mrs Weston thought for a moment. 'When he first went into prison, he was worried that some of the other inmates might go after him. It seems like even hardened criminals believe some things are off limits, especially when they relate to hurting children. I know he was kept away from the general prison population, and to my knowledge, he wasn't attacked or anything like that.' She shrugged. 'Maybe everyone thought he was just another murderer and didn't know what he'd done to children.'

'Was he worried about what might happen to him when he was released from prison?' Bowker asked. 'In the sense of being physically harmed.'

Mrs Weston chuckled. 'I don't think that would've entered his head, Detective. In his mind, he was the one wronged. He was the victim.'

Bowker nodded. 'That's often the way in these cases, unfortunately.' He sighed loudly. 'Can I trouble you for Adrian's house key before we leave, Mrs Weston? We'd like to check his old car as well.'

She struggled to her feet and shuffled off down the passageway towards the back of the house. Bowker stood up as Holmes returned.

'Tomlinson owns a white 2014 Toyota Corolla,' Holmes reported.

Bowker raised his eyebrows. 'Small white sedan. Any other cars registered at that address?'

Holmes smiled. 'A 2018 red Mazda MX-5.'

Bowker rolled his eyes. 'We'll have a talk to him, but I doubt he's involved,' he said. 'Not in the murder, anyway.'

'Maybe he drove Weston up there.'

'Cowan didn't see him in Chinky.'

'True,' Holmes said.

Both detectives turned as Mrs Weston shuffled back into the lounge. She held out two keys on a ring. 'Here, Detective. The address is on the tag.'

Bowker took them. 'Can we hold onto these for a while?'

'You can keep them, if you'd like. They're no good to me, and they're certainly no good to my son.'

'Just one last question, Mrs Weston,' Bowker said. 'Did Adrian have a mobile phone?'

She shook her head. 'Not that he told me about. I didn't see him use one while he was here.'

After thanking the old woman, Bowker walked with Holmes to the decaying garage in the backyard. Bowker dragged open one of the old timber doors, his efforts freeing the rusty hinges. Holmes entered first. Immediately, he was enmeshed in spider webs. He clawed the delicate white threads from his face, then used his arms to chop his way deeper into the structure. Bowker followed. The door swung closed behind him, leaving the darkness punctuated only by thin shafts of daylight piercing through rifts in the iron roof above.

'Bugger this, Sherlock,' Bowker said, returning to the door and propping it open with an empty steel jerry can. With the shed illuminated, Adrian Weston's pride and joy, his pillar-box-red Chrysler Valiant Charger, materialised in all its glory. The vehicle was layered in thick dust and cobwebs, a metal chrysalis dormant inside a gossamer cocoon. The tyres were flat, their rubber cracked. A decapitated koala was all that remained of the registration sticker. Two suitcases, one large and the other smaller, sat on the backseat.

Bowker removed a pair of rubber gloves from his coat pocket. After forcing his hands into them, he dragged the larger case out onto the ground. The lid came open easily to reveal clothes and footwear. Bowker had a quick search through before closing the lid and returning it to the vehicle. The smaller case was heavier than the first and contained books, most of them textbooks relating to science. In among the collection was a teacher's chronicle, which was a day-to-day planner and student assessment record.

Bowker opened the chronicle and flipped through. Most pages

contained brief lesson plans or meeting reminders. He read one page, then flipped over a few that followed. His face lit up with a huge grin. 'Listen to this, Sherlock. Remember, Weston was a reluctant ag science teacher.' He quoted from the planner. '*Chicken project underway. Six healthy hens.*' He flipped a couple of pages. '*Fox took two chickens last night. Need to improve fencing.*' He turned two more. '*Fox back again, two more chickens taken.*' A few more pages were flipped. '*Fox back again. But only took one chook. Project in jeopardy.*' Over another few pages. '*Fox took last fowl. Chicken project stalled!*'

Holmes burst out laughing. 'Not just stalled, I'd say. More like chicken project totally fucked!'

Bowker kept reading and chuckled. 'Here's a lesson he gave. Remember, he's talking to country kids. It's about installing a fence post. *Number one, dig hole. Number two, place post in hole. Number three, fill in dirt around hole and tramp down.*' Bowker looked at Holmes. 'You're a farm boy, born and bred, Sherlock. Bet you didn't know that.'

Holmes shook his head in mock wonderment. 'Who would've thunk it?'

Bowker leafed through to the back of the book, where student names and assessment outcomes were recorded in grids. His attention was suddenly grabbed, and his jocular mood darkened. He moved to the front of the Charger and placed the chronicle on the bonnet in a shaft of light so Holmes could see. 'Look, on these pages, there's a student list for each of the classes Weston taught and space to fill in marks. There's this column for each of his Form Three and Four kids that has no header. Notice there's a few ticks against some of the girls' names. Nothing for any of the boys.'

'What do you reckon it means? His targets?'

'Well, Yvonne Bryant's column is marked, as well as a few other girls whose names I don't recognise. Could just be coincidence. Who knows? The fucker's dead now anyway. Might take this book with us, just in case it becomes relevant later in our investigation.'

The two detectives returned to their vehicle. Holmes looked back at Mrs Weston's house. 'God's waiting room in there, Greg. Bloody depressing,' he said, as he snapped on his seatbelt.

'I noticed the Hobsons Bay Council offices as we came in – I think I'll drop in and request that one of their welfare people pay her a visit. She'll be eligible for all sorts of services. Cleaning, for a start, and Meals on Wheels would also be a help. She's had a pretty shitty life, the poor old bird. Adrian for a son and a fuckhead for a husband.' Bowker completed a U-turn and headed back towards the council offices.

Holmes looked across at him. 'Do you reckon she pushed her husband under the train?'

Bowker's eyes remained on the road ahead. 'Yep.'

'You going to follow it up?'

'Nope. The shithead got everything he deserved.'

Holmes hesitated for a moment. 'That's what people in Manangatang are saying about his son. Got what he deserved. Let sleeping dogs lie.'

'His killer's probably not in their nineties, and the murder isn't forty years in the past. But you're right. I'm possibly guilty of a little hypocrisy.'

* * *

At this time of day, traffic was light on the Princes Freeway, which connected Melbourne to Geelong, Victoria's second-largest city. Absent were the annoying lane changers who believed veering in and out of traffic sliced a minute or two off their journey, rather than simply heightening the risk of an accident.

The police vehicle's GPS quickly found Weston's address in the north of the city. His nondescript unit was located at the rear of an ugly white brick block of flats. Bowker pulled in under the carport adjacent to the front door of Unit Nine, and the two detectives alighted. Both scanned the building's carpark, more from habit than the expectation of spotting anything of interest. The steel security door unlocked easily, but Bowker needed his shoulder to convince the heavy wooden front door to open.

The unit consisted of a combined dining-lounge-kitchen with a bedroom and a bathroom off to the side. A small laundry was located inside the back door, which opened onto a narrow backyard running the length of the building. The residence was modestly and sparsely furnished, Holmes suggesting a bulk purchase from a local op shop. The main living area contained just a sofa, a wooden kitchen table with two chairs, and a small-screen TV. Holmes checked the bedroom and discovered little of interest — just a few clothes in a wardrobe and in a chest of drawers.

Rifling through the kitchen, Bowker found more op shop purchases in the form of crockery, pots, pans, and a small amount of cutlery. In a flat dish on the corner of the bench were a handful of papers. One was a copy of Weston's lease, another was paperwork related to his prison release, and a third was a written valuation of his mother's house in Altona. But it was the fourth document that grabbed Bowker's attention. He yelled to his partner, who was still searching the other rooms, 'Sherlock, I think we've hit pay dirt.' When Holmes re-entered the kitchen, Bowker handed him the papers of interest.

'Europcar,' Holmes said, as he looked up from the receipt with a smile. 'He rented a vehicle.'

'Yep. White Toyota Yaris,' Bowker replied. 'Should've been returned ten days ago.' He retrieved a small key from the windowsill over the sink and under-armed it to Holmes. 'Check his mailbox and see if there's anything else we should know about.'

While Holmes walked down to the white brick cube that housed a grid of the residents' mailboxes, Bowker sat down at the table and read the details of the car rental agreement. In his mind, they'd finally identified the small white sedan seen in Chinkapook the morning of the Back-To.

Holmes returned within a couple of minutes and threw a pile of junk mail on the table. In his right hand was a white envelope. He held it up so Bowker could read the company name printed in the top left-hand corner.

Bowker grinned. 'Europcar. Bet it's a *where-the-fuck-is-our-car* letter. Open it up and see if I'm right.'

Grabbing a table knife from the kitchen drawer, Holmes slit the envelope open. He removed the one-page letter inside and confirmed Bowker was correct.

Bowker took his mobile phone from his coat pocket and rang the number on the letter. After identifying himself and being shuffled between a number of different departments, he was able to establish that the car still hadn't been returned and the police were already involved. He thanked the company representative for her help and passed on his number so he could be informed if the car turned up. He then phoned his colleagues at headquarters in Melbourne, quoting the registration and details of the rental. They informed him that they'd made no progress in locating the vehicle, despite numberplate matching on toll roads, speed cameras and police radar stations confirming the Yaris had left the city heading north. Again, Bowker passed on his thanks, and asked to be informed if the car was located.

He finished the call and grimaced at Holmes. 'That car has disappeared off the face of the earth.' Looking back at the Europcar agreement, he began punching numbers into his mobile.

Holmes sat down opposite. 'Who are you ringing now?'

'Adrian Weston,' he said, with a smile. 'But I'll give you even-money he doesn't answer.' He listened for a moment, then hung up. 'Not ringing. And no voicemail, apparently. Bet it's a cheap prepaid SIM.'

Holmes raised his eyebrows. 'You didn't expect anyone to answer, did you?'

Bowker shrugged. 'Probably not. But you never know your luck. It may have been dropped, or found in his car. Or, someone may have stolen the car, along with the phone, and be stupid enough to answer an unfamiliar number. Maybe someone innocently picked it up and is waiting for the owner to track it down.'

Leaning back in his chair, Holmes clasped his hands behind his head. 'We've had a good morning, really. We've ID'd the white car and now have his mobile number as an extra piece in the puzzle.'

'Yeah. We'll get the techs onto that number before we finish up this afternoon. With a bit of luck, they'll track down its service provider, which should get us a call log.'

'If the phone was switched on during the weekend Weston

was murdered, we should also be able to find out which towers it pinged.'

Bowker nodded. 'We're definitely making progress, Sherlock. Small steps, but we'll get there in the end.' He thought for a moment. 'I reckon we can assume Tomlinson's white Corolla wasn't the car in Chinky. I still want to talk to that bastard, though. If he's a contemporary of Weston's, he's probably retired by now if he stayed in the teaching game. We'll go back to Melbourne, whip around the ring road to Niddrie, and see if he's home.'

CHAPTER 13

Tomlinson was mowing his lawn when the detectives parked behind his white Corolla in the street outside his triple-fronted cream brick veneer. He was of medium height, wearing long, baggy shorts more fashionable among younger males, a canary-yellow tee-shirt, expensive Ray-Ban sunglasses and Nike runners without socks. Even from the car, his hair appeared unnaturally dark for a man of his age. The Mazda MX-5 in the carport with the top down completed the portrait of a man flailing desperately in the contrails of a long-passed youth.

'Fuck me! Check out the car,' Holmes said, as he undid his seatbelt. 'Sugar daddy or what?'

'I'll bet you a thousand dollars he's not married,' Bowker replied. 'By the time a female reaches marriageable age, he'd no longer be interested.'

Tomlinson stopped the mower when Bowker and Holmes opened his wrought-iron front gate and walked up the concrete path towards him. 'What can I do for you, officers?'

Bowker grinned. 'That obvious, is it?'

'Only other suits you see around here are on undertakers or Jehovah's Witnesses,' Tomlinson replied. 'Since there are no dead people inside, and you're not carrying a bible, I figured you'd be coppers. And because Adrian Weston was killed in the last few weeks, I suspect you'll want to have a chat with me.'

Bowker introduced himself and Holmes before asking for a more private place where they could talk. Tomlinson ushered them past the Mazda and invited them to sit at an outdoor setting under grapevines at the rear of the house.

'Nice car,' Holmes said, then added, straight-faced, 'Housing it for your grandson?'

'Just because a man's getting on in years, doesn't mean he has to forfeit the delights of his younger days,' Tomlinson replied.

Bowker wondered if this was Tomlinson innocently making polite conversation, or whether he was taking the piss, playing mind games around his purported history with younger girls.

'So, what was your relationship with Adrian Weston?' Bowker asked. 'Barwon Prison said you visited him regularly.'

'Friend. We've known each other since our first year of teaching. Met at a combined school camp in the snow at Harrietville. He was teaching at Kilmore High, and I was at Heathcote HES. We got on well. Lot of shared interests.'

'Schoolgirls?' Holmes said.

Tomlinson refused to take the bait. 'Yeah. And schoolboys. All schoolkids. That's what teachers are paid to do. It's our passion.'

Bowker let the comment go through to the keeper. 'When did you last see Weston, Mr Tomlinson?'

'When I moved his stuff from his mother's place to his flat in Geelong.'

'And before that?' Bowker asked.

Tomlinson thought for a moment. 'I picked him up when he was released from prison and delivered him to his mother's in Altona. We've been out and had a few drinks at the pub since then.'

'Did he mention anything about driving up to Manangatang?'

Holmes asked.

Tomlinson shook his head. 'Not that I remember. I wouldn't have been caught dead in the place, if it had been me.'

'Well, he was, wasn't he?' Bowker replied.

'Are you saying you thought he'd be in danger if he showed his face up there again?' Holmes asked.

'No. It never occurred to me that his life would be at risk,' Tomlinson said, as he leaned back in his chair, crossing his legs. 'I would've stayed away because that place turned his world to shit. Cost him thirty years of his life. Ruined his career. Wrecked his marriage. Destroyed his reputation.'

Bowker bristled. 'So, the *place* wrecked his life, did it? Nothing to do with him rooting underage schoolgirls, including his own stepdaughter? Nothing to do with him killing some poor innocent girl to cover his tracks?'

'Stop trying to rewrite history, Detective,' Tomlinson replied angrily. 'The Bryant girl was about as innocent as Satan himself. She had sex with anything with a dick and probably a lot that didn't. Her boyfriend was twenty-three, and they fucked like rabbits. She charged Adrian ten dollars a screw, did you know that? She was over sixteen. Everything was legal. So how about we leave off with the *innocent* crap?'

Bowker struggled to keep it together. 'Then in your mind, it was okay to kill her, was it?'

Tomlinson shook his head vigorously. 'No, it wasn't. He shouldn't have done that, but let's not pretend the girl was Sister Theresa, okay?' He took a deep breath. 'Ten years, and out in seven on parole, should've been his right whack. Thirty-one was a bloody disgrace. That's the sort of sentence you'd expect for common criminals.'

'You conveniently forget the incest conviction rolled up in his sentence,' Bowker shot back. 'And his history of predatory behaviour with pubescent girls.'

Tomlinson guffawed. 'You blokes don't get it, do you? The hormones are pumping through these girls. They're practically asking for it. Adrian isn't the first, and he certainly won't be the last, to fall foul of these manipulative little bitches.'

Holmes stood quickly, thrusting his chair backwards. 'Where's your toilet, Mr Tomlinson? I'm busting for a leak, but I've suddenly got an overpowering urge to vomit as well.'

Tomlinson pointed to the back door. 'Down the passage to the right, then second door on the left.'

'What subject area did you teach, Mr Tomlinson?' Bowker asked him, as Holmes strode away.

'Phys ed.'

'How long did you teach at Heathcote?'

'Two years. Then I transferred to Kyneton.'

'How long were you there?'

'One year. After that, I went to three different secondary colleges in the city, before I got out and started lifeguarding at the Moorabbin aquatic centre.'

Bowker looked him in the eye. 'Get moved from each school, did you? Like your mate Weston. Slinking around the girls a bit too often.'

Tomlinson didn't react. 'Variety's the spice of life, Detective. I wanted to see how different schools operated.'

'Bit of eye candy at the aquatic centre, I presume?' Bowker asked sarcastically.

Tomlinson didn't answer.

Bowker rested his elbows on the table and steepled his fingers in front of his face. 'Obviously, Weston took little responsibility for his own actions. Did he ever mention who he felt was responsible for his time in jail?'

'The retarded kid, mostly,' Tomlinson replied.

'Lovely term to use, especially coming from an ex-teacher,' Bowker said, annoyed.

'The kid with the intellectual disability, then. Happy?' Tomlinson said, then added, half under his breath, 'Bloody PC gone mad.'

'Just for the record, the boy's name – well, he's a man, now – is Jimmy Cobb.'

'Yeah, that rings a bell. The Cobb kid dobbed him in to the flatfoot up there, who Adrian said wouldn't know his arse from his elbow. The case was closed and Adrian was free as a bird until the kid opened his mouth.'

Bowker wasn't sure whether to laugh out loud or just get it over with and knock Tomlinson off his chair. He decided to take the neutral route. 'So, to Weston, getting caught was the reason for his imprisonment? Not the crimes he committed?'

'That's about it.'

'Was he planning to kill Jimmy Cobb?'

'Buggered if I know. To my knowledge, he didn't own a gun. Maybe he just wanted to verbally rip through Cobb and get thirty-one years of built-up frustration off his chest. Maybe he just wanted to punch him in the face.'

Bowker smiled inwardly, thinking about the likely outcome of a physical altercation between the farm-fit Jimmy Cobb and the wimpish Adrian Weston. Before he could push the conversation further, Holmes returned through the back fly-wire door.

'Nice collection of photos you've got on your walls in there, Mr Tomlinson. Bikini-clad girls frolicking around on the sand. Very young bikini-clad girls.'

'I'm not a paedophile, Detective. I think you'll find none of those photos are of individuals under twelve,' Tomlinson replied defensively.

'For anyone over eighteen, the relevant age is *sixteen*,' Holmes said. 'I think you fall into that demographic. Physically, anyway.'

Tomlinson was becoming irate. 'Those pictures are not pornographic. Just young ladies having fun.'

'Nice collection of old *Dolly* magazines in the rack by your toilet, too,' Holmes snarled.

'No law against that either. They used to be available in all the supermarkets and newsagents.' Tomlinson smirked. 'Flick through some, did you?'

Holmes shook his head. 'Wouldn't have been able to get the pages unstuck.'

Bowker pushed his chair back and stood up. 'Thanks for your time, Mr Tomlinson.' He took a business card from his wallet and slapped it on the table. 'If you think of anything that might aid in the apprehension of your esteemed friend's killer, give me a call.'

As the detectives walked into the carport, Holmes turned back to where Tomlinson was still sitting at the wrought-iron table. He pointed at the Mazda and called, 'Why don't you go the whole hog and put P plates on this thing?'

* * *

As they grabbed a late lunch in a Southbank café close to their Spencer Street headquarters, Bowker and Holmes were still fired up over Hayden Tomlinson's attitude, even though they'd discussed the interview on their way back to the city.

'Except for wanting to contact every school he's ever taught at, and interview every principal he's worked under, and speak to every parent who's had worries about his relationship with their daughter, and do everything to nail the prick for things he thought he's gotten away with, I think we can forget about Tomlinson,' Bowker said. 'I believe he knows nothing about Weston's trip to the Mallee and even less about the murder.'

'I'd just like to deck the juvenile old prick,' Holmes said, unwrapping his salad roll. 'Blokes like him make me want to pack up the kids and head back to Murrayville. Give the old man a hand on the farm and let the kids spend their days in the fresh air.'

'You can find blokes like Tomlinson anywhere, mate. Look what Weston did to a little place like Manang.'

'Yeah, I suppose,' Holmes replied.

The two detectives sat in silence as they quickly consumed their lunch.

* * *

There was a sheaf of papers held together by a paperclip on Bowker's desk when he returned. The cover page told him the documents had been forwarded by Senior Constable Parker at the Manangatang station. Bowker pulled the top sheet away to reveal the contents. 'Good lad, Shane,' he said to himself, before calling Holmes across.

'Our boy at Manang has done well, Sherlock. Got the bank statements for Weston's two cards.' He gave the NAB debit card transcript to Holmes and perused the ANZ credit card statement himself.

'The Back-To was on the eighth, right?' Holmes enquired, as he dragged up a chair from the neighbouring desk.

Bowker glanced up from his reading. 'Yep. Saturday August eighth.'

Holmes handed him back the NAB statement. 'This won't be useful. There's been no activity on this account since the first of the month. Payment at a Thirsty Camel in Geelong. Two hundred and eleven dollars. He either had expensive tastes in wine, or he was buying in bulk to make up for being a prison-based teetotaller.'

'Either way, it doesn't help us at the moment.' Bowker took the sheet and placed it in a manilla folder on the shelf above his desk. 'But this ANZ statement is a bonanza. Five payments were made with his credit card after the time we think he was killed. All five were on the weekend after, all in the metropolitan area. And they were all under a hundred dollars, so a PIN wasn't required.'

Holmes retrieved a blank sheet of paper from Bowker's top drawer and took his pen from his shirt pocket. 'Okay, shoot.'

'The first payment was at the Liberty servo on Flemington Road on Saturday the fifteenth at 11.37 in the morning. Ninety-four dollars. If most of that was for fuel, then you'd think the car was probably near empty.'

Holmes had drawn up a grid with *Date*, *Time*, *Place*, and *Money* on the column headings. He filled in the first row. 'Got it.'

'The next purchase was at the MCG at 1.09. Twenty-seven dollars. I reckon that would be a general admittance ticket. Then, ten minutes later, he spent twenty-four dollars at a Spotless outlet.'

'They do the catering inside the Ground,' Holmes replied, and smiled. 'Twenty-four dollars. Must've bought a pie, a Coke, and a bucket of chips.'

Bowker laughed as he looked back at the statement. 'Next payment is ninety-eight dollars at the Peking Duck Restaurant and Takeaway in Camberwell at 10.08 that night.'

Holmes filled out the next row of his matrix. 'Got it.'

'And the last one is for fifty-three dollars at Coffee 'n' Eggs in Hawthorn at 9.53 the next morning.' Bowker waited for Holmes to complete his record. 'Okay, Sherlock. What does all this tell us?'

Holmes leaned back in his chair and folded his hands behind his head. 'Well, stating the bleeding obvious first, this person filled up with juice on Flemington Road late Saturday morning, drove to the MCG and attended the footy. They then ate dinner in Camberwell, stayed the night somewhere, then had breakfast not far away in Hawthorn.'

'What about the non-bleeding obvious? What does your gut tell you?'

Holmes closed his eyes, thinking deeply. 'My gut tells me it's a male. Can't see a female going to the footy by herself unless she was meeting someone there. Ninety-seven dollars in a suburban Chinese restaurant with takeaway sounds a bit steep for one person, so I suspect he had dinner with someone else. For the same reason, I reckon he had company for breakfast as well. If he had the same companion for both meals, it's logical to assume he stayed overnight with them.'

Bowker nodded. 'Agreed. Plus, I reckon the servo on Flemington Road is significant. If our subject came down from the Mallee, and if he came by the quickest route using the Calder Highway, that would've brought him into central Melbourne using the

Tullamarine Freeway, which runs into the top of Flemington Road. The fact that he probably filled his tank there would indicate he'd driven a fair way that morning.' He shrugged. 'That's a big assumption, of course. He could've just come from the northern suburbs and been low on fuel.'

Holmes leaned forward. 'A northern suburb like Niddrie, perhaps?'

Bowker screwed up his face and inhaled audibly. 'Fuck. Never thought of bloody Tomlinson. Do you think he's the type to go to the football?'

'Depends if there's a pubescent girl there, I s'pose.'

'If Tomlinson had the card, why would he have waited a week to use it? More likely to be someone from around Manang, someone who didn't want to be caught using that card locally, don't you think?'

Holmes nodded. 'Sounds logical, but we can't be sure, can we?'

'Can't be sure of anything at this stage, my friend. Can't be sure he didn't eat on his own, can't be sure he stayed with a companion that night. Maybe he stayed at a hotel or motel and the cost was more than the hundred bucks he could put on the card without a PIN. Hell, we can't even be sure it *was* a he!'

'There's a good chance there'll be some CCTV footage,' Holmes said. 'Especially at the servo.'

'There are cameras everywhere at the G, too, but trying to get footage for the gate our mate entered won't be easy. I reckon there's a better chance the Chinese restaurant might have something more specific, and with a bit of luck, the breakfast place as well. Can you give each one a call and see what's available for the times the payments were made?'

'No worries.' Holmes stood. 'I wonder who played at the G that day?'

Bowker opened the AFL site on his computer and scrolled through the list of results. 'Collingwood and Essendon.'

'Shit. Magpies and Bombers. The crowd would've been massive.'

* * *

Holmes struck gold with his CCTV enquiries. The petrol station staff agreed to search their footage for the Saturday in question, while the two eateries were happy to make their systems available, but neither felt they could spare staff to find the few seconds the detectives were seeking. Holmes and Bowker would need to do the search themselves. Their schedule for the next day thus wrote itself.

CHAPTER 14

Since the home address of Adrian Weston's ex-wife Belinda was in West Melbourne, en route to the servo in Parkville, Bowker decided to visit her first, allowing the Liberty staff more time to conduct their CCTV search. Belinda's Rosslyn Street address was an impressive nineteenth-century terrace with an iron picket fence topped with ornate arrowheads. Opened shutters adjoined the high front window, which had a barred grid on the outside. The second storey featured a balcony accessible by double glass doors, its white lacework balustrade running the width of the building.

'Worth a pretty penny, this place,' Holmes said, looking out his window as Bowker parallel-parked the car.

'In the millions,' Bowker replied. 'Fifty years ago, it wouldn't have been worth two bob – regarded as a working-class relic, an inner-suburban slum, compared to the new triple-fronted cream brick veneers replacing the orchards in outer Melbourne.'

'Where'd Belinda get the cash for this?' Holmes asked.

'Family house, I reckon. She came from a humble background, but she'd be laughing now, by the looks of this joint.'

Bowker led Holmes through the gate, up the short, tiled garden path, and to the front door. He rang the illuminated doorbell and took a step back as he waited for the footsteps he heard to arrive at the entryway. A pair of locks clicked, and in the lee of the partly opened door was a grey-haired, time-wearied woman who Bowker judged to be in her late sixties.

'Belinda?' Bowker asked.

'Yes,' the woman replied, with a puzzled look.

'It's Greg Bowker, the copper from Manang. Remember?'

Her face brightened with recognition. 'Greg. But you're not at Manang anymore. Not for years, from what I've heard.'

'No, I'm with the homicide squad now. This is Detective Sergeant Holmes.'

Belinda nodded, before her face darkened once more. 'This isn't a social visit, I presume?'

'Afraid not,' Bowker said. 'We're investigating Adrian's murder. Can we come in?'

'Of course,' she replied, as she opened the door wider and stood aside to allow them to pass. 'Straight up the passage to the back.'

The rear of the house had been totally renovated. A large bright kitchen-living area with expansive skylights extended from the original building into the backyard. A horseshoe-shaped white leather lounge suite decorated the living area, with bookshelves on opposite walls. A very elderly man sat in a recliner at one end of the couch.

'Take a seat, officers,' Belinda said. 'This is my father, Malcolm. Dad, this is Detective Bowker and Detective Holmes.'

The old man nodded. He pressed a button on his chair, an electric motor whirred, and he was lifted to his feet. He shuffled away towards the kitchen, using a walking stick that had rested against his chair.

'Dad's just about past it,' Belinda whispered. She sat down in the bend of the horseshoe, the detectives on each side of her, opposite one another. 'I'm not sure I'll be much help with your inquiries, but I'm happy to answer any questions you might have.'

'We're mainly trying to establish timelines at this stage, Mrs Weston,' Holmes replied. 'Working out where everyone was and when.'

'Call me Belinda, Detective. And it's Belinda Coghlan. I've dropped the Weston and reverted to my first married name. Sophie's taken it, too – she was a product of my first marriage, before her father was killed in Vietnam. Bernadette was happy to become an Urdevic when she married Travis, so the Weston stain has been erased from the family.'

'I couldn't believe my ears when I heard that Bernadette had settled in Manang,' Bowker said, with a smile. 'Last place I expected to see one of your daughters.'

'Teaching jobs are hard to come by, especially for graduates. She thought if she toughed it out up there for a year, she could transfer somewhere else.' She grinned. 'But she was swept off her feet by Travis. She got married, had a couple of kids, and now she's as happy as a pig in mud. She was only twelve when we left there, so she hasn't got the traumatic memories of the place that Soph and I have.'

'I have to ask you this, Belinda, so please don't feel affronted,' Bowker said quietly. 'Where were you on the weekend Adrian was killed?'

Belinda didn't flinch. 'I knew you'd ask me that, so no need to apologise. I had a pretty big motive to wish him dead. But I didn't kill him. I was here in Melbourne, as I normally am. Haven't been back to the Mallee since I packed the girls up and left, thirty-something years ago. I see Bernadette and the kids pretty regularly, but it's always when she and Trav come to Melbourne. Travis tries to squeeze in a footy game if he can work it. Mad Bombers supporter.'

Holmes flashed a glance at Bowker. 'Were they down last weekend?' he asked.

'No. Haven't been down for a month or so.'

'Do you know where Sophie was on the weekend Adrian was killed?' Bowker asked.

Belinda shook her head. 'No idea. She lives on the other side of the city, near where she works. I only see her occasionally. Perhaps once every two or three weeks.'

'How's she getting on?' Bowker asked. 'Bernadette said she's done it pretty tough.'

Belinda crossed her arms and leaned back on the couch. 'Yeah. Had a lot of counselling, been through a few relationships that have gone belly-up. To be quite honest, there have been times when I thought we might lose her.'

'Suicide?' Bowker asked softly.

'Yes. But she seemed to work through it all somehow. Last time I saw her, she was on top of the world, so she has her ups and downs, that's for sure.' Belinda stood, walked to one of the bookshelves and collected a framed photo. She handed it to Bowker. 'Not the fifteen-year-old kid anymore, eh, Greg?'

Bowker took the picture. 'Not a fifteen-year-old kid, that's for sure. How old is she now?'

Belinda sat down. 'Forty-six. That photo was taken last Christmas.'

'Forty-six,' Bowker said, shaking his head. 'It seems like yesterday that she and Yvonne Bryant were the stars of Rachael's dance class.' He continued to stare at the pretty woman in the photo, her dead eyes disclosing what Weston had stolen from her. Not just her innocence, but her childhood, her love of dance, her future, her living essence. Maybe everyone was right about this case. Maybe they should let Weston's killer run free. There was no doubt, even in Bowker's mind, that the world was now a better place for what the unknown assassin had done.

Holmes's next question brought him back into the present, and he handed the photo back to Belinda.

'Have you got any idea who might have killed your ex-husband, Mrs Coghlan?'

Belinda placed her right hand on her chest. 'With my hand on my heart, I can say I have no idea. I know there are many people who had very good reason to want him dead, including myself. But as to knowing who actually carried out the murder, I have no idea.'

'You mentioned your first husband was killed in Vietnam,' Holmes continued. 'Is there anyone on his side of the family who might've been sufficiently upset by Adrian's abuse of your daughter to kill him?'

Bowker raised his eyebrows at Holmes. That was an angle he hadn't considered. *Good thinking, Sherlock*, he thought.

'He had a brother, Des. Older than him by a few years. Des would be well into his eighties by now. I've only spoken to him a few times over the years, but I couldn't imagine him murdering anyone. Especially at his age.'

'Does he have any offspring?' Holmes asked. 'Cousins of Sophie's?'

'No. He and his wife tried for years, but couldn't have kids.

It's a pity, because they would've made great parents.'

Belinda's father shuffled back into the room and slowly made his way to behind where Bowker was seated. He was breathing heavily when he leaned over the back of the couch. Bowker slid forward and turned so he could look the old man in the face.

'Detective Bowker, I served in the army during the war. I landed on Borneo and nearly drowned when I stepped off the landing barge. I fought the Japanese there and later in New Guinea.' He held up a tarnished bronze medal attached to a striped ribbon. 'I was awarded this for outstanding bravery under fire.' Taking Bowker's hand, he turned it over, allowing the medal to gently drop into the detective's palm. 'Take this. If you find the person who killed Adrian Weston, I want you to pin it on his chest.'

*　*　*

'Were you tempted to keep the medal, Greg?' Holmes asked when they'd returned to the car.

'Nah,' Bowker said, as he adjusted the rear-vision mirror. 'I was happy to humour the poor old bugger by taking it, but it belongs to the family. That's why I slipped it to Belinda on our way out.'

'Certainly no love lost for Weston in that household,' Holmes said.

Grimacing, Bowker turned on the engine. 'Good riddance to the bastard, as far as they're all concerned. Can't blame them for holding that view. I feel the same way, though I'm not directly affected.'

'You can add me to the club, and I never even met the prick.'

Bowker headed east down Rosslyn Street, turned left, and followed Peel Street to the giant roundabout where Elizabeth

Street became Royal Parade. The intersection was one of the trickiest to negotiate in Melbourne, with the Elizabeth Street tram line branching into Flemington Road as well as continuing north through Carlton and beyond. Bowker's turn was the easiest. A simple left into Flemington Road took him past the Royal Melbourne and Royal Children's Hospitals. When they arrived at the Liberty servo, Bowker parked in a *Staff Only* bay to the side of the brick building, and the two detectives made their way to the cashier, each taking note of the array of CCTV cameras around the bowsers and inside the spacious retail area.

Bowker walked to the counter and introduced himself, showing his ID to a middle-aged woman, who immediately called another colleague. A young dark-skinned man emerged from a nearby office and introduced himself as Raj. He ushered Bowker and Holmes to a small area at the rear of the office, where a computer screen and keyboard sat below a shelf of blinking electronic storage devices.

'Sorry to bother you with this stuff, mate,' Bowker said. 'You're probably flat knacker without having to do the coppers' work for them.'

Raj shrugged. 'Works both ways. We often have to call the police when we get a drive-off from the petrol pumps.'

'Many of those?' Holmes asked.

'Too many,' Raj replied. 'Wastes our time and yours.' He glanced at a slip of paper beside the keyboard. 'Now, you were asking for the footage for August fifteenth, 11.37 a.m., correct?'

Holmes consulted his notebook and nodded. 'Correct.'

'I have that vision cued up to save us time,' Raj said, as he opened a file on the screen. 'I'll play from 11.36.'

Bowker and Holmes bent down to peer at the screen, which

displayed a view from behind the counter, looking towards the station's main door. At 11.36, the shop was empty except for a young woman making a choice of lollies at the end of a shopping aisle. A few seconds passed before a male entered the station wearing a short-sleeved Collingwood football jumper over a grey polo shirt. At this stage, he had his wallet in his left hand, head down as he removed cash or a card for payment.

'It's not Travis Urdevic. He's an Essendon tragic,' Bowker said.

As the man on the video looked up to address the cashier, his face was clearly visible.

'Freeze it there,' Bowker said urgently. The vision stopped. Bowker was taken aback. 'Well, fuck me. Didn't see that coming.' He tapped a finger on the screen. 'Leigh Davidson.'

'Urdevic's shearing partner?'

'Yeah. And Jimmy Cobb's spotlighting mate. The same Jimmy Cobb who's reported his shotgun missing.' Bowker handed a thumb drive to Raj, who'd been staring absently at the keyboard, but was no doubt taking it all in. 'Can you copy those couple of minutes onto this stick, please?'

Raj inserted the USB stick, and after some manipulation of the video file, was able to copy the segment Bowker required.

'Can you get up the corresponding view of the petrol pumps?' Bowker asked. Following several minutes of high-speed scrolling through footage from half a dozen outside cameras, they found what they were looking for. A grey Nissan Navara drove in beside one of the diesel bowsers, the door opened, and out stepped Leigh Davidson. Holmes jotted down the numberplate details, while Raj copied this segment to the thumb drive.

* * *

'Sherlock, my friend,' Bowker said, as soon as he closed the door of their car, 'of all the possible scenarios we've considered, none have involved Leigh Davidson being Weston's killer.'

'I don't get it.' Frowning, Holmes did up his seatbelt. 'What's the connection we've missed?'

Bowker made no attempt to start the car. 'Maybe he was doing the dirty work for someone. Someone like Travis Urdevic, or maybe Jimmy Cobb. They're both his mates.'

'Or maybe he didn't get the bank cards directly from Weston. Maybe someone passed them on to him.' Holmes sighed. 'Fucked if I know how or why that might've happened, though.'

'We'll print him later in the week when we return to Manang. If his prints match the ones found on Weston's wallet, that'll put him with Weston at some point.'

'Not necessarily. What if the wallet became separated from Weston and was returned sometime later?'

'And we still haven't explained those female prints. I wonder if their owner's associated with Davidson?'

Holmes shrugged. 'His wife left him and took his two kids down here to Melbourne. Could that have anything to do with all this?'

'I reckon some of the answers might lie in the CCTV records at the Chinese restaurant or the breakfast café. We'll head out to the eastern suburbs now. Meanwhile, can you contact Citylink and see if their toll points picked up his Nissan on Saturday the fifteenth?'

As Holmes made his call, Bowker turned on his own phone and was alerted to a pair of missed calls, both with associated voicemail memos. The first was from an agitated Jimmy Cobb, advising Bowker that he still couldn't locate his shotgun and needed help searching for it. Bowker climbed from the car, leaned his elbows on the roof and dialled Jimmy's number. The call went straight to Jimmy's message bank. He left a brief missive confirming he and Holmes would be back in the area later in the week and would investigate the disappearance of the gun. He didn't add that locating it had taken on a new importance since the discovery of a link between Weston and Jimmy's shooting mate, Leigh Davidson.

The second message was from Erin O'Meara at the forensics centre in McLeod. Bowker turned to lean his back against the car and rang O'Meara's direct number. O'Meara, who was obviously busy, got straight to the point as soon as she answered the call.

'Greg. Those fingerprints you lifted from the bottle at the cemetery – we got a match.'

Bowker exhaled heavily. 'Bloody beautiful. Who do they belong to?'

'Can't help you with that, I'm afraid,' O'Meara replied. 'The match is with the female prints from where your victim was found.'

After thanking O'Meara for her work and her promptness in getting back to him, Bowker ended the call. He climbed back into the car as Holmes finished his conversation with Citylink.

'Those prints we lifted off the bottle in Manang match the unidentified female set from Cocamba,' Bowker said.

Holmes smiled. 'Sort of tells us she had an emotional link to Yvonne Bryant, don't you think?'

Bowker nodded. 'That's the way I read it. I was hoping the prints might belong to Weston himself. If he'd left the flowers, it might've helped explain his motives for returning to the scene of his crimes.' He pulled on his seatbelt. 'But this is the next best outcome. It gives more weight to our theory of a revenge killing.'

'Whoever owns those prints placed the flowers on Yvonne's grave as a sort of message to her dead friend, I reckon,' Holmes said.

Bowker started the car. '*You can rest in peace now, Yvonne, because your death has been avenged.* That's what you're saying?'

'Yeah. A sign of respect, like when people put flowers on a grave to mark the dead person's birthday. It's not really about the dead person. It's more about the living honouring the dead.'

Turning left onto Flemington Road, Bowker executed a U-turn at the next set of lights to take them back towards the city. 'I'm willing to bet that Davidson left the MCG via Punt Road then took the Monash Freeway out to Camberwell.'

When they reached the Peking Duck restaurant, Bowker got his answer. Holmes's phone rang as they pulled into the carpark. He rested his notebook on his knee and jotted a few lines. After closing the call, he looked at Bowker and smiled. 'Citylink ran his rego through their system. At 11.28 a.m., he went under the toll point on the Tullamarine Freeway near the Brunswick Street exit. At 5.13 in the afternoon, he passed the toll point on the Monash opposite St Kevin's College. On Sunday morning, he made the opposite journey. Monash at 10.31 and the Tulla at 10.54.'

'So we've got his journey pretty well nailed,' Bowker said, with a grin. 'He came in on the Calder to the top of the Tulla, then onto Flemington Road, where he filled up with diesel. He then went to the G for the footy and headed out to the eastern suburbs via the Monash Freeway. We next place him here at the restaurant. Hopefully the CCTV footage gives us a clue about where he went between the football and eating here.'

Inside the Peking Duck, the detectives were ushered to an office at the rear of the building, where a staff member explained that the restaurant had just two security cameras: one over the till area near the front door, the other capturing an overview of the dining room. All footage was recorded on a thirty-day loop in chronological order. She taught them how to roll the vision forward and back in real or accelerated time, then how to operate slow motion and freeze-frame. Before leaving them to their task, she demonstrated how the footage could be copied to their USB device.

Bowker nominated his partner as their chief video manipulator. Holmes quickly located the file containing the over-the-till vision for August 15. He scrolled the footage at the highest available speed, stopping at 20.05 that evening. A young couple were sitting at a row of chairs near the restaurant entrance, the male absorbing the wonders of his mobile phone, his companion flicking through a magazine.

Bowker pointed at the screen. 'My guess would be they're waiting for takeaways, those two. The credit card transaction went through at 20.08, so we're close. Let it run at normal speed.'

After a minute, another couple approached the counter, the male removing his wallet from an inside pocket of his jacket. 'Stop it there, mate,' Bowker said.

Holmes obliged, then looked at Bowker. 'That's Davidson. Who's the woman with her arm through his?'

Bowker closed his eyes and leaned back in his chair, putting his hands behind his head. 'Sophie Weston,' he said quietly, 'or Sophie Coghlan, as she's known now.' He moved his hands to his temples and massaged them in a circular motion. 'Fuck, this is getting complicated, mate.'

'Are you sure it's her? You haven't seen her since she was sixteen.'

'That's her. Belinda showed me her photo this morning, remember?'

Holmes nodded, then asked, 'Why the hell is Davidson squiring around Weston's stepdaughter? By the grip she's got on his arm, it doesn't look like it's a simple reunion of old school friends.'

'I bet I can guess where Davidson spent the night after he left here,' Bowker said. 'Bernadette gave us Sophie's address. I reckon it'll be close by.'

Holmes took out his notebook and leafed through it. 'Unit Six, Fourteen Clifton Avenue, Malvern. Bingo. Malvern is five minutes away.'

Bowker thought for a moment. 'If Davidson is thick with Sophie, then we suddenly have a motive for him killing Weston.'

'You thinking what I'm thinking about those unidentified female prints?'

'Yep.'

Holmes reversed the footage to find the point where Davidson and Sophie entered the restaurant. It was timestamped at 20.07, or 8.07 p.m. From the dining room view, the detectives observed the couple being shown to a table on the far side of the restaurant. They held hands like young lovers until a waitress arrived and they ordered their meal. Since there was no sound, little was to be gained by watching the remainder of the footage in real time, so Holmes accelerated the frame rate. Except for the occasional holding of hands, and the arrival and consumption of food, there was little more of interest to observe. Nevertheless, Holmes copied the full two hours of their visit, in addition to the relevant footage from behind the counter.

'I reckon, as a gesture of appreciation, we should order a takeaway lunch each,' Bowker said, with a wide grin. 'What do you think?'

'As a gesture of appreciation, I'll be forced to agree. What I was really hanging out for was a quiche and a salad.'

They both burst out laughing.

*   *   *

The visit to Coffee 'n' Eggs in East Hawthorn yielded identical results to the Chinese restaurant. The café only had one CCTV camera, but its footage clearly showed Davidson and Sophie arrive hand in hand and leave thirty-five minutes later after using Adrian Weston's credit card to pay the bill. There was now little doubt that Davidson had spent the night with Sophie and that the two were in an intimate relationship.

'Do we visit Sophie while we're out this way?' Holmes asked, when they got back to the car.

Bowker checked his watch. 'She'll be at work, probably. How about we slip out after tea? Can you swing that with your missus?'

Holmes nodded. 'She's hosting her women's book club tonight, so it'll suit her if I'm not around listening in. *Fifty Shades of Grey*!'

'You never know,' Bowker said, raising his eyebrows. 'You might pick up a few pointers.'

Holmes chuckled. 'Develop an inferiority complex, more like.'

'How about we meet outside Sophie's place at 7.30 and hope she's home? I'd like to talk to her without her knowing we're coming.'

'How much do we tell her?'

'Bugger-all, I think. We'll say we're just there for a routine interview. Her mother or her sister have probably told her we've spoken to them already and that she can expect a visit. Let's see if she volunteers anything about Leigh Davidson. I don't want to push his name forward in case she tips him off that we're interested in him. I want to hit him cold when we talk to him on Thursday.'

'So we're not planning to fingerprint her?' Holmes asked.

Bowker smiled as he opened the car door. 'Not formally, no.'

CHAPTER 15

When Bowker arrived home in Caulfield North, Rachael was in her office assembling teaching aides for her next day of work at the kindergarten. As soon as she heard her husband enter through the back door, she moved quickly to the kitchen, put her arms around Bowker's neck and kissed him firmly on the lips. 'Cracked the case, have you, big boy?'

Smiling, Bowker put his arms around her waist. 'We made some real progress today, actually. We chased up those credit card transactions I mentioned last night.'

Rachael pulled out a kitchen chair and patted the seat. 'Sit down and tell me what was on the CCTV while I make us a coffee.'

Bowker sat. 'I can give you fifty tries and you won't guess who used those cards.'

'Do I know the person?' Rachael asked, as she spooned coffee into matching mugs.

'Yep.'

'Well, it won't be Travis or Jimmy, if you think I'll need more than fifty guesses.' Rachael rested her backside against the bench and folded her arms. 'Have you got a hint?'

'He was at school when you worked there,' Bowker said, intertwining his fingers on the tabletop.

Rachael rolled her eyes. 'That narrows it down to about two hundred.'

'He was in Yvonne Bryant's form.'

Frowning, Rachael searched her memory.

'Caught smoking dope with Travis Urdevic at school,' Bowker said, with a smirk.

Rachael's jaw dropped. 'Leigh Davidson?'

'Leigh Davidson,' Bowker confirmed.

'I don't get it,' Rachael said, oblivious to the electric kettle whistling behind her. 'Why would he be tied up in this?'

'Finish making our coffee first. You need to be sitting down when I tell you the rest of the story.'

It took Rachael less than thirty seconds to hastily pour water and milk into the mugs and sit at the table, eagerly awaiting her husband's next revelation. 'Okay. Shoot.'

'Leigh is in a relationship with someone you know from the past,' Bowker said, teasing.

'Come on, Greg,' Rachael replied abruptly. 'Just tell me.'

'Sophie Weston.'

Rachael was stunned. 'Bullshit.'

'Got footage of the two of them playing lovey-dovey at dinner and at breakfast the next morning.' Bowker took a tentative sip of his steaming coffee.

Rachael shook her head. 'Isn't Leigh married?'

'Wife packed up and left him a while ago,' Bowker replied. 'Took the kids with her.'

'But Sophie? I thought she was a broken woman.'

'They were in the same class together at school. May have been an attraction, even back then. Two ships in the night, as they say.'

'So, you suspect Leigh killed Adrian Weston because of what he did to Sophie?'

'We've got some unidentified female prints at the crime scene. Maybe they were both involved.'

Rachael sipped her coffee, then cradled the mug in two hands. 'Well, there's my surprise for the day. Unexpected blast from the past.'

Reaching down, Bowker fished around in his briefcase, which stood beside him on the floor. He removed a glossy, A4-sized copy of the photo he'd taken of Jimmy Cobb on his property in Bolton. The print was enclosed in a plastic protective pocket. 'Speaking of blasts from the past.' He handed the photo to Rachael. 'Leave it in the sleeve, Rach.'

Rachael perused the picture closely, before her face lit up. 'Is this Jimmy Cobb?'

'Yep. He was sad to have missed you last week, so I took his photo to show you.' Bowker chuckled. 'Male model potential, eh?'

Rachael laughed. 'Love the pose. Straight out of a Myer catalogue.' She put the photo on the table. 'Any other big surprises you've got to show me?'

Bowker smirked. 'Yep. But it'll have to wait until I get back from Sophie's.'

Rachael picked up the photo sleeve and playfully slapped him with it.

* * *

Holmes's Toyota Land Cruiser was already parked in the street outside Sophie Coghlan's block of units when Bowker arrived. Seeing Bowker's Subaru pull up to the curb, Holmes met him on the nature strip across the street. They briefly reviewed their plans before locating Unit Six.

Bowker gently knocked on the door. After a moment, the outside light came on and the door opened as far as its safety chain would allow. Through the gap, Bowker could see a tallish, middle-aged woman with a pretty but emotionless face. She had shoulder-length brown hair and the empty eyes that had so disturbed Bowker when he saw her photo the day before. She was dressed in blue jeans and a white skivvy, with a hand-knitted pink jumper over the top.

Bowker displayed his identification, introduced Holmes and asked to come in. Sophie briefly closed the door while she released the safety chain, before opening it again and leading the detectives into a small but comfortable living area. A kitchenette adjoined it, and a TV played quietly.

'You're the policeman who arrested my stepfather,' Sophie said, with a faint smile.

Bowker raised his eyebrows. 'Did you recognise the name or the face?'

'Neither. Mum rang and said you'd probably be in touch. She told me about you being the officer in Manangatang. It was a long time ago, and I've tried to forget what happened up there.' She turned off the TV and sat down. 'Take a seat, please, officers.'

Bowker sat on the couch beside her, with Holmes taking the armchair opposite. 'Just some routine questions, Sophie. Firstly, did you attend the Back-To-Manangatang a couple of weeks ago?'

Sophie shook her head vigorously. 'No way. Not after what happened up there.'

'You haven't been to visit Bernadette?' Bowker asked.

'No. Bernie and Travis visit me. That's how we keep in touch.'

'When did you hear that your stepfather had been murdered?'

Holmes asked.

'Bernadette rang to tell me the local policeman had been around to inform her.'

'What was your reaction?' Holmes asked.

'I won't lie about it. I was absolutely delighted. It was a dream come true, really. I can't tell you how many times I've lain in bed praying that someone in prison would kill him.' Tears welled up in her eyes. 'It wouldn't have been just if he'd died of natural causes at some ripe old age. Not after what he did to me, let alone Yvonne.' She took a hanky from her jeans pocket and blew her nose.

Bowker flashed a glance at Holmes. 'I have to ask you this, Sophie. Did you kill Adrian Weston?'

Sophie sniffed. 'No, I didn't, Detective. As I just said, I haven't been to the Mallee in over thirty years. Did I get pleasure out of hearing he'd been killed? Yes, I did. If I'd been pointing a gun at him, would I have taken the shot? Yes, I would've. But I didn't have that chance. Whoever pulled the trigger did it on behalf of me, Yvonne, and who knows how many other unfortunate girls.'

'Do you know who did it?' Bowker asked.

Sophie shook her head. 'No. But if I did, the first thing I'd do is nominate them for Australian of the Year.'

Holmes stroked his moustache. 'Do you keep in touch with any of your school friends from the Mallee?'

The tiniest hint of a smile crossed her face, before it disappeared as quickly as it came. 'Bernadette and Travis, of course. Most of the kids I was friendly with no longer live up there. The rest I've forgotten about. It's been a long time since I was fifteen.' She looked directly at Holmes. 'Why do you ask?'

Holmes played a straight bat. 'Just wondering if you had any contacts who might've passed on local gossip about the murder.' He shrugged. 'You know, something we haven't heard that might help us with our investigation. Do Bernadette and Travis have any theories?'

'As far as I can tell, no one has any idea who killed the bastard. Including you, by the sounds of it.'

'You're not wrong there, Sophie,' Bowker said, with a smile, before becoming more serious. 'Has Travis or Bernadette mentioned the name Jimmy Cobb?'

Sophie frowned. 'The intellectually disabled kid in my class at Manang?'

'Yeah,' Bowker replied. 'The kid who finally led us to your stepfather and the truth of what happened to Yvonne. And of what had been happening to you.'

Sophie smiled fully for the first time. 'He was the only boy in Miss Stow's dance class. He said he was another John Travolta.' Her smile disappeared. 'Surely you don't think he committed the murder.'

'He was really upset about what happened to Yvonne,' Bowker replied. 'We're just checking him out, that's all.'

'I hadn't heard his name in decades, until you brought it up a minute ago. Bernie and Trav haven't mentioned him. To be honest, I couldn't have told you if he was alive or dead.'

'Oh, he's alive, alright,' Bowker said, with a broad grin. 'He runs a property a few miles out of Manang.' He took the picture from his briefcase. 'He wanted to be remembered to Rachael, so I took this photo and blew it up for her. I'm going to present it to her when I finish work tonight. She loved those dance classes, you know. Still talks about Yvonne and Jimmy, and you, of course.'

Sophie sniffed back tears.

Holmes stood. 'While you two are reminiscing, I'll take the opportunity to use the toilet,' he said. 'Can you point me in the right direction?'

Sophie nodded towards the passage. 'Second door on the left.' She looked back at the sheet in Bowker's hand.

'This is the forty-seven-year-old version of the new John Travolta.' Bowker pulled the glossy photo from its opaque pocket and handed it to Sophie. She took it in both hands.

'Does he think he's in *Vogue* or something?' Her mouth curved slightly. 'Same cheeky smile. He looks a lot fitter than he was at school. Not as much hair, though.'

'He's doing well. He seems happy.' Bowker hesitated for a moment. 'What about you, Soph? How are you doing?'

She shrugged. 'There's ups and downs. I'm going through a good patch at the moment. Might help that there's some closure with my stepfather. Hope so, anyway.' She handed the photo back to Bowker. 'Say hello to Jimmy if you see him again. And thank him for rescuing me from that life of hell.' Straightening, she looked Bowker in the eyes. 'And I've never thanked you for what you did, either. It's a bit late in coming, but thank you, from the bottom of my heart.' She touched him on the forearm. 'Thank you.'

Bowker was glad he had the photo to return to its sleeve, otherwise emotion may have overwhelmed him. 'You're welcome, Sophie. You deserved all the help you were given.'

Holmes's return broke the emotional tension.

Bowker stood up. 'Thanks for your time. It's honestly been great to see you again.' He handed her his business card. 'Call me if you think of anything that might help our inquiry. Or just if you need help with anything.'

Holmes shook Sophie's hand. 'Glad to meet you.'

As she showed the detectives to the door, she suddenly clasped Bowker's arm. 'Can you remember me to Rachael and pass on my apologies for leaving her dance class? Tell her I loved those classes and she was a fantastic teacher. Tell her I couldn't stay in the class because of what my stepfather was...' She started to cry.

Bowker put a hand on her shoulder. 'I know. And I'll pass on what you said to Rachael.'

Sophie nodded and walked back into the lounge room, sobbing quietly, leaving the detectives to let themselves out.

On the nature strip, Holmes handed Bowker a small plastic evidence bag containing two long strands of brown hair. 'Hairbrush,' he said.

Bowker opened his briefcase and threw in the zip lock pouch. 'I'll come into work via Forensics in the morning. I'll drop off these samples, as well as Jimmy's photo. See what Erin comes up with.'

Holmes nodded towards Sophie's flat. 'A bloody sad case if ever I've seen one.'

'Yeah,' Bowker replied. 'I can't help feeling sorry for her, whether she's tied up in this or not.'

CHAPTER 16

The Victoria Police Forensic Services Centre was located in the northern Melbourne suburb of McLeod, on the imaginatively named Forensic Drive – which, perhaps worryingly for many investigations, was a dead-end street. The centre gave the outward impression of a prison, with its high wire fences and the sliding steel security gates on each side of a mirrored guardhouse at the main entrance. Inside the compound, beyond the ubiquitous carparks, the environment was more relaxing, with tall eucalypts among modern single-storey brick buildings.

It took Bowker over an hour to make the run from Caulfield North to McLeod, predominantly via the busy suburban arteries of Tooronga, Toorak and Burke Roads. Wednesday morning peak-hour traffic was heavy, but most vehicles were city-bound, making his journey reasonably hassle free.

When he finally passed through security, he found Erin O'Meara sitting in her office. She was late middle-aged, tall, and skeletal. With her pinched face and pallid skin, she gave the impression of a walking corpse. The nicotine stains on the fingers of her right hand added to the stereotypical picture of a woman in the last throes of life. She had to be ill, but nobody knew her true malady. Rimless glasses were balanced on the tip of her nose, and she spoke in a gravelly smoker's voice.

She motioned for Bowker to sit down. 'What can I do you

for this time, Greg? You're here in person, so you must be after something ASAP.'

Bowker smiled. 'Yeah. Thought I could get a couple of things here quicker if I brought them myself.'

O'Meara frowned. 'So, why the big hurry?' she asked, then coughed several times.

'I think we're close to breaking the Weston case,' Bowker replied. 'I'm looking to find out if our suspect had an accomplice.'

'Okay. What have you got for us?'

Bowker put his briefcase on the desk and snapped open the lid. He removed Jimmy Cobb's photo and the evidence bag containing strands of Sophie Coghlan's hair. 'I've got some informally obtained samples,' he said, as he passed over the picture, still in its plastic pocket. 'The subject in the photo is irrelevant. We want to check whether the prints on it match the unidentified set found at the crime scene.'

'Okay.' O'Meara placed the picture on the desk in front of her. 'What else have you got?'

'Strands of hair.'

'Where were they found?'

'On a hairbrush in our person of interest's bathroom,' Bowker replied.

O'Meara took the evidence bag. 'She live alone? I'm assuming it's a she, by the length of the hair.'

'Yeah. Forty-seven-year-old female,' Bowker replied. 'Unmarried, but may have had a male stay over in recent nights. But he has short hair.'

'DNA will tell us whether the hair is from a male or female,' O'Meara replied.

'Yeah, of course,' Bowker replied, a little embarrassed. The simplest thing DNA testing could determine was gender. If X and Y chromosomes were present, the subject was male. A pair of X chromosomes established they were female.

'So why do you need this yesterday?' O'Meara asked, raising her eyebrows, her glasses lifting on her nose.

'Holmes and I are returning to the Mallee tomorrow to confront our suspect, face to face. It'd be good to have all the information we can on a possible accomplice. If it can't be done by then, it can't be done.'

'To be totally honest, Greg, we're flat out like a lizard drinking at the moment. There's a ton of stuff from a terrorist raid earlier in the week, and the big dogs are putting the heat on us. They're under the griller from the pollies, I suspect. But I'll see what I can do.'

Bowker smiled. 'Thanks, Erin. If you have any luck, I'll shout you a bottle of whisky. I know you fancy a drop. You name the label.'

O'Meara stared at him with a stern countenance. 'That would be encouraging favouritism,' she said. 'You know the rules.'

Bowker was suitably chastised. 'Sorry, I know all cases are important.'

'Make sure it's Johnnie Walker Red,' O'Meara said quickly, before her laughter precipitated a long fit of coughing.

* * *

By the time Bowker arrived at Spencer Street, Holmes had documented their interview with Sophie Coghlan and uploaded the copied CCTV footage to the police mainframe and to his own laptop. Bowker approached his desk, and Holmes handed over the USB stick. 'How'd you go with Erin?' he asked.

'She'll do her best to get it done quickly,' Bowker said. 'They're buried in work up to their ears, as normal. Hopefully we'll have something before we talk to Davidson tomorrow.'

Holmes leaned back in his chair. 'What time do you want to leave?'

'Sparrow fart, if we can. That should get us up there by lunchtime and give us the afternoon to deal with Davidson. I'll book us a room at the pub for a couple of nights. If we need to stay longer, I'm sure we'll be able to extend.'

'We'll need to fit in Jimmy Cobb as well,' Holmes said. 'Try and track down that shotgun of his.'

'You never know. That might get sorted when we talk to Davidson.' Bowker chuckled. 'Kill two birds with the same gun, so to speak. Shit, Davidson might even tell us where that fuckin' Yaris is.'

Holmes thought for a moment. 'What should we do about Allender? See if we can track him down this afternoon?'

'Skeeta?' Bowker shook his head. 'Nah. I think we'll sit on that one for now. If Davidson is the killer, we'd be wasting our time chasing Skeeta. Creating a lot of angst for nothing.'

Holmes smiled. 'Can't disagree there. Confronting a bikie gang isn't my idea of a good time.'

'Can you put a copy of this on your phone?' Bowker asked, looking at the memory stick on his palm. 'It'd be nice to show Davidson if he starts denying where he was.'

'Sure,' Holmes replied.

'I'm gonna try to get a hold of Bryan Stapleton and check if

Davidson's still shearing at his place. If he's not, I'm sure Bryan will know whose shed he's moved on to.'

Bowker rang Rachael at her kindergarten to retrieve Anne Stapleton's number, who in turn would be able to give him a contact for Bryan, whose number had been blocked when he'd sent Bowker the bootleg photos of the crime scene. *Why isn't it like the old days?* Bowker thought. *Used to be able to just look up the bloody number in the phone book.*

As it turned out, he didn't need Bryan's number. Anne was able to inform him that shearing had finished a few days before at their place, and that Travis and Leigh had moved onto Bluey Keene's shed on the Chillingollah-Tyntynder Road, a few miles east of Gollah.

Bowker walked back to Holmes's desk and updated him on Davidson's location for the next day. 'This will work out perfectly,' Bowker said. 'We'll drop into the shed and see him on the way up. Total surprise.'

*   *   *

There was no easy southerly approach by road to Chillingollah, although it was located on the rail link between Bendigo and Robinvale. Originally a thriving regional centre with extensive shopping facilities and the impressive Railway Hotel, the town's main structures were now giant silos. The hotel had burnt down in 1963, the shops and newspaper were long gone, and the number of houses could easily be totalled on one hand. The public hall stood naked beside the once-vaunted gypsum tennis courts, which had long been reclaimed by nature. The sporting oval, with its tree stump on the half-forward flank, once the scene of great football victories for the Chillingollah team, was now impossible to discern, lost to history and native scrub.

The best roads into the fossilised remains of Chillingollah came from Swan Hill via Tyntynder to the east, and Manangatang via Chinkapook to the north. But as the crow flies, the shortest route from Melbourne was following the Calder Highway as far as Berriwillock, then tracking north on unsealed surfaces, ultimately reaching Chillingollah via Springfield Road from the south. Bowker decided to take the latter route, stopping at Wycheproof for an early lunch. He knew no food or refreshments would be available before they rolled into Manangatang later in the afternoon.

Light rain was falling when the detectives left Melbourne, but as they travelled north, the rain cleared. By the time they reached Wycheproof, the sky was cloudless and the temperature was in the low thirties. The town was famous for two things: the railway line ran up the main street, and the settlement sat on the slope of the forty-three-metre-high Mt Wycheproof, the world's smallest registered mountain. Bowker and Holmes picked up food from the local bakery, and the carpark at the top of the mountain proved a spectacular dining room, with 360-degree vistas across the town and the Wimmera-Mallee plains.

'Pretty specky view,' Holmes said, as he sat on a bench and unwrapped his salad roll.

'Only forty-three metres above the flats down there,' Bowker replied. 'Steep little bastard, though. One-in-six slope. I wouldn't like to walk up the road, let alone carry a seventy-kilo bag of wheat on my shoulders.' He took a bite of his sandwich.

'You talking about the King of the Mountain race?' Holmes asked.

'Yeah.'

'They don't run it anymore. Pulled the pin in 1988, apparently.'

'Heard that. Pity, though. Events like that put these little towns on the map.'

The two men sat in silence for a while as they ate their lunch and took in the view. After a minute or two, Bowker pointed out to the northeast. 'Gollah's out that way somewhere. If we had a telescope, we'd probably see the silos.'

There was another stretch of silence before Holmes spoke. 'How do we handle this?'

'Introduce ourselves to the boss cocky first,' Bowker replied. 'Then have a chat to Davidson outside the shed, where it's a bit quieter.'

Holmes scrunched up the cling wrap from his roll. 'Heavy him from the start?'

'Let's see what he volunteers first. We'll begin with a few routine questions about where he was on the weekend of the murder and who he may have noticed in town for the Back-To. Make it sound as if we're tracking someone else before we throw in a few hand grenades relating to the wallet and the credit cards. We can always put the heat on him if we're getting nowhere.' Bowker took a long swig of his iced coffee.

'You knew him when he was a kid. Do you reckon he'll spill his guts?'

Bowker shrugged. 'Dunno how he'll react. To be honest, I'm surprised he's even tied up in all this. He comes from a good family, and except for the marijuana business at school, I had no reason to speak to him in the twelve years I was a copper up there.'

'They say love is blind, mate. It's unbelievable what blokes will do to keep a female onside. It wouldn't be the first time a murder has been committed in the name of love.' Walking to the rubbish bin, Holmes deposited his lunch wrapping and orange juice container.

Bowker nodded and took out his phone. After a few seconds, he disconnected the call. 'Still can't get hold of Jimmy Cobb. Wanted to make sure he'll be home tomorrow.' He finished his flavoured milk and binned his refuse.

Holmes stretched. 'Pity they don't still have that King of the Mountain. I'd give it a go, I reckon.'

Bowker laughed. 'While we're here, should I ask them to resurrect the event so you can compete?'

Holmes smiled. 'I don't think so.'

*   *   *

Bowker hadn't seen Chillingollah for twenty years, and it was even more depressing than he remembered. 'Hard to imagine that early last century, this was a prosperous little commercial and social centre.'

'It's called progress, mate,' Holmes said sadly. 'It kills off these once-happy little places and takes the community spirit with it. Most people end up in a big, soulless city where even their next-door neighbour is a stranger.'

Bowker nodded his agreement but didn't answer. He continued up what had once been the main street and turned right over the railway line, onto Tyntynder Road. A few miles further along, Holmes spotted a house with surrounding outbuildings through his passenger-side window. Its yards were filled with sheep in full wool, and a paddock close to the road contained recently shorn animals clustered around a small dam.

'This'll be it, mate,' Holmes said.

Bowker slowed down and turned past the mailbox, which displayed an RMB number and the Keene surname. The property carried the moniker *Hillcrest*, but there seemed more crest than hill. The track to the sheds was in dire need of a grader, with deep corrugations all the way along its length, while the farmhouse required either a team of tradesmen or a bulldozer. Typical of its time, the house had wide verandahs, a high gabled roof, ancient asbestos-cement-sheet cladding and the obligatory oversized evaporative air conditioner on the roof. There was no garden. Sections of the wire-netting fence around the house lay on their side. It was difficult to assess whether the house was still occupied or whether it had been abandoned for a modern residence in Swan Hill. Or maybe it was like many other homes in the district, vacated when the property was bought to increase the acreage of another landholder.

Bowker parked outside the shed, alongside a late-model Toyota one-tonner. A grey Nissan Navara sat beside Travis Urdevic's battered Ford. 'We've got the right place, mate.'

Holmes nodded. 'And Mr Davidson is in attendance, so we're right to go.'

The scene inside the shed could've come from any one of the thousands of small-scale shearing sheds in Australia. Urdevic and Davidson were at stands each side of an old-style Cooper single-piston engine, its cooling water in a twenty-gallon cylinder at its side. The exhaust was connected to an inch-and-a-half-diameter galvanised water pipe, which initially went vertical, before curving at right angles to make its way through a hole in the shed's corrugated iron wall. Flywheels-cum-pulleys on each side of the engine drove belts. In turn, those belts drove the shearing apparatus, via a series of worm drives that powered the hand pieces. At the opposite end of the assembly was an emery wheel, where shearers would sharpen cutters and combs at the end of the day. With the *pop-pop-pop* of the engine and the high-pitched whirr of the shearing machine, it was virtually impossible to hear anyone speak inside the shed.

As the detectives entered via the oversized door, the first person to see them was the rousie Matty McIver, who was loading fleeces into an old Ajax wool press. His face lit up, and he strode across to them.

'Can't keep away from us, huh?' McIver said. 'Do you want to talk to Trav again?'

'We'd like to introduce ourselves to the boss first,' Bowker said. 'Didn't see anyone outside, and there's only you and the shearers here.'

'He's filling up the catching pens.' McIver walked to the other end of the shed and pushed his way through the swinging western-saloon-type doors. After a moment, a short, nuggety man came back through them and approached the policemen. Bluey Keene was true to his name, with flaming red hair and a ruddy, weather-beaten complexion. His green eyes appraised the visitors, and he warily proffered his hand. 'What can I do for you? Matty said you'll probably want to talk to Trav.'

Bowker introduced himself and explained that it was Leigh Davidson they were after.

'Hope this won't take too long,' Keene said. 'Showers are forecast for tomorra, and I need to get most of these wethers shorn so I can shed the ewes that are still outside.' He wandered off to the board and spoke to Davidson, who looked back at the detectives, then proceeded to finish the animal he was shearing. He pulled a cord to throw his machine out of gear and used his knee to push the shorn sheep down the chute and out of the shed.

Bowker looked at Holmes. 'I think whichever way this goes, Travis will have to finish the wethers on his own.'

CHAPTER 17

The three men moved from the cacophony of the woolshed to the relative quiet outside. The buzz of the machines was still audible, but moderated by distance, and softened by its fusion with the bleating of sheep, the barking of dogs, and the twittering of birds. Davidson appeared relaxed and unaware of anything ominous on the horizon as he lifted his backside onto the top rail of the yard fence. 'What can I do for you blokes?' he asked breezily.

Bowker put his hands in his trouser pockets. 'Just tidying up some details around the weekend Adrian Weston was killed. We've got a few gaps we hope you might be able to help us fill.'

'Okay. Shoot.'

'Did you go to the Back-To celebrations at the racecourse on the Saturday afternoon?' Bowker asked.

'Yep,' Davidson replied.

Holmes nodded. 'How long were you over there?'

Davidson thought for a moment. 'Arrived around ten in the morning. Stayed until six, probably. The footy club were running the drinks tent. I'm on the committee, so I was on deck most of the day.'

Holmes leaned backwards against the Navara's bull bar. 'Did you leave the racecourse at any time during the afternoon?'

'Nope,' Davidson said, suddenly serious. 'Why are you interested in where I was?'

Bowker waved away a fly. 'We're more interested in where Adrian Weston was. If you were there all day, did you see him around the reunion area?'

Davidson relaxed a little. 'Nope. Probably wouldn't have recognised him anyway. Haven't seen the bastard since you carted him from school and sent him off to prison.'

'Many strangers at the Back-To?' Holmes asked.

'Shitloads. Occasionally, one would introduce themselves when they were buying a beer and explain their connection to the town. But that was more the exception than the rule.'

Bowker chased another fly from the corner of his mouth. 'Did you have EFTPOS facilities there, or was it all cash?'

'All cash. Not worth setting up EFTPOS for one day.'

'Anybody drop a credit card near the tent while they were fishing around for cash?' Bowker asked, keeping a straight face.

Davidson's expression visibly tightened. 'Not that I heard, anyway.'

Bowker nodded slowly for effect. 'What did you do on the weekend after the Back-To? Most people would've been looking to have a quiet one, I'd imagine.'

Bowker glanced at Holmes as Davidson stared down at the grass. After a moment's contemplation, he looked up. 'Actually, I went to Melbourne for the footy. Watched Collingwood at the G. Good game. Pies won by three points.'

'Beat the Bombers, right?' Holmes asked.

Davidson was now sweating more than he had while shearing. 'Yeah. Beat Essendon.' He paused for a moment. 'Where are you heading with all of this?'

'After you left the footy, where'd you go?' Bowker asked.

'Came home,' Davidson snapped. 'What else would I have done?'

Holmes put his foot on the rail of the fence. 'Didn't pick up a meal somewhere?'

'Yeah, I did, actually,' Davidson said, giving a broad smile that was clearly forced. 'Lashed out on some Chinese takeaway.'

Bowker folded his arms. 'You went all the way out to Camberwell to get Chinese takeaway? The Peking Duck must serve fantastic food.'

Davidson's face blanched.

'Apparently, the Coffee 'n' Eggs in East Hawthorn does a great breakfast as well,' Holmes added.

Davidson became defiant. 'I've got no idea what you blokes are on about. I went to the footy at the MCG, bought takeaway on the way home, and arrived back at the farm about one o'clock on Sunday morning.'

'I'll put our cards on the table, okay, Leigh?' Bowker patted the bonnet of Davidson's Nissan. 'Citylink cameras captured this Navara inbound on the Tullamarine Freeway that Saturday morning–'

Davidson interrupted. 'That's the way I went to the footy!'

'We also have you on the Monash outbound early on Saturday night, and at the same point inbound on Sunday morning. You were then caught on camera half an hour later on the Tullamarine Freeway, outbound. Obviously on your way home.'

Exhaling loudly, Davidson stared into the distance. 'Alright, I'll level with you. I've been on my own for years now after my wife pissed off to Melbourne. I've reconnected with a girl I knew at school, and so far, we're getting on pretty well. But we promised each other we'd keep it quiet until such time that we're confident something permanent will come out of it.'

'How'd you get Adrian Weston's credit card?' Bowker asked bluntly.

Davidson's eyes widened. 'What credit card was that?'

Holmes took his foot off the rail and hitched up his trousers by the belt. 'The credit card you used to buy fuel on Flemington Road and at the food outlets we mentioned a minute ago.'

Slipping down off the fence, Davidson took up a defiant stance, hands on hips. 'I didn't use any credit cards other than my own. You're looking for someone else who was in Melbourne that weekend. What's that fancy saying they use? Just because things happen at the same time doesn't mean they're connected?'

'Correlation doesn't equal causation,' Bowker replied.

'Yeah, that's it,' Davidson shot back.

Holmes removed his mobile phone from his jacket pocket and pressed a series of keys. He then turned it so Davidson could view the screen. 'Well, let me show you a big coincidence, Leigh. At the very time a transaction is time-stamped on Adrian Weston's card at this service station, you are on camera at the cashier counter at the same location. And if you're not convinced with this one, I can show you equally damning pictures at the Peking Duck and the Coffee 'n' Eggs.'

Bowker lifted his chin and scratched his neck. 'So, my question still stands, Leigh. How'd you get Weston's credit card?'

Davidson visibly struggled to find an explanation. 'It was handed in by someone at the Back-To,' was the best answer he could come up with. 'I saw the name on the card and thought I'd take advantage of the prick, after he'd taken advantage of so many people up here all those years ago. I didn't know he was going to be murdered, did I?'

Holmes smirked. 'Who handed in the card?'

Davidson shrugged. 'Never seen the lady before. Relation of a local, I guess.'

'Why hand it in to the boozer?' Holmes asked, raising his eyebrows. 'Why wasn't it handed in to the office where lost property normally goes? I presume there was one.'

'The lady said it was found near our tent, so she thought it might've been dropped by someone buying a beer.'

Bowker closed his eyes and inhaled deeply before speaking. 'The problem that I have with all of this, Leigh, is that there are unidentified prints on Weston's wallet. At the end of this little talk, we're going into Manang, where we'll fingerprint you. I'll bet anything you'd like to put up that your prints will match those on the wallet.'

Davidson blinked rapidly, his Adam's apple bobbing. 'Actually, now I think of it, the lady handed in the wallet itself. I took the card and binned the rest.'

Bowker laughed. 'And how'd the wallet get back onto Weston's person at Cocamba?'

Davidson shrugged. 'Maybe, when I took a break, he came back looking for it and one of the boys found it in the bin and returned it to him.'

'Let's get the name of Sophie Weston, or Sophie Coghlan, as she's now known, on the table,' Bowker said. 'The security footage from the two eateries shows you and her attending together, and your body language strongly suggests a romantic relationship. Detective Holmes and I are assuming you spent the Saturday night at her flat. If the need arises, we can acquire CCTV footage from the entrances to Sophie's block of units to confirm the depth of your relationship. That's entirely your affair, but it does provide a motive for your involvement in her stepfather's murder. So, perhaps it's time to stop fucking us around, Leigh. Most of what you've told us is absolute bullshit.'

Davidson took a long breath. He squatted down onto his haunches, then sat on the grass, his back against the timber rails of the sheep yard fence. Bravado all but dissipated, he looked up at the detectives. 'You're right. All the stuff about finding the card is bullshit.'

'That's a promising start,' Holmes replied. 'Keep going.'

Before Davidson could continue, Bluey Keene appeared on the landing outside the shearing shed door. 'You blokes nearly finished with Leigh?' he yelled above the din from inside. 'I'm tryin' to run a business here.'

Before anyone could answer, Keene disappeared inside, having subtly made his point. Bowker smiled as he watched the shed door close, knowing shearing was over for Davidson. At least for today, anyway. He looked down and saw the same little boy he'd put the wind up over smoking pot all those years ago. 'You were saying, Leigh?'

Davidson stared straight ahead. 'I worked all day at the racecourse, then had a barbecue tea in the big shed there with a couple hundred other people. We all adjourned to the Manang hall for a reunion ball, but for a lot of us, it was just stage two of the piss-up. I stayed there till after midnight, then headed home to Chinky. I needed to stop somewhere for a leak, so I pulled into the Cocamba silos.'

'Was Sophie with you?' Bowker asked.

Davidson shook his head. 'I was on my own. There's no way Sophie would go anywhere near the Mallee. If something permanent comes out of our relationship, the plan is to sell my place here and buy something smaller down in Gippsland, or over in the northeast, where there are no memories for Soph. She's been through enough already. She deserves something better.'

Bowker felt a twinge of sympathy for Davidson, but right now, he was looking down the barrel of a murder charge. 'So, you stopped for a leak at Cocamba?'

'I pulled in behind the silo and saw something on the ground in the headlights. I got out of the car, and here was this dead bloke with his face blown off. I just about spewed up. I had no idea who he was, so I fished around in his pockets to find some ID before I'd head back into Manang to knock up the lazy bastard who masquerades as a copper there. I found his wallet, looked at the contents in the car lights, and realised it was Weston. The same fucking prick who killed Yvonne Bryant and rooted Sophie when she was a little girl.'

'So, your plans changed?' Holmes asked.

Davidson fired up a little. 'Too right, they bloody changed. Nobody owes that arsehole anything. As far as I was concerned, he could stay there and be eaten by foxes and crows and maggots. Leave him the same way he left Yvonne.'

Bowker nodded. 'Why'd you take the credit cards, then?'

'I did that for Sophie,' Davidson replied. 'Have Weston shout her a couple of decent feeds. More symbolic than anything. Just a way of sticking it up the filthy pervert.'

'Does Sophie know about the cards?' Holmes asked.

Davidson shook his head. 'I told her nothing about seeing him at Cocamba or about the credit cards. We get on like a house on fire. Why risk something like that backfiring?'

Bowker swatted away another fly. 'And it never entered your head that the credit cards could be traced?'

'Yeah, it did. That's why I cut them up and put them in the rubbish when I got home. After just one weekend in a place where no one knew me, I never thought they could be traced back to me.' He gave a mirthless chuckle. 'Forgot that every square metre of the fuckin' earth is covered by CCTV, didn't I?'

Bowker was struggling to know what to believe. Davidson's story sounded plausible, but would it check out? 'The weekend of the murder, you were at the racecourse from ten in the morning until six?'

'Yep,' Davidson said. 'On the drinks table all day, except for a couple of breaks. Check with the blokes I was working with.'

'We will,' Holmes replied. 'Anyone with you when you took those breaks?'

Davidson thought for a moment. 'I grabbed a sausage and a chop around lunchtime. Spent a while talkin' to the blokes there. Red Cameron, Heifer Delahunty, Bullpup Graham. They were running the barbie.'

'Where'd you go on your other breaks?' Bowker asked.

'Only had one other. Went over and watched the kids' novelty races. Ask Prong. I talked to him for most of it.'

'When you left the racecourse, you went straight to the Manang hall for the reunion ball, you say?' Holmes asked.

'Yes. With the same blokes I'd worked with during the day.'

'Pretty early for a ball,' Bowker said.

Davidson closed his eyes and shook his head. 'The footy club was doing the drinks there too. We had to set up, didn't we?'

'You're the one telling the story, mate,' Bowker replied sarcastically.

'Well, it's true. You can ask the other blokes,' Davidson replied quickly. 'And I didn't leave there until after midnight. Walked to my car with Jungle Mills. You might remember him from your time here. Big bugger. Called Jungle 'cos he's tall, thick, and dense.'

Holmes suppressed a smile. 'How'd you fill in the Sunday following?' he asked.

'Came back into Manang. Had the big clean-up at the racecourse.' He looked straight at Holmes. 'Plenty of people to vouch for that, too. Once we got everything packed up and the area was clean, I sat around with a few blokes and knocked down some stubbies. Cooked the leftover meat on a portable barbie and had a good chinwag.'

'You tell them about what you found at Cocamba the previous night?' Bowker asked.

Davidson rolled his eyes. 'I'm not a complete fuckin' idiot.'

'You don't think?' Holmes asked, smirking.

Bowker decided to change tack. 'Ever used Jimmy Cobb's shotgun?'

Davidson's face didn't change. 'Plenty of times, when we go spotlighting. Beretta. Twelve-gauge. Under-and-over. Belongs to Jim's old man, actually.'

Bowker scratched his temple. 'What size shot do you use?'

'BBs, usually,' Davidson said. 'You're not going to knock down a fox with anything smaller. We might use smaller shot if we're chasing rabbits.' He paused for a moment. 'You're not thinking

I used Jimmy's gun to blow Weston away, are you? 'Cos if you are, you're fuckin' wrong.'

'The gun's gone missing,' Bowker said. 'Jimmy says the last time he saw it was when you were at his place spotlighting.'

'Well, I know nothing about that, I swear.'

Bowker thought for a moment before addressing Davidson. 'This is the way it's going to work from here, Leigh. After I explain to Mr Keene that you won't be shearing again today, and that he'll likely have wet sheep in the morning, I'll drive you to the Manang police station. Just so you're not tempted to take off on us, Detective Holmes will follow us into town in your Nissan.'

Davidson stood and faced the fence before resting his head on his arms on the top rail. Bowker walked to the shed to inform the boss that he was one shearer down for at least the remainder of the day.

* * *

When they arrived in Manangatang, the local police vehicle was absent, and Bowker found the station locked with the now-familiar *Station Closed* sign on the door. He used the key Parker had given him to enter, and instructed Davidson to take a seat while they waited for Holmes to park the Nissan. Bowker collected a series of forms from a filing cabinet and sat behind the desk, opposite Davidson, who then dictated his name, address and relevant personal details. When Holmes arrived, the detectives took Davidson's formal statement. It varied little in detail from the account he'd finally given at the Keene property.

After Davidson signed the document, Bowker leaned back in the swivel chair, arms folded across his chest. 'Leigh Jeffery Davidson,

I am charging you with theft and perverting the course of justice through interference with a crime scene. I should also warn you that you are a major suspect in the murder of Adrian Weston.'

Davidson dropped his head into his hands. 'Am I going to be locked up?' he muttered.

Bowker looked at Holmes. 'At this stage, you'll be released, pending further inquiries. You'll receive a summons in the mail to the Swan Hill court to face the charges I've just mentioned.'

Bowker retrieved a kit from a steel cupboard against the side wall, and Holmes proceeded to take Davidson's fingerprints.

'You're free to go now, Leigh,' Bowker said. 'But don't leave the district without letting me know first.'

When Davidson looked up, he had tears in his eyes. 'I didn't kill him. I really didn't.' He stood, and Holmes handed him the keys to his car.

'We'll be in touch,' Bowker said.

When Davidson closed the door behind himself, Holmes looked at Bowker. 'What do you reckon? Is he telling the truth?'

Bowker shrugged. 'Probably. We'll chase up the people he claims can vouch for his movements. If his story checks out, I can't see him having a window of time to kill Weston and dispose of the body. What do you think?'

'He initially lied through his teeth, but my gut tells me he's not our man.' Holmes upturned his palms. 'I could be wrong, though. Wouldn't be the first time.' He stood up from his chair and stretched, arms above his head. 'What's the penalty for perverting the course of justice these days? Still a twenty-five-year maximum?'

'Yeah. But it depends big-time on the seriousness and impact of the action, of course. Witness tampering is likely to get you twenty-five. Davidson will be at the lower end, I'd imagine. Except for wasting our time, his actions probably won't influence the outcome. As far as we know, anyway.'

Holmes returned the fingerprint kit to the cabinet and rifled among the items inside.

'What are you chasing?' Bowker asked.

'Digital camera. I'd like to get Davidson's prints to Forensics ASAP.'

After opening each desk drawer in turn, Bowker finally located the camera among various electrical chargers in the bottom drawer. Holmes carefully photographed each print while Bowker searched for the cable to connect the camera to his laptop. Within five minutes, an email containing digital images of Davidson's fingerprints arrived at the forensics centre in McLeod.

CHAPTER 18

The detectives had barely packed up their gear and signed their reports when Senior Constable Parker barged through the station door pushing a handcuffed Jimmy Cobb in front of him. He shoved his distraught captive down into a chair.

'History repeats itself, eh, Detective Bowker? Local copper solves a murder for the Homicide boys.'

'I didn't kill nobody, Consable Bowker!' Cobb yelled urgently.

'Don't talk unless you're asked to, arsehole!' Parker screamed in his face.

Bowker held up both hands. 'Whoa, whoa, whoa, everybody. Let's just settle down a minute.' He paused while everyone took a deep breath. 'Can you take the cuffs off Jimmy, please, Senior Constable Parker? He's not going anywhere.'

Parker shook his head and reluctantly removed the handcuffs.

'Now tell me what's the go here, Shane,' Bowker ordered.

'Mr Cobb here called me reporting his shotgun missing,' Parker replied. 'Said he'd rung you, but you hadn't been out to his place to help.'

Bowker frowned at Cobb. 'I told you I'd be back later in the week, Jimmy. I've tried to ring you twice since then, but you didn't answer.'

Cobb lowered his head. 'I left my phone in the ute. I forgot about it. Had to use the house phone,' he muttered

Bowker looked back at Parker. 'Okay. Jimmy rang. Then what happened?'

'I drove out to his farm to discuss the gun. Thought it might have something to do with Weston's murder. We checked the sheds, but found no sign of the murder weapon–'

Bowker interrupted. 'The Beretta shotgun, you mean?'

Parker rolled his eyes. 'Same thing.'

'Not at this stage, it isn't,' Bowker responded sharply.

Parker heaved a sigh. 'Okay, the fuckin' shotgun. I went for a walk around the yard and down the back of the sheds. Under a lean-to where some hay is stored, I found a big pool of blood and small indentations in the galvanised iron wall. In my opinion, that's where Weston was shot. Blood spatter, pellet marks, it all fits.'

Bowker nodded before turning to Cobb. 'How'd the blood get there, Jimmy?'

Cobb shook his head. 'I don't know, Consable Bowker. I don't go behind there very often. I never seed it until Consable Parker showed me.'

'Bullshit, Cobb,' Parker said angrily. 'You were getting revenge for the Bryant girl, and you shot Weston in cold blood.'

Bowker held up his hand. 'Let's calm this down a bit, Shane. Have you contacted Forensics?'

'I was going to do that as soon as I locked up this fucker.'

Bowker thought for a long moment. 'I want to see the blood and pellet marks before we call them in.'

Parker exploded. 'Thanks for the fuckin' confidence, Bowker! You don't think I'd know a crime scene if I saw one, is that it? I've heard stories about you city big dicks getting all upset when someone else shows you up. I solve your bloody case, and what credit do I get? Fuckin' zilch.'

'Detective Holmes,' Bowker said calmly, 'can you go with Jimmy into the kitchen and take a statement, please? May as well take his prints as well, if he's happy with that. Shane and I need to have a little chat.'

Holmes nodded and grabbed the fingerprint kit from the cupboard. He motioned towards Cobb, who was already out of his chair, evidently keen to exit the uncomfortably tense atmosphere in the office. When they'd left, Bowker indicated for Parker to take a seat. Bowker settled on the front of the desk.

'Let's get a few things straight here, Senior Constable,' he said forcefully. 'I will not be spoken to in that manner, whether it be by you, Detective Sergeant Holmes, or the chief commissioner. I am in charge of this case, and I decide where to take the investigation. I routinely view any potential crime scene before I call in extra expertise. That is the case whether it was discovered by an experienced Homicide detective or by a recently promoted senior constable who, by his own admission, has only witnessed the aftermath of two murders. It's a matter of common sense.'

Parker rolled his eyes up to the ceiling.

'And you'll need to give me a hell of a lot more before you can declare this case solved. Do I make myself clear?'

'Yes, sir,' Parker said through gritted teeth.

'Good. And you can forget the sir. All I'm asking for is common courtesy. I'm not big on the formal stuff.'

'Oh, yeah.' Parker half-chuckled under his breath.

'So, let's start again,' Bowker said, with a strained smile. 'You responded to Jimmy's phone call, searched his sheds and found what you believe is the original murder scene at the rear of the buildings.'

'That's about it,' Parker mumbled, arms crossed tightly across his chest.

'And you thought that was enough to arrest Jimmy for murder?'

'I arrested him on *suspicion* of murder. I thought I'd get him back to the station and sweat him for a few hours. If he'd done it, hopefully I'd get him to confess.'

Bowker smiled. 'Sweat him? Been watching a bit too much American TV, I think, Shane.'

'Well, *grill* him, then,' Parker snapped back.

'Didn't consider waiting until you got confirmation that it was Weston's blood?' Bowker asked.

Parker exhaled loudly. 'It's his blood. Cobb has no explanation for blood being there. No shot foxes or slaughtered sheep.'

'If he'd killed Weston as you suspect, don't you think it strange that he hadn't come up with some sort of story to explain the blood?'

'He's a couple of sandwiches short of a picnic, you know that,' Parker replied. 'Look, he had a motive to murder Weston because of the Bryant girl, and we know Weston was looking for him when he came up here that weekend. So there's good reason to believe he arrived at Cobb's farm. Cobb had a shotgun, and there are boxes of BB cartridges in his garage, so that matches the weapon that killed Weston.'

'But you couldn't find the Beretta out there,' Bowker said.

'That's because he's disposed of the gun somewhere,' Parker replied irately. 'Bloody obvious, isn't it?'

'Then why did he ring both of us saying the gun had gone missing and pleading for help to find it?' Bowker asked.

Parker stared into space. 'Like I said, he's a retard.'

Bowker stood up. 'As soon as Sherlock finishes Jimmy's statement, the four of us will take a trip out to Bolton and look at what you found.'

'Why not leave Cobb here in the cells?' Parker asked, frowning.

'Unless we find something out there to change my mind, there's no grounds to hold him.'

'What about motive, means and opportunity?' Parker retorted quickly.

'There's not enough. Surely you can see that.'

Parker scoffed. 'Who the fuck else could it be? Cobb lives on his own and has bugger-all visitors.'

'If it turns out Weston was killed where you say, there are other possibilities. Someone could've followed him out there, or heard he was looking for Jimmy and waited for him.'

'Sure you're not biased, Inspector?' Parker said. 'Just because Cobb helped solve the girl's murder doesn't mean you owe him anything.'

Bowker was seething inside but kept it under control. 'I follow the evidence, Shane. Nothing else. You might be proven correct in the end, but right now, there's nothing that would support a conviction.'

*   *   *

It was midafternoon by the time the four men arrived at Cobb's property on the Bolton-Kooloonong Road. Holmes parked behind Cobb's ute, which was nosed into the workshop-cum-garage. As Bowker climbed from the car, he noticed an opened packet of shotgun cartridges on the bench. He picked up the box. 'BBs, Jimmy?'

'Yes, yes,' Cobb replied, as he slid from the backseat. 'We need big shotter for the foxes.'

'Ammunition should be locked away,' Bowker replied.

'It was, Consable Bowker. I was going shooting but couldn't find the gun.'

'Still should've put them away,' Bowker said.

Cobb nodded, but said nothing.

Parker led them to the lean-to at the rear of the sheds and indicated a patch of what appeared to be dried blood among the grass.

'You did well to see this, Shane,' Bowker said. 'If it was here last week, Sherlock and I missed it when we drove past here looking for Weston's car.'

Parker placed his hands on his hips. 'Wouldn't see it from a vehicle. I only spotted it because I was on foot searching for Cobb's shotgun. Thought it might've vibrated off the back of his ute.'

Holmes moved to the wall and carefully examined the indentations in the corrugated iron. 'Looks like the edge of a shot pattern.' He dropped down onto his haunches. 'And I can see at least one lead pellet here in the grass.'

Bowker took out his mobile. 'Okay, nobody touches anything. I'll ring for a crime scene van to attend. Won't see them till the morning, I'd say. Nearest one's in Bendigo.' He looked at Cobb. 'Jimmy, I don't want you near this spot until we come out with the experts in the morning, alright?'

'No, no, no. I won't go near it, Consable Bowker.'

Parker spun around and faced Bowker. 'Come on, Detective. You're not seriously going to release him, now you've seen what happened here?'

'As I said at the station, Senior Constable, it isn't sufficient grounds to hold him,' Bowker said calmly. 'You're not going anywhere, are you, Jim?'

'No, no, no,' Cobb replied quickly. 'This is my home.'

Bowker removed his phone from his jacket pocket, selected a number from his list of contacts and requested the attendance of a crime scene van the following morning.

Overhearing the call, Cobb turned to Holmes. 'What's a crime scene van?' he asked.

'It's a vehicle carrying people who are experts at gathering evidence from where crimes have taken place. They have special equipment that helps solve crimes.'

Cobb nodded. 'I hope they find Dad's shotgun.'

Parker rolled his eyes. 'I doubt they will,' he muttered under his breath.

'Maybe they can find out who been driving around my dam,' Cobb said.

Holmes immediately pricked up his ears. 'What do you mean, driving around your dam?'

'Near the edge of the water,' Cobb said. 'Make tyre marks in the mud. All gone hard in the sun. Buddy dangerous, it was. Could've slipped in.'

Bowker closed off his call. 'What's bloody dangerous, Jim?'

'Some stupid idiot coming in the front gate and drivin' round the big dam. Stirrin' up the mud.'

Bowker beckoned the others to follow him the few hundred metres to the dam near the road. Once there, it was immediately obvious what Cobb was referring to. But the tyre marks weren't so much circling the dam as going straight into it.

'Sort of tyres you'd find on a small sedan, Sherlock?' Bowker asked, looking at Holmes.

'I'd presume so,' Holmes said. 'But I'm no expert.'

Bowker turned to Parker. 'They're nowhere near as wide as the ones on your Commodore.'

Parker shook his head. 'Mine are oversized mag wheels. These tracks are still smaller than what you'd get from road tyres on one of your larger vehicles, though.'

Bowker climbed the dam bank to its highest point. 'Any tyre tracks would've been obliterated by the sheep that camped up here.' He walked back down the slope. 'This bank is pretty bloody steep. How deep to the bottom of the water, Jimmy?'

'Very, very, very deep,' Jimmy said, stretching his arms above his head. 'When Dad had it cleaned out, it was twice as deep as the big Catpilla tracta.'

Holmes pointed to where the windmill's intake pipe entered the dam. 'Look at how steep that pipe goes into the water, Greg. There'll be a foot valve at the end of it, and that usually sits on the bottom, in the deepest part.'

Parker raised his eyebrows. 'You reckon Weston's car is in there?'

'Yep. And my bet is, that's where Jimmy's gun will be, too.' Bowker took out his mobile and redialled. 'We're gonna need a diver.'

* * *

Both Bowker and Holmes ordered the mixed grill for dinner in the Manang pub lounge. When Bowker visited the small counter to refresh his Coke Zero and Holmes's Carlton Lite, he spotted Prong Lyon chatting to Red Cameron and several other elderly locals in the main bar next door. He recognised most of the men, although their faces were older and more weather-beaten. He signalled to Holmes to follow, and they joined the jovial group. After five minutes of chat and reminiscence, most of it exaggeration, Bowker was able to confirm Leigh Davidson's account of his movements on the weekend Weston was murdered.

Back at their lounge table, Holmes attacked the remains of his cold lamb chop. 'Sounds like Davidson's alibi holds up,' he said.

'Yeah,' Bowker replied. 'Thought it would. Guilty of being a dickhead rather than a murderer.'

'What about Jimmy Cobb? Is he smarter than he makes out?'

'Nah. Jimmy didn't kill Weston. He's always been easier to read than *John and Betty*. There's no way he'd be calling the police about his shotgun if he'd used it to kill someone. And if he'd driven the car into the dam, why tell us about the tyre tracks?'

Holmes picked up a now-glazed fried egg on his fork. 'Parker seems to think Cobb had something to do with it.'

'Parker just wants the whole thing to go away so we'll piss off back to Melbourne and he can sit on his arse playing computer games.' Bowker washed down a forkful of cold chips with his Coke.

'Not much of a bloody copper,' Holmes replied.

'It's like every profession, I guess. You get good ones, and you get half-arses. When I went to school, I had teachers who dedicated their lives to helping kids, and I had a couple who were slack as all shit. Didn't correct your work, told you to piss off if you asked for help at lunchtime or recess.'

Holmes smiled. 'Sounds like the town was spoilt when you worked up here.'

'Stories get embellished over the years, mate. I just did my job. I bet most of the guys who followed me have done the same thing. When you get a dud like Parker, it makes earlier blokes look like Officer of the Year.'

Their conversation was interrupted by Red Cameron approaching their table.

'Doin' anything at six in the morning, Greg?' he asked. 'Got a two-year-old Art Major filly needing a few miles of jog work.'

Bowker's eyes lit up, and a big smile seized his face. 'I'll be there at quarter-to,' he said.

CHAPTER 19

The sun was only a faint glow below the eastern horizon when Bowker arrived at Red Cameron's stables just before six. Under the floodlight, he could see two horses tied to the rail, each already yoked into its own heavy jogging cart. The chestnut filly Red had mentioned the night before shied sideways when Bowker entered the lit area, showing her big baldy face and white forelegs. The bay gelding beside her just flicked his ears as if wondering what all the commotion was about.

Red emerged from an empty horse box and smiled. 'I wondered if you'd make it this morning,' he said, with a chuckle. 'You're a bit longer in the tooth now than when you lived up here. I thought the detective's life might've turned you a bit soft. Especially when I see you dressed in that sort of clobber just to work a horse.'

Bowker looked down at his new Nikes and tracksuit, compared his outfit with Red's weathered old riding boots, dung-covered dungarees, and torn flannelette shirt, then burst out laughing. 'I'm only in town for a couple of nights. Brought mainly work clothes. Just lucky I threw in a tracksuit in case I decided to go for a run. Otherwise, I might've been working this filly in a grey pinstriped suit and leather dress shoes.'

'Would've been worth a photo, I reckon,' Red replied. 'Might've taken the edge off the rugged sportsman reputation you still have up here.'

Bowker pointed towards the horses. 'These two raced yet?'

'The bay bloke's had a few starts, but he's not much good,' Red replied, without a hint of disappointment. 'Pretty slow. Can time him with a calendar. I keep him around as company for the filly and to help with her education.'

Bowker nodded. 'What's his name?'

'Back Lawn, would you believe? Pedigree goes all the way back to Lawn Derby.' Red chuckled. 'When I named him, a few blokes said Back Lawn was a shit choice because he'd always get mown down. But I've had the last laugh, 'cos he's never been close enough to the lead for that to happen.'

Bowker laughed. It was good to be back with the smell of horses in his nostrils. He nodded towards the filly. 'She raced yet?'

'In at Swan Hill in a fortnight.'

'What have you called her?'

'Paleface Aloha,' Red replied, with a grin.

Bowker raised his eyebrows. 'Well, if she's half as good as Paleface Adios, you'll have a great one.'

Red chuckled. 'She'll have to go a lot faster than Paleface Adios to win even one race these days. Remember when he won the Miracle Mile in Sydney? Rated 1.58 and a bit. You'll be lucky to win a race anywhere going that speed now. A horse rated 1.49 the other night at Bendigo. Would've beaten Paleface Adios by the length of the straight.' He shook his head. 'Unbelievable, really. The two-year-olds are now going 1.53 or better.'

Within ten minutes, they were outside Manang, ploughing through heavy red sand on a backroad northeast of the town. The filly was fractious, to say the least, keeping Bowker on high alert as she shied at every quivering leaf or bolting rabbit. *She's a bit of a nutcase*, Bowker thought, but didn't say. *Still, some of the better racehorses are highly strung individuals.* By comparison, Back Lawn wasn't about to waste energy jumping at shadows; he just rhythmically ploughed on ahead, concentrating on dragging the heavy motorbike wheels of Red's cart through the sand.

'Remember that morning we saw the Min Min light?' Bowker asked.

'Yep,' Red replied, without looking across. 'They still scare the shit out of me.'

'Seen many since?'

'A few. But none as close as that one. Not liftin' out of the trees, either.'

'When I tell people about it, they say I'm talking bullshit. But I know what I saw.'

They were quiet for a few hundred metres. The sun rose above the horizon, the horses pulling hard on the traces as they climbed a sandy rise. Red was now an old man, but he still sat confidently in his recycled metal plough seat. He slapped the gelding on the rear to encourage him to attack the crest with a bit more enthusiasm.

Bowker had promised himself that he'd buy a horse when he retired so he could enjoy these early morning work-outs. But becoming ensconced in city living had made that more and more unlikely. Working a horse around a racetrack also lacked the essence of what he was experiencing now: the sky, the trees, the serenity.

'Having any luck tracking down who killed Weston?' Red asked out of the blue.

'We're making progress establishing who *didn't* do it, but I can't say we're any closer to finding who did.' Bowker laughed.

'I s'pose if we eliminate enough people with a motive, the one left standing will be our killer.'

Red grinned across at him. 'You'll have to eliminate a shitload of people to get to that point, Greg. I don't know of one person who's not happy the bastard is dead.'

For a while, the only sounds were birdsong and the metronomic beat of hooves.

'It'd be interesting to know if he made it out to Jimmy Cobb's,' Red said, finally.

Bowker frowned. 'What makes you think he was going to Jimmy's? You been talking to the Urdevics, or that bloke who bought the Weston's old house in Chinky?'

Red shook his head. 'No. Doug Palin told me Weston was asking for directions at the Back-To shebang on the Saturday afternoon. Doug lives out towards Kooloonong, so he knows the Cobb place.'

'Who's Doug Palin? Name means nothing.'

'Bought Meathead Morrison's place about fifteen years ago. Had to be three or four years after your time in Manang.'

'And fifteen years after Weston was put away,' Bowker replied. 'How'd he know it was Weston?'

'He didn't. He was in the pub last week, and he mentioned this stranger he'd come across at the Back-To who was wearing an old-fashioned lairy shirt. One of the blokes showed him the photo of Weston's body that's been circulating. He said it was the same shirt.'

'Did he mention anything else Weston might've said?'

Red shook his head. 'Nah. Pretty brief conversation, apparently.'

'Might take a run out to Kooloonong and have a chat to him,' Bowker replied. 'Meathead Morrison's old place, you say?'

'Yeah, on the left of Boundary Bend Road, a few k's north of the silos.'

Nothing more was said for a few minutes as Bowker mentally reconstructed Weston's movements on the day he most likely met his fate. Weston had arrived in Chinkapook on the Saturday morning and spoken to Peter Cowan, chasing information on the whereabouts of his daughter and Jimmy Cobb. He'd later shown up at the Urdevic residence on Pioneer Street seeking reconciliation with his daughter and again enquiring about Cobb. From the contents found in Weston's stomach during his post-mortem, Bowker suspected that he'd eaten at the Back-To celebrations. If the account of Doug Palin's encounter with Weston was accurate, then Weston had known where to find Jimmy. Bowker was becoming more convinced than ever that the blood-soaked patch found at Cobb's was where the murder had occurred.

Bowker was shaken from his musings when a metre-long goanna scurried across the road and climbed one of the taller mallee gums nearby. His filly reared, then spun sideways. The cart's left wheel hit the steep edge of the roadside drain. It tipped, throwing Bowker into the scrub.

His instincts kicked in. His first priority was to maintain his grip on the reins. The filly lunged forward, snorting and throwing her head in the air, making every effort to bolt up the dirt road ahead. But he held on tight.

After being towed through the sand on his stomach for twenty-five metres, Bowker was able to bring the horse to a halt. She stood in the middle of the road, quivering all over, her ears twitching in every direction. Bowker climbed to his feet and slowly edged towards her head, keeping the reins taut as he went. When he reached her withers, he patted her on the shoulder and talked to her calmly. Finally, he took her by the bridle and waited for her to settle.

A huge laugh echoed from behind Bowker. He turned to see a smiling Red Cameron sitting comfortably in his seat, his bay gelding picking at a few green shoots on the side of the road. Bowker edged back to the upturned cart, flipped it back onto its wheels and climbed gingerly aboard. Red trotted his horse up alongside and pointed to Bowker's filthy attire. 'Just lucky you didn't wear the suit, Greg. No drycleaners in Manang.'

'Fuckin' goannas,' Bowker said. 'I don't blame the filly. They scare the shit out of me too.'

Red laughed again. 'Could've been worse. It could've ended up in the cart with you.'

'Couldn't see that ever happening,' Bowker replied, his heart still thumping.

'The bastards will run up anything if they get stirred up,' Red said. 'Few years ago, an old cocky at Kulwin was riding his horse around the sheep. Stirred up a goanna, and the bloody thing climbed up the rear of his horse, hooking its claws in as it went. The horse bolted, of course. The old bloke was trying to pull it up when he felt the goanna climbing up his own bloody back.'

'Bullshit.'

'No, this is dinkum. Finished up, the poor old bugger was sittin' atop an uncontrolled horse going flat strap with a goanna's head lookin' over his shoulder. It happened, Greg. I swear.'

Bowker didn't answer for a moment as the two horses broke into a slow trot. 'Been scared of goannas ever since I was a kid. We went camping somewhere down in Gippsland, and when we started cooking, the bloody things invaded the area. They were stepping up over the fire onto the hotplate and pinching our meat. You could hear the bottoms of their feet sizzling, but they didn't seem to feel it. I ran away and stood against a big gum tree. My dad started laughing and pointed to something above my head. I looked up, and there was another big fucker coming down the tree, headfirst.' Bowker exhaled loudly. 'I'll tell you something, Red. I've never bloody well got over it. Wake up in the night dreaming about the pricks sometimes.'

Red chuckled. 'Rather them than snakes.'

Bowker shook his head. 'Neither are on my list of favourite animals.'

The pair trotted along in silence for several hundred metres before Red had another anecdote. 'You were talking about goannas swipin' meat off the barbie. Pam took the Grade Sixes on a camp to the Grampians a couple of years ago. They cooked up a swag of sausages for tea over a campfire. A kookaburra sat on a branch a few feet away and watched every move they made. There was another teacher who was with them… forget her name now. She transferred to Melbourne after a year up here. Anyway, she said she wasn't eating shitty old sausages, so during the day, she went over to the Hall's Gap supermarket and bought a piece of fillet steak. When the snags were just about done, she produced the beautiful steak and proudly laid it on the hotplate. Quick as a flash, the kookaburra dived down, grabbed the steak and pissed off with it. Pam reckons the kids didn't stop talkin' about it for a week.' Red laughed. 'Apparently, the other teacher didn't see the funny side.'

'Serves her bloody right,' Bowker said, grinning. 'It's called karma.'

Red was suddenly more serious. 'Do you think it was karma, what happened to Weston?'

'Well, he probably got what he deserved, if that's what you mean.'

'Most people around here say it was karma. They think maybe you should let sleeping dogs lie.'

'Can't do that, Red,' Bowker replied. 'Maybe it was karma, but it's still my job to find out who drove the karma bus.'

They finally reached the turnaround point, from where they would canter the horses home. 'Notice many strangers over at the Back-To?' Bowker asked.

'Quite a few I couldn't put a name to, yeah,' Red replied. 'If it's any help to you, Pam took quite a few photos. Not only of the people we knew, but some of the crowd as well.'

'That could be a great help, actually,' Bowker said. 'Could she email them to me? I'll write down my address when we get back to your stables.'

Both slapped the rumps of their steeds with the reins, and they returned to the town at a lively canter. Bowker smiled as the sun caught his face and the wind rushed through his hair. Except for the absence of his family, he was in heaven.

* * *

The crime scene van arrived at the Manangatang police station at ten that morning. The forensic crew were quickly escorted to the Cobb property by the three officers and shown the area to be examined. Parker walked up to the house to inform Jimmy Cobb that the police were in attendance. After a thorough search, he returned, his anger palpable.

'He's done a runner, Detective. Just like I warned about yesterday.

But of course, you wouldn't listen, would you?'

Bowker ushered Parker away from the forensic work area. 'Settle down. Did you check inside?'

'Course I did. Went right through the house, checked all the sheds. He's pissed off. Simple as that.'

'He's a farmer, Shane,' Bowker said coolly. 'He could be anywhere on the property. It's over five thousand acres. Is his ute there?'

'Yes, in the garage,' Parker replied.

'Well, he's on the farm somewhere. He's hardly going to do a runner on a tractor or a quadbike.'

Parker shook his head and wandered back to where the fully kitted-out forensic techs were working. Blood was carefully collected from the grass, then samples of the grass were bagged and labelled. Measurements were taken of the indentations in the corrugated iron wall, and shotgun pellets were retrieved from various points around the area. Also collected were short fragments of fine gauge wire and small splinters of glass, the likely remains of Weston's spectacles. The wall was dusted for fingerprints, and a series of high-resolution photographs were taken of the scene.

As the team were finishing up, a Mitsubishi Pajero sped up the track and stopped abruptly where the police vehicles were parked. There was an urgent series of blasts from the horn. Bowker jogged across to find Jimmy Cobb's white-faced mother behind the wheel.

'Jump in, please, Greg,' she yelled through the open passenger-side window, any questions about the police presence seemingly extraneous to her in that moment. 'It's Jimmy.'

'What's going on, Marilyn?' Bowker said, as he quickly climbed in beside her and buckled his seatbelt.

'Jim's had an accident on the quadbike.' She slammed the

vehicle into gear and sped off towards a gate to the north. 'He's trapped underneath it down in the back paddock, where he's been ripping rabbit burrows.'

'How do you know?' Bowker asked.

'Jimmy rang my husband's mobile, but Mark's in Swan Hill. He called me, and said Jimmy sounds *compos* – with Jimmy, though, who knows what condition he's in? I rang the Robinvale ambulance before I left, so they shouldn't be far away.'

It took them ten minutes to negotiate the rough, sandy tracks and a trio of gates to reach the old rabbit warren on the scrubby crest of a rise. The upturned quadbike was visible from several hundred metres away, but it wasn't until they were on the scene that Bowker saw the cause of the rollover. The machine had obviously hit the area at speed, and its wheels had dropped into a trench of soft dirt that Cobb had gouged out with a tractor and ripper in the days prior.

Cobb was conscious, but in pain. Luckily, the quadbike lay across his hips rather than his chest. His mobile phone lay in the sand to his right.

Marilyn kneeled beside him, stroking his forehead and talking to him in a soft, reassuring voice. 'The ambulance will be here soon. Where does it hurt, love?'

'My ankle,' Cobb replied in a fatigued voice. 'My ankle really hurt.'

Bowker placed a hand on Marilyn's shoulder. 'Believe it or not, it's a good sign that he's feeling pain in his legs.'

Cobb placed his hands against the machine. 'Help me lift this off, please, Consable Bowker. It's too heavy for me.'

Bowker looked at Marilyn. 'He doesn't seem to be losing any

blood. Externally, anyway. And he's having no trouble breathing. I think we should wait for the ambos to arrive before we move anything.'

Marilyn nodded her agreement.

'You must've been going pretty fast, Jimmy,' Bowker said.

'Yes, yes, yes. I saw the police cars come up the road and I got away before I got arrested again.'

Bowker frowned. 'We weren't coming to arrest you, Jimmy. I told you yesterday afternoon we'd be back with some experts to look at the blood behind the shed.'

Marilyn blinked, her mouth falling open. Cobb shook his head vigorously, making a depression in the soft sand beside his face. 'No, no, no. When you said that, Consable Parker said once they got proof, I'd go to jail.'

Marilyn's gaze shot straight up to Bowker. 'What's he talking about, Greg?'

Bowker turned away so Cobb and his mother didn't catch the anger on his face. He put his hands on his hips and, after taking a few seconds to regain his composure, turned back. 'You're not going to be arrested, Jimmy. I'm the boss policeman, so you can believe what I say. Okay?'

Jimmy nodded. 'Yes, yes, yes, Consable Bowker. I believe you.'

Bowker looked down at Marilyn. 'It's got nothing to do with Jimmy, Marilyn. But we think Adrian Weston may have been murdered behind the sheds near the house. That's why the police vehicles are there now.'

Marilyn's brow furrowed. 'Why would that happen on our farm?'

Bowker didn't want to frighten Cobb further. 'I'll explain later,' he replied, before walking away a few paces to call Holmes and explain his sudden departure.

The ambulance arrived soon after. Cobb's head was placed in a brace, and the quadbike was lifted off his body. The ambulance officers suspected a broken left ankle was his only major injury, but scans would be needed to assess if he'd suffered internal bleeding. After twenty minutes, the vehicle departed for the Robinvale hospital, Jimmy's mother following closely behind.

By the time Bowker had returned to his police duties, the focus of attention had shifted to the dam. A police diver had arrived after a long drive from Melbourne and was presently submerged in the dark, murky depths. The forensic team sat in their van, awaiting a call on whether their skills would be further required. Holmes and Parker leaned against the steel windmill tower, following the diver's progress via a line of bubbles surfacing near the centre of the dam and the faint glow of a powerful light some twenty feet below. Bowker approached them for an update.

'Cobb alright?' Holmes asked.

Bowker nodded. 'Busted ankle and a shitload of bruises, but he'll survive. Luckier than hundreds of others who've rolled one of those bloody death traps.'

'No danger of brain damage, anyway,' Parker said, laughing at his own joke.

Bowker spun around and stepped into Parker, who backed off but found himself trapped against the windmill tower. 'You know why he was under that quadbike?' Bowker said, slowly and quietly, but with unmistakable venom. 'He took off because you told him you were coming out to arrest him this morning. Why'd you say that, Shane, when I specifically told you that wasn't going to happen?'

'Just trying to keep the pressure on him,' Parker said. 'See if he'd crack. Obviously he did. That's why he did a runner.'

'He took off because you scared him, not because he's guilty,' Bowker said. 'You leave any accusations to us from now on. Do I make myself clear?'

'If that's the way you want to play it, you'll get no more input from me,' Parker said, straightening his shirt, even though Bowker hadn't touched him. 'I was under the impression we were a team, but I'm happy to be your errand boy.'

Bowker stepped back. 'Being a team means working together, not going off half-arsed on your own.'

Holmes broke the tension. 'The diver's surfacing.'

Once he was waist-deep in water, the diver confirmed that a small white hatchback sat at the bottom of the dam, but his search had located nothing else of interest. Bowker was assessing his options when Mark 'Corn' Cobb arrived in a panic, looking for his wife and son, who he'd been unable to contact via phone. Bowker explained Jimmy's satisfactory condition and that he and Marilyn were on their way to the Robinvale hospital. Once Corn had relaxed, Bowker explained their activities at the property, much to Corn's bewilderment. He asked one favour before Corn departed for Robinvale.

Corn arrived back at the dam atop a mammoth four-wheel-drive tractor dragging a heavy metal chain. As Corn backed the machine down the dam bank, the detectives lugged the chain to the water's edge. The police diver grabbed its end and submerged. After a couple of minutes, he surfaced, swam to the side, and gave a thumbs up. Corn put the tractor in gear and easily dragged the Toyota from its resting place, then over the bank and onto flat ground. The car disgorged hundreds of litres of water as it went. Bowker unhooked the muddy chain and thanked Corn for his assistance. Within minutes, the farmer was on his way to more important matters in Robinvale.

The hire car was still partially filled with water when the forensic team took over. Bowker doubted whether anything of assistance would be gleaned from their efforts. However, once drained, the backseat of the car gave up an ultra-cheap mobile phone, along with a Beretta under-and-over shotgun.

CHAPTER 20

After a ham and salad roll from the Five Star Café for lunch, Bowker decided against the hour-and-a-half round trip to Kooloonong just for a quick chat with Doug Palin, instead electing to ring him using the number Red had supplied earlier in the day. Palin confirmed he had been approached by a man, likely in his seventies, who'd asked where he might locate Jimmy Cobb. A regular user of the road adjoining the Cobb farm, Palin was able to give precise directions and offer an accurate description of Jimmy's residence. He confirmed that he'd never previously met Weston, but was able to identify his shirt from the ubiquitous photo of Weston's body at the Cocamba silos.

Bowker had barely finished his conversation when he received an incoming call. He smiled as he answered. 'Erin O'Meara. Good afternoon from warm and sunny Manangatang.'

'Good afternoon to you too, Gregory. From cold and windy Melbourne.'

Bowker heard her cough loudly, then blow her nose. 'By the sound of that, you should be at home in bed, my friend.'

'Today's one of my better days. Haven't thrown up yet, and I've only used the one box of tissues.'

Bowker laughed. 'Have you got any good news for us?'

'Depends what you're looking for. The prints on the photo and the strands of hair you dropped in yesterday morning don't match anything in our fingerprint or DNA databases. And they don't match anything from where the body was found.'

In a way, Bowker was relieved that Sophie didn't appear to be involved. 'Thanks, Erin. Appreciate you expediting the analysis.'

'I've also got the results for the prints you emailed down yesterday afternoon. As you suspected, they match a set lifted from the wallet at the discovery scene, though they don't match anything on our database. We'll hold onto them, pending whether Mr Davidson is charged.'

'In spite of what everybody says, I think you're a bloody ripper,' Bowker said, with a smirk.

'Flattery will get you nowhere, Bowker. But that bottle of Johnnie Walker will.' O'Meara devolved into another bout of coughing, and Bowker waited while she regained her composure.

'Your work's not finished quite yet, though,' he said. 'We think we've found the actual murder scene. The forensic team has recovered a shitload of stuff for the lab to check out.'

'Well, don't expect any results until next week, whisky or no whisky. We're still flat-chat here.'

* * *

Back at the station, Bowker summarised where their investigation stood. 'We now have four witnesses confirming that Weston was chasing Jimmy Cobb's whereabouts. With what motive, we can only speculate.'

'Given the car in the dam with the shotgun, and the bloodied area that Shane found, I reckon we can assume Weston did find his way out there, but was killed for his trouble,' Holmes said.

236

Bowker nodded, then looked at Parker. 'You happy with that, Shane?'

'Pretty bloody obvious, I'd say,' Parker replied, without looking up.

Bowker ignored his pique. 'Forensics will have to confirm a lot of our assumptions, of course. There are plenty of questions requiring definitive answers. Is it human blood? If it is, does it belong to Weston? Do the shotgun pellets match the ones removed from Weston's body? Does the vegetable matter match? Did Cobb's Beretta fire the shots? Can any information be salvaged from the mobile phone found in the car? Are there usable prints on the car or the gun?'

'They've been underwater for more than a fortnight,' Parker said. 'Won't get prints off them.'

'You might be surprised,' Holmes replied. 'Especially in a dam like that. Fresh water, no currents. Best conditions for a submerged print to survive.'

'If you say so,' Parker replied tersely.

Bowker ploughed on. 'We started this investigation with more questions than you could shake a stick at. If our assumptions are confirmed by Forensics, then we've found answers to most of them.' He chuckled. 'Except the main one, of course. Who killed the bastard?'

Rolling his eyes, Parker theatrically slumped back in his chair. 'We know who killed him. Jimmy Cobb did it. Why can't you accept that? Weston was looking for Cobb, he visited Cobb's farm, and he was shot behind Cobb's shed using Cobb's shotgun. The car was driven into Cobb's dam. Cobb was close to the Bryant girl who Weston killed, so he probably had revenge on his mind.

Or maybe he was threatened by Weston, grabbed his gun, and killed him out of fear for his own life.'

'I just can't see it,' Bowker replied.

Parker shook his head. 'I saw this thing on tellie where they talked about a theory called Ocker's razor, or something like that.'

'*Occam's* razor,' Holmes corrected.

'Okay, then. Occam's razor,' Parker replied, with a snarl. 'According to that, the simplest explanation is usually the right one. The more assumptions you make to explain something, the more likely you are to be wrong.' He glared at Bowker. 'If it's not Cobb, you have to assume someone with an axe to grind saw Weston in town, followed him out to Cobb's property, found Cobb's gun, and just happened to know where to dump him out at the silos. That's a lot of fuckin' assumptions.'

Bowker could begrudgingly admit that Parker was making at least some sense. Were his prior dealings with Jimmy the young boy clouding his judgment about Jimmy the adult? Was Jimmy holding something back, like he had for months in the Bryant case?

'Okay, Shane,' Bowker said. 'I'm happy to leave Jimmy on our suspects list. You alright with that, Sherlock?'

Holmes nodded. 'Logically, he's always been on there, Greg. But I trust your instincts.'

Parker smiled, appearing satisfied with his small win over the big boys. Bowker asked him for a sheet of paper, removed a pen from his top pocket, and scribbled down a list of all the suspects they'd identified before the investigation began.

'Stop me if you think I'm missing something,' Bowker said. 'I've added Leigh Davidson to the original list.' He started from the top. 'Percy Bryant. Confessed to the crime, but he's too old to have carried it out unless he had help. Got the pellet size way wrong, and wasn't in Manang the day of the murder, so wouldn't have known Weston was even in town, let alone at Cobb's place. If he'd planned to kill Weston, he would've taken his own weapon. For mine, we can cross him off.'

Holmes folded his arms across his chest. 'We still haven't identified those female prints, so he could've had help.' He shrugged. 'But from who? You said his daughter-in-law is in the final stages of cancer, so she'd be weaker than him.' Frowning, he paused for a moment. 'Yeah, cross him off, I reckon.'

'Shane?' Bowker asked.

Parker shook his head. 'You know what I think. It wasn't him.'

Bowker looked back at his list. 'Belinda Weston, or Belinda Coghlan, as she is now. Absolutely no indication she was in Manang that weekend. Hasn't been back since I locked up Weston thirty years ago. There's no way she'd have known he was up here. Besides, why travel all this way to kill him when she could've popped him when he was first released? And like with Percy, you don't go to all that trouble without bringing a weapon.' He thought for a moment. 'Unless, of course, you *do* bring something, and then stumble on Jimmy's gun and use that to help cover your arse. Very unlikely. Cross her off?'

'I think you can rule Sophie out for exactly the same reasons,' Holmes replied. 'My gut tells me this murder wasn't long in the planning. Weston unexpectedly crossed someone's radar, and he or she saw the chance to settle an old score.'

'So, Belinda and Sophie are off?' Bowker asked. The others nodded, and he drew a line through the women's names. 'Travis and Bernadette? Both attended the Back-To celebrations but weren't at the reunion ball. Spent the night at home with their kids, they said. Both had motive, particularly Travis, whose first love was killed by Weston. He had a violent temper when he was young but seems to have mellowed with family life. With the involvement of Leigh Davidson, all the male prints at the silo have now been accounted for, but that doesn't preclude Travis from being there. I tend to doubt it, but it's possible he's implicated. And with Bernadette, you have to remember that Weston was her biological father, she wasn't interfered with, and she was quite young when the family was torn apart. If she had a motive to kill Weston, it would've related to what he did to her mother and half-sister.'

'I say we cross off Bernadette, although the female prints still worry me,' Holmes said. 'Leave Travis on for the moment. He's a shearing mate of Davidson's, and we know for sure that Davidson was at the scene.'

Bowker looked at Parker. 'Happy with that, Shane?'

'I'm happy with whatever you do as long as Cobb stays on that list,' Parker replied, without meeting Bowker's eyes.

Bowker returned to his notes. 'Well, that leaves Skeeta Allender and Leigh Davidson. Davidson's alibis all check out, and his story about stealing the cards makes sense in a warped sort of way.'

Holmes leaned forward and clasped his hands together on the desk. 'I'd keep Davidson on. He's the only one we can connect directly to Weston's body.'

Parker snapped back, 'What? Cobb's farm, his gun, and his dam aren't connections?'

Holmes raised his palms. 'I know what you're saying, mate. But we still haven't got evidence he even knew Weston had entered his property.'

'This is bullshit,' Parker said, under his breath.

Bowker ignored the comment. 'I was hoping the breakthrough with Davidson would solve this thing without the need to track down Skeeta Allender. But given our stalemate here, I think we better talk to him.'

'It's only a stalemate because you blokes are making it one.' Slapping the table, Parker stood up. 'I need to visit the shitter.'

He left quickly. Bowker threw his head back in annoyance. 'Sometimes I'd like to grab that bastard by the throat and give him a good shake. He's got Jimmy in the frame, and he can't see outside it.'

'Don't forget you have a history with some of these people, Greg,' Holmes replied. 'You have some insight into their character and make-up. Parker doesn't. Neither do I, for that matter. I trust your instincts, don't get me wrong. But in the cool light of day, and on the verifiable information we have so far, Cobb fits the evidence better than any of the others.'

Bowker stared into space. 'I don't want another Skeeta Allender, that's all. Everything around Yvonne Bryant's murder pointed straight to him, and Homicide charged him, then it turned out he was innocent. I always felt his involvement in Yvonne's death didn't add up. I couldn't stand the prick, so it wasn't a case of looking after someone I knew personally.'

Holmes nodded. 'So, where to now?'

Bowker thought for a moment. 'May as well go back to Melbourne this afternoon. See if we can find Allender tomorrow. But if Forensics confirm the murder scene was at the Cobb farm, then I doubt he's involved. If he was, how the hell did he transport the body to Cocamba on a motorbike?' Bowker chuckled. 'Unless he did his own version of *National Lampoon's Vacation* and straddled it over his fuel tank.' He inhaled loudly. 'But he's a man with a motive, so let's see what he's got to say.'

'And if he's no help?'

'We'll come back here and redo all the interviews. But you never know. We might get lucky – Forensics could give us something from this morning's work. Maybe some new DNA, or–'

Bowker was interrupted by a ping from his mobile. He retrieved it from his pocket and scanned the message. 'Red Cameron, letting me know his wife has emailed me photos of the Back-To.'

He took his laptop from his briefcase and placed it on the desk. More than thirty photos were attached to Pam's email. Most of them were of small groups comprising people Bowker didn't recognise. Half a dozen were general shots of various festivities at the event.

As Bowker clicked through the photographs, Holmes spoke up. 'Whoa. Go back one, Greg,' he said, and Bowker obliged. 'There, in the background. The motorcycle. Is that a Harley?'

Bowker enlarged the photo, but it disappeared into pixels. 'Not sure. Could be, though. Got the *Easy Rider* handlebars and the big silver mufflers. Even if it is, there's no guarantee it belongs to Skeeta. Make a note of the time stamp: 11.55. When we finish here, I'll email a copy to Melbourne and see if they can ID the model of the bike.'

They scanned through the remainder of the photos until they reached the very last. Behind Red Cameron, who was posing with a few elderly mates in the foreground, was a figure in the distance. It was the brightly coloured shirt that caught Bowker's attention. The man stood with his back to the camera, his hands frozen above his shoulders. He seemed in animated conversation with a woman of average height sporting shoulder-length brown hair, jeans, and a white top. She also faced away from the camera. She stood with hands on hips, but with her thumbs pointing forward, the very opposite to most people adopting that aggressive pose.

'That's Weston in the lairy shirt,' Bowker said. 'I'll bet my left knacker on it.'

Holmes squinted at the photo. 'Who's the bird?'

Bowker shrugged. 'Fucked if I know.' He looked more closely, then increased the magnification. 'She doesn't ring any bells. Even if she's a local, I haven't seen most people up here for twenty years.'

'Whoever she is, it's bloody important we talk to her,' Holmes said, as he scribbled in his notebook. 'Photo taken at 13.55.'

Parker returned to the room. 'You two still here?'

'Don't worry, Shane, we'll be out of your hair soon enough,' Bowker replied. 'We're off to Melbourne this afternoon to see if we can track down Skeeta Allender. With a little bit of luck, we might have the case wrapped up before you see us up here again.'

Parker rolled his eyes but said nothing.

Bowker pointed to the unknown woman in the photo. 'Any idea who this might be? We think it's Weston she's talking to.'

After looking at the picture, Parker shook his head. 'Nah. Who are the blokes in the front?'

'Red Cameron and some old mates,' Bowker replied, resisting the temptation to tell Parker he should have a handle on all the locals. Some in the picture may have been visitors, but Parker should've at least known Red.

* * *

On their way back to the pub, Bowker and Holmes visited Red and Pam Cameron's home to see if they could attach a name to the mystery woman in the photo. They couldn't. Bowker also asked if they'd seen Skeeta Allender at the Back-To, again getting a negative response. Prong and Lenore Lyon, a few doors further up on the Coghill Street corner, were asked the same questions. Their responses were identical.

For the time being, at least, the identity of the mystery woman remained just that. But Bowker had a gut feeling she held the key that would unlock their case.

CHAPTER 21

Rachael was eager to hear the latest developments in Bowker's investigation when he arrived home in Caulfield that evening. Their conversation at the kitchen table mirrored the discussion he and his colleagues had conducted earlier in the day. As Bowker had anticipated, Rachael was horrified when she heard Jimmy Cobb was still a major suspect in the case.

'I just can't have it, Greg,' she said. 'I worked with Jimmy for three years, and he's just not capable of something like that. He's one of the gentlest people I've ever met.'

Bowker raised his palms. 'You're preaching to the choir, here. I don't think he did it either. But like you, I'm relying on my prior knowledge of Jimmy. For what it's worth, Parker's convinced he's guilty, and Sherlock's only trusting my gut feeling that he didn't do it.'

'So, when do you head back to Manang?' Rachael asked.

Bowker shrugged. 'Tomorrow, we'll look for Skeeta Allender and see what he can tell us about his movements on the Back-To weekend. That might determine where we head next.'

'Tomorrow's Saturday,' Rachael replied. 'Surely you're allowed the odd weekend off.'

'We're more likely to find him at the bikies' clubhouse on a weekend.' Bowker chuckled. 'There's a chance some of those blokes might work during the week.'

'Where to with the mystery woman in the photo?'

'We'll chase that lead after we speak to Skeeta. Not sure where to start, but it'll mean another trip to the Mallee, I'm sure.'

Rachael stood up and walked behind Bowker's chair. She leaned down, her face against his cheek, her arms around his shoulders. 'It's good to have you home, Detective Inspector.'

Bowker took her hands in his. 'It's good to be home. What have you got lined up for tea?'

'It's what I've got lined up for *after* tea that you'll be more interested in,' she replied coquettishly.

'Actually, I'm not all that hungry right now,' Bowker replied, with a lecherous grin.

* * *

Bowker and Holmes arrived at the Barbarians' clubhouse in Northcote around ten on Saturday morning. The building was an old warehouse or automotive repair shop, with the front wall abutting the footpath. The original front windows were boarded up, and the central roller door was closed, with two heavy steel poles cemented into the ground to prevent the door being hit by a vehicle. A smaller, heavily reinforced door gave members direct access to the interior from the street. Beside the building was a parking area secured behind a heavy steel fence, accessible via a sliding steel gate. Around the yard and in the front of the building was a suite of security cameras. Within the compound were a dozen or more motorcycles, the majority Harley Davidsons. There was another entrance to the clubhouse building from the fortified yard outside. Two American pit bulls patrolled the perimeter, snarling at passing pedestrians.

Bowker parked the unmarked police vehicle on the street opposite. He and Holmes alighted and surveyed the scene. Holmes shook his head. 'Shit, these pricks have delusions of grandeur. Two-bob crims play-acting at soldiers and forts.'

They crossed the road, and Bowker knocked on the door. There was no answer, so he pounded it with his fist. The guard dogs growled and threw themselves against the fence. There was still no response. Holmes tapped him on the shoulder and pointed to a security camera above. Removing his ID from his pocket, Bowker held it up towards the camera. After thirty seconds, a skinny, late-middle-aged man in a black tee-shirt appeared behind the gate of the compound, donning a leather jacket. He sported long hair and a beard, and spoke in a gruff voice. 'What do you arseholes want? This is a pig-free zone.'

Bowker kept his temper, but spoke sternly. 'Watch your mouth, mate. Who am I talking to?'

'None of your business, unless you suspect me of something,' the bikie snarled.

'I'm not chasing details,' Bowker replied. 'Just trying to be civil.'

'Cement Head is all you're getting.'

'Cement Head it is, then,' Bowker replied. 'Can you quiet those bloody dogs? Can't hear myself think.'

Cement Head turned and threw a leg at the closest animal. 'Shut the fuck up, you two!' he screamed. The two hounds stopped barking, but stood at attention, hoping for an attack command.

Bowker nodded his appreciation. 'We're looking to talk with a bloke named Daryl Allender.'

'You fuckers from the drug squad?' the bikie asked gruffly.

'Expecting them, were you, Mr Cement Head?' Holmes asked.

'Not especially, no.'

'So, Daryl Allender?' Bowker asked again.

'Never heard of him, mate.'

'He used to go by the name Skeeta,' Bowker said.

'Nobody here by that name.'

Bowker put his hands in his pockets. 'We might come in and have a look for ourselves.'

'Not without a warrant, you won't,' Cement Head shot back.

'At the moment, you're interfering with a murder investigation,' Bowker said sternly. 'We can do it the easy way, or we can go down the official path, and I'll come back with a warrant and a busload of uniforms to turn this place upside down looking for evidence. Probably take those dogs away as well. Prohibited breed, from memory.'

While Cement Head assessed his options, a dozen bikies with their molls burst from the clubhouse, laughing and jostling each other. Among the cacophony, Bowker recognised a familiar voice. He put two fingers in his mouth and whistled sharply. The bikie group went silent, the dogs spinning angrily in circles.

'Hey, Skeeta!' Bowker yelled, not sure from who the voice had originated. On first glance, none of the men fitted the skinny, light-framed and fair-haired Daryl Allender who he'd last seen twenty years prior.

An overweight man in leathers, his gut hanging over his belt, wandered across to the gate with a contrived swagger. A younger woman in a white tee-shirt with dyed green hair followed him across, carrying a leather jacket over her arm and chewing aggressively on a mouthful of gum.

'He's Rooter. Never heard of Skeeta,' Cement Head said

offhandedly.

Holmes raised his eyebrows. 'Rooter?' he asked, with a smirk.

'Comes from the Mallee,' Cement Head replied. 'You city blokes have probably never heard of mallee roots, but that's why we call him Rooter.'

'I was born and raised in Murrayville, mate,' Holmes said.

Cement Head shrugged. 'Never heard of it.'

Allender took a moment to recognise Bowker. 'What the fuck are you doing here, Bowker?'

'Nice to see you too, Skeeta,' Bowker replied. 'Who's your lady friend?'

'None ya business,' the woman said.

'Glad to meet you, Nunya,' Bowker replied, winking at Holmes.

'It's Janine, if you must know,' Allender said irately.

'I like the hair,' Bowker said, noticing her uncanny resemblance to Yvonne Bryant, especially with her coloured hair.

'Rooter likes my hair bright. Any colour but purple. He doesn't like purple hair.'

Yvonne had purple hair the night she was killed, Bowker remembered. He pointed at the gate. 'Can one of you blokes open this gate so we can have a chat with Daryl and Janine without staring through bars?'

Cement Head commanded the dogs to heel, then took a key from his pocket and turned it in the heavy-duty padlock. 'Don't take too long. We're takin' a run up to Yarrawonga for the weekend.'

'You come over to the car with me, Daryl, and Detective Holmes can have a chat with Janine on the bench up there near the corner,' Bowker ordered.

Allender immediately protested. 'We're not going anywhere

until I find out what all this is about, because I've done nothin' wrong. I'm not going to prison again for something I didn't do.'

Bowker shook his head. 'If it wasn't for me, Daryl, you would've stayed inside, so let's drop the preaching. We're investigating the murder of Adrian Weston.'

Allender appeared surprised. 'The dude who killed Yvonne in the eighties? Didn't know he was murdered.' He smiled. 'Can't say I'm disappointed. Why do you want to talk to me?'

'Because you had a motive,' Bowker replied. 'He killed your girlfriend and was happy to let you rot in jail on his behalf. And we know from your sister that you and the lovely Janine here were in the district the weekend of his murder.'

Holmes wandered up the street with Janine, while Bowker and Allender crossed the road and leaned against the police vehicle.

'You visited your sister on the morning of August eighth?'

'That's right. The club was doing a run up to the Murray and we camped at Merbein.'

'Janine was with you?'

'Yeah. We live together in Faulkner.'

'You took a detour at Ouyen and headed east to Kulwin?'

Allender snorted. 'Out to my fuckin' sister's place. The bitch owes me three quarters of a mil.'

'How's that?' Bowker asked, already knowing the answer.

'The old man ripped me off in his will. Left the fuckin' farm to Cynthia. She's not even a real Allender. Bloody adopted.' Allender gave a sour laugh. 'I work my guts out to help the old man keep the place going, and what do I get? Sweet fuck-all.'

'You've got a different memory than me, Skeeta. What I remember is your parents scratching out a living while you travelled the district drinking piss and selling dope.'

Allender shook his head but didn't comment.

'Your sister told you to piss off. So, where'd you go? Back to Ouyen?'

'Went on to Manang so Janine could see what a shithole I'd come from. Then went out through Winnambool to show her the farm that should belong to me. Rode on to Robinvale, crossed the river, and followed the Sturt Highway to Mildura. Met up with the rest of the club on the river and sat around drinking piss for the rest of the day. Came back to the city on Sunday arvo. Satisfied?'

Bowker thought for a minute. 'Did you stop in Manang?'

'Went to the pub and bought a sixpack of stubbies. Café wasn't open, so we went over to the big shebang at the racecourse and bought a couple of sausages. Ate them, downed a beer, then rode out to Winnambool, like I said.'

'Talk to anyone at the racecourse?'

'A couple of young blokes I didn't know who were serving on the barbecue.'

'What time did you leave Manang?'

'I dunno,' Allender said, scratching his receding hairline. 'Probably around one-ish.'

'Did you stop in Robinvale?'

Allender shook his head. 'Did a few laps of the main street. Janine had never been there before, not that she'd missed much. Another shithole.'

Bowker glanced towards the street corner and saw that Holmes was still in conversation with Janine. 'Whatever happened to that hotted-up ute you were so proud of? The golden Holden?'

Allender glared at Bowker. 'Got repossessed when you put me in jail for trafficking weed. I loved that car. That's another thing I lost up there.'

'So, what do you do for a quid nowadays?'

'Casual labouring, mostly,' Allender replied.

'Keeps you in shape,' Bowker said, with a straight face.

'Puts food on the table.'

'Where'd you meet your lady friend?'

Allender turned and looked over the roof of the car. 'Moe. The club had a weekend at Mallacoota. Have to be ten years ago now. We stopped in Moe to top up with grog.'

And drop off the drugs, Bowker thought but didn't say. 'And what? Your eyes met across a room, and it was love at first sight? That's the way it happens in most great romances, I hear.'

'Nope,' Allender replied, clearly sensing Bowker's sarcasm. 'She was in the street when we mounted up and saw I was on my own. Said nothing, just climbed on the bike behind me, and off we went. Had a root in the public toilets in Orbost, and we've been together ever since. She's good company, likes a beer, and puts out on a regular basis. Can't ask for much more than that in life, can you?' Allender straightened as his prized catch began to make her way back towards the clubhouse and Holmes crossed the street towards them. 'If we're finished reminiscing here, I might leave you to it, Bowker. Yarrawonga won't wait.'

'Making deliveries up that way?' Bowker asked.

Allender put his hands on his hips. 'Over thirty years, and you're still on my fuckin' back. Ever thought of giving a bloke a break every now and then?'

'What? Like saving you twenty-five years inside for murder?' Bowker snapped back.

'That's all you've got to hang your hat on with me, isn't it, Bowker?'

Allender crossed the road, narrowly avoiding being run down by a gravel truck, with its driver giving a long blast on the horn.

The detectives climbed into the car for a debrief. 'What'd you find out from Princess Janine?' Bowker asked.

'They were part of a ride to Mildura and camped at Merbein on the river. Took a detour at Ouyen and went to visit Allender's sister to ask for the money that Janine said really belonged to Allender. Had no joy there, so they went on to Manangatang to let Janine see Allender's hometown. She went into great detail about what a hole it was and how lucky Allender was to escape from it.'

Bowker chuckled. 'Escaped via the Ararat prison. Did she say if they stopped in Manang?'

Holmes nodded. 'Yeah. Bought grog at the pub and went over to the Back-To celebrations for lunch. Didn't speak to anyone. Left there about one, she thinks. Headed out to the family farm, where Allender described how he'd virtually run the place with minimal help from his parents.'

Bowker shook his head. 'Fuck me.'

'After that, they rode up to Robinvale, chucked a few laps, then went through the desert across to Mildura. Got booked for doing ninety up Deakin Avenue. Joined the rest of the gang on the riverbank at Merbein and drank grog all night.'

Bowker raised his left hand. 'Whoa, whoa, whoa. Back up a bit. Skeeta was booked for speeding in Mildura?'

Holmes nodded. 'That's what she said.'

'Skeeta failed to mention that little detail,' Bowker replied. 'Everything else tallies, though.'

Taking out his mobile, Bowker searched for the phone number of the Mildura police station and made a call that confirmed Allender's speeding infringement. When finished, he looked across at Holmes. 'He was booked at 3.15 on the Saturday afternoon, so the time they say they left Manang sounds about right. What was the time stamp on that photo of Weston talking to our mystery woman?'

Holmes opened his notebook and leafed through several pages. 'It was 1.55.'

Bowker leaned back in his seat. 'At that time, Skeeta would've been in New South Wales, somewhere between Robinvale and Mildura.'

'So he's right off our list?'

'As far off it as you can get,' Bowker replied.

Further conversation was interrupted by the enormous roar of a dozen Harleys being started and revved. The iron gate opened, and a leather-clad phalanx spewed out into the real world.

CHAPTER 22

The detectives were back in Manangatang by early afternoon on Monday. Bowker was sure that the solution to the murder lay hidden among details they'd already assembled.

'We've missed something, Sherlock,' he'd said on the way up. 'You know that feeling when there's something banging on the door of your conscious mind, but you can't find a way to let it in?'

Bowker had spent much of Sunday rereading notes and witness accounts and reviewing forensic reports. He'd again laid the case out in front of Rachael, hoping her sharp mind might perceive something he'd missed, something that would break the case open. But all to no avail. Except for the unidentified woman in the photo with Weston, they were back to square one.

It seemed business as usual at the local police station when Holmes and Bowker made their way up the front path after unloading their gear at the pub. The police vehicle was missing, and the *Station Closed* sign was back in place on the front door. Bowker rifled around in his pocket, retrieved his key, and opened up. He placed his briefcase on the desk and picked up a handwritten note. He raised his eyebrows, glanced at Holmes, and read out:

'Detective Bowker. Just in case you return early from Melbourne, I'm letting you know I'm using up a few of my days in lieu for a bit of R and R in Mildura. I'm meeting up with an old friend from Hamilton who works in an irrigation business up there. If you need

me for anything urgent, you have my number. Plan to be back on Friday, or Monday at the latest. Hope you've nailed Cobb by then. Shane P.'

Bowker screwed up the paper and threw a perfect three-point shot into the wastepaper basket between the filing cabinets. 'Time in fuckin' lieu? How do you get time in lieu when you do jack shit?'

'It'll be easier without the prick, I reckon, Greg. And how much time do we waste putting up with his carping about Jimmy Cobb?'

Bowker slumped down into the office chair behind the desk. 'Can you write up the interviews with Skeeta and his bird? I want to go through the paperwork again. The answer's in there somewhere.'

Holmes went through to the kitchen. 'The lazy fucker!' he yelled through to Bowker. 'Dirty dishes and cutlery everywhere. He could've cleaned up his mess before he took off for his hard-earned R and R. Notice he took the police car too, thank you very much. Limits our movements a bit.'

'Guess he was worried about taking the Commodore without a spare tyre,' Bowker called back. 'But you're right, it would've been handy to have the two police vehicles.'

Opening his briefcase, Bowker placed a pile of notes on the desk. He was about to close the lid when he spotted the red cover of Weston's thirty-year-old teacher's chronicle. He pushed his notes to the side, opened the chronicle, and looked for any annotations Weston had made.

The first few pages contained calendars and other commercially printed information. Weston's annotations began in early February with the beginning of the school term. There were three timetables filled in with different biros, which Bowker assumed were his teaching schedules for each of the three terms. The bulk of the pages were designed for day-to-day use in recording lesson plans and other class information. A small section down the bottom was reserved for managerial notes, such as meeting reminders, sport commitments and other administrivia.

Bowker quickly scanned each page, picking up snippets of information about science topics and various experiments planned for individual lessons. He began to see the patterns in the rotation of subjects and classes, and could anticipate which lessons would be described on coming pages. He also began to appreciate which students caused Weston trouble, with Jimmy Cobb's name appearing on a regular basis. About halfway through Term Two was the first time he noticed the name *Kate* scribbled in the administrative notes section. The name appeared again about a month later, and then on a semi-regular basis throughout the final term.

Bowker flipped over to the back of the book, finding Weston's class lists, where each student's assessment results were recorded. He carefully perused each of Weston's five individual classes and failed to find a Kate, or any given name that could be logically abbreviated to one. After repeating the exercise to be totally sure, he stared into space, trying to remember the staff who'd worked at the school three decades ago. He couldn't remember a Kate teaching in any of the years he was stationed in Manang. Through Rachael, he'd socialised with the teachers, so surely he'd remember if there was one.

Bowker stood up and strode through to the kitchen, where Holmes was buried in his paperwork. 'Just shooting up to the school for half an hour, mate. I'll explain when I get back. If you finish that, feel free to have another look through that pile of stuff on the desk in there.'

Holmes raised the pen in a goodbye gesture and resumed writing.

* * *

Bowker greeted the school receptionist and flagged his intention to visit the library. She ushered him through the staffroom, where two young teachers were discussing a lesson plan, and into the empty library. Bowker thanked her and introduced himself to the young female librarian, who he found working in the adjoining glass-fronted office.

'Just wondering if I could take a look at your old school magazines,' he said. 'I presume you keep one each year for your records?'

The librarian nodded. Taking him to a bookshelf parallel to the back wall, she pointed to the bottom shelf. 'Should find what you're looking for among them. We've got something for each year since the school was consolidated in 1947.'

Bowker thanked her, and she returned to covering infant picture books. Bowker sorted through the collection until he found the year he was after. He adjourned to a table under a window overlooking the quadrangle outside to read the *Quandong*, another copy of which he knew probably existed among Rachael's memorabilia at home in Caulfield. As he flipped through the pages, he took particular note of student photos and the names underneath. Class photos would be his best chance of finding what he was looking for. He doubted he would uncover Weston's Kate among the primary school students, but checked each picture nevertheless. No luck. He moved on to the photos of the secondary classes, with the same negative result. There were no Kates in the staff photos either.

One picture did catch his eye, but it had nothing to do with a Kate. It was part of a staff montage the Year Twelve students had put together. The photo had been taken as staff members and their partners boarded a school bus for a social outing at the now-defunct Oasis hotel in Swan Hill. Featured were Rachael and senior English teacher Judi Wikman. Judi wore a pink satin dress and Rachael the shortest of miniskirts and high heels. *Shit, she's got great legs*, Bowker thought, as he stared into space.

His libidinous reverie was broken by the arrival of Bernadette Urdevic and her Grade Six class. 'Penny for your thoughts, Detective Bowker,' she said, as her students filed past her, coming in through the library door.

'G'day, Bernadette. Just checking an old school magazine, looking for a student. You might be the right person to help me out.'

'Hold on a moment while I hand the class over to Melissa,' Bernadette replied.

When the students had taken their seats, and the librarian had started a spiel on library etiquette, Bernadette returned and sat down next to Bowker. 'Okay. How can I help?' she asked.

'I found your father's teacher's chronicle among some personal stuff at your grandmother's place. The name *Kate* is written at the bottom of quite a few pages. I can't find a Kate in the school population of that year.'

'That'd be Kate Olsen. Her family were pretty staunch Catholics, so they sent her to Mary McKillop in Swan Hill. My father tutored her in maths at her family's farm every couple of weeks. Her mother occasionally babysat us, and Dad or Mum sometimes looked after Kate if her parents went away to the wool sales or down to Melbourne.'

The hair stood up on the back of Bowker's neck, but he ploughed on calmly. 'Does Kate still live around here?'

'Sophie knows more about her than me. They're the same age. Occasionally, Soph will mention that she's been talking to Kate and tell me what she's up to. Last I heard, she and her husband were running a bakery in Horsham. Pretty successful business, apparently.'

'Do you know if Kate attended the Back-To?' Bowker asked.

Bernadette shrugged. 'Don't think so. Then again, I wouldn't know her if I fell over her.' She stared at Bowker. 'You don't think Kate had anything to do with my father's murder, do you?'

'I doubt it,' Bowker replied. 'But we're drawing blanks everywhere we go, so we're just chasing up any tenuous link we can find.' Smiling, he changed the topic. 'I've got something I'd like to photocopy.' He found the page and pointed out the picture of Rachael.

Bernadette's eyes widened. 'Woo hoo! Check out the skirt. You'd be locked up if you wore something that short nowadays.'

'Depends who the arresting officer is,' Bowker joked.

* * *

The moment Bowker entered the police station, Holmes jumped to his feet with a photo in his hand. 'You know how you said we're missing something in this case? I think I might've found it.'

'I've got news too,' Bowker replied, 'but you go first.'

Holmes handed him a photo of Weston's body. 'Picture taken by the forensic team at Cocamba after the body was discovered.'

Bowker scanned it briefly. 'Yep,' he replied. 'Half his head blown away.'

'The bloke we interviewed at Chinkapook. The bloke Weston visited, chasing an address for his daughter and for Cobb. Peter Cowan. What did he say Weston was wearing?'

Bowker thought for a moment. 'Retro clothing. Lairy shirt, wire-rimmed glasses, and...' – then it hit him – 'a heavy gold chain around his neck.' He looked at the photo again. 'So where the fuck is that chain?'

'That's what I'm asking myself,' Holmes said, with a smile of satisfaction.

'You're certainly living up to your name, Sherlock.' Bowker took out his mobile and searched for the bootleg photo of Weston's body that had circulated in the district. Once he located it, he used two fingers to enlarge the area around Weston's neck. He held out the photo and showed Holmes. 'Shitloads of blood, but definitely no gold chain. What are our possible scenarios?'

'It wasn't at Cobb's place,' Holmes replied. 'Not at the site where we think he was killed, or in his car.'

'And the techs didn't find it at Cocamba with the body,' Bowker said.

'I reckon we need to talk to our credit card thief, Mr Davidson.'

'Agreed. It won't hurt to chat with the Netcor workers, either. All we've got is their statements to Parker on the day they found the body, which are pretty basic at best.'

Bowker rang the school and briefly spoke to Bernadette, who was still on a break, with her class being taken by the librarian. When the call ended, Bowker explained its contents to Holmes.

'Bernadette Urdevic confirmed her father was wearing the gold chain when he visited, so Cowan's description was accurate. She also confirmed that Travis and Leigh Davidson were still shearing at Bluey Keene's place.'

'We tackle him this afternoon or in the morning?' Holmes asked, as he sat in the chair behind the desk.

Bowker looked at his watch. 'It'd be gettin' on a bit by the time we made it out there. Plus, we need all our ducks in a row before we front him with stealing the chain. We don't want to rush it and fuck it up. Might let you handle that one in the morning, Sherlock.'

'No worries,' Holmes replied, with a puzzled look. 'You got something else on the go?'

Pulling up a chair, Bowker explained his discovery of Kate Olsen's name in the teacher's chronicle and Bernadette's subsequent confirmation of her link with Weston.

'You suspect this Olsen girl might've been another one of Weston's victims?' Holmes asked.

'It's a possibility,' Bowker replied. 'She's the right age. He tutored her, presumably alone, and Bernadette said her mum *or* dad sometimes babysat.' He shrugged. 'I dunno. We're making a hell of a leap from her being tutored by Weston in the eighties to surmising that, thirty-one years later, she made a special trip from Horsham, where she has a family and a successful business, to blow his brains out in Manang.'

Sighing, Bowker scratched at his forehead. 'To be honest, I think we're probably grasping at straws. But straws are about all we have at this stage. I think we have to follow it up. So, in the morning, while you're at Bluey Keene's place, I'll take a run down to Horsham and see if I can catch up with her.'

Holmes smiled. 'I'll toss you to see who has to walk. I had a scout around for the keys to Parker's Commodore, but no joy.'

'I'll ring Prong and see if we can borrow one of his vehicles. You're only going as far as Gollah, so you'll be back midmorning. You'd better hold on to the key to the station.'

'Are you going to ring Kate to make sure she'll be in Horsham? It's a long trip for nothing if she's not.'

'I'll risk it, I think,' Bowker replied. 'I'd like to hit her cold. If by chance she *is* involved, I don't want to give her time to construct an alternate narrative.'

CHAPTER 23

The weather was warmer than normal for this time of year, with the temperatures nudging the high thirties. A blustery north wind sent ripples through the crops as Holmes turned off the Tyntynder Road and drove Prong's Ford Territory up the potholed track to Bluey Keene's sheep yards.

When Holmes entered the adjacent woolshed, Keene's reaction was immediate. 'Fuck me, mate,' he said, throwing his hands in the air. 'Surely you're not gonna pinch one of my shearers again. I'm already a day behind because you took Leigh away last Friday and the sheep got wet. They're due to start at Ned Kelly's on Wednesday morning, so I can't afford any more delays.'

'I'm not here to take anyone away,' Holmes replied. 'I just want a quick word with Leigh. Shouldn't need more than five minutes.'

Keene's mood lightened immediately. 'Flying solo today?'

'Yeah. Splitting the workload.'

With a nod, Keene hurried off to fetch Davidson. He tapped Davidson on the shoulder and yelled something in his ear. After looking over his shoulder, Davidson finished the sheep he was shearing, pulled the machine out of gear, and pushed the animal headfirst down the chute, into the counting pen outside. He adjusted his groin as he wandered towards Holmes, who motioned him outside.

Holmes got straight to the point. 'Where's the gold chain, Leigh?'

Davidson seemed taken aback. 'What gold chain?'

'The one you took from Adrian Weston's neck when you stole his credit cards.'

Shaking his head vigorously, Davidson lifted his arms in front of him, palms facing out. 'No, I didn't take any chain.'

'Come on, Leigh. Admitting you souvenired it for Sophie won't get you into any more trouble than you're already in for taking the cards. But it will help clear up a few things in our investigation.'

Davidson remained adamant. 'I didn't even *see* a gold chain. Honest. I promise. I don't reckon he was wearing one.'

Holmes was inclined to believe him. Davidson had nothing much to gain by lying. 'Okay, I'll record your denial. If you have a change of heart, you be sure to ring me.' He handed over his card, and Davidson returned to the shed.

For a moment, Holmes stood still, watching a hawk circle something unseen on the ground a few hundred metres away. He smiled to himself. In this tiny slice of the natural world, some poor creature was about to get a very big surprise. By comparison, he and Bowker were yet to identify their target.

As Holmes opened the door of the Territory, Travis Urdevic exited the shed and jogged across. 'Leigh told me you asked him about the gold necklace,' he said, when he reached Holmes. 'Just for the record, I believe what he said about it not being there.'

Holmes nodded. 'Noted.' He put one foot into the car.

'But the prick was definitely wearing it when he lobbed in at our place on that Saturday morning. I remember thinking what a wanker he was for wearing something like that. Especially nowadays.' Urdevic was silent for a moment. 'Just thought I'd tell you, that's all.'

'Thanks, mate,' Holmes said. He climbed into the Territory and headed back down the pitted gravel track. In the rear-vision mirror, he noticed Urdevic watching him drive away, hands on hips. As he turned onto the road and back towards Chillingollah, he saw the hawk dive earthwards.

*   *   *

Meanwhile, Bowker was passing through Birchip, with Morton Plains the next waypoint on his journey south. There, he would turn southwest to Warracknabeal, and ultimately Horsham, some forty minutes further on. All up, without stops, the drive would take him over two and a half hours. That would be a five-hour round trip, plus his time in Horsham.

This better be worth it, he thought. The big risk was that Kate Olsen wouldn't be in Horsham and his journey would be a complete waste of time. But he'd never travelled this route before, and he was determined to enjoy the countryside. He watched as the mallee scrub gave way to the more substantial trees of the Wimmera. The soils became heavier as he journeyed south, and with them, the crops became denser and the yields dramatically increased, partly also due to higher annual rainfall. However, while the light, sandy soils of the Mallee would never support the yields common across the Wimmera in good years, they were able to produce a crop on very little rain, making complete wipe-outs less common in the north.

Around lunchtime, Bowker rolled into Horsham, a regional centre of about seventeen thousand people set on endless flat plains. He turned left at the lights, onto Firebrace Street, and quickly found Olsen's Family Bakery between the two roundabouts, just

266

where the internet predicted it would be. He parked half a block down, decided against wearing his suit jacket and tie, and strolled to the well-patronised shopfront. He was inspecting the varieties of salad roll in a glass display case when a middle-aged female shop assistant approached from behind the counter.

Bowker glanced at her name tag. 'Hi, Rosa. Just after a ham and salad roll to take away, please.'

Rosa handed him a cling-wrapped roll in a brown paper bag, and he paid by card. He thanked her and, as if it was an afterthought, asked if Kate was in the shop.

'That's her working the coffee machine,' Rosa said, pointing deeper into the bakery. 'Do you want me to grab her for you?'

Bowker shook his head. 'No, don't interrupt her work. I'll just wander down and say hello.'

He made his way to where Olsen was stirring what appeared to be a latte in a takeaway cup. 'Kate Olsen?' he asked in a friendly tone.

The woman looked up and smiled. 'That's right.'

Bowker opted not to display his ID in the crowded shop. 'I'm Detective Greg Bowker of the homicide squad. Are you in a position to have a brief chat?'

A puzzled look crossed her face, and he held up a hand. 'Don't worry, you're not in trouble,' he said. 'I'm just after information that might help with an inquiry I'm conducting at the moment.'

'Okay,' she said slowly. 'I'm about to take my break. This latte's for me. Can I get you something to drink? On the house.'

'Same as you would be terrific, thank you.'

Olsen pointed to a table at the rear of the shop. 'If you take a seat down there, I'll be over as soon as I've made our drinks.'

Within a couple of minutes, Olsen appeared from behind the counter, a takeaway coffee in each hand. She stood about a hundred and seventy centimetres in height and was in good physical shape, with a round, friendly face and short ginger hair. Big silver rings dangled from her ears. Her hands were carefully manicured, her nails painted a deep red to match her lipstick.

'Has someone been killed in Horsham?' she asked grimly, as she sat opposite Bowker and placed his latte on the table.

Bowker nodded his thank you. 'Actually, I'm investigating a murder that took place a few weeks ago. Further north, in the Mallee.'

Olsen took a mouthful of coffee. 'Adrian Weston. I read about it. He used to tutor me when I went to school at Mary McKillop.'

'What else do you know about him?' Bowker asked, amazed at how quickly they'd moved to the nub of his questioning.

'He killed a girl from the Manang school with whom he was having an affair. I found out later he was molesting his daughter Sophie, whom I've kept in touch with. We're the same age, and even though we went to different schools, we spent time at each other's places.' She frowned. 'How come you want to talk to me?'

'We found Weston's old teacher's journal for the year Yvonne Bryant was murdered. There were occasional references to a Kate in there. I checked records at the school, and there were no students named Kate attending in that calendar year. Sophie's sister works as a teacher in Manang. She told me about her father tutoring you in maths, and we're running out of leads on the case, so I thought I'd go for a drive in the sun and see if you had a recollection that might help.'

'Long drive,' she said, with a chuckle.

'I realise that now,' Bowker replied. 'Would've been simpler to ring.' He smiled and held up his coffee cup. 'But then I would've missed my free latte.'

Olsen laughed. 'My advice is to stay out of the business world with that sense of economics, Detective.'

'There's a couple of questions I need to ask you. Sorry if they're a bit upsetting.' Bowker took a deep breath. 'Did Weston ever try to molest you?'

Eyes widening, Olsen shook her head. 'No. Never. Dad would've killed him!' She paused and smiled. 'You know what I mean.'

Bowker grinned. 'Yeah. Bernadette said that occasionally, Adrian or Belinda Weston babysat you if your parents went away for a night.'

Olsen screwed up her face, evidently trying to think back. 'Mrs Weston stayed over once, but I can't remember him ever being at our place. I stayed with the Weston girls a few times at their house.'

'It was a long time ago, and Bernadette was just a primary school kid, so her memories of that time are probably a bit hazy,' Bowker replied.

'I can't remember much about her, to be honest. Just a little kid hanging around Sophie and me while we were playing. If I'd gone up to the Back-To, I might've been able to catch up with her. I'd hoped to go, but unfortunately, Saturday mornings are our busiest time here.'

'Does your husband work at the bakery as well?'

Olsen shook her head. 'Nah. Anthony's a truck driver. Away a lot of the time.'

Bowker was becoming increasingly convinced Olsen wasn't

involved. She was very open and matter-of-fact, and seemed comfortable with his visit.

'Are you related to the Officer Bowker who was in Manang when Yvonne's murder happened?' Olsen asked. 'You remind me of someone, maybe.'

Bowker smiled. 'One and the same Greg Bowker, Kate. Was in Manang for twelve years. Loved every minute of it.' He scanned her face. 'Actually, you look a little familiar too, so we might've crossed paths at the footy or tennis or somewhere. Small world, eh?'

They exchanged contact numbers and reminisced about the old days as they gradually consumed their coffee. Bowker was hungry and keen to break out his salad roll, but decided it would be rude to eat in front of his host. After ten minutes, their discussion was interrupted by a call from a staff member behind the counter, who needed Olsen to attend to some perceived emergency. Bowker watched her stride to the counter to take charge, impressed by her quiet control over the business. But a bolt of electricity shot through his spine when she placed her hands on her hips, thumbs pointing forward.

Bowker's coffee cup was almost empty, but Olsen's was still a quarter full. He surreptitiously took a serviette from the holder on the table, picked up her latte, and tipped the contents into his own cup. He pushed his cup across to where Olsen had been sitting, took the salad roll from the brown paper bag, and used the serviette to carefully insert her now-empty cup into the bag. He climbed to his feet and hurried past the counter.

'I'll leave you to your crisis, Kate. Lovely to meet you.'

'Great to meet you too, Greg,' she called back. 'Drop in and say hello next time you're in town.'

'Will do,' he said over his shoulder.

Back in his car, Bowker headed south rather than north. From here, Melbourne wasn't much further away than Manang. He pulled under a tree in a truck stop a few k's out of Horsham and ate his salad roll while he and Holmes apprised each other of their recent interviews. Bowker had resolved that personally delivering Kate Olsen's coffee cup to the forensics centre in Melbourne was the quickest method available, and certainly the simplest in maintaining an accurate chain of custody for what might turn out to be case-busting evidence.

As he skirted the eastern edge of the Grampians, he called Rachael on his hands-free to advise her he'd be home that night, so she wouldn't get a fright when the front door opened unexpectedly. She was likely with her kinder group, as her mobile went to voicemail. Bowker left a brief message, short on details of his day but dripping with double entendres.

Just under three hours later, Bowker entered metropolitan Melbourne via the Western Freeway and followed the Western Ring Road all the way around to the Bundoora exit onto Plenty Road. From there, he quickly circled La Trobe University and delivered his potentially precious cargo to the forensic science centre in McLeod. Driving against the peak-hour traffic, it was a relatively hassle-free journey back to his home in Caulfield North.

Rachael threw her arms around him when he entered. 'This is an unexpected surprise, big boy.'

Bowker kissed her lightly. 'Surprise for me too. We might have the breakthrough we've been waiting for. I'll explain over tea.'

'Not much planned, I'm afraid,' she replied. 'I thought I'd be on my own, so it was going to be soup and toast.'

They walked through to the kitchen, where Bowker opened his briefcase on the circular wooden table. 'Got something to show you.' He took out the photocopied picture of his wife and Judi Wikman boarding the bus to Swan Hill. Smiling, he passed it over, waving his hand as though fanning away the heat.

Rachael grinned. 'That skirt was a bit short, don't you think?'

'Nope,' Bowker said instantly.

'Just lucky the weather was warm up there,' she said, with a chuckle, 'otherwise I would've got my bum frozen off.'

Bowker put his arms around her, placing his hands on her buttocks. 'You were too hot for that, baby. Still are.' He kissed the end of her nose. 'Let's forget about the soup and head down to the Italian place on Glenferrie Road.'

'Sounds like a plan,' she said. 'I'll just change out of this tracksuit. Bit underdressed to be accompanying a man in a suit.'

Bowker sat down at the table and contemplated where analysis of Kate Olsen's coffee cup might lead the investigation. The biggest likelihood was nowhere. His theory that Olsen was their mystery woman was based solely on the unusual way she put her hands on her hips. Other than that, he had nothing. Olsen's hair was shorter, and it was the wrong colour. Even if she *was* the woman who'd talked to Weston at the Back-To, it didn't mean she was involved in his killing.

Any fingerprints or DNA that Forensics could garner from the cup wouldn't prove one way or another whether Olsen was the mystery woman. But a positive match with the crime scene samples would place her at the site of the murder, and that was more crucial than proving she'd spoken to Weston at the racecourse. It would be a couple of days before he'd get the results, but in the meantime, he expected that an equally important forensic report wasn't far away. Analysis of the evidence acquired at the Cobb farm was still pending, along with the verdict on the prints Holmes had taken from Jimmy Cobb. Bowker was sure the latter would prove unrelated to the murder.

'I'm ready, if you're right to go,' Rachael said from behind him.

Bowker stood, turned around, and had to grab hold of the chair. Rachael stood before him wearing basically the same outfit she'd worn to Swan Hill on that night thirty-one years ago. He was struck dumb.

'Never pays to throw things out, does it, Greg?' she said flirtatiously.

'Let's go back to the bedroom and get you out of that thing,' Bowker said, basically panting.

'Am I too old for this?' she asked, running her palms slowly down her hips. 'You don't like it?'

'Oh, I like it,' Bowker said quickly, as he led her up the passage. 'I like it too much.'

CHAPTER 24

Bowker was on the road early the next morning, still wondering if it made more sense to stay in Melbourne until the forensic results arrived and let Holmes cover the Mallee end of their investigation. Eventually, he resolved that since all the main players in this puzzle were based in northern Victoria, the case would be solved up there. If, indeed, it was ever to be solved. But his gut told him they were close.

The forensic report for Cobb's farm arrived by email a couple of hours after Bowker hit town and was printed on the police station's Epson. Bowker sat down behind the desk, with Holmes at a chair opposite. He scanned the document quickly.

'Firstly, the blood by the lean-to at the Cobb farm belongs to Adrian Weston,' Bowker quoted from the report. 'The quantity of blood and the large amount of facial tissue recovered are consistent with the victim dying instantly at the scene.'

'We've been assuming that, but it's good to have it confirmed,' Holmes said.

'Yeah. Takes out some of the ifs and buts.' Bowker read further down the page. 'Shotgun pellets match the ones embedded in the victim's skull at Cocamba. Vegetation and soil samples match those found on the victim's body. Forensics' conclusion is the same as ours. Weston was killed at Cobb's place, and the body was transported to Cocamba and dumped at the silos.'

Bowker flipped the page. 'Now for the interesting stuff.'

Holmes smiled. 'What was found in the dam, you mean.'

'Yeah,' Bowker said. 'Nothing of value was obtained from the exterior of the car, but a few prints were lifted from the seatbelt buckle inside. They match Adrian Weston's. Prints were lifted off the steering wheel but were too smeared and water-damaged to be identifiable.'

'Fuck!' Holmes slapped his palm on the table.

Bowker raised a hand. 'Don't give up too early, my friend. Fingerprints were recovered from the stock and the fore-end of the shotgun that matched the unidentified female prints found with the body.'

'Bingo!' Holmes exclaimed.

'Can't argue with you there,' Bowker replied. 'Two fingerprints matching those of a James Mark Cobb were recovered from the barrel of the gun. These prints didn't match any sample in the national database or any lifted prior in this investigation.'

'It was Cobb's gun, so you'd expect to find his prints on it.'

Bowker nodded and silently read the last page of the report. Looking up, he summarised: 'There were no identifiable prints on the mobile phone. It's a cheap pay-as-you-go. Forensics traced the number from the SIM card. Voicemail wasn't part of its plan, so there's nothing there. There's a short list of incoming and outgoing calls, all to and from Hayden Tomlinson. By the dates of the calls, it doesn't sound like Weston had the phone very long.' Bowker threw the report on the desk. 'That's about the size of it, mate.'

Holmes leaned back, balancing his chair on two legs. 'Seems pretty clear now, doesn't it? Whoever owns those un-ID'd prints found at Cocamba is the one who pulled the trigger.'

Bowker smiled. 'If Forensics are right about it being a woman, I wouldn't want to be her husband if he came home a few dollars short in his pay.'

Holmes burst out laughing.

Drumming his fingers on the desktop, Bowker absently stared at the report in front of him. 'You know what a dead weight a corpse can be, Sherlock,' he said. 'Weston wasn't a big man, but he wasn't a skinny twig either. Lifting his body into a car would be a big ask, even for a large, fit bloke.'

'If a woman killed him, you reckon she had help somewhere along the line?'

Bowker shrugged. 'Just surmising.'

'Where do we go from here?' Holmes asked.

'We'll get a clearer idea once we get the lab results on Kate Olsen's coffee cup. In the meantime, let's have a chat to the Netcor crew who discovered the body. But finding where the hell they are will be our biggest challenge. I think this end of the state is run from Mildura, so that's where we'll start.'

The Mildura Netcor office advised that Damien Cowton and Campbell Kilmartin were part of a crew replacing power poles beside the Sunraysia Highway, ten kilometres to the south of Ouyen. It was a leisurely forty-minute drive for the detectives, especially on this sunny day with just a zephyr drifting in from the northeast. The landscape here was identical to most of the northern Mallee, with rolling sandy rises sown down with wheat or barley between lines of remnant mallee scrub, punctuated occasionally by dry saltpans surrounded by dead trees. The cluster of Netcor trucks and vans made the worksite impossible to miss, and within ten minutes, Cowton and Kilmartin were in separate conversations with the detectives. Bowker walked Cowton to the police car while Holmes and Kilmartin chatted at the rear of one of the trucks.

'Good job, Damien?' Bowker asked as an icebreaker.

'Yeah. Love it.' Cowton smiled, leaning against the car with arms folded. 'I've worked for Netcor since I left school, cruising the countryside with a mate, doing the occasional maintenance job. I'm my own boss, within reason.'

'What took you to Cocamba on the day you found the body?'

'Replacement of the feeder cable from a transformer to the switchboard in the silo complex control room. The weather was windy as buggery, and I remember the overhead wires whistling and swinging about in the breeze. But up to that point, it was just a normal day with a pretty simple repair to carry out.'

'Who found the body?'

'Me, unfortunately,' Cowton replied, screwing up his face.

'Take me through what happened leading up to its discovery.'

'Cam drove the truck into the silo reserve. We were piss-farting around a bit as we picked our way through the long grass. You know, pretending we'd stepped on a snake or goanna. There was a bit of a stink in the air, but we put that down to a dead animal we saw close to where we parked the truck.'

Pausing, Cowton rubbed at his mouth. 'Cam went and opened up the control room, while I followed the supply cable back towards the transformer. As I passed between the two silos, with my eyes still focused on the cable, I tripped arse-over through a swarm of flies. When I stood up and my eyes adjusted to the shadows, I saw the poor bastard lying on the ground. Reeked to high heaven.'

'What'd you do next?' Bowker asked.

'Yelled at the top of my voice to Cam and tried to steady myself against the silo.'

'Then what happened?'

'Cam ran across, thinking I'd been bitten by a snake or something. He turned white when he saw the body. I walked back to the truck and spewed up on the ground.'

Bowker nodded. 'Who called the senior constable in Manang?'

'Cam. The copper arrived about fifteen minutes later. He asked our names and what work we were doing there. He wrote down a few notes, then told us we couldn't do our maintenance that day, because the area would be sealed off as a crime scene until all the forensic stuff was finished.'

'Who took the photos?' Bowker asked without warning.

Cowton cleared his throat. 'Photos?' he asked, unconvincingly.

'Come on, Damien. I've seen them. They've gone viral right across the Mallee. I'm not going to arrest you or anything. I just want to get a handle on what happened that afternoon.'

'Cam took them,' Cowton replied quietly. 'He took two or three of the body and one of me spewing my guts out.'

Bowker frowned. 'He thought it was all a big joke, did he?'

Cowton shook his head vigorously. 'Not at all. We couldn't believe what we'd found. Cam just took photos like people do when they see stuff they'll talk about later.'

'Are the photos on your phone as well?' Bowker asked. Cowton nodded, and Bowker handed over his business card. 'Send copies of them all to my email.'

'No worries,' Cowton replied, as he slipped the card into his top pocket.

'Did you or Campbell remove anything from the scene?'

'What do you mean?'

'Did you keep any souvenirs of your big discovery?'

'Souvenirs? Like what?'

Bowker folded his arms. 'Like a gold chain the victim had around his neck.'

'No way!' Cowton replied. 'To be honest, I didn't even notice he was wearing a chain. All I remember is dried blood and millions of flies and maggots.'

'When did you get fingerprinted?'

'The next day, at the police station in Mildura. But they told us it was only for elimination purposes.'

'Okay, that'll do for today,' Bowker said. 'We might need to talk again. Just in case, I'll grab your mobile number.' He took a notebook from his pocket and wrote down Cowton's contact details. 'Don't forget to send those photos, and have a really good think about that necklace.'

Cowton nodded and strolled back to his workmates, as Bowker leaned against the bonnet of his car, enjoying the warm sun on his back. After five minutes, Holmes wandered across. Following a short discussion, it became obvious their interviewees had identical stories, about both the discovery of Weston's body and the absence of a gold chain necklace. The detectives were content that they were telling the truth.

*   *   *

The forensic report Bowker had so eagerly awaited came via email on Thursday morning. When he read the results, he leaned back in the office chair and raised his arms in the air. 'Prints on the coffee cup match those on the gun and at Cocamba. Saliva traces contained skin cells that matched the DNA extracted from the hair sample adhered to the blood on Weston's skull.'

Holmes rested his elbows on the desk in front of him, forearms crossed. 'So, Kate Olsen did it. Wasn't even on our suspect list.'

Bowker nodded. 'Certainly appears that way.'

'She'd need a serious reason to do something like that. You'd have to assume Weston molested her as a child.'

'That would be my guess,' Bowker said, grimacing. 'She'd hardly kill him because she failed maths.'

'She told you she was pretty good mates with Weston's stepdaughter when they were kids. Perhaps Sophie told her about her own abuse and Olsen decided justice hadn't been served with a jail sentence.' Holmes upturned his palms. 'Just a thought.'

'My money is on him getting at her when she was a kid,' Bowker replied. 'I think she came up here to celebrate the Back-To and, by a quirk of fate, recognised Weston as soon as she arrived. She confronted him, as we can see in the photo, then followed him when he went looking for Jimmy Cobb.'

Holmes pursed his lips. 'Do you reckon she planned to kill him? As far as we know, she didn't have a weapon. And Cobb's gun was likely the one used.'

'From her aggressive pose in the photo, I suspect she was verbally unloading on Weston earlier at the racecourse. Maybe he fobbed her off, and she followed him so she could finish having her say. Perhaps matters got out of hand at Cobb's farm.'

Holmes nodded. 'Yeah. So, I presume we're off to Horsham this afternoon. Do we bowl into the bakery and arrest her on suspicion, or do we get the local coppers to quietly take her to the station and wait for us to arrive?'

'The latter, I think. Don't want to create a big kerfuffle if we can avoid it. Besides, I'd like to visit the bakery without her there to sort a few things out before we talk to her.'

'I'll contact VicRoads before we leave and check if there are any cars registered in her name.'

Bowker stood up. 'Check if there's anything for an Anthony Olsen as well. When you're finished, I'll ring the details through to Forensics, and they can send a crime scene van over to have a look-see.'

CHAPTER 25

By the time Bowker and Holmes arrived at Olsen's Bakery, the shop was abuzz with speculation on why the local constabulary had quietly escorted their friendly and popular boss from the store. Bowker introduced himself and Holmes to the woman seemingly in charge, opting not to add they were from Homicide. He requested to see the diary where each day's staffing was listed, before adjourning with Holmes to the table he and Kate Olsen had used on Tuesday.

Bowker opened the diary and flipped back to August 8. Unexpectedly, Kate Olsen's name was listed, but unlike every other occasion, where her name was at the top of the page, on this day it appeared at the bottom of the staff roster. A slightly different-coloured pen had been used to record her name, giving further weight to the assumption it had been added posthumously. Posthumously for Adrian Weston, anyway. At the foot of each page was a designated space for miscellaneous notes, where Olsen had recorded holidays taken by staff, her husband's trips interstate, events to be catered for, and other business information. On the page for August 8, something had been written in this space, but later completely obliterated using the same biro that had been used to add Olsen's name. Bowker placed the diary in his briefcase before handing a written receipt to the woman in charge.

Horsham Police Station was a two-storey red-brick-and-concrete box wedged between the city offices and the magistrates court on

Roberts Avenue, in the town's central business district. External concrete pillars and beams seemed an attempt to ameliorate the building's cubist appearance, but any attempt at aesthetic improvement was negated by the numerous white air-conditioner units lining the walls that faced the street.

Kate Olsen was sitting quietly at a table in an interview room, head in her hands, when Holmes and Bowker entered and sat down opposite her. A local solicitor scribbled on a notepad to her left. A recording device lay on the end of the table. The interview would be videoed via a camera on the wall above the door. Bowker introduced himself and Holmes and formally started the interview for the benefit of the recording.

'Good afternoon, Mrs Olsen. Want to tell us what really happened on August eighth? The day Adrian Weston was murdered?'

'I told you everything on Tuesday,' Olsen replied, calmly. 'I would've liked to go to Manangatang for the reunion, but I had to work. As I said, Saturday is our busiest day. When you asked me about Adrian Weston, I told you that he tutored me in maths when I was at Mary McKillop. That was it.' She shook her head. 'I honestly don't know why I've been arrested.'

Bowker opened his briefcase and removed the photo of the mystery woman speaking to Weston. He placed it on the table in front of Olsen, who dismissed it immediately. 'That's not me. My hair's shorter and a different colour.'

'I noticed there's a hairdresser three doors up from your shop,' Holmes said casually.

Olsen blinked rapidly, clenched her hands and swallowed. 'I wasn't there. I was in Horsham working. Check the roster if you don't believe me.'

Bowker removed the bakery's diary from his briefcase and opened it at the page for August 8. 'Looks to me like your name was an afterthought, written with a different pen than the others.' He pointed to the effacing at the bottom of the page. 'And I'm sure our forensic people will find that underneath all this scribble is a note saying you were off to Manangatang for the day.'

For a moment, Olsen stared fixedly down at the diary, before she straightened and swept her hair from her face. 'Okay. I planned to go to Manang. But then I realised we'd be short-staffed, so I decided to stay here.'

'Do we have to interview all your staff, Mrs Olsen?' Bowker asked. 'I'm sure at least one will remember being in charge on the eighth.'

Olsen threw up her hands. 'You can't prove I was up there. You've got nothing except a photo of a woman's back, which I swear to you is not me.' She folded her arms indignantly.

Bowker again reached into his briefcase. Retrieving the forensic report, he placed it on the table in front of him and flicked to the second page with a flourish. 'You see, we have your fingerprints. On the gun that killed Weston, and on the silo where his body was dumped.'

Olsen's mouth dropped open. 'What? How?'

'We also have your DNA,' Holmes added. 'And guess what? It's a match for DNA garnered from strands of female hair found on the victim.'

Olsen struggled to speak.

'You don't have to answer any of these questions if you don't want to, Mrs Olsen,' her young solicitor advised.

'This is all rubbish,' Olsen said, ignoring her. 'I haven't provided fingerprints or DNA samples. This is a big stitch-up. You told me Tuesday that you were running out of suspects.'

Bowker leaned forward with the tiniest of smiles. 'They were on your coffee cup, Mrs Olsen. Fingerprints and saliva containing DNA.'

Olsen shook her head vigorously. 'No. I threw my cup in the bin after you left. In the bin behind the counter.'

Again, Bowker smiled, more openly this time. 'You threw out *my* cup. I took yours with me. Thought you'd finished with it.'

Olsen shot a glance at her lawyer. 'Is that legal? I didn't give him permission to have tests done.'

The solicitor nodded. 'It's called the informal collection of genetic material. Unfortunately, there are many precedents he can quote.'

'So, we've got you holding the gun, and in physical contact with the victim,' Holmes said. 'Plus, we can place you at the silo where the body was dumped.' He raised his eyebrows. 'Perhaps it's time to come clean and tell us what really happened.'

Olsen took a deep breath and glanced at her solicitor, who moved her chair a few centimetres so she could look directly at Olsen. 'You don't have to answer any more questions if you don't want to. You have the right to remain silent.'

After a moment, Olsen moved her gaze back to Bowker. 'It was an accident, alright? I just tried to scare him, and the gun went off. I was worried about being charged with murder, so I dumped him at Cocamba so it would look like he killed himself out of guilt.'

'Blew his own face off without a gun?' Holmes said, with a chuckle. 'You mustn't think coppers are too bright if you believed we'd fall for that one.'

'I wasn't thinking straight,' Olsen said, becoming increasingly upset. 'Got out to Cocamba and remembered I'd thrown the gun in the dam, so I just dumped him there.'

Bowker shook his head. 'I think you dumped him there to tie him to revenge for Yvonne Bryant's murder. You knew there were half a dozen people who'd become likely suspects once Yvonne's killing was brought into play. I'd say you were covering your tracks.'

Olsen put her hands out. 'I told you, I wasn't thinking straight.'

Closing his eyes, Bowker thought for a moment. 'So far, we haven't discussed a motive. Detective Holmes and I suspect he molested you as a child.'

Olsen's face crumbled. 'He raped me when I was just fifteen!'

'When he tutored you?' Holmes asked softly.

Olsen shook her head, tears rolling down her cheeks. 'When he babysat me. My parents went to the wool sales in Melbourne, and Mrs Weston took both her daughters to the city, when Bernadette had one of her check-ups at the children's hospital.'

'Did you tell anybody about what he did?' Holmes asked.

Removing a hanky from her apron pocket, Olsen blew her nose. 'No. I was too ashamed. He said it was my fault for wearing a silky nightie. He said he wouldn't tell Mum and Dad what a wicked girl I was if I just kept quiet about it.'

Inwardly, Bowker was sympathetic, and part of him felt like justice would be best served by letting her go and stamping the case as unsolved. However, he knew full well that this wasn't an option.

'Better tell us the whole story, Kate,' he said quietly. 'And this time, the truth would be appreciated.'

Olsen sniffed heavily and drew in a deep breath. 'I drove up to Manang for a social day out, hoping to catch up with people

I hadn't seen for years. As soon as I parked the car, I saw Weston talking to a man I didn't recognise. All the hatred I thought I'd long forgotten bubbled up, and as soon as he'd finished his conversation, I confronted him. He didn't even remember who I was. As soon as I told him, he just fobbed me off with a wave of his hand. He'd just spent thirty-one years in jail, he said, and here I was carrying on about a few minutes of sex a lifetime ago.'

'He certainly sees himself as a victim,' Bowker said. 'I've heard similar stories from others. So, what happened next?'

Olsen wiped her face. 'I saw him leave in his car, and I followed him out the Robinvale Road. He turned off at Bolton, went into a farm, and pulled in behind a ute in a garage. He walked around behind the sheds as I drove up the track. When I got out of the car, I could hear him yelling out, looking for someone.'

'What was he yelling? Do you remember?' Holmes asked.

'*Where are you, you bastard? Where are you, retard?* Things like that,' Olsen replied. 'He was so angry.'

'Okay,' Holmes said.

'There was a gun on the bench in the garage. I picked it up. Didn't realise it was loaded. I found him around the back, in a sort of hayshed, and I pointed the gun at him.'

Bowker folded his arms. 'How did Weston react to that?'

'He taunted me, for a start. When it dawned on him that I might actually kill him, he offered me a million dollars to let him go. He said he was getting the money in his mother's will and was willing to sign it over to me if I just let him walk away.' She inhaled deeply. 'I was so upset that he thought he could put a price on my suffering that I pulled the trigger, and the gun went off.' She paused for a moment and looked up at the ceiling.

'Then I panicked. Brought my car around next to his body and bundled him into the back of it.'

Bowker nodded.

'I threw the gun on the seat of his car and drove it into the dam so no one would know we'd even been there. Not for a while, anyway.'

'How'd you drive the car into the dam?' Holmes asked. 'Pretty tricky manoeuvre, I'd suggest.'

'Not really,' Olsen said. 'I just drove it really slowly to the top of the dam bank, where it nearly stopped moving, and climbed out. As soon as it crept over the top, it accelerated down the hill and into the water. It floated for a little while, then sank as it filled up.'

'What did you do next?' Bowker asked.

'Took the body to Cocamba,' Olsen replied, still sniffing. 'Dragged it out of the car and left it beside the silo. Then I drove back to Horsham, shaking like a leaf all the way home.'

'No you didn't, Kate,' Bowker said, folding his hands on the table. 'You drove back to the Manang cemetery and put a bottle of flowers on Yvonne Bryant's grave. You left prints.'

Olsen's eyes closed for a moment as she drew in a long breath. 'I found the bottle at Cocamba, where someone might've placed a little memorial years ago. Picked a few flowering gum blossoms off a tree on the edge of the cemetery. Just a way of saying to Yvonne that the ledger has been squared.'

Bowker chuckled sarcastically. 'Very noble of you, Kate. I think it was just a way of telling investigators that they should be looking to Yvonne Bryant for the motive of the killing.'

'Do you really think I'd be that calculating?' Olsen asked.

'Yeah, I do, Mrs Olsen,' Bowker said. 'It's hard to totally condemn you for killing Weston after what he did to you, but you lose my sympathy when you try to implicate others.' He glanced at Holmes. 'And as for this rubbish about believing the gun wasn't loaded – you're a farm girl. Handling firearms comes second nature. Forensics have your prints on the cartridges found in the Beretta.'

Holmes raised his eyebrows.

'Okay,' Olsen said. 'I loaded the gun. I was scared Weston might do to me what he did to Yvonne. But the gun went off by accident. I was trembling all over.'

'Well, it'll be up to the courts to decide if it was an accident,' Bowker replied. 'But I don't like your chances.'

'So, who helped you move the body?' Holmes asked.

'Nobody helped me,' Olsen replied. 'I loaded the body into the car on my own.'

Bowker frowned. 'I think you must've had help. Weston's body would've been too heavy to handle on your own.'

Olsen shook her head. 'He wasn't a big man. Once I got his shoulders into the back of the car, I only had to lift his legs in.'

'Pretty small car, a Ford Laser hatchback,' Bowker said. 'That's what you drive, isn't it? Or did you bring the old Camry wagon?'

'I was in the Laser,' Olsen said, blowing her nose. 'It was a tight fit, but I got him in there.'

'Our forensic people will find blood and other bodily tissue in the back of the car, then, will they?' Bowker asked quickly.

'Probably not. There was a plastic tarp laid out in the back. I often transport supplies for the bakery, and it protects the carpet, especially from flour dust. The tarp was covered in blood, so I rolled it up when I got home and threw it in the rubbish.'

'Did you ring your husband for help?' Holmes asked.

'No,' she said indignantly. 'He was on his way to Wentworth with a load of sheep.'

'Use the Calder Highway, did he?' Bowker asked. 'Up through Mildura? Not a massive trip across to Manang in a crisis.'

'I didn't ring anyone. You can check my phone records if you don't believe me,' Olsen replied feverishly, before she began to cry in earnest again. 'Look, I've admitted to killing him by accident. Nobody else was involved. Weston was heavy, but I somehow manoeuvred him into the back of my car. You hear about people having superhuman strength when they panic. And let me tell you, I was panicking.'

'Well, we might leave it there for the moment, Mrs Olsen,' Bowker said, looking at his watch. 'By now, our forensic people will have arrived in Horsham to examine your vehicles. Detective Holmes and I will await their report before deciding when we should interview you again.'

Olsen's face relaxed a little. 'So I can go for now?'

Bowker shook his head. 'I'm afraid not.' He stared straight into her eyes. 'Kate Olsen, it is my intention to charge you with the murder of Adrian Weston. You have the right to remain silent. If you do say anything, what you say can be used against you in a court of law. You have the right to consult with a lawyer and have that lawyer present during any questioning. If you cannot afford a lawyer, one will be appointed for you if you so desire.' He nodded towards the solicitor present. 'You've done the right thing and sought legal advice from the outset.'

Tears rolled down Olsen's cheeks. 'What happens next?'

'You'll be held overnight to appear in Horsham Magistrates'

Court in the morning, where you'll be remanded in custody, awaiting trial,' Bowker said.

'Will I get bail?' Olsen choked out between sobs.

'It's not usual in murder cases. But given the circumstances, I probably won't oppose it. You won't reoffend, and I don't see you as a flight risk.' Bowker paused. 'But that's up to the magistrate.'

CHAPTER 26

As it turned out, Kate Olsen appeared before the magistrate in an out-of-sessions hearing later that afternoon. She was placed on bail under strict conditions, needing to report to the police station every morning and afternoon. The early hearing allowed Holmes and Bowker to return to Manangatang to wrap up their investigation, although neither was convinced the case was totally solved. They had their killer, but not necessarily all who were involved.

'She had to have had help,' Bowker said, as they drove north. 'You and I both would have trouble lifting a dead body into a little car like a Ford Laser. Can't see her being able to do it.'

'Should we go back to our original list, you reckon?' Holmes asked from behind the wheel. 'Or do you think her involvement now brings new actors into play?'

'Like who?'

'Like the husband. He was heading north. Would've passed through Ouyen on his way to Wentworth. Only half an hour across to Manang.'

Bowker shrugged. 'Yeah, but he was in a semi full of sheep. And it would've been a fluke if he was contacted as he approached Ouyen. If he'd still been south of there, or had already been through the town, it could've been hours before he arrived to help.'

Holmes nodded. 'And in all our inquiries, no one has mentioned a semitrailer loaded with sheep.'

'We can probably check when he left Horsham and when he arrived at his destination. And there'll be a camera somewhere in Mildura that will have picked him up. A highway patrol probably has him on their dashboard camera too. Before we go to all that trouble, let's see if we have more likely alternatives.'

'Okay, then. Back to our well-worn list. Percy Bryant.'

Bowker laughed. 'Not a chance. He's so frail he'd be more a nuisance than a help moving the body. Besides, how would Kate Olsen ever have met him?'

'Agreed.' Holmes flicked on his blinker and overtook a slow-moving ute that was towing a flat trailer topped with two large round hay bales.

'We can forget Skeeta Allender,' Bowker said. 'He was halfway to Mildura with the lovely Janine. And we can put Leigh Davidson in the same category. His alibi for the day Weston was killed checks out. I doubt Mrs Olsen knew either of them, anyway.'

'She knew Sophie and her sister. And their mother, of course.'

'Sophie and her mother weren't in Manang, I'm sure of that. Haven't been there for decades.' Bowker hesitated for a moment, watching the old ute recede in his side mirror. 'Bernadette is a different kettle of fish, and with her, we have to bracket Travis Urdevic. They both claim to have attended the Back-To at the racecourse, but we haven't really nailed down that alibi. I've never seriously considered they'd plot to kill Weston, but perhaps helping an old friend move his body is a horse of a different colour.'

'You know who that leaves, though, don't you? Johnny on the spot.' Holmes grinned. 'Or should I say *Jimmy* on the spot? Let's say Weston's shot on the Cobb farm while Jimmy is down the paddock working somewhere. He returns to the sheds and finds Kate Olsen with the dead Weston. He's scared shitless and wants to get the body off the farm. Or perhaps he's happy to help Olsen because he hates Weston's guts for killing Yvonne Bryant.'

Bowker thought for a long moment. 'I can see Jimmy panicking if he found Weston lying dead on their farm, and helping lift the body into a car just to get rid of the damn thing. If Olsen asked him to keep quiet about it, he probably would. Especially if she told him his parents might get into trouble for a dead person being on their farm.'

Holmes nodded. 'If it did unfold that way, I'd say he came across Olsen after she'd put the car and the gun in the dam. He appeared genuinely upset that he couldn't find his gun, and he seemed to know nothing about a car at the bottom of his dam.'

'We need to talk to him tomorrow,' Bowker said, looking out his side window before turning to Holmes. 'He's one of those people, perhaps because of his disability, who will only volunteer information when he's asked directly. But Jimmy's able to keep secrets really well too. It was weeks before he told us about Weston and Yvonne Bryant in the eighties.'

'If Cobb does turn out to be involved, we'll never hear the end of it from our local senior constable,' Holmes said, with a grin.

Bowker remained po-faced. 'Don't assume I haven't imagined that smirk on his face already.'

*　*　*

The detectives drove into Manangatang right on sunset. Outside their motel room, they stood transfixed by the panorama to the west. Reds, oranges and yellows morphed into purples as the glowing orb of the sun slipped below the horizon. Patches of an eerie blue were unwrapped above them, and a line of pillowy, low-level clouds traversed the wash of colour like a string of mauve pearls.

'You don't see anything like that in the city, mate,' Holmes said, hypnotised by the golden tapestry above him.

'It's the same on a moonless night,' Bowker replied. 'I could stand outside and look at the stars for hours.'

After five minutes, Mother Nature packed away her lightshow for another evening, and Bowker's thoughts turned to a cold drink and a counter tea. It had been a long but successful day. As he and Holmes changed out of their suits and into civvies, his phone rang. He smiled while he retrieved it from his bed, anticipating his daily chat with his wife. His smile evaporated when a male voice greeted him.

'G'day, Greg. Shane here. Just checking if you're up in Manang or still in Melbourne. I'm in Mildura.'

'Yeah, I read your note,' Bowker replied.

'So obviously, you're back in Manang.'

'Came back Monday.'

'Shit, you're keen. I didn't expect you till later in the week. I was gonna stay over here till Sunday. Planned to take the whole week off. Just ringing to see where you were at, and whether you wanted me back earlier to help with the investigation.'

'All done. We've made an arrest.'

'You nailed the cunning little retard, then?' Parker said. 'Told you he was lyin' through his teeth.'

'It wasn't Jimmy Cobb, Shane,' Bowker replied quickly.

'Well, who was it? Urdevic's my next pick.'

'A woman called Kate Olsen.'

'Who the fuck is that?'

'She's from Horsham. Abused by Weston when she was a kid. Was at the Back-To and just happened to see him there. Followed him out to Jimmy Cobb's and shot him.'

'Cobb see her, did he?'

'Nope. Nobody saw her out there.'

'How'd you find her?'

'Her name was in one of Weston's old teacher's chronicles. One thing led to another, and we nailed her. I'll explain the details when you get back.'

'D'you want me to drive down tomorrow and help finalise things?'

'Nah,' Bowker said. He looked at Holmes and winked. 'You stay there. You've earned a bit of R and R. Sherlock and I have pushed you pretty hard, and you deserve a break.'

'Will you still be there Monday morning, if I come back on Sunday?'

'Probably. We suspect Olsen had assistance moving the body. We'll see if we can make any headway on that.'

'Weston wasn't a big bloke,' Parker said. 'Wouldn't take a lot to move him.'

'He'd have to be seventy-odd kilos. Takes a lot more strength than you'd think.'

'Then I'll bet my arse it was Cobb,' Parker replied quickly.

'Perhaps. Listen, Shane. You try to forget about the case and just relax, okay? If we leave early, we'll make up a sign to put on the door telling people to ring Robinvale if they need police assistance.'

'There should be one of them there already.'

'Really?' Bowker retorted, with faux surprise.

'Yeah, should've been on the door when you arrived.'

'That's right. Forgot.' Bowker said, again winking at Holmes. 'Catch you next week, possibly.'

He clicked off the call and tossed the phone back onto his bed. 'Fuckwit,' he said under his breath.

*   *   *

With Jimmy Cobb nursing a broken ankle, he was most likely convalescing at his parents' farm, and that was where Bowker and Holmes found him Friday morning. The original Cobb family home was on another of their square-mile blocks, the one now being used by Jimmy. With his maturity into adulthood, Corn and Marilyn had grabbed the opportunity to shout themselves a more modern residence, at the same time providing their son with a degree of independence.

The new Cobb house was no mansion. A neat, simple, relocatable building, it had been trucked in from Ballarat like a few others Bowker had seen appear in Manangatang itself. The garden wasn't extravagant, but it was well-maintained, and offered a green oasis for when the summer heat and wind rendered the neighbouring countryside barren and dusty.

Marilyn Cobb took the officers through to the living room, where her son was resting on a couch, his plastered foot up on a kitchen chair. Bowker and Holmes sat on lounge chairs opposite Jimmy while his mother withdrew to the kitchen to fetch tea and coffee.

It was obvious that Jimmy was apprehensive about his visitors. He was quick to start a conversation. 'Have you come to see if my ankle alright, Consable Bowker?'

'Yeah, Jim,' Bowker replied. 'How is it, mate?'

'Pretty good.' He nodded. 'Hurts at night in bed sometimes, but.'

'It'll gradually get better, though,' Holmes said, with a smile. 'You'll be up and about in no time, I reckon.'

Bowker leaned forward, forearms on his knees, hands folded in front of him. 'Jimmy, on the day that Mr Weston was shot, you said you were down the paddock rabbiting.'

'Yes, yes, yes,' Cobb replied. 'With the ferrets.'

'Did you see any strange cars at the farm that day?' Bowker asked.

Cobb shook his head vigorously. 'You can't see very far from the rabbits, 'cos of the scrub.'

'Did you see Mr Weston on the farm that day?' Bowker asked.

'No, no, no,' Cobb said.

Holmes followed up quickly. 'Did you see his dead body?'

'No, no, no,' Cobb replied, becoming upset. 'I didn't see nobody except Mum.'

Bowker sat back in his chair. 'Your mum was there, that day?'

'Yes, yes, yes,' Cobb replied. 'She was the only one I seed.'

Bowker glanced at Holmes, then looked at Cobb. 'Whereabouts did you see her, mate?'

'Down at the rabbit burras. She brought me some lunch.'

'Did she stop down there with you while you ate lunch?' Holmes asked casually.

'Yes, yes, yes. We eated it together. Sausage rolls and sauce.' Cobb smiled. 'She make the best sausage rolls.'

'I think you might be biased, Jim,' Marilyn said, chuckling, as she entered the room carrying a tray of coffee mugs and homemade jelly slices. She put the tray on a small coffee table and dragged it over between the three men. After allocating the drinks, she sat down beside her son.

Bowker took a sip from his mug. 'You over at Jimmy's place the Saturday of the Back-To, Marilyn?'

'I dropped in some groceries and a casserole for his tea. On Saturdays, he often goes ferreting, so I drove down the back paddock and found him. We had lunch together.'

'You didn't mention that the other day when Jimmy rolled the quadbike,' Bowker replied.

'Why would I, when I was worried Jim might've killed himself on that damn machine?' Marilyn replied.

'When I told you the forensic team were at the farm investigating whether Weston was killed there, you might've made mention that you'd been there that day. I might've been able to ask you if you'd seen anything.'

Marilyn shrugged. 'Had other things on my mind, obviously.'

Holmes picked up his second jelly slice. 'So, did you see anything out of the ordinary that day, Mrs Cobb?'

'There were no stray cars or people wandering around, if that's what you mean.'

'Didn't pass any cars on the road when you were coming or going to your son's place?' Holmes asked.

Marilyn shook her head. 'Not much between here and Jimmy's in terms of houses. If people did come to Jim's that afternoon, they would've come from the opposite direction. From Bolton and the Robinvale Road.'

Bowker took another mouthful of his coffee. 'Well, people did come that day, Marilyn. At least two strange vehicles entered the property on August eighth, and Adrian Weston was killed there.

We know that for certain now. We also know who committed the murder–'

Jimmy lurched forward. 'Who was it?' he asked urgently.

'We can't tell you at the moment, Jimmy, but that person has been arrested,' Bowker replied.

'If it's all done and dusted, why are you here questioning my son, then?' Marilyn enquired, her voice slightly sharp.

Bowker put his mug on the tray. 'Because we think someone helped the killer load Weston's body into a vehicle. Probably someone who had nothing to do with the shooting. Jimmy was here all day, so we were keen to ask him a few questions.'

Cobb shook his head. 'No, no, no. It wasn't me, Consable Bowker. I didn't see no bodies or no other cars. I wouldn't touch Mr Weston's body, no way.'

Holmes downed the dregs of his coffee. 'What about you, Mrs Cobb?'

Marilyn glared at him. 'Of course I didn't have anything to do with it. It's preposterous to even suggest I might've. After I had lunch with Jim, I drove straight past the sheds, out the gate and home. I helped Mark draft lambs in the afternoon. You can check if you want.'

Bowker stood and hitched up his trousers. 'Good to see you again, Jim. Look after that ankle.'

Holmes climbed to his feet as well. 'Be careful on that quadbike next time, too.' He looked at Marilyn. 'Thanks for the coffee. And those jelly slices are to die for.'

As Marilyn showed them to the back door, she suddenly turned and faced Bowker. 'Look, neither Jim nor I had anything to do with any of this. But I'll tell you one thing. If I had come across someone trying to load Weston's body into a car, I can't guarantee I wouldn't have given them a hand.' She placed her hands on her hips and spoke with more venom. 'That man didn't deserve to live. Not after what he did to Yvonne Bryant. A lot of people up here thought she was a gutter rat. But do you know what, Greg? That girl showed a kindness to Jimmy that nobody else did. She never judged him like a lot of the others. She knew what it was like to be at the bottom of the pile.' Her voice softened, and her eyes moistened. 'Do you remember she planned to ask Jimmy to be her partner in the deb because she was worried nobody else would? And as fate would have it, she was right. Your wife had to step in and partner him.'

Bowker nodded but said nothing.

'How many millions of dollars have been spent on that bastard, Greg?' she continued, her voice rising again. 'Thirty-one years in jail, police investigations of his misdeeds and now his own murder. How much more will be wasted locking up someone whose only crime was doing the world a massive favour? Why dig any further?'

'Because it's my job, Marilyn,' Bowker said.

*   *   *

'What do you reckon?' Holmes said, as he started the car.

'Dunno.' Bowker dragged on his seatbelt. 'Don't think Jimmy had anything to do with it. You see how quickly he wanted to know who killed Weston? That was an automatic reaction. He doesn't know.'

'And his mother?'

'Not sure she would've crossed paths with Olsen or Weston.

We know Weston bought a hotdog at the Back-To, and we have a photo of him in Manang at 1.55. If Marilyn had lunch with Jim and then went home, she'd have been well gone before Weston and Olsen arrived.'

'Where to now?'

Bowker checked his watch. 'It'll be recess at school. Let's have a quick chat with Bernadette.'

When they arrived, she was on yard duty at the front of the school, bypassing the need for them to track her down through the office. She was in the quadrangle, standing among raised timber flowerboxes and chatting with a group of very young children. As the detectives approached, she hustled the children along, and they sprinted away towards the playground.

'Nice day to be outside, Bernadette,' Bowker said. 'Sun shining, breeze blowing, birds singing.'

She smiled as she nibbled on an apple. 'Yeah, hard to imagine how brutal summer can be when you get days like this.' She looked at Holmes. 'Ever experienced a Mallee summer, Detective?'

'Born and raised in Murrayville, so I've got a fair idea.'

Bernadette touched him lightly on the arm. 'Sorry. Didn't know that. Thought you were probably a city slicker.'

'No,' Holmes said, with a chuckle. 'Got red sand in my veins. Probably will end up in the bush when I retire.'

Bowker became more serious. 'Now, Bernadette. Can I take you back to August eighth, the Saturday of the Back-To? You and Travis spent the afternoon over at the racecourse. Correct?'

'That's right.'

'Can anyone verify that?'

'Yes,' Bernadette replied, her eyes darting between the detectives.

'Travis and I supervised the kids' activities for much of the day. Novelty races and things like that. The rest of the time, we sat with other teachers and had a few drinks. There are plenty of people who can confirm we were there all day.' She frowned at Bowker. 'Why? What's all this about?'

'We've found out who killed your father, Bernadette,' Bowker said. 'We've got a confession. But we think the killer may have had help moving the body to Cocamba. We're verifying people's movements on that day. It's just routine. We don't believe you or Travis were involved.'

Slowly, Bernadette sat down on the edge of the flowerbox. 'So, who did it?'

'The girl he tutored in maths. The Kate from his diary, who you helped me track down.'

'Kate Parker killed him?' Bernadette asked, her voice high with disbelief.

'No. Kate Olsen,' Bowker corrected.

'Olsen is her married name. She's Andy and Lorraine Parker's daughter.'

Bowker's mouth dropped open as he digested the sudden implications. 'Kate's maiden name is Parker?'

Bernadette nodded. 'Katherine's her proper name, but she's always been called Kate.'

Bowker's mind was running at a thousand miles an hour, connecting all the new dots that had suddenly appeared on his page.

'Why would she kill my father?' Bernadette asked, but before Bowker could answer, she must've read his expression. 'Not her too!' Her head dropped onto her chest.

'I'm afraid so, Bernadette,' Bowker said. 'When he babysat her.'

She looked up, tears running down her cheeks. 'He deserved to die, didn't he?'

Bowker didn't answer, but he put a reassuring hand on her shoulder.

With a shake of her head, Bernadette got to her feet. 'I'd better get back to my yard duty. It'd be just my luck if some kid had an accident while I was distracted.'

'Can we get someone to relieve you while you come to terms with all this?' Holmes asked.

'No, I'll be right. Just never thought my opinion of my father could get any lower, but here we are.' She smiled weakly.

Bowker inhaled deeply. 'Bernadette, do you know if Kate Parker has any relation to the local copper? Shane Parker?'

Bernadette shrugged. 'Don't know. Pretty common name, Parker. Lots of them around.' With a feeble wave, she wandered off into the playground.

Bowker looked at Holmes. 'Fucking Parker! It all fits now. He told me he applied for Manang on the recommendation of family who used to live up here.'

Holmes raised his eyebrows. 'He's a copper. Surely he wouldn't let himself get tied up in something like this?'

'That's what we're going to find out,' Bowker said, as they walked back to their car. 'Shane Parker's prints are all over the scene at Cocamba, but we put that down to his slack protocols when he found the body. I reckon those prints were from when they dumped Weston at the silos.'

'Do we call him back for questioning?' Holmes asked.

'Nope. We'll get our ducks lined up here before we talk to him.' Bowker thought for a moment. 'It now makes sense that the lazy bastard rang us last night asking where the investigation was placed and whether he needed to come home early. The prick would've already known we'd arrested Olsen. She would've called him to tell him and warn him we were looking for an accomplice.'

'Also makes sense why he was so keen to put Jimmy Cobb in the frame.' Holmes paused at the car door. 'Everything seems to fit. But what if it turns out he's got no relation to Kate Olsen?'

'It's him,' Bowker said determinedly. 'I'll bet my left knacker on it. In fact, I'll throw in my right one as well.'

Holmes smiled. 'Maybe you should check Rachael's opinion on eunuchs first.'

CHAPTER 27

On their return to the police station, Bowker immediately called Rachael, who he thought was likely tied up with kids at her kindergarten. He was preparing to leave a voicemail when she answered. 'Is this a booty call?' she said, with a chuckle.

'Wish it was,' he replied, smiling to himself. 'I thought you'd be with the kids somewhere.'

'Alison's reading them a story, so I've got a few minutes to have a coffee and clear my head before we start making paper hats. I presume you're still living in the afterglow of busting the Weston case. After I got off the phone last night, I couldn't stop wondering how many other girls' lives Weston has destroyed. We'd never heard of Kate Olsen.'

'That's why I'm ringing. I just found out that her maiden name is Parker. Kicking myself that we didn't nail that down earlier. Slack detective work.'

There was silence on the line for a few seconds. 'Parker? As in Senior Constable Parker?'

'That's my thinking,' Bowker said.

'Remember that night in the pub a fortnight or so ago? I had a chat with him while you and Darren were off talking to your old footy coach.'

'Yeah. You said you had a heart-to-heart.'

'He said his mum was from the district and she encouraged

him to apply for a cushy job in a one-man police station. I'm pretty sure he said the family originally owned a farm on the Chinky-Nyah West Road. This might be stretching the memory a bit, but I reckon he said his parents were Andy and Lorraine.'

'Bingo!' Bowker said excitedly. 'Same parents as Kate Parker, or Kate Olsen, as she is now. So obviously, Shane's her brother.'

'That would be the Katherine he was talking about. She was quite a few years older, apparently. Went to school at Nyah West, then in Swan Hill.'

'Yeah. Mary McKillop College.'

'I think Shane said he was born in the Western District.'

'That's right,' Bowker replied. 'They sold their place up here and bought a sheep farm down near Hamilton.'

'Anything else I can help you with, big boy?'

Bowker chuckled. 'Yeah, but unfortunately, it's not possible over the phone.'

After the conclusion of the call, Bowker and Holmes discussed their options. They decided Holmes would ring Forensics requesting a team attend the next day to go over Parker's Commodore, the vehicle they felt would most likely have transported Weston's body. Holmes's other task was to track down Parker's mobile phone service provider and request a copy of his incoming and outgoing calls for the date of Weston's murder and the days that followed. Meanwhile, Bowker would call Damien Cowton, the Netcor worker he'd interviewed earlier in the week.

Holmes adjourned to the kitchen to make his calls. It took Bowker three tries to get hold of Cowton, with his phone going to voicemail on the first two attempts. Bowker feared the maintenance team were in a remote area and out of mobile reception, but he held some hope that Cowton was involved in a brief task and was only temporarily away from his phone.

The third attempt found Cowton atop a power pole removing an electrocuted possum that had caused a local blackout during a thunderstorm the night before. He apologised for the missed calls before describing the 360-degree panorama around him. 'Pity I haven't got an iPhone, Detective, otherwise I could show the view with Facetime. Can see right across the sunset country.'

'Whereabouts are you?' Bowker asked.

'Told you. Top of a pole,' Cowton replied, without a hint of humour.

'No, I mean where are you geographically?'

Cowton laughed at his own misinterpretation. 'Halfway between Torrita and Underbool. Anyway, what can I do for you, mate?'

'Just got another couple of questions about what happened when you found the body at Cocamba,' Bowker said.

'Okay. Go for it.'

'When the local copper arrived, what was his reaction to the body?'

'Not as repulsed as we were, that's for sure.'

'What do you mean by that?'

'Well, I spewed my guts out, and Cam went so white I was sure he was about to faint. The copper just looked at the body and basically went *Ho-hum, dead guy with no face.* I suppose the police get desensitised to these things after a while.'

So much for Parker's account of staggering around when he saw Weston's body, Bowker thought. 'Did he put his hands on the silo to steady himself?'

'Nah. The body didn't seem to worry him at all. Besides, I don't think he wanted to touch anything if he could avoid it.'

'Fingerprints?' Bowker asked.

'Probably. But he was also whingeing about his sore thumb. He'd cut it on a beer glass breaking up a fight at the Manang pub, apparently.'

At that moment, Bowker's mind finally grasped what his subconscious had been desperate to tell him since the start of the investigation. He put that aside for later and continued his questions. 'You mentioned something about a dead animal on the ground when you first arrived in the truck. Something you thought was creating the smell until you found Weston's body. Did you get a look at what it was?'

'It was a hare,' Cowton replied. 'A big bastard. Been there for a couple of days, at least. Covered in flies and maggots.'

'Wasn't an echidna?'

'Definitely wasn't an echidna, mate. Unless an echidna has big floppy ears.' Cowton chuckled.

Bowker thanked Cowton for his time, ended the call, and immediately punched in Erin O'Meara's personal number.

'Calling me to tell me when my Johnnie Walker is due to arrive, are you, Gregory?' O'Meara said, without a greeting.

'It's on its way, Erin.' He smiled as he heard her trying to suppress a cough. 'Just need something else. Won't take long.'

'Shit, Greg. This unit has done nothing for the last month but analyse stuff from your investigation. Do you want us to come out and do the legwork for you as well?' She paused for a moment and cleared her throat. 'Okay, what do you want?'

'Can you get the Weston murder case up on your computer?

More specifically, the prints lifted at the scene where the body was found?'

Bowker could hear the clacking of computer keys. 'Okay,' she said, 'got 'em. Five sets. Which ones do you want me to look at?'

'Shane Parker's.'

'The dumb-arse copper who doesn't understand crime scene protocols?'

'Yeah. That's him. Have you got a print from his right thumb?'

'Got a couple, clear as crystal. Why?'

'Does the print show any evidence of the skin being sliced, cut or sutured?'

'Don't you think we would've put that in the forensic report?' O'Meara replied, before coughing and spitting out the product.

Bowker tried not to imagine where the phlegm had ended up. 'Just checking.'

'That's the second time you've rung up to check on our work. I'm starting to get a complex.'

'Yeah, well, the Allender prints were missing, so I was right on that one,' Bowker replied, with a chuckle.

'We haven't made a mistake with Parker's prints, so we're one-all.' O'Meara paused for a moment. 'Just out of interest, why the question about a cut?'

'Keep this under your hat, because it'll possibly result in charges against a serving police officer,' Bowker said seriously, knowing full well that O'Meara's sharp mind had already deduced the implications of his query. 'When the body was discovered, Parker had a badly cut thumb, so there's no way he left those prints then. In fact, witnesses say he had the thumb bandaged at that time.'

'Obviously, he left them sometime earlier,' O'Meara said.

'Yeah.'

'I see by my screen that we finally got a match for those mystery prints and DNA. A Katherine Lorraine Olsen.'

'Yeah. She's confessed to the murder. But we reckon she had help from Parker moving the body.'

'Very obliging policeman,' O'Meara said dryly.

'He's her brother.'

'I need that whisky!' was all O'Meara said.

Bowker's next call was to the local hospital, where the duty nurse consulted casualty records and confirmed that Parker had been treated for a badly cut thumb at 6 p.m. on August 9.

Just after Bowker finished writing up notes of his calls, Holmes returned to the office with his own tidings. 'I got lucky,' he said. 'Parker's with Telstra, so I didn't have to ring around a dozen other providers. They're going to email me a record of incoming and outgoing calls for his phone. The bird had his account on the screen in front of her, so I asked her about any calls on August eighth.' Holmes pushed a sheet of paper over the desk to Bowker and pointed to a number. 'He got a call from this number at 4.07 in the afternoon.' He moved his finger to a second number. 'Rang this one that same evening, and according to the Telstra sheila, there were multiple calls back and forward with it over the following days. She couldn't ID it, though. It's with another carrier.'

Bowker flipped through his notebook. 'I would've thought that second number would belong to Kate Olsen. There'd be no surprise if there was a flurry of calls there. But that's not the number Olsen gave me.' He pointed at Holmes's sheet. 'The 4.07 call is from a local landline number. And I'll bet my arse it came from Jimmy Cobb's house.'

Holmes smiled. 'Better be careful about betting your arse. You may have already lost your balls. But you're right.' He took back his sheet of paper and flipped it over. 'The Telstra bird said it belonged to a J. M. Cobb on Bolton-Kooloonong Road.'

Bowker laughed. 'Bingo.'

Holmes tapped his knuckles on the table. 'Maybe it wasn't Kate Olsen using that phone. Maybe it was Weston calling for help. Or Jimmy Cobb, maybe.'

'Calling Parker's mobile? No way. Neither would know his number. They'd call the station or triple zero if they wanted the police.' Bowker shook his head. 'No, it was Kate Olsen who used that phone, trying to avoid a call from Bolton being linked to her own number.' He grinned broadly. 'We're all over this, Sherlock. All over it like a fat kid on a cream bun.'

Holmes chuckled. 'You find out anything of value from the Netcor bloke?'

'Yeah. Remember that story Parker gave us about how he nearly flaked when he saw Weston's body, then steadied himself against the silo? It was all bullshit. Cowton said Parker was cool as a cucumber and didn't touch a thing. He also mentioned Parker's bandaged thumb, and I finally realised what had been eating away in the back of my mind since we started this investigation.'

A light went on in Holmes's eyes. 'The prints lifted by the techs showed no sign of an injury. They were left there before he cut his thumb. Fuck me, how did we miss that?'

'I double-checked with O'Meara to make sure there were no blemishes on his thumbprint, then rang the local hospital. Their records showed Parker attended late on Sunday the ninth.' Bowker leaned back in his chair and clasped his hands behind his head. 'I think we've got the timeline pretty close. Olsen comes to Manang for the Back-To, and to possibly catch up with her little brother. Sees Weston at the racecourse, confronts him, is fobbed off, and finally follows him to Jimmy Cobb's. There's another confrontation, where she shoots him. She panics and rings her brother for help. He arrives, they transport the body to Cocamba. The next night, he cuts his thumb breaking up a fight at the pub.'

'My guess is they used the Commodore to transport the body, but Forensics will nail that down tomorrow, hopefully,' Holmes said.

'We're still waiting on the lab report for Olsen's Laser, but like you, my money is on the Commodore out there in the carport.' Bowker smiled at Holmes. 'Come on, I'll shout you lunch. Then we might head off on a wild goose chase.'

*   *   *

They were travelling very slowly when they passed the Myall reserve. 'It was just along here, somewhere near that culvert,' Bowker said, pointing to the scrub to the side. 'The crows lifted into that taller mallee tree over there, remember? You had to swerve a bit to miss the roadkill. May as well stop here.'

Holmes pulled the police vehicle to the side of the road, and they alighted, their suited figures a strange juxtaposition to the ancient landscape. Bowker searched the verge on one side of the road, Holmes the other. It was Holmes who found what they were looking for.

'Over here, Greg,' he called. 'There's not much left of him, but more than we'll need.'

Bowker wandered over and surveyed the echidna's remains in

the lightly grassed sand. 'Must've been dragged off the road by the crows. Or foxes, maybe.'

'Not freshly killed, but hasn't been here for months either, by the look of it,' Holmes replied.

Bowker walked back to the car and returned with a medium-sized evidence bag. 'There's a one-in-a-hundred chance that this poor bastard was run over by Parker, but if its DNA matches the spikes in his tyres, then we can place his Commodore on this road. Won't tell us exactly when, but it will help build our case. He'll have a lot of trouble explaining why the fuck he was on this backroad a mile from Jimmy Cobb's.'

Bowker held the bag open, while Holmes lifted the hollowed-out monotreme with a stick and carefully dropped it inside. 'Be ironic if a prick helped convict the prick,' Bowker joked, as he zip-locked the bag.

'Be fuckin' karma from the echidna's point of view, too,' Holmes replied.

*   *   *

The forensic team arrived at eleven the next morning, in bright sunshine between icy skiffs. A roaring southerly had rendered the day decidedly unpleasant. Over the road from the police station, the wind howled loudly between the silos, but thankfully, recent showers had settled the dust. While it appeared Parker had taken the Commodore's keys with him to Mildura, its tailgate was unlocked, allowing the forensic technicians easy access. Bowker welcomed them, thanked them for attending on a weekend, explained his suspicions concerning the car, and adjourned to the office, leaving them to their work.

When Bowker entered, Holmes was standing facing the door, his backside leaning against the desk. 'Email just arrived from Forensics about the Olsen cars. The old Magna wagon came up clean in the sense of anything relating to our case. Full of dirt and dust that doesn't seem to have been disturbed in yonks.'

Bowker smiled. 'How do Forensics define yonks?'

'Months, at least,' Holmes replied, with a grin.

Circling the end of the desk, Bowker sat in the office chair. 'And the Laser hatchback?'

Holmes stood up and turned to face him. 'Absolutely no traces of blood or cleaning agents on the rear deck. But there was a very faint smear of blood in the driver's footwell. The techs were able to lift enough to match it to Adrian Weston.'

'So, the driver was at the scene, but it's highly unlikely the vehicle transported the body.'

Holmes pulled up a chair. 'That's the way I read it. Looking more and more like the Commodore, isn't it?'

'Unless he used the police car,' Bowker said. 'That'd be a bit cheeky, though, wouldn't it? Using a police vehicle in the commission of a crime?'

'What's cheeky is a policeman being involved in a crime in the first place,' Holmes replied.

Bowker grinned. 'You're not wrong there, my friend.' He leaned back in his chair. 'But you have to remember that from Parker's point of view, he and his sister were home free. Kate Olsen's connection to Weston was unknown, and so far back in history that her name would never be raised in this investigation. Particularly when there were so many more obvious suspects. And if Parker believed his sister was at arm's length from the case, then there was no reason for anyone to suspect he was involved. He could afford to be slack.' Bowker laughed. 'And that comes naturally to him, anyway.'

'His assumptions were pretty right, you know. If we hadn't found that teacher's chronicle, we'd still be pissing into the wind.'

'Can't put anything over the Bobbsey twins from Homicide,' Bowker said, with a smirk.

Holmes chuckled. 'You read too much *Dave Robicheaux*.'

There was a knock on the glass door, and a forensic tech entered. He dropped an evidence bag on the desk between the detectives. 'We're just about to start testing the Commodore for blood and cleaning products. Found this wedged down below the flat tyre in the spare wheel well.'

Bowker picked up the bag and stared at the gold neck chain, spattered with blood. 'Well, this solves one mystery. Any clues on how it got down there?'

'The mag wheel is slightly too wide for the well, so the cover sits up an inch or two. If a body was transported in there as you suggest, this chain might've snagged in the gap and ripped loose as the body was dragged out. It would've dropped down into the well, and vibrations from the vehicle would've caused it to move under the tyre.'

Bowker nodded. 'You blokes are solving one mystery after another in this case.'

The tech pointed his thumb outside. 'Don't refer to us as blokes when Leanne is around. She gets a bit touchy about people assuming this is all men's work.'

'Note taken,' Bowker said. He slid open the bottom drawer of the filing cabinet and removed the sealed bag containing the echidna remains. 'Got a present for you too. Can you grab sample spines out of that flat tyre for comparison with this baby? If they match, it'll put our mate near the scene of the crime.'

The tech took the bag, then pointed to the necklace. 'We'll need that back too. The lab has to analyse the blood and check if there are prints.'

'Just a tick,' Holmes said, as he took out his phone. 'I'll take a pic. Might need to show a suspect.' He took several photographs, before the technician left the office carrying the two plastic bags.

Bowker put his hands behind his head. 'For days and days, we had nothing, Sherlock. Now it's all fitting together like pieces in a Swiss clock.'

'A week ago, I thought we may not solve—'

Holmes's response was interrupted by a chorus of raised voices outside. He climbed to his feet and looked out the window.

'Fuck,' he said. 'Parker's back!'

CHAPTER 28

The moment Bowker and Holmes exited the police station, Parker was in their faces. 'What the fuck is going on here?' he asked angrily. 'Why are these clowns all over my car?'

'Better come inside, Shane,' Bowker said, touching him on the arm.

Parker pulled away. 'Not until you call off the dogs.'

'Just come inside,' Bowker replied, more sternly. 'This team is here until their job is done.'

Parker shook his head, then reluctantly followed them into the station.

'Sit down,' Bowker said, walking behind the desk. Parker remained standing. Holmes leaned against the filing cabinet.

'Back earlier than you thought, mate?' Bowker asked, as he sat down.

'Missed the place after a couple of days,' Parker replied sarcastically.

Holmes folded his arms. 'Bit worried we were getting close to the truth about Weston's death?'

'What are you talking about? You got your killer, according to your esteemed colleague here.' Parker nodded towards Bowker. 'Some woman from down at Horsham.'

'Let's cut the bullshit,' Bowker said abruptly. 'We know Kate Olsen is your sister, so let's get that on the table first.'

Parker raised his eyebrows. 'She had every right to kill the bastard. Do you know what he did to her when she was just a kid?'

'She told us,' Bowker replied. 'Absolute tragedy, and it makes me sick to my guts. But it doesn't give her the right to murder him.'

Parker swiped a hand down his face. 'Why can't you just let it go, Bowker? She's a good woman, and what's to be gained by putting her in prison? How wrong can it really be to exterminate that prick? Even the Bible talks about an eye for an eye.'

'It also says *Thou shalt not kill*,' Holmes replied dryly.

Bowker leaned forward, hands folded on the desk in front of him. 'Let's get to your part in all this, Shane. After she shot Weston, your sister rang you and asked for help.'

Parker gave a forced smile. 'What are you talking about?'

'She called you from Jimmy Cobb's house,' Bowker replied. 'We've got your phone records from Telstra. And don't try and say it was Jimmy calling, because there's no way he would've known your private number.'

'Okay. She called me,' Parker shot back defiantly. 'Doesn't mean I helped her. My advice was to get the hell out of there.' He lifted his hands, palms facing out. 'I know as a policeman I should've investigated, and probably placed her under arrest, but she's my sister. My family loyalties took priority.' He shrugged. 'Advising her to flee the scene will probably cost me my job, but right now, I couldn't give a dead rat's clacker. Especially if it means I get out of this shithole.'

'You did more than tell her to flee the scene,' Bowker said. 'Your prints were found at Cocamba with Weston's body.'

Parker rolled his eyes. 'I fucked up the crime scene protocols and forgot to wear gloves. We've already been over that! Why bring it up again now?'

'Because you didn't fuck up when Weston's remains were found,' Holmes said. 'You fucked up when you and your sister dumped his body.'

Parker looked at the ceiling and expelled air through his lips in mock amusement. 'Pfft. Forensics got a new whiz-bang process, have they? Can date fingerprints?'

'No, but they can detect whether a print has a cut or a scar on it.' Bowker folded his arms across his chest. 'You know the one I mean, Shane. The one you got when your thumb was sliced by a beer glass, which was still healing a week or so later when you pretended to see Weston's body for the first time.'

Parker slumped down into a seat, dropping his head into his hands.

Holmes took out his phone and found the photo of the blood-spattered necklace. 'You might be interested in what the techs found in your car a few minutes ago. Was worn by Weston on the day he was killed. We've got at least two witnesses who described him wearing it.' He handed the phone to Parker.

'Where was this?' Parker said quietly, his bravado evaporating.

'Under the flat tyre in the back of the Commodore,' Holmes said. 'Must've got snagged when you dragged the body out at the silos. The techs are running tests for blood and cleaning agents in your car right now. What do you reckon they'll find?'

Parker closed his eyes and didn't answer.

'In summary,' Bowker said, 'we've got your sister contacting you, your prints on the silo at the time the victim was dumped, and evidence that his body spent time in your car. That all adds up to being an accessory to murder. Maximum five years, or up to half the time your sister gets if she's given more than ten. It's pretty serious stuff, Shane, so it's probably in your interests to come clean with us.'

Parker inhaled deeply and sat back in his chair. 'Okay. I knew Kate was coming up to the Back-To and was planning to drop in to say hello. Hadn't seen her for nearly a year. Not since I've been in this shithole, anyway. I got this call from a strange number, and it was Kate saying she'd followed this bloke out to Cobb's farm, and after an altercation, she'd grabbed a loaded shotgun from the shed and accidentally shot him.'

Bowker nodded. 'What'd you do?'

'She's my sister, so I told her to sit tight and I'd be straight out to Cobb's. She gave me directions, and I drove as fast as I could to get out there. Fucked a tyre in the process.'

'You didn't take the police car?' Holmes asked.

Parker looked at him with steely eyes. 'Of course I didn't take the fuckin' police car. I wasn't going out there as a policeman. I was going out there as her brother. My aim was to get her out of the place while all the attention was on Manang at the Back-To. There was so little traffic, the police car would've stuck out like dog's balls on the back roads.'

'So, when did you hatch the plan to dump the body at Cocamba?' Bowker asked.

'When I got out there. I figured we had two options: leave the body where it was and let Jimmy Cobb explain how the fuck it got there, or take it to Cocamba and let people think it was a revenge killing for Yvonne Bryant. To be quite honest, I thought by leaving it at Cocamba, you Homicide blokes would grill all the suspects, get nowhere, and record the killing as unsolved. Thought because Weston was such a lowlife, you'd just go through the motions.' Parker ran his fingers through his hair. 'But you just kept at it, and at it, and at it. In the end, I was forced to push you towards Jimmy Cobb by showing you where Weston was shot.'

Bowker shook his head. 'Then you were happy to see an innocent man – an innocent man with an intellectual disability, no less – go down for Weston's murder?'

Parker frowned. 'Not happy, no. But it was a better alternative than letting my sister go to jail. Especially for doing everyone a favour by ridding the world of that piece of shit.'

Bowker was becoming visibly annoyed. 'You're a policeman, Shane. It's your duty to uphold the law, family or no family.'

Parker stared at him. 'Let's swap places, Detective. Say it was your missus who rang you up and pleaded for help for something she'd done. Would you do your duty and charge her, or would you find a way to fix the situation? Especially if what she'd done made the world a better place?'

Bowker didn't answer.

'Just as I thought,' Parker said. 'Get off your fuckin' high horse.'

'So,' Holmes said, to break the tension, 'you used the Commodore to transport the body down to Cocamba?'

'Wouldn't fit in the Laser, would it?' Parker replied. 'Not without a lot of manipulation, anyway.'

'Why'd you drive Weston's car into the dam?' Bowker asked.

'There were too many cars for us to remove from the scene. If we were going to move the spotlight to Cocamba, we couldn't leave a car sitting around at Cobb's.'

'It would be found eventually,' Holmes said.

Parker shrugged. 'Not necessarily. Those dams are filled by the

Grampians pipeline. They don't dry up when the channels stop running like in the old days. Besides, if the dam did dry up at some time down the track, any trail for the killing would've long gone cold. And I'd be way gone as well. At that stage, it would be up to Cobb to explain how the car got in his dam.'

Bowker looked at Holmes. 'You can do the honours, Sherlock.'

Holmes stood up. 'Shane Parker, it is my intention to charge you with being an accessory to the murder of Adrian Weston.'

Parker exploded. 'This is all bullshit! Why can't you just let the whole fuckin' thing drop? Weston deserved what he got, and my sister shouldn't have to pay a price after what he did to her. This is not fuckin' justice. Justice would've been to keep the bastard locked up until he died. In fact, justice would've been to hang the prick when he was found guilty.' He took a deep breath. 'Weston should've been happy he got an extra thirty-one years before he got his right whack.' He pointed at Bowker. 'And I'll tell you one thing, Bowker. I'm not going to prison. No way! I know what happens to coppers in there.'

He jumped to his feet and made for the door. Moving quickly, Holmes grabbed him by the arm and pushed him back into his chair.

'Don't be stupid, Shane,' Holmes said. 'You can't run away from this.'

'I'll have the keys to the police vehicle, please,' Bowker said. 'Since you've been charged with a criminal offence, you're automatically stood down from the force pending the outcome of any relevant trials. I may as well have your Commodore keys as well.'

Parker retrieved the keys from his jeans pocket and threw them angrily on the desk. There was a gentle knock on the exterior glass door, and Holmes turned to see one of the forensic technicians beckoning him outside.

Bowker nodded to him. 'Can you get an update out there? I'll take a written statement from Shane.'

As he closed the door behind himself, Holmes asked the technician, 'Anything more of interest?'

'Yeah. Looks like some pretty potent cleaner was used on the carpet, but we found traces of blood in some of the stitching. We've taken samples. Found a couple of strands of human hair hooked on a plastic fastener holding the mouldings around the tail-light, too.'

Holmes nodded. 'Good stuff.'

'We've also removed three echidna spines from the flat tyre for comparison with the remains you supplied. Should have the results back to you in a couple of days.'

'Before you go, we've just arrested Senior Constable Parker on suspicion of being an accessory to the murder. Can you take a DNA swab, please?'

The tech nodded and departed to his van to retrieve a DNA kit. When Holmes returned to the office, Parker was sitting opposite Bowker, who was transcribing his statement.

'They found traces of blood and heavy-duty cleaner in the back of your Commodore, Shane,' Holmes said. 'They've taken a couple of hair samples as well.'

Parker stared into space. 'Should never have come to this fuckin' hole. Nothing's gone right since I got here. Weather's so fuckin' hot you think your head's gonna explode half the time. Full of inbred hillbillies who think the greatest event in the world is half an inch of bloody rain. Thought it would be the biggest bludge ever, but fuck me, did I get that one wrong. Bloody girlfriend pissed off on me, and now I'm in this shit.' He shook his head. 'You try to do the right thing, and what do you get for it? Fuck nothing. Thank you, fuckin' Manangatang.'

Another bloke playing the victim, Holmes thought, but said nothing.

After a moment or two, the tech entered and took a swab from the inside of Parker's cheeks. He gave the thumbs up to Bowker as he slid the sample into a plastic vial. 'We'll be gone in five minutes, unless there's anything else.'

Bowker stood up and shook his hand. 'Thanks, mate. Safe trip home.'

Holmes walked the tech to the door while Bowker continued taking Parker's statement. Five minutes later, the forensic van departed, as a violent squall passed over, painting the streets of the little town white with marble-sized hailstones.

*   *   *

The drumming of hail on the Colorbond roof made hearing difficult inside the police station, with Bowker and Parker practically yelling to make themselves heard. Within minutes, however, the heavy shower had disappeared as quickly as it'd arrived, the sun slowly breaking through outside.

'While you blokes are finishing that, I might slip into the dunny,' Holmes said, as he walked towards the room at the back, which held a cell and a toilet.

Bowker picked up the sheet of paper on which Holmes had noted the calls to and from Parker's phone. He pointed to the mobile number associated with numerous incoming and outgoing calls. 'Whose number is this?'

'It belongs to Kate. Why ask me when you already know?'

Bowker frowned and flipped open his notebook. He tapped his finger on the number Kate Olsen had supplied when they first spoke in Horsham. 'Your sister gave me this number. Who does it belong to?'

Parker closed his eyes. 'The bakery in Horsham. I sometimes ring that mobile if she's not answering her own.'

Bowker rubbed his chin. So that was why nothing suspicious had come up in the analysis of the number she'd given him. And that was why the phone had only pinged the Horsham tower and nothing further north.

'I don't feel very well,' Parker said, opening his mouth wide and gulping in breaths. 'Think I'm gonna spew.' He slapped his right hand over his mouth, stood up, and made for the toilet in the back.

'Sherlock's in there,' Bowker called out. 'You'll have to use the toilet in the house.'

Dry-retching into his hand, Parker changed direction and hurried through the connecting door into the police residence. Bowker heard heaving sounds coming from the house as Holmes returned.

'Where's our mate?' Holmes asked.

Bowker pointed over his shoulder with his thumb. 'Driving the porcelain bus. In the end, it's all got a bit too much for him, I think.'

'He's certainly shitting himself about going to jail,' Holmes replied, an instant before the room was filled with the unmistakeable sound of a V8 rumbling to life.

'Fuck me! The bastard must have a spare key,' Bowker said urgently. He jumped to his feet, snatching the police car keys from the end of the desk.

By the time they leapt into their car, Parker was on Wattle Street, accelerating quickly past the shops. As they turned the corner to follow, they saw him cross the main intersection.

'He's heading south,' Bowker said, as he turned on the siren and flashers.

'Heading home to Hamilton would be my bet,' Holmes replied.

Once they cleared the town, the speedo read a hundred and forty kilometres per hour and increasing. Bowker could see Parker's car in the distance but didn't feel he was gaining. 'He's going like a cut cat. Has to be doing a hundred and sixty per hour.'

'Back it off, I reckon, Greg,' Holmes advised. 'The road's not built for these speeds, and there's still piles of ice here and there. And don't forget he's on three mags and a bald standard tyre.'

Bowker took his foot off the accelerator, and the vehicle immediately started to slow. 'Yeah, you're right, Sherlock.' He shook his head as he turned off the siren and flashing lights. 'Just don't like the prick putting one over on us. Especially when he's a shit copper and drags us all down with him.'

Holmes was quiet for a moment. 'I'm a bit worried about you, mate. I reckon you might be taking this whole inquiry a bit too personally. It's like you see it as unfinished business from thirty years ago. It's a different case, Greg. Related, but separate.'

Bowker pondered this. 'S'pose it's brought in a lot of the same people. Brought in a lot of memories.' He looked at Holmes. 'One of my greatest satisfactions as a copper was solving Yvonne Bryant's murder. Against all the odds, we nailed the killer. I guess

I've felt that if we didn't solve this one, it would be like undoing some of that effort.'

There was silence in the car for a while.

'Radio Sea Lake and get them to pull up Parker when he goes through there,' Bowker said. 'He must be headed that way. There's nowhere else to go.'

They had now decelerated to the speed limit, the wet road glistening in the sunshine. Holmes picked up the radio handpiece while they followed a slight bend in the road. As the straight stretch beyond came into view, he slowly placed it back in its cradle. 'Fuck me!' was all he said.

Bowker braked as he approached the accident site, stopping in the middle of the road with his blue and reds flashing. Parts of the Commodore were strewn across a large area, and there was a long gouge in the bitumen where the blown tyre had rolled off the rim. The V8 wagon lay on its pancaked roof among mallee scrub thirty metres from the road, steam rising from the front.

Even from the most cursory observation of the scene, the sequence of events was obvious. Parker's high-powered Commodore had blown its driver's side front tyre at high speed. It had flipped and bounced numerous times, shedding countless components on its final odyssey to disintegration.

Holmes ran to the vehicle and squatted down on the driver's side. Bowker didn't need to be told Parker's fate. As he looked across, Holmes leaned with his forearms atop the overturned vehicle, the Cocamba silos towering behind him.

CHAPTER 29

Tuesday was Bowker's first genuine day off in nearly three weeks, and his first opportunity to relax without an investigation annexing his brain by stealth. But the Weston inquiry wouldn't dissipate like other solved cases. This one was different.

An open newspaper sat in front of him on the kitchen table as he stared into space. Rachael was quick to notice his ruminative mood when she sat down opposite. 'You're normally high as a kite when you crack a big case, Greg. What's wrong?'

Bowker raised his eyebrows and shrugged. 'Normally it's a win for the good guys, Rach, where the bad guy's been caught and will pay the price in prison. But the Weston case isn't that black and white. If we hadn't worked so hard to solve the case, what would've been the likely outcome? Weston would've still been dead, much to the community's satisfaction. But Kate Olsen would've remained happily working in her Horsham bakery, and Shane Parker would still be alive.'

Rachael reached across and took his hand. 'You're a homicide detective, Greg. It's your duty to solve murders. You can't just pick and choose.'

'Sometimes I wish we could. Whichever way you look at it, solving that murder destroyed one life and ended another's. Is that justice?' He spread his hands. 'I'm not so sure.'

'You're becoming too maudlin over this case,' Rachael said quietly.

'In the cool light of day, regardless of the terrible things Weston did to her, Kate Olsen took a human life. Her brother covered for her, even though he'd sworn an oath to uphold the law. The outcomes have been tragic, but you can't hold yourself responsible.'

Bowker was about to reply when his phone rang beside him. He looked at the screen and saw the caller was Erin O'Meara.

'Sorry to bother you at home,' O'Meara said, 'but I thought you'd like the results of our work in Manangatang last Saturday. I rang Spencer Street, and they told me you had a few well-earned days off.'

'Appreciate that, Erin,' Bowker replied. 'Final pieces in the puzzle. What have you got?'

'Blood found on the gold neck chain and on the carpet in the rear of Parker's car belongs to Adrian Weston. Two strands of hair retrieved from the wagon DNA-tested as belonging to him as well. Given the strength of the cleaners applied to its carpets, there's little doubt Weston was transported in that car and Parker was trying to clean up the mess.'

'So, our assumptions were right,' Bowker replied, with a slight grin.

'Yep. But you get the gold star for your hunch about the echidna. DNA from the samples the techs took from that flat tyre are a match for the dead animal you retrieved.' She laughed. 'First time we've been asked to do DNA testing on a prick that wasn't a human.'

'You're a bloody genius,' Bowker said. 'I better get that bottle of whisky over to you *tout de suite*.'

'Are you sitting down?' O'Meara asked.

Bowker frowned. 'Yeah, sitting at the kitchen table. Why?'

As O'Meara replied, Bowker's mouth dropped open. He slowly leaned back in his chair, his left hand moving to the back of his head, where he grabbed a fistful of hair. Finally, he took a deep breath. 'Thanks for that, Erin. I might have to hit your whisky and buy you another bottle.' He nodded, then tapped the end-call button on his phone. Dropping the mobile on the table, he stared up at the ceiling and exhaled loudly. 'Fuck me,' he said, to nobody in particular.

'What is it, Greg?' Rachael asked.

'They sequenced Shane Parker's DNA sample. He's not Kate Olsen's brother.'

Rachael stared at him, bewildered. 'Then why—'

'He's her son,' Bowker said.

Rachael shook her head. 'But that means she would've been just a kid when—'

'Adrian Weston is the father.'

Rachael's mouth was agape. 'The rape?' she asked, after a moment.

Bowker nodded. 'Yeah, I assume.'

It was all too much to contemplate, so they sat for what seemed like minutes before Bowker broke the silence. 'Her pregnancy is probably why they up and left the district. Strict Catholics, and all that. Weston would've been arrested by the time they found out, so there was nothing to gain by going to the police.'

Rachael closed her eyes. 'So, they left the district and bought in down near Hamilton. Presumably, Lorraine and Kate didn't move to that area until after Kate's child was born and a new family history was fabricated, with Lorraine being an older-age mother and baby Shane a little brother for Kate.'

'I've heard of the same thing happening before.'

'You think Shane was aware?'

'Don't reckon. But who knows? Doesn't really matter now, I suppose.'

'No, it doesn't,' Rachael said quietly.

After a pensive moment or two, Bowker swallowed heavily, but said nothing.

'Come on, Greg, there's something eating away at you,' Rachael said. 'Get it off your chest.'

Bowker hesitated slightly before replying. 'When I grilled Parker about the wisdom of going to Kate's assistance, he threw it back on me and asked what I'd do if our positions were reversed and *you* had killed some monster from your past.'

Rachael's eyes never left her husband. 'And what was your answer?'

Bowker shrugged. 'I didn't say.'

'That's not what I asked.'

He took a long, deep breath.

'I would've done the same thing.'

Reader comments on the author's previous novel PURGATORY.

"I cannot recommend *Purgatory* highly enough for fans of this genre, especially if you enjoy unique angles and mysteries jam-packed with plenty of unexpected surprises. Robert M. Smith shows a remarkable talent, and I look forward to his next novel."

"Very engaging book to read. Finished it in a day as it was so easy to connect with characters and read the story line. Most impressed. Keep up the great writing."

"I thought I'd put *Purgatory* on my summer reading list. I'm so glad I did… this is gold, a novel by Robert M Smith using actual characters you might know, and some using creative license. *Purgatory* is set in Manangatang in the 80's, and a touch of nostalgia and (not-so-true) crime mystery all together. I know the roads travelled and described very well so I was more than happy to go down the rabbit holes it takes you down…"

"Congratulations Robert. I loved the book and look forward to the next one."

"Really enjoying your book Robert and can recognise some of the characters. Great work!"

"Puts you in the Mallee Country of Australia. Loved the way climate and remoteness are key characters in a terrific murder mystery that creates as many questions as it solved. A thoroughly enjoyable and addictive read. 5 out of 5 Stars."

"I'm sure my partner will love to read it as he went to school there!! I actually started to read a few pages before I wrapped it up and didn't want to put it down!!! Enthralling Robert."

"Received my book, meant to be a Christmas present for my sister. Absolutely loved the book. Brought back so many memories. My Dad was posted there in 1946 to bring the small schools into Manangatang to create the consolidated school. He taught there till 1952. Mice plague, dust, footy, tennis all very vivid memories. Well done for a great book."

"Just read this while on holidays. It's a good easy read. Good work Robert Smith."

"My husband is from Manangatang and I'm from Sea Lake. Been away a long time. It's surreal reading a book about places you know! Well written though!"

"Loved it."

"*Purgatory* captures so much of the Mallee in the eighties. Such a great read especially the way it combines the way of life with the mystery. It is a can't-put-down book. It's up there with Jane Harper."

"I loved that the story was set in the 80's and is back to basics like reading actual maps to find a place, no internet and good old-fashioned police investigating."

"A good read. Congratulations!!! Really enjoyed it."

"I finished *Purgatory* last night. WHAT A READ...! Beautifully written; Great story line. Had me giggling and shedding a tear. Manangatang and district described beautifully. Loved the characters. I read lots of books, an eclectic bunch of authors and subjects, and I must say *Purgatory* has become a favourite. Hope to see more of Bowker. I'm tipping there's more to the silhouetted figure placing flowers on Yvonne's grave..."

"Thoroughly enjoyed the book thanks Rob. Read it without putting it down. Very well done. Great reading."

"I finished the book in 2 days, I couldn't put it down! Highly, highly recommended if you love a murder mystery! Well done Robert, huge achievement."

"It's a great read!!"

"A great book. The descriptions of the Mallee where the book is set were wonderful, you could feel the heat and see the dust. The characters were all well drawn and the writing was excellent. The story line was cleverly thought out and executed, It kept me guessing to the end. I hope the author writes more in this genre I will be lining up to read it if he does. I won't say anything about the story as you need to read it and find out for yourself sufficient to say a wonderful read, well done."

"Halfway through and loving it. Well done Robert."

"I took the book away with me on holidays. I enjoyed it so much. Very easy to read. Loved the characters and I wasn't expecting who did it. Lol. Congratulations Robert. Can't wait for the next one."

"Just finished. Really enjoyed it. Waiting for the next one to come out. Loved all the things that I could relate to your life – teaching, tennis and the trotters. Also the characters names and places that were mentioned. Good stuff."

"Halfway through and can't stop reading it. What a wonderful book. I'm enjoying it so much. I'm usually in bed by 9pm but had to force myself to go to bed after 1am. Congratulations Rob. Will definitely recommend your book to others."

"As a retired country copper, *Purgatory* is very realistic and got the feel of country towns and policing. Really nailed it. Very readable and authentic."

"Started it this afternoon. Can't put it down. Just cleaning up after tea so I can get back to it. It is a very descriptive piece of writing. I feel it all around me. – Just finished the book. Loved it. Would like to read the next one when published. It is now 11.30."

"I really enjoyed your book Robert Smith. Can't wait for the next one."

"Great talking to you Rob about your book. We both enjoyed it."

"I really enjoyed the book Robert."

"Finished and now cannot wait for the next one, how long Robert?"

"Loved the book and the Winnambool side of the novel."

"Just finished this cracking read. Murder mystery with lots of twists and turns and a vivid portrayal of life in a small Mallee town. Can't wait for the sequel."

"Really enjoying your book, well done."

"Obtained a copy of the book *Purgatory*. Just started reading. It's a classic. Hilarious writing."

"Cannot wait for the sequel. Was not expecting the ending but excited."

"It was bloody fantastic!"

"Thanks Robert, Great read. I too hope you have another on the way."

"Fantastic read. Can't wait for the sequel."

"Just finished reading it & loved it. We lived in Manangatang from mid-60s to mid-70s & 80s. Manangatang still felt familiar. Look forward to the sequel."

"Got it a bit over a week ago, just finished reading it. Kept me hooked from chapter to chapter, engaging and enjoyable read. Thank you!"

"Congratulations on such a fantastic book. You certainly captured the Mallee and Manang. My kids are now reading it and loving it as previously local kids. So lovely to read and remember the adventures of that time. I cannot wait for the next one."

"Book arrived today. I have started reading it and loving it. Probably finish it tonight. Looking forward to the sequel. Well done Robert."

"Loved the book. Will spread the word."

"Have enjoyed reading *Purgatory*, particularly the second half which is suspenseful and tightly written and got me turning pages very quickly. Thanks for the read. Any of us who taught in country towns really related with the setting, especially when arriving."

"Just picked up a copy of *Purgatory* from the library and can't put the bloody book down – not getting any farm work done!! Well written with lots of quirky humour delivering streams of quiet chuckles. Finished it in six days which is a record for me."

"Nice yarn Robert. Loved the anecdotes!"

"Really enjoyed reading this book."

"Great read, loved it. Looking forward to the next one."

"Great read."

"Great read. Get into it."

"I love this book. Such a great read."

"Awesome read."

"Loved it is your next novel continuing the story?"

"Really enjoyed this book. Recommend it to everyone."

"Loved it."

"Thank you Robert for taking me back to my youth. Dad was the local policeman at the time, and I worked briefly at the Cocamba silo under a long-suffering boss. Your descriptions and humour resonate so well."

"Great read."

"I'm enjoying the novel *"Purgatory"* very much. Well Done, Robert, you are a magnificent author in my humble opinion."

"I thoroughly enjoyed reading *Purgatory*. Well done on a good job and I can't wait until the next one is published."

"Reading the book on kindle at the present. Loving the characters and often have a giggle at the conversations. Congratulations on a book that I'm finding hard to put down."

"Great job! Loved the book. Can we expect one about Ararat, next?"

"I really enjoyed *Purgatory* on so many levels. What a great start to Robert's crime writing career."

"It's such a fabulous book, loved every page... enjoyed working out the locals, and the references to all the local streets and locations."

"Loved immersing myself into the heat, flies and characters. Do you have more books coming please Robert?"

"Reading and enjoying *Purgatory* at the moment."

"Loved the book."

"What a great read your book has given me, congratulations Robert, a job well done. Looking forward to your next publication."

"Great story."

"*Purgatory* was great to read. I couldn't put it down."

"Well done, loved your book especially all the nicknames – so Aussie and the story of course."

"We'll done, loved the book."

"I read *Purgatory* and I loved it."

"I really connected to this book. Being the partner of a police officer also sent up to the Mallee I felt so connected to Senior Constable Bowker and his partner Rachael. The author did an amazing job at writing from the setting of the Mallee and I really resonated with each word."

"Cannot wait for the next one Robert…don't leave us hanging too long."

"Loved your work."

"I had a great deal of difficulty putting it down. Congratulations. It was a brilliant read. I had previously finished the 6.20 Man by David Baldacci and in my opinion your novel was far superior."

"Just brought your book and started to read it. Really enjoying it so far."

"It's a great read Robert. Well done on your book."

"Just finished *Purgatory* today and I really enjoyed it, as an ex-Manangatang local (I went to the school in 1959-61 when my Dad was Principal). The book brought back so many vivid memories of the town, the crazy but warm-hearted people who lived and still live there, the sandy roads around town, the school, the sporting culture. Apart from the local colour, it's a great yarn and it captures the atmosphere of a small, isolated bush-school in the 80s (as it certainly was in the 60s when I was a Grade 6 student!) I probably spent Grade 6 in the old 'Winnambool' primary school building!"

"More power to efforts to keep paper books alive!"

"Loved the way climate and remoteness are key characters in a terrific murder mystery that creates as many questions as it solved. A thoroughly enjoyable and addictive read."

"It's an excellent read, especially if you know Manangatang, the streets and surrounding bush, and the school! (Did grades 4-6 1959-61, dad was school principal)."

"I bought *Purgatory* for my brother-in-law for his birthday last month. He absolutely loved it and can't wait for the next one."

"Just finished reading… congratulations on a great yarn. Couldn't put it down."

"Just finished your book which was a great read."

"Congratulations. Was a great read didn't want to put it down."

"Reading it now… Really, really enjoying it. I feel like I'm there! Well done Robert."

"Great read Robert. When driving back from Mildura we made sure we drove through Manangatang and we even met some locals who remembered you."

"I grew up in Manang and have enjoyed the book so much."

"Three of us have read your book and we all loved it! We are on a trip and saw a few of the places mentioned in your book! Is your next book out?"

"Congratulations. Loved the easy-to-read writing and can't put down story."

"Really enjoyed your book, Robert. Have passed the book on to other members of the family who also are enjoying it. Congratulations!"

"Congratulations. It's a great read."

"Loved your book Rob, it was a fantastic read I couldn't put it down."

"Fabulous book highly recommended to all crime and mystery readers."

"I am reading the print copy at the moment and enjoying it very much."

"I have just finished reading *Purgatory*. Loved it, a great read! When is your next one available?"

"*Purgatory* is a great read with evocative scene setting, excellent character development and like all good thrillers it is full of suspenseful excitement."

"All the locals have nicknames which I found amusing and descriptions of the countryside and small towns gave a feeling of actually being there. It was interesting too, to read of Greg's encounter with the Min Min lights and how the community dealt with a mouse plague."

"Robert M. Smith's novel *Purgatory* is a great 5 star read and one I thoroughly enjoyed."

"Many twists and turns in this amazing book by Robert M. Smith, the epilogue at the end made me laugh. Karma. What goes around, comes around."

"Reading it now. Loving it!"

www.ingramcontent.com/pod-product-compliance
Lightning Source LLC
Chambersburg PA
CBHW071403200726
48294CB00002B/281